THE WATER'S EDGE

BOOK THREE
MODERN LEGENDS of DRAGONS & SHADOWS

TRISTA RICKETTS

The Waters Edge © Copyright <<2025>> Trista Ricketts

Copyright notice: All rights reserved under the International and Pan-American Copyright Conventions. No part of this book may be reproduced or transmitted in any form or by any means, electronic or mechanical, including photocopying and recording, or by any information storage and retrieval system, without permission in writing from publisher.

This is a work of fiction. Names, places, characters, and incidents are either the product of the author's imagination or are used fictitiously, and any resemblance to any actual persons, living or dead, organizations, events, or locales is entirely coincidental.

Warning: the unauthorized reproduction or distribution of this copyrighted work is illegal. Criminal copyright infringement, including infringement without monetary gain, is investigated by the FBI and is punishable by up to 5 years in prison and a fine of $250,000.

For more information, email: trista@tristaricketts.com

Contributions:

Editor: Caroline Goldsworthy

Cover Art: WhiteRose Publishing Service   IG: @siennas.coverart

Warning: *Here there be Dragons!*

Join forces with the Dragons and Wielders!

The Modern Legends are all about the ongoing battle for ancient magical creatures working to defeat their enemies while facing the challenges of modern society mixed in with the whims of a few old Gods along the way. If you love Vaughn and Bridget's story and want to see what happens with the rest of the clan, then sign up for my newsletter! You'll be the first to know about the launch of the next books in the series, get sneak peeks at other series coming out, deleted scenes, short stories, and more.

Sign up for my newsletter at: www.tristaricketts.com

Want to send me your feedback? You can do that through my site as well. Just beware, the snark dragon sometimes visits my house so if you snark me, it may just snark back.

Dedication

This one is for the thirsty readers who never fail to amaze me with the things they want to read about.

It's also for the readers who have ever felt different, singled out, self-conscious, unaccepted for who they were, and somehow despite that struggle, are still out there making it through each day. <u>I see you, and I'm proud of you!</u>

Contents

1. Chapter 1 — 1
2. Chapter 2 — 9
3. Chapter 3 — 17
4. Chapter 4 — 25
5. Chapter 5 — 35
6. Chapter 6 — 42
7. Chapter 7 — 51
8. Chapter 8 — 57
9. Chapter 9 — 65
10. Chapter 10 — 74
11. Chapter 11 — 82
12. Chapter 12 — 94
13. Chapter 13 — 105
14. Chapter 14 — 115
15. Chapter 15 — 126

16.	Chapter 16	131
17.	Chapter 17	141
18.	Chapter 18	151
19.	Chapter 19	159
20.	Chapter 20	167
21.	Chapter 21	178
22.	Chapter 22	187
23.	Chapter 23	197
24.	Chapter 24	206
25.	Chapter 25	215
26.	Chapter 26	224
27.	Chapter 27	235
28.	Chapter 28	245
29.	Chapter 29	256
30.	Chapter 30	266
31.	Chapter 31	275
32.	Chapter 32	280
33.	Chapter 33	289
34.	Chapter 34	299
35.	Chapter 35	310
36.	Chapter 36	319
37.	Chapter 37	325
38.	Chapter 38	332

39. Read More! 333

Chapter 1

"DIO, WE DO NOT steam our brother's butt!" Jorrie sighed wearily, putting her hand over her eyes in the way of all mothers of toddlers. That was item number 8,714 on the list of phrases she'd never thought she'd utter in her lifetime. Then again, she never imagined being married to a dragon and having triplets, yet here she was, killing it.

The little dragon in question turned to his mother and grinned innocently, "But Mommy, Fwank took my cwayons again."

She sighed again, deeper this time. "Frankie, baby, please give Dio his crayons back, you have your own set," she called uselessly as he ran out the door giggling like a maniac. She noticed Dio was still having trouble with his Rs, but Shepard said Davis did too, and he turned out alright. She wasn't so sure that last part was true as she sent an evil glare towards the sound of her brother-in-law's voice in the other room.

Davis, her husband's identical twin brother, was quite the jokester. Her triplets loved getting visits from Uncles Jack and Davis, but that usually meant they ended up sugared up and wild. She loved both men fiercely — Jack had been her friend since college, and Davis was irresistible — but sometimes they made her life difficult. As if she needed any help in that regard.

Serenity tiptoed to her and tugged on her mother's skirt. Jorrie obliged and picked her up, hugging her closely. Sighing yet again, this time in relief that at least one of her children was not acting like a hooligan. Serenity, like her name, was quiet and calm, but not speaking much yet. Barbara, Shepard's mother, said she was a lot like Shepard as a child. She knew *he* turned out just fine.

A few minutes later, the man responsible for the fact that Jorrie had three children three years of age, strode into the room carrying Franklin by his feet, the child laughing hysterically. Jorrie gazed lovingly at her husband and as always, caught her breath at how handsome he was. She still settled happily into the feeling of warmth and love that filled her all over again every time she gazed at him. Knowing he was hers. Her husband. Her mate. She had brought him back from the brink of death, she loved him so much. Shepard smiled at her; she knew he adored her beyond all things in this world. The squirmy child in his grip was a close second.

"Found this interloper trying to ride Bubbles into the pool." Bubbles was the family dog, a sweet and patient black Labrador that fortunately loved children. They named her Bubbles because, as a puppy, she would put her snout in the water dish and blow bubbles in it like the babies did. The babies did it because they were water dragons, and control over water was part of their inherent magic.

They wouldn't be able to fully shift into dragons until they were around eighteen, which was fine by Jorrie. They were already a handful, and she couldn't imagine what she would be facing if they could fly at their current age. That didn't stop them from using the powers they did have. Jorrie felt she was forever wiping up random puddles, and she bought towels in bulk.

"Dio was steaming Frankie again," she relayed to Shepard as if it was an everyday occurrence. Which it was.

Her good-natured husband laughed and held Franklin up at eye level, "What did you do to Dio?" Franklin just smiled his cute baby-toothed smile, his cheeks rosy and adorable. He had the sweetest blonde curls like his mother and ocean-colored eyes like his father. Franklin and Dio were very similar in appearance, making the two troublemakers look like a pair of cherubs. Serenity also had blue eyes like her father, a trait of all blue dragons, but she had silky mahogany tresses like him as well. A true Daddy's girl, she had him wrapped around her fingers.

Shepard lowered his son to the ground, and Franklin promptly ran off to get into more mischief. Shepard went to his wife, his mate, his soul, and the love of his life. He brushed her hair from her face in a tender manner that he knew melted her.

"Are you all packed?" he said with a low rumble in his voice that always soothed her, as she rubbed her cheek on his palm.

She smiled gratefully; he was anxious to go on this trip, too. They were traveling back to Australia to do a small two-week tour for Brett and Quentin's hometowns and supporters. This would be the first time they'd been away from the children since they were born. They didn't have a honeymoon as Jorrie was already expecting when they got married, and they were looking forward to having time alone. As alone as a platinum-selling singer and her rock-star husband could ever be. Still, it would be just the two of them, no kids.

Jorrie was the latest musical sensation to hit the stage. Her powerful singing voice and stage presence captured the hearts of audiences all over the world. Shepard played drums in their band, Still Waters. The other two members of the band, Brett and Quentin, had relocated to the United States from Australia two years prior. It wasn't the most organic start to a band, considering their origins were filled with subterfuge. For some reason, the two Aussies had clicked with the two Americans, and they were still together. Now, she was living her original dream for her life while balancing it out as a wife and mother of three dragon toddlers.

"Just about. I have a couple of more things to grab, but I got interrupted, I'm sure you can guess how," she rolled her eyes and grinned. The children were a handful, but he knew she wouldn't change a thing about her life.

Shepard threaded his fingers into her long blonde hair, pulling her close to him and kissed her tenderly. "Go finish packing, sweetheart. I'll wrangle the miscreants."

Jack, her close friend, sailed into the room, scooping Serenity from Jorrie's arms and shooing her away. "Honestly, Shepard, distracting that poor woman while you should be letting her pack," he teased, his tone overly dramatic and scolding.

Shepard grinned, "Jack, I can't tell you enough how much we appreciate this. Are you sure you guys are ready for this?" Jack and Davis were going to watch the kids while their parents were gone. Shepard knew the Triple Threat, as they call the kids, were a lot for anyone for one day, much less two whole weeks.

Jack rolled his eyes, "Please, we so have this under control, they won't even know you're gone. You two just have fun and maybe spend some time working on the next batch since Barbara is making noise at Davis again."

Shepard chuckled. When the triplets were born, Barbara was over the moon, finally being a grandmother after waiting over two hundred years for one of her boys to take a mate. She was thrilled that Shepard had triplets, three at once, to make up for them taking so long, she declared. Now, she wanted even more.

"I don't know how Jorrie feels about that, she's focused on her career, which is hard enough with three little ones around, you know they're her first priority. Doesn't mean we won't have fun trying, though." He didn't bother keeping his voice low, making sure his wife knew his intentions.

"I heard that!" she shouted from the other room, right on cue.

Jack and Shepard both laughed at the expected response.

"Sorry Mom is being hard on you guys," Shepard told Jack quietly, putting a hand on the other man's shoulder in support.

Jack was Davis' boyfriend, so there would be no grandchildren from them. Jack huffed out a sharp breath, "Well, if Davis would just make an honest woman out of me, she would understand how serious we are." His tone was light and nonchalant, but Shepard could see pain in the set of his mouth and eyes.

Shepard snorted, "Well, that's one way to put it, let's hold him down and force him." He knew his mother still held out hope that Davis might meet a woman and take her as a mate, giving her more grandchildren. She loved Jack dearly; she just wanted them to carry on their water dragon line. Blue dragons and wielders were the second-rarest color, brown being the first. With their strong magic and abilities, Shepard and Davis were highly revered and sought after. The triplets were already showing signs of being just as powerful. They were, after all, favored by the ancient Sea God Mac Lir, who gave Jorrie her powers. He popped in occasionally to check on them.

Even though Davis put her off, Barbara still leaned on him about it. Even more so lately. Shepard felt terrible for Jack. It wasn't anything to do with him as a person. Davis wasn't solely attracted to men the way Jack was. As Shepard had once told Jorrie, his brother was someone who appreciated life and beauty in all forms. He'd had both men and women as partners throughout his long life. Jack was charming, loyal, loving, and handsome.

When the two met years ago, it was an instant overwhelming attraction between them. They'd been inseparable ever since, even living together. But they hadn't made a move towards a more permanent relationship. Shepard thought it was why Barbara still held out hope.

Davis strolled into the room and gave his signature cocky grin, "Do I hear my dear brother, my own blood, dastardly plotting against me in here? With the one who holds my heart, nonetheless? Shepard, you wound me!" He placed his hand over his heart in dramatic fashion as if he couldn't bear the pain in his chest a second longer.

Shepard rolled his eyes and studied the face that matched his own so much it was like looking into a mirror. They both had the same chiseled features, ocean blue eyes that changed to reflect their moods and rich mahogany hair. Shepard wore his hair long, letting the natural waves fall to his shoulders. Davis wore his much shorter, faded in the back with feathered layers on top. Shepard's face was leaner, sometimes harder than Davis', but it was the result of hardships Shepard had faced in the Shadow battle years before.

Shepard, Davis, Jack, and a wielder friend named Dio joined forces on a special mission to rescue Vaughn's mother who was a prisoner of the now-dead Shadow King. Dio was Shepard's rider, and the two of them fought off Shadow forces while Davis and Jack had rescued the captive dragon. Davis was relatively unharmed, while Jack sustained some serious injuries. Shepard, unfortunately, was gravely injured and almost didn't survive the mission. Dio had not made it back at all. Shepard held himself responsible for Dio's death for years, suffering from nightmares, panic attacks, and serious survivor's guilt.

Only with Jorrie's help was he able to move forward and let go of some of that guilt, finally able to begin healing. They named one of their children in his honor. Davis was a mess afterwards, too, having almost lost his twin, a special bond no one really understood without experiencing it.

Jack and Davis leaned hard on each other to work through it, and it cemented their affection for each other. For all their joking playboy exteriors and charm, they were very serious when it came to their relationship. At least, they were. Shepard sensed some trouble in paradise.

Shepard pulled his twin close and hugged him tightly, "Brother, would I ever do that to you?" he asked as if he was offended, his tone light and joking. He eyed Jack's retreating form as the man left the room with Serenity whispering in his ear.

Davis hugged his brother back then smirked at him with his ever-present impish smile. "All the time!" he laughed. Davis studied Shepard's face, he knew he was just as exasperated with their mother as he was, but when Barbara was on a roll, there was no stopping her. He often wondered how his father had managed to stay sane all these years with her. Oh, right, because they were mated, soul mates bonded forever. Davis sighed softly. Shepard found his own mate, but he was pretty sure that was off the table for him.

Problems brother? He heard Shepard ask him softly in his mind. Being twins, they could communicate with each other via their mind link. All dragons could link when in dragon form, but only mates could do it in human form. The brothers hid their secret that they could link as humans; there were a lot of things they could do that others couldn't, and it was all kept quiet to reduce the chances of any of their enemies targeting them. Their parents worried the Council would take them when they were younger, under the guise of studying them.

Just the usual, Davis replied, *Mom meddling, causing turmoil and strife. I've got a lot on my mind, that's all. Don't worry about me, go take that gorgeous wife of yours on her trip before I convince her she married the wrong twin.*

Shepard snorted. *As if. Jerk. I love you.*

Davis grinned and hugged him again, feeling a little lighter. *Love you, too.* He also loved Jack, loved him dearly. But he sadly knew they would never have a mating bond because it was magic reserved only for those who would reproduce and carry on the dragon genetic line. Unless there was some kind of medical miracle development he was unaware of, that was not happening. Which also made him sad because he loved being Uncle Davis to Shepard's kids, and he adored his friend Vaughn's little girl Celeste. But he wouldn't have his own children unless he left Jack and searched for a woman willing to help with that. It churned his stomach with tension and anxiety, and lately, it was getting worse, watching everyone around them growing their families, raising the next generation.

He just didn't know how to share his worries with Jack.

Chapter 2

"BYE, BABIES, MOMMY AND Daddy love you so much! We will be home before you know it! I'll call you every day!" Jorrie kept calling out farewells to the point Shepard picked her up over his shoulder and carried her to the car. She screeched in indignation until he smacked her behind and whispered something in her ear. She immediately calmed down, and Jack heard a giggle before the door shut.

Jack rolled his eyes. Despite Jorrie's protests, he had a feeling Barbara might get those extra grandchildren sooner rather than later. Those two never seemed to stop touching each other. Jack sighed wistfully. "Must be nice," he murmured sadly. Although nothing was said out loud, he was fully aware that Davis was pulling away from him. It was slowly ripping his heart into dragon-shaped confetti. And not the fun kind. The kind that was full of so many tiny, jagged pieces there was no hope of ever putting the puzzle back together. A feeling of hopelessness began to wash over Jack, threatening to engulf him completely. He took a deep breath to steady himself, so he didn't show it to the children.

"What must?" asked Davis, popping up behind him as if Jack summoned him with merely his thoughts.

"Going on a trip, an adventure, having some fun. They haven't been able to do it in a while, so... good for them!" Jack said with a bright smile. He wasn't sure Davis believed him, but he was saved from explaining by Bubbles running out the door, barking and snarling. "Shit!" Jack shouted and ran after her.

"Uncle Jack!" came Dio's wail, "Get Bubbles!" His little arms were wrapped around Davis' leg in the doorway while his brother and sister peered around the other one.

Davis pushed them back inside, reassuring them and hollering for Serena to get them as he closed the door in their worried faces. He hurried after Jack to help corral the growling escaped Labrador.

"Davis," called Jack, snatching the dog by the collar. "What the hell do they feed this thing; she won't budge!" He was pulling on her collar to herd her back to the house, but she was staring at the bushes alongside the driveway, her hackles raised and snarling. He paused, pondering what she was reacting to. He thought, at first, she was chasing the car that carried Jorrie and Shepard away, but she ignored the retreating taillights and ran to the other side of the smooth expanse of concrete.

A rustle came from the bushes, and Jack reached back to hold up a hand to tell Davis to stop. He narrowed his eyes and studied the sway of the leaves, noting with concern, the area wasn't moving like it should. It was the same spot where Bubbles was growling. He glanced down at her; she was quiet now, but her teeth were still bared. She was fiercely protective of the children and wasn't the type to bark at random squirrels.

"Davis," Jack called again, but this time, quietly pitched so only the dragon could hear him. "I've got Bubbles. I think there's something or someone in the bushes here. Can you check?"

He heard Davis' stealthy feet sweeping behind him, and the dragon quietly slipped into the landscaping surrounding the premises. Jack pulled the dog back some and shushed her when she whimpered at him. "I know Bubbles, Davis is scarier than you, though, he's got this."

"Clear," called Davis shortly. "But you need to see this." His tone was serious and concerned, which was far from his usual careless attitude.

Jack stepped into the bushes, too, still gripping Bubbles firmly as she eagerly followed him. He found Davis in a small gap between the tall plants and discovered what had the dragon's interest piqued. He noticed broken branches and a depression where someone had certainly been kneeling. "Someone was here, watching the house," Jack murmured.

Davis nodded absently, his brow furrowed. "Whoever it was, they hauled ass in a hurry once the mighty Bubbles went on the attack." He grinned, his impish smile back in place.

"Sure," Jack rolled his eyes, "I'm sure it was Bubbles that scared them and not the sight of you coming after them with fangs."

Hissing, Davis flashed those fangs but ruined the intimidation factor by letting his laughter bubble out. "Nah, I wasn't growly, but…" he trailed off and looked confused, scrunching his nose and frowning now.

"What?" Jack huffed, dragging Bubbles back towards the house.

"It's just that whoever was here, I heard them moving around in here, but I didn't hear them leave. I should have heard footsteps at a minimum, maybe the branches creaking." Davis shook his head. "I didn't hear anything. It's like they disappeared."

Now, it was Jack's turn to frown. "Maybe it was paparazzi after Jorrie and Shepard. Or some crazy fan. I've heard they do that kind of thing. Look, let's get Bubbles back inside and we'll keep an extra eye on things."

Nodding, Davis moved to kiss Jack on the cheek, but Jack turned quickly and hurried off, leaving Davis alone in the bushes, looking surprised, his dark eyebrows winging into his hairline.

Davis waited for a moment longer, watching the puffy white clouds in the bright sky drift by lazily. He would love to be flying through them right about now instead of facing this swirl of confusion tearing him up inside. He could tell Jack wasn't being completely honest with him. He thought he knew why, too. Barbara's constant badgering for Davis to take a 'real mate' and carry on the line, was very hurtful to Jack. Davis knew she loved Jack and would accept him should Davis indicate that this was a permanent match. He couldn't bring himself to do that yet because of the uncertainty of their future. What if there was someone out there that was fated for him? He couldn't hurt Jack like that.

He often felt like the issue made him hold part of himself and his heart back from this man he loved. For all his jokes about it, he knew Jack was deeply hurt before by a former fiancé. Darren hadn't understood Jack's deep ties to his family and the traveling he had to do with his job. Darren also wasn't aware of dragons and wielders, so it had left Jack torn that he couldn't share that part of his life with him.

Davis smiled fondly, thinking about the day he met Jack. It was just before they left for Italy to approach the Dragon Council. He was introduced to Jack and figured he must be with Jorrie; they were both such beautiful people. He was immediately impressed with Jack's loyalty to his family, his charm and humor, his quick wit, and his determination. Add that he was gorgeous, and an instant wave of desire had washed over Davis. It was a refreshing, cleansing feeling, and he was unable to tear his gaze away from the beauty of the man in front of him. He loved watching the way the sun glinted on Jack's golden hair. He was well put together but seemed very laid back, as if his looks were effortless.

That evening, as he packed for the trip, Davis' thoughts kept returning to Jack, and he looked forward to spending more time with him. He noticed a concerning change in the man from that day to the next. He'd overheard Bridget talking to Jack about it in Vaughn's kitchen before they departed. Davis' heart had leapt into his throat. Jack *wasn't* with Jorrie, and was, in fact, engaged to another man. The dumbfounded dragon had leaned against the wall. He was torn because he hated what Jack was going through, but also undeniably excited, that there might be a chance for him with Bridget's handsome brother.

It came down to an ultimatum from Jack's fiancé, Darren. Stay engaged or go with his family to help stop a menace that was threatening to wipe out all dragon and wielder kind. Jack chose his family. Bridget was the widow of Jack's younger brother, and after Brian's death, the two were as close as blood brother and sister. He wouldn't have chosen any other way. His fiancé, the one who had promised to love him forever, simply left.

It made Davis furious that someone would use love as a weapon. To make a person choose like that. He didn't understand how this man, who claimed to love Jack enough to want to spend his life with him, would throw him away so easily. He wanted to immediately rush to Darren's home and rip the man's heart from his chest but knew that would cause more problems than it would solve. Davis made it his mission to try and cheer Jack up on their journey. As he got to know him even better, the attraction grew, and he found he wanted to spend all his time with Jack. His soft smile, his easy charm, and tender heart fully enraptured the blue dragon. Jack had his moments when he was a little theatrical and flamboyant, but that was mostly for fun or to cover his true feelings. Otherwise, he went with the flow, and Davis felt like he could always be himself around Jack.

Davis sighed, but wasn't that what he was doing now? Holding his feelings for ransom. Or what his mother was doing? Shaking his head, he turned to go inside, trying to calm the storm in his eyes that reflected the turmoil of his mind.

He took another glance around and frowned at the faint whiff of ocean he smelled. Shrugging, he wandered back inside.

In the children's playroom, Davis found Jack lying on the floor, Dio and Franklin sprawled over him, screaming about monster attacks while Serenity colored at her little table. Davis laughed at the boy's roughhousing and wandered over to see what his niece was doing. He studied the image and realized she was trying to draw her dog, Bubbles. He praised her efforts and got a shy smile in return. She was not a Picasso just yet, but she was remarkably talented for her age. *Must get it from her father*, Davis mused. Shepard was talented in so many things. He was always the one that studied and practiced, honing skills. Davis had always been the bad boy, the party guy, just looking for fun. He was two hundred and forty-four now. He should probably settle down.

A particularly loud scream made him glance over and laugh heartily as the boys were now attacking Jack with foam swords. Jack wailed like he was being slaughtered. It was adorable. A sense of warm longing rose in Davis, filling him with a pleasant glow. He wanted this. He wanted days where they could share their lives with their own family, not just borrow the children of their friends. Davis rolled his eyes about how maudlin he was getting. *If I were a woman, I'd be moaning about my biological clock ticking away over here.* He smiled tentatively at Jack, holding his breath. Jack caught him staring and smiled back. Davis relaxed his lungs with a slow, steady stream of relief. They were okay for now, it would seem.

Serena, the young silver wielder who lived with Shepard and Jorrie, came in to check on them. A delicate young woman who suffered too many years of abuse at the hands of the Shadow Claw before she was rescued, she was a gentle soul. They all found her truly delightful and still somehow innocent in the ways of the world. She was doing much better than when she first became part of the family. Although she still had dark moments crossing her face when she thought no one was looking, those moments were getting fewer and farther between. She was having dreams off and on lately that she had a sister, but no one knew if these were actual memories or wishful thinking. Killian, Vaughn's best friend who was also a silver wielder, was helping her refine her magic and determine the truth about her background.

Her light, tinkling bell laughter echoed throughout the room. She smiled softly at the chaos unfolding before her. "I see you are settling in well with the triple threat," she called, amusement coloring her voice.

Jack grinned from the floor before jumping up and gliding over to take her hand. "My lovely lady," he said before kissing the backs of her fingers, "The way you light up a room does my heart a world of good."

She blushed sweetly and stared at her toes. "Oh, Jack, you stop that! Be serious," she admonished him.

"I am serious, Serena. You are a beautiful young woman; you shine brighter every time I see you. I'm so happy to see you smiling," he told her as he ran a hand over her long silvery hair.

Davis' eyes stung, Jack was a beautiful soul as well. He loved people deeply, and he cared about their well-being despite having been shunned by others most of his life. He deserved better than someone not able to commit fully to him.

"Did you need something, darling?" Davis said, clearing his throat around the lump there. "Or are you checking to be sure we aren't letting them burn the house down," he smiled to let her know he was playing.

She returned his smile; Jack was right, it did light up the room. "Davis, you are such a silly thing. I know they wouldn't burn it; they'd flood it! But I came because Vaughn called to remind you of their play date with Celeste tomorrow. And he said to bring their swimsuits. Also, Jack, Bridget asked me to let you know she needed some gummy bears, Vaughn doesn't get the right ones." She relayed her message and smiled again serenely as she left the room.

Jack chuckled. Bridget was pregnant again, and when she was pregnant, she craved gummy bears like crazy. Vaughn bought the same kind he did, but Jack always put them in a brown paper bag, which she swore made them taste better. Pregnancy cravings were strange like that, and you didn't dare say no to a pregnant wielder. Especially one who could zap you across the room with merely a flick of her wrist.

Davis moved closer to Jack and quietly asked, "Do you already have them, or do you need to go get them?"

Turning, Jack gave him a considering look, "I'll need to go pick some up. Why don't I do that while you get the creatures ready for dinner? I'll bring back some pizza to see if we can appease their voracious little appetites."

The kids cheered, "Pizza!" It was a sometimes treat in their house, but Jack's philosophy was, what's the point of getting spoiled by Uncles Jack and Davis if you didn't start off with junk food?

Davis nodded and gave Jack a gentle kiss on the cheek, "Be safe, I love you."

Jack's smile, in return, did a lot to lift some of the heaviness in his heart. He resolved he was going to have that conversation with Jack soon, maybe after the kids went to bed.

Chapter 3

DAVIS STARED AT JACK'S shoulders as they lay in the bed, listening to his breathing, which was even and smooth, like someone deeply asleep. Davis had hurried through brushing his teeth and changing his clothes, but when he came in, Jack was already in bed, eyes closed. He turned off the lamp, giving a soft sigh. He'd wanted to talk with Jack about the push from Barbara and apologize, but Jack was so tired he didn't have the heart to wake him. At least, he hoped it was because Jack was tired and not because he wanted to avoid him. Davis gritted his teeth; he was sick of himself and disgusted in his inability to communicate with this amazing man he loved so much. It took him a long time to fall asleep.

He finally drifted off after a while but slept fitfully and suddenly jolted, wide awake again. Tense. Waiting. Something had set his nerves on edge. He listened quietly in the dark. He sat up, watching shadows from the moonlight flit across the room. Something about them gave him a chill, raising the tiny hairs on his body and creating a vague sense of unease in his stomach. Even though they'd eradicated the Shadow Claw, in the deepest parts of the night, some shadows still took him back to harder times.

Davis listened, the still of the night closing in on him. Then he realized Bubbles had woken him. She had crept into their bedroom and was staring out the window. A slight growl escaped from her throat, barely audible except for his sensitive ears. Her hackles were raised. Davis slipped quietly from the bed and dropped to the floor next to her. He peered through the glass, surveying the yard, looking for the source of her distress. The dog sat and huffed, seeming disgusted by her inability to get to whatever was drawing her attention outside. Davis sat and huffed, too. Amused at the disgruntled expression on her furry face, he rubbed between her ears. "I know Bubbles. I hate the shadows too," he admitted quietly.

Although he wasn't as injured as Shepard in the original battle, he felt much of Shepard's pain through their link. Too much. He hadn't shared that with Jack. No one knew about their abilities, not even Jorrie. He'd been terrified his brother wouldn't make it out of the compound alive, but he had to get Jack and Mirra out of there as well. He'd been vastly relieved when Shepard had made it back. His brother was fierce and determined in a way that Davis admired. He wished he had some of that right now.

The shadows, empty as they were, still made his skin crawl. A rustle of the covers drew his attention back to Jack, who had turned in his sleep to face him. Davis crawled back into bed and lay on the twisted sheet beneath him. He studied Jack's long lashes and how they fell on the graceful curve of his cheeks. The way his full lips were slightly curved in a soft smile, and the lock of his golden hair slanted across his forehead. Davis moved the hair so he could trace the lines of his lover's face and across that wonderful lower lip.

Jack stirred slightly. He opened his eyes and focused on Davis as they lay facing each other, Davis continued running his thumb across the faint smile on Jack's lips. He shifted restlessly and saw Jack's expression soften.

"Feeling lost?" Jack whispered.

He always knows, Davis thought as he nodded once. Jack was there when he needed him and comforted him in the night when the shadows were the strongest. Davis began to trace the scar on Jack's side where he'd been stabbed with the dark blade, it had healed well, but since Jack was not a dragon or wielder, Siobhan had done her best to close it. Thus, the constant reminder of that day in Maui.

Davis hated the scar and what it represented. It was the only thing marring his partner's otherwise perfect body, and he remembered the pain they'd all felt. He remembered how brave and fierce Jack had been. He had no claws, no wings, no magic powers, only his cunning and sometimes scary knife skills. He'd fought just as hard as the rest and was badly hurt in the process. But that didn't stop him from carrying Vaughn's mother out of that dark, musty prison cell and back to her son. Back to her family.

Davis felt his body heat up, remembering how amazing Jack had been. He glanced up and saw Jack was now fully awake and watching him intently in return, a sad smile on his face, knowing Davis was struggling.

"Davis, it's okay, are you having trouble sleeping?" Jack inquired before yawning.

Davis nodded and at once felt bad for waking Jack up, he'd obviously been very tired.

Jack stroked his hand over Davis' cheek, "C'mere," he whispered, pulling Davis to him, wrapping him up in his arms.

Davis gratefully snuggled up to him, his head on Jack's chest. He settled down and listened to his breathing and thrum of his heart, letting the steady rhythm soothe him.

Jack stared at the ceiling. His heart flip-flopping in his chest, he worked to control his breathing, so he didn't give away how worried he was. He loved

Davis, but he held part of himself in reserve. Darren's leaving and ending their engagement the way he had was brutal and made Jack more cautious with his heart. Meeting Davis right on the heels of that split seemed too good to be true. They'd gotten so close, though, he knew Davis was who he wanted to spend his life with. Of that part, he had no doubts. What he doubted was if Davis wanted the same.

He knew Davis loved him, but Davis wanted a family. He wanted children. His mother was constantly pushing him as well. Jack knew Davis thought he wasn't aware of his desires, but there were signs. The way he looked at his brother's kids with such longing, it was obvious to anyone who wasn't blind. Jack felt like Davis had one foot out the door, and he was guarding himself for that inevitable pain to come.

Jack felt the dragon rumbling against his chest the way he did when he was content and happy. It made Jack smile. Bridget had once likened it to a giant cat's purr when her husband Vaughn did it. Jorrie had told him the sound was an instant turn-on for her when Shepard did it. And when Davis did it? Jack agreed with both of them. It was like a giant, sexy cat.

A sharp bark had them both sitting up, startled and breathing heavily. Jack grinned at Davis and laughed quietly. "This is why I don't want a dog," he whispered.

Davis shook his head. "She did that earlier. It's what woke me up. Do you think that bush lurker is back?" He glanced towards the window and shuddered when a cloud covered the moon, casting more shadows through the room.

Jack smirked, "Well, if they want a show, they can have one." He pulled Davis closer and gently kissed him. When Davis didn't immediately engage, he became concerned. The dragon was normally very passionate and eager to participate in any and all pleasurable activity. Maybe the shadows were too strong tonight. Jack tightened his arms around Davis, "Hey," he murmured, "Give me your fears." It was their code for Davis to know that Jack had him and he was safe. He could let go of whatever was bothering him. The dragon rumbled again and reached up, placing a kiss on Jack's lips, biting lightly where he'd been running his thumb earlier.

Sighing contentedly, Jack deepened the kiss. He felt Davis' body stir in response and was now very eager to continue. The hard length of him was pressed firmly against Jack's thigh, and it made his pulse quicken. He stroked his hands down Davis' back, encouraging the passion that was building between them. Davis responded immediately by settling himself across Jack's thighs and grinning down at him. He had that look that Jack knew meant he was going to fall into the bliss that only this gorgeous blue dragon could offer him. Davis wrapped a strong fist around them both and stroked, bringing them both to the edge before backing off. He let Jack take over then, and he repeated the process, building each other up again, but this time, he didn't stop. When Davis' thighs clenched around Jack's and a hoarse cry ripped from his throat, Jack pulled him close and held him while they both trembled. Jack slipped from the bed and got them both cleaned up. By then, Davis was finally able to fully relax and fall deeply asleep in Jack's arms.

The next morning, Jack woke up feeling refreshed. He thought back on what Bridget told him years ago; that dragons were very passionate and generous lovers. She was absolutely right. He turned and saw Davis was still asleep. He placed a tender kiss on his temple, currently covered by his mess of dark hair, and got up, letting him have the extra rest he needed. After he showered and dressed, he noticed Davis was no longer in bed. He heard giggling and found him in the kitchen with the kids, flipping pancakes in the air to the delight of the little ones. As they finished, he floated them over to the table, dropping them on their plates with a flourish.

"Good morning, little chickens!" Jack cheerfully called out to them. The boys laughed wildly, and Serenity smiled.

"Uncle Jack!" yipped Dio, "We not chickens! We feiwce dwagons!"

Not to be outdone, Franklin added in the scariest little "RAWR!" he could manage, holding his hands up, fingers curled like claws. It wasn't at all scary. In fact, it was absolutely freaking adorable. But, of course, Uncle Jack couldn't laugh at the ferocious tiny beast.

"Oh, my goodness! That was super scary!" he said in mock terror, trembling with one hand thrown dramatically across his brow as he stumbled to the table.

The young dragons cheered at their success of scaring Uncle Jack. Davis grinned at him and winked, letting him know his performance was on point. Jack smiled, too; Davis seemed in a better mood today. He was glad, he loved him and wanted him to be happy. His smile faltered, that was the problem, he loved him, sure, but he wanted him to be happy, and he was concerned Davis couldn't be happy with him long term, they couldn't be mates and couldn't have children.

He'd considered mentioning adoption, but that wouldn't continue the dragon bloodline. The other problem was that Davis was aging very slowly, and Jack was aging at a normal human rate. Davis was two hundred and forty-four, Jack was forty-three, even though he was blessed with good genes and didn't look a day over thirty. Eventually, age was going to catch up to him, and there's no way Jack expected a young-looking Davis to stay with an old, infirm man.

Davis watched Jack's expression change and saw sadness filling his eyes. He wasn't entirely sure what had caused it, but had a sneaking suspicion it was related to him and their relationship. He pressed a hand to his chest, feeling it tighten in response. He hated that look and cursed himself for most likely being the cause. His stupidity was interfering in the best thing to happen to him in centuries. He felt sudden calmness and resolve creep in and overtake his mind. Certainty filled him head to toe. He promised himself that he and Jack were going to talk today, they were going to air this out. He thought back to the way Jack held him and cared for him last night, the way he always was there for him, no matter what. The passion they'd shared for each other and the way they made love. Dragons were reported to be generous lovers, but Davis had met his equal in Jack.

He firmed his lips; he wasn't letting Jack go anywhere, and his mother was just going to have to deal with it. He loved Jack, and that was that. He was the one he wanted to be with for the rest of his life. Shepard had been on his ass about it, and although Barbara thought she was the queen of pressure, she had nothing on Shepard. The difference was Shepard was pushing him to follow his heart. That path led him to Jack. Bless Shepard, he knew his brother would stand firm with him against their mother. It would take both of them to convince her to back down. Either way, Jack was his.

"Jack," he called, his voice shook, thick with emotion. He noticed three pairs of eager eyes watching him and decided he'd rather not have an audience. He cleared his throat. "I checked outside this morning. Near where there was a concern. Some interesting indentations in the landscaping by the windows," he said in a calculated, careless tone. He didn't want to alarm the children, but someone had indeed been watching the house the night before. Bubbles must have warned them off, but it still made him uneasy. Someone watching the house for Jorrie would know she was gone, so why were they still lurking? Who were they really watching? He decided he would speak to Vaughn about it when they went there this afternoon. "We should take Serena with us, I bet she'd like to see Bridget and Celeste, while we talk to Vaughn," he casually added.

Jack nodded once, tersely, understanding Davis' point and went to find the quiet young wielder.

Chapter 4

"OH, MY GOODNESS, LOOK at you, darlings!" Bridget gushed as Jorrie's children came to visit and play with Celeste. She stood and rubbed her small baby bump. She'd told them all when Jorrie had her triplets, Vaughn was going to push for more. She'd been right, and now they were expecting a boy. She gave Serena a quick hug as the young woman chased the triplets down the hall, reminding them not to run in the pool room.

Jack stomped in, and as he kissed his sister perfunctorily on the cheek, he whispered, "Monsters, not darlings, monsters," and kept marching straight to the kitchen to get a beer. His fists clenched tight, and a frown between his normally smooth eyebrows.

Davis followed him, laughing sheepishly, "Jack's a little miffed that Bubbles threw up pancakes in his shoes. Guess where she got the pancakes." He grinned innocently, as if he'd had nothing to do with it. Technically, he hadn't given the dog any pancakes, but he also didn't stop the kids from doing it. He didn't realize Bubbles wouldn't have enough sense not to overeat. He asked after Vaughn, intending to tell him about their nighttime visitor, but Bridget said he was on the phone talking to his friend Killian and would be a minute.

Bridget stifled a giggle as Jack shuffled back over, a sheepish expression and a paper bag in hand. "I'm sorry, Bridge, I don't mean to be an ass." He sighed, "Here are your drugs, don't take them all at once." He took a swig of his beer and winked.

She squealed and ran off to dig into the gummy bears before her husband took them and rationed them.

Davis laughed and threw an arm around Jack's shoulders before kissing his cheek loudly. "You dirty enabler, you!" he teased.

Jack smiled a little and kissed Davis back just as loud, "We all have our crosses to bear!" he smirked.

Davis ran a finger slowly down Jack's cheek, "I'm happy to bear them with you," he whispered, gazing purposefully at Jack, hoping he got the meaning behind it.

"Are you?" Jack whispered back, his voice full of hope.

"Yes, my love, I am."

The two stood there grinning and holding hands until Vaughn wandered by. "You two joining us, or you just going to stand there looking starry-eyed?"

Jack laughed and turned to follow, but Davis pulled him back and kissed him hard before letting him go. "I am!" he repeated firmly.

Liam and his sister Siobhan showed up to visit and provide moral support for watching the triple threat. The two strolled in without knocking since they were basically family. Liam was Vaughn's right-hand man, so he maintained a room here as well as a house in a nearby city. Siobhan worked at Vaughn's gaming company as a developer. Vaughn was their godfather and had essentially adopted the siblings when their parents were taken out by the Shadow Claw.

Jack greeted them both, then asked Siobhan, "Where's Lorenzo? Haven't seen him around in a while." She grumbled something unintelligible and stormed off to find the children.

Liam blew out a deep breath, "He went home, to visit his family a few weeks ago. Said he needed to recharge for a bit away from this country. She didn't take it well. I think he was just homesick, but you know how he sometimes struggles with his Italian-to-English translation. She took it as he needed time away from her. I don't think that's it at all, but... it's Lorenzo."

Jack nodded. Lorenzo was usually very quiet and reserved, although he'd come out of his shell a bit after the mission to Australia, where he had helped rescue Serena and end the last of the Shadow Claw. They also knew he tended to be very literal.

While Jack and Liam continued to discuss the Lorenzo situation, Davis approached Vaughn and pulled him aside. "Hey, couple of things. Someone was lurking around outside Shep's house yesterday after Jorrie and Shepard left. Whoever it was, they were hiding in the bushes. Bubbles cornered them, and we could hear them moving around, but when I checked, they were gone. It was really weird because I didn't hear them leaving. They were there one second and gone the next. I couldn't really sense much about them at all. They came back last night and were peeking in the windows. Bubbles heard them again. I didn't see anyone in the dark, but this morning, I found signs someone had been there. The only thing I smelled was salt water. It's why we brought Serena with us; I didn't want to leave her alone at the house. What do you think?"

Vaughn rubbed his chin, his black eyebrows raising like raven's wings. "Weird, for sure. And you don't think it was some fan of the band or paparazzi?"

Shaking his head, Davis replied, "At first, yeah, but they would have seen Jorrie and Shep leaving. So, for them to come back, it made me concerned."

"You're right," Vaughn nodded. "I'll put someone on patrol and install some cameras. I'm glad you brought Serena. I'd hate for anything to happen to her." He clapped Davis on the shoulder. "You said a couple of things, what else?"

Fidgeting now, Davis asked, "Do you mind if I take Jack up to the rooftop for a bit? I need to talk to him about something serious and could use some privacy and distance. When we get back, we'll go arrange that security."

Vaughn studied him for a minute, "Okay, but if you make my wife cry, I'm going to rip your wings off."

Davis was taken aback at first, then realized what Vaughn was thinking, and quickly reassured him, "Well, it's nothing bad, so I can't imagine she would. She's more likely to cry if you take away those gummy bears Jack gave her."

Vaughn laughed and handed over a key card for his private rooftop terrace. "Thanks for the tip!" he tossed over his shoulder as he went to take the candy from Bridget before she ate it all.

Davis found Jack in the pool room, laughing as the triple threat were paddling circles around their cousin Celeste and generally causing a ruckus. Celeste loved every second of it. Davis quietly slipped his hand into Jack's and pulled him out of the room. Jack stared at him quizzically, about to ask, but Davis just shook his head and motioned him to follow.

They took the elevator up to the highest level, then used the key card to access the private terrace stairwell. Once on the rooftop, Davis led Jack over to the patio seating area, Vaughn kept there. Davis knew the rooftop was warded and had perception filters on it so no one could see them. Anyone looking out or down from surrounding buildings would only see the usual rooftop of a residential tower in Dallas. After Jack was seated, Davis pulled off his shirt and let his wings unfurl, stretching them and enjoying the light breeze across them.

"Oh, man, that feels good," he rolled his neck and shoulders, stretching his arms over his head. He noted that Jack was watching him with interest and grinned at him, "Sorry, just needed to do that. It's been a minute." He winked at Jack and got a sly smile in return.

"Did you bring me up here to show off?" Jack asked him. He stood and slowly moved to Davis before circling behind him. He ran his hand over one of the blue wings, stroking the arch where it came from Davis' back. He knew it was intensely pleasurable for the dragon, so he did it every chance he got. As expected, Davis shivered and rumbled, enjoying the touch.

"No, but since you are enjoying the view, I'm glad I did."

Jack circled back around and lightly kissed him, "Then, before I get too distracted, why are we up here? Did you talk to Vaughn?" he asked as he sat again, leaning forward with his forearms on his thighs, hands dangling between his legs in an attempt to look casual, but Davis saw the tension in his limbs.

Suffering a moment of slight disappointment that Jack had stopped touching him, Davis took a deep breath, followed by a rush of nerves. He wanted to be sure this was said correctly. "Jack, I brought you up here so we could talk." He sighed then kneeled on the ground in front of him. Having his wings out made sitting in a chair difficult, but he wasn't quite ready to put them away yet. He felt steadier, as if they gave him the courage to be strong like the ferocious beast he could be.

Jack eyed him warily; it was obvious he was not expecting this to go well.

Davis took Jack's hands into his own and took another deep breath. "Jack, we've been through a lot together these past five years, and I know that you love me, right?"

Jack nodded, his eyes going shiny and damp.

"I think that lately you've felt me pulling back from you, and I wanted to tell you I'm sorry about that. I didn't want to burden you with what's been going through my head."

"So, is this it?" Jack let out a shaky laugh. "Where you tell me it's been fun, but it's time for you to move on and find someone your mother approves of? Someone you can have children with and be a true mate to?" he asked softly in a voice thick with emotion and unshed tears.

Davis rocked back on his heels, stunned. Apparently, he hadn't been as good at hiding his concerns from Jack as he thought. He hated seeing the tears in Jack's eyes; Jack hated crying. He shook his head, "No, I mean yes to some of it, but not all of it."

Jack stood and strode quickly away, leaning against the rail around the edge of the building, arms wrapped around his stomach as if he were in pain. He whispered to himself, "It's Darren all over again, the ultimatum, give me something you can't, or I'm leaving you and taking my love away." He tensed when Davis hurried over behind him.

Jack has to know I heard that, maybe he wanted me to, Davis thought. He softly whispered, "Jack, my darling. I'm not Darren." He laid a hand gently on Jack's shoulder.

Shrugging it off, Jack sniffed, saying, "Let's not waste breath on extra words. I'll just go back to Shepard's with the kids, and you can pack your things and move back to your old condo. Shepard kept it, right?" He was referring to the condo Shepard and Davis shared before Davis moved in with Jack. Neither of them lived there now but they kept it so Serena could move in when she was ready to try living on her own.

Davis gasped, "Jack, no, please listen!" and pulled him around quickly to face him. He gazed at the hurt dulling Jack's normally bright blue eyes and smacked himself on the forehead, "This is not going the way I planned. Jack, my love, please, just… hear what I need to tell you. I've been struggling to really tell you how I feel and what I've been trying to decide. I'm not leaving you!" He saw Jack was listening, but with tears gathering again in his eyes, threatening to spill at any second. "I'm not leaving, Jack. I never wanted to hurt you like this." He pulled him close and kissed him deeply, trying to put all that he felt into the moment. Trying to show him without words what he couldn't seem to say correctly.

Jack slowly untensed and began to respond, the kiss building until they were both breathless.

Finally, they pulled apart, and Davis put his forehead on Jack's. "My love," he whispered again. He looked up and put his hands on Jack's face, "I'm so sorry, I didn't mean to make you think I was leaving you, far from it, please, forgive me."

Jack stared at him with the beginning of hope now blooming over his face. His expression was wary but obviously still wanting so badly to believe.

"My darling Jack, you have no idea how wonderful you are. You sweet, incredible, amazing man. The things you do to me. I've been so torn up about this whole thing, thinking it was my responsibility to find a mate and carry on the line. With how much I want a family and how hard my mother is pushing me, it's overwhelming. I didn't want to burden you with it, but I can see now that I was stupid. You knew anyway. After lying there with you last night, after you chased the shadows away for me, I realized that none of that other crap matters. If I don't have you in my life, the rest of it is useless. I can't help the way I am. I can't help that you are who I want. All that matters is that I love you, I want you, I choose you, and I hope that you still want me, too."

Jack drew in a deep, shuddering breath, trying to make sense of the revelations swirling through his head. Davis just confirmed all that he'd feared and wondered about. He said he was pulling away at first because of assumed responsibility, but was he now saying to hell with that... for him? Was he saying he was going to stand up to his mother, was this forever? "What are you saying, Davis? I'm too tired for games and riddles. I need to know where we go from here."

Smiling tenderly, Davis answered, "Jack, I'm saying that I choose you, that I am so in love with you, and screw that mating nonsense, the heart wants what it wants, and my heart... it wants you. Forever. Barbara can get the hell over it." He brushed his hand across Jack's cheek again, holding his chin still and placing another gentle kiss on his lips.

Jack sighed, emotions swirling like a hurricane through his body and his thoughts bouncing around like a flock of pigeons fluttering in his mind. "Davis, I do love you, so very much, but if we are going to stay together, you can't hold things back from me anymore. It's been hell wondering if you're going or staying. Waiting to see if a woman turns your head because she's the one you're supposed to be with, to be your mate. Not knowing if we are end game or just a game. It's maddening. I can't—"

"Stop it," Davis interrupted sharply, putting his hand over Jack's mouth.

His head jerked back in startled surprise. Davis almost never interrupted him. It was one of the things he loved about Davis. He was always so interested in anything Jack had to say. He swallowed hard and waited for Davis to clarify why he'd stopped his rambling.

Smiling softly, Davis shook his head, "Jack, what do I need to do to prove to you that regardless of some magical bond that, let's be honest, it's been over two hundred years, and I haven't found it, you are the one I want? You want reassurance?" he lowered his hand and dropped to one knee. "Marry me, Jack. Be my husband, my forever. Let's get married, hell, right now, let's run off to Vegas."

Staring at Davis, Jack's mouth opened in shock, his eyes wide. *Did he really just ask me to run away with him and elope?* He studied the sincerity in Davis' eyes and almost wept, he really did mean he would leave right now and get married.

Now it was his turn to stroke Davis' face, as he pulled him back to his feet, his expression softening to one of wonder. "Davis... I, that's so sweet of you. I would love nothing more. But do you really think if we just disappeared and got married, our friends would ever forgive us? Not to mention, we can't run off to Vegas, we have the triple terror to watch." He sighed wistfully, *I want to so badly, but still...* "Davis, I love you, but don't marry me just because you want to prove a point."

Davis shook his head emphatically and squeezed Jack's hands tightly. "No, it's not to prove a point. If we could just choose our mates, I would choose you. Over and over, I would always choose you. In another lifetime, I would choose you. You are the reason I wake up with a smile every day. You are the one person in this entire world that I would give everything up for. The sun rises and sets on you. You take away the shadows for me. I love you beyond everything and all reason. That's what Shepard and Vaughn told me the mating bond feels like. We may not have that magical binding or a silly little tattoo, but I feel that way about you. I hope you feel that way about me," he searched Jack's eyes, questioning and hopeful.

Jack smiled softly, watching the storms swirling in Davis' ocean-blue eyes the way they did when he was anxious. "You know I do. It's enough that you offered. But I need you to make it clear to Barbara as well. I know she adores me, but I can't stand it when she talks about your future mate and children as if I'm not going to be in the picture."

Davis nodded, "Done. She's going to understand it, because I could never love anyone more than I love you. But Jack, are you saying you don't want to marry me?" His lower lip trembled.

"God, no," Jack laughed, "I want to more than anything, but we have to 'adult' here," he grinned while making air quotes. Stroking his hands over Davis' fluttering wings, he offered, "How about we announce it to our friends, and then we plan a small wedding?"

Davis smiled, kissed his fiancé, and they turned, hand in hand, to break their big news. "Small wedding?" he snorted, "Have you *met* my mother?"

Chapter 5

WHEN THE NEWLY ENGAGED couple made it back downstairs, it was suspiciously quiet in the house. They found Bridget sitting on the couch, watching a movie and pouting. "Hey, Bridge, what's wrong? Where is everyone?" Jack asked her.

She smiled wryly, "Vaughn and Liam took the kids to that park down the street, to let them run off some energy since being in the pool only feeds that. I think he's also hiding because he took my gummy bears." Her earlier smile was now a frown, "Claims it's for my health," she snorted disdainfully. "Siobhan and Serena went to pick up some sandwiches for lunch."

Jack kissed his sister on the cheek and handed her a second bag from his jacket pocket. "Love you," he smiled.

"Yes, you do!" she chuckled and popped a green bear in her mouth.

Davis laughed at them both, everything was wonderful to him right now.

Bridget narrowed her eyes at them, then pointed accusingly at Davis. "You two are up to something, what's going on? You know you have to tell me. You don't want to upset the pregnant lady!" She shook her finger in a threatening but playful manner.

Jack and Davis laughed, excited to break the news. They glanced at each other and clasped hands.

Davis smiled happily at Bridget, his eyes a light blue that rivaled the sky outside. His voice breathless, he rushed out his words, "Well, I've been a bit of an ass to Jack lately, and I need to explain it, so we went upstairs. I finally told him how I felt, how much he means to me and how much I love him."

"We talked it through," Jack picked up the next part, "And Davis asked me to marry him."

"He said yes!" Davis cheered.

"I said yes!" Jack added, bouncing on his toes.

Bridget squealed and jumped to her feet, the gummy bears forgotten. She grabbed them both in a tight hug, jumping up and down and cheering. "Oh, you guys, I'm so happy for you! I can't wait, and Jorrie is going to be so excited, too! And Shepard! Oh wow!" she burst into tears, and Davis stared at her in alarm, remembering Vaughn's earlier threat.

Jack waved him back, "It's okay, Davis, these are hormonal, happy tears. She's fine."

She nodded, wailing through her tears, "I'm so happy! Two of my favorite people! Finally getting married! Love is wonderful!" She sat, covering her face with her hands.

Davis laughed, "Wow, that's fantastic, I didn't know I was one of your favorite people."

She nodded, sniffling, "Yeah, from the day we met. I saw that sparkle of mischief in your eyes. I knew you were going to be trouble, and then you were just so wonderful to my brother. You made him so happy when he was sad, and you keep making him happier than he's ever been. And now here you are, making him your husband! I love you, Davis!" She bawled again, starting to hiccup as she jumped back to her feet and threw her arms around the dragon's neck.

Seeming overcome by her admission, Davis gladly accepted the hug and spun Bridget around as he held her tightly. He buried his face in her coppery hair and closed his eyes. A peaceful smile crossed his face as he relaxed his shoulders.

Jack shook his head in amusement and went to get her some water.

When he came back, Bridget smiled gratefully at him, as he held out the glass. She reached for it, and just as he let go, the glass slipped through her fingers, shattering on the ground. "Vaughn!" she screamed. Her eyes flashed solid black. "*No, Vaughn, no!*" she continued to scream. Blue arcs began snapping across her arms and lifting her hair, like a static charge was rolling over her. A sudden hum filled the air, and every light in the home flickered off and on before brightening to an almost blinding level. She swayed heavily before her eyes rolled back in her head, and she collapsed. The lights dimmed to their normal levels.

Jack dropped to the floor to catch her and eased her back onto the sofa. He looked frantically at Davis, "What happened, what's going on?" he begged him, terror filling his eyes and raising his voice half an octave.

Davis already had his phone out and was trying to call Vaughn. He shook his head rapidly, "I don't know, he's not answering." He growled and slammed his fist against his leg. "Didn't she say Liam went with him?" he demanded, holding the phone up again.

Nodding quickly, Jack held Bridget's head in his lap, his face pinched with fear, growing pale as it hit him what this might mean. "This can't be happening, not again," he whispered.

Davis tried Liam, and still no answer. He was about to try Vaughn again when his phone rang, showing Liam was calling him back.

"Liam!" Davis shouted, "Are you okay, is Vaughn with you?" He began pacing in his agitation.

Jack could hear shouting from the other end of the line.

"What?" Davis said, all color draining from his face as he halted mid-step. "No, not possible," more shouting in the background, "What about the kids?" Davis asked, his heart racing in fear. His eyes were swirling again like a hurricane was building inside of him. "Yes, Jack and I are with Bridget now. She must have felt it. She fainted. Get back here as soon as you can. Once we have the kids safe, we can go back. I'll call Marco." He hung up and stared at Jack, lines of horror etched across his face, his voice trembling as he told him, "Vaughn's been taken."

Jack was pretty sure he was having a nightmare. His sister's husband? Again? It just couldn't be! "Davis," his voice was shaking and held an edge of denial, "What the hell happened?"

Davis relayed what Liam told him. They were walking, watching the kids in the park, when a large shadow appeared behind them. A man they'd never seen before jumped out at them. He moved as quick as a snake, striking Vaughn down without warning. He then tried to snatch Celeste, too.

Liam stopped the attacker from grabbing the little girl, but during the ensuing fight, he'd knocked Liam down as well with some sort of spell. The triplets hid Celeste and themselves, keeping their cousin safe. The man cursed and dragged Vaughn into the shadows, taking him who knows where. Liam tried to grab him from the ground, but the man kicked him in the head, and he passed out. Dio and Franklin used their powers to pour water on Liam and bring him around. Serenity helped keep Celeste calm. The little girl was understandably shaken and terrified at seeing her daddy taken.

"So, Bridget must have felt or heard him being attacked and taken. It overwhelmed her. I don't think he's dead, or she wouldn't…" Jack trailed off and looked to Davis for confirmation, biting his lip to keep it from trembling harder than it already was.

"No, he's alive, if he wasn't," Davis shook his head, "She wouldn't still be with us. But we don't know where he is. Once Liam gets here with the children, we're going back out to see what we can find out about who took him and where. I'll call Marco to get here ASAP to track them. Can you call Siobhan and Serena back? I'm worried someone might be after Serena, too."

Jack nodded; Davis was handling this well. He was often described as a party boy and someone who couldn't be taken seriously, but when it was time for action, he was all business. He got things done. Jack called Siobhan, explained what had happened, and after she was done growling curses, assured him they were on their way.

Bridget slowly woke and gazed around, overwhelmed. She was lying in her bed, her face damp with tears. She remembered Vaughn frantically calling her name and screaming, then nothing. Just blackness and emptiness. An endless hollow pit was centered in her body. It felt like someone had carved her soul out through her chest. It was the worst feeling imaginable. She sat up quickly, a wave of nausea coming over her. She grabbed her head with one hand and put the other over her mouth.

"Here, Bridget, here," she heard Siobhan saying, as she placed a bucket under Bridget's head and held her hair back while she emptied her stomach. "Okay, there we go, I've got you," Siobhan whispered, laying her back and wiping her forehead with a cool cloth.

Bridget moaned, "Vaughn, Celeste."

"I know, sweetie, it's going to be okay, they're going to find him and get him back. Celeste is fine, she's safe."

"My head," Bridget moaned again, hating how weak she sounded, but her world was collapsing in on her.

"I've got that." Siobhan put her hands on her temples, concentrating until a soft green wave pulsed over Bridget, easing the pain and letting her breathe easier.

Finally, Bridget was able to sit up and gaze bleakly around her. Her lip quivered, "Where is everyone?"

"Liam, Davis, Jack, and Marco are back at the park, gathering every bit of information they can. Serena is here, and she's got the kids back in Celeste's room, they're taking a nap. The excitement wore them out. Killian's watching the door. Mirra and Ivan are on their way," Siobhan supplied. She sighed, "We don't have any word on Vaughn yet, but we are going to find him, Bridget. We are going to find him and bring him back to you. And then we are going to kill the sorry bastards who took him."

Bridget nodded and narrowed her eyes. "I want first crack at him," she said with steely resolve in her voice. "The kids, you said they are alright?" she asked after a minute of breathing. She knew Vaughn was alive, she could feel it because of their mating bond. She just couldn't sense him anywhere near at all. She couldn't reach him through their connection, and it felt like she was missing a lung. She wasn't able to take a full breath.

Siobhan smiled softly, "Yes, they're fine. Celeste was a little shaken up, but she's better now that she's home. She was asking for her Daddy. We told her he had to go away for a bit to get better, but that he was going to come back. I'm sure she will be ready to see you when she wakes up."

"Was Liam harmed?" Bridget asked, knowing Siobhan would be worried about her brother as well.

She shrugged, "A few bumps and bruises, nothing major. You know my brother, he's got a hard head. He was more pissed than anything. We all are. Whoever it was that took Vaughn and tried to grab Celeste, caught them both off guard, and you know that is a rare thing." She shuddered, "I've never seen Liam that angry in my life." She glanced up at Bridget, who was now clenching her fists and making a fair impression of a dragon's growl.

"That asshole better make his peace with his maker; he has no idea who he's messing with." Bridget raised her hand and studied it, then frowned. She shook it like it was numb and turned a wide, horrified gaze on Siobhan, "I can't call my magic," she whispered.

Chapter 6

LIAM AND DAVIS STOOD near some scuffs in the grass, where the initial struggle had occurred. They spoke in low tones; Liam describing exactly how the attack happened before he was knocked out. Jack crouched, examining some blood nearby, and Marco scouted the surrounding areas for additional clues.

Jack rose and made his way quickly to the others, "Vaughn was certainly alive when they took him, the amount of blood was small. Based on the pattern, it looks like the person was to his right and hit him with something, probably blunt. He twisted when he fell and didn't fight back when he was dragged. A single blow, does that match up with what you saw, Liam?"

The two dragons stared at Jack in surprise. "You can tell that from looking at the blood?" Liam asked, nodding that Jack was correct.

"Yes, well, that and the scuff marks and the angles," Jack confirmed, "It's like a puzzle you have to work backwards from. Liam, did you get a good look at the attacker's face?"

Liam dropped his head and shook it slowly, "I was so focused on keeping him from taking Celeste I didn't get that good of a look at his face. I can give you a general description, he seemed a little familiar, though. Then he hit me from behind with that spell while I was trying to get the kids to hide. Thank goodness the little ones were able to get away," he grimaced like he had a terrible taste in his mouth. They knew he was more upset about his Godfather being taken than anything. He felt he'd let him down.

Marco came back and shook his head quietly; indicating he hadn't found anything to help in the surrounding area. "How the hell did someone get the drop on Vaughn?" he demanded, "Vaughn is the most powerful dragon in the past thousand or more years, right? Do you think that's why he was targeted? Liam said it was a Shadow person that grabbed him, but we killed them all or revoked the powers of those who surrendered. Didn't we?" He looked around at his friends, "*Esta no es bueno*, not good."

"Yes!" Liam insisted, "When we went to Australia a few years back, Jorrie, and uh, Shepard," he paused, his eyes wide as if remembering something terrifying, then shook himself, "Yeah, dispatched that last Shadow. All our intel indicated he was the last. So, either that was wrong, or there's some new threat." He shook his head again, biting his thumbnail in frustration. "Mac Lir said it, there was still Darkness out there. But it's been years. Why now?"

Davis was shaking his head as well. "I smell ocean, salt water. Marco, do you get that too?"

Jack squeezed Davis' arm with a gasp.

Marco slowly nodded. "Yes, *amigo*. Like the beach."

Growling, Davis' eyes filled with a blizzard. "I think we need to call everyone together and pool our resources."

Jack added, "And we need to reach out to the remaining members of the former Council to see what insight they may have as well."

They regrouped at Vaughn's to discuss the next steps and to start making calls. Jack went to the main bedroom to check on Bridget.

She was sitting in bed, holding Celeste in her arms and rocking her. She glanced up when Jack came in, a hopeful expression on her face. He shook his head slightly to indicate they had no news, hating to let her down. She gave him a watery smile, then squeezed her eyes shut, the pain on her face like a fire brand directly to the center of his heart. He sat next to her and gathered her in his arms, kissing the top of her head, feeling a sense of déjà vu.

They'd been here before when Jack's brother, Bridget's first husband Brian, was killed long ago. That awful day, she'd comforted him when he'd arrived to tell her the news. Now, it was his turn to care of her. They knew Vaughn wasn't dead, but they didn't know when or if they would get him back despite the reassurances of the others. They sat that way for a long time before Jack noticed Davis standing in the doorway watching them.

"Hey, sorry to intrude," the dragon started softly.

Jack waved him in.

Davis continued with uncharacteristic timidness, "Liam was able to work with Siobhan to sketch the man that grabbed Vaughn, he feels the man looks familiar somehow but can't really place him. I was wondering if you would look and see if you recognized him, Bridget?"

She nodded, and Davis held out a pencil sketch to her. She frowned, her breath quickening as she got her first look at the man who had taken her mate, "You know, I see what Liam means, he looks familiar, but I can't place him."

"His nose was smaller, Mommy," Celeste spoke up then. They all turned to look at the little girl who was peeking at the picture over her mother's arm. They glanced at each other, the man had almost grabbed Celeste, could she have seen him more clearly?

Davis dashed out of the room to grab Siobhan, and she rushed in, ready to make alterations, while Bridget praised Celeste's recall. With her help they refined the face; making the nose smaller, the ears bigger, the mouth thinner and added color.

Soon, Bridget stared in shock at the picture before her. She looked to the others, "Where's Circe?"

Jack, who had called her, answered, "She's on her way, should be here any minute. Why, do you recognize him?"

Bridget stared at the picture harder. "Not quite, but I swear this looks like Baltrus, the traitor on the Dragon Council. But I thought he was executed, and this man looks much too young to be him," she finally said. The others shrugged, besides Bridget, none of them except Liam had ever seen Baltrus.

Twenty minutes later, Circe, Ivan, and Mirra all rushed into the home, adding another layer of noise and concern to the already chaotic environment. Mirra went to check on the babies while Ivan and Circe conferred with Bridget in the dining room.

"Yes, that is a great likeness to Baltrus, but the Council executed him for his crimes," Ivan declared with a vicious bite to his tone. Baltrus held Ivan hostage for years as part of his plot to gain control over Vaughn. When his ploy failed, he leaked information about the planned attack on the Shadow King, which almost resulted in Bridget being captured by the evil madman. Only the intervention of another elder dragon, Tar'n, saved her from that fate.

"Perhaps there is a relationship," came a quiet lilting voice from the corner. Bridget jumped and put a hand over her heart. It was Killian, Vaughn's wielder friend. The man was spooky quiet and had a habit of sneaking up on people. He didn't do it to be mean, they just didn't notice him until he was right there. She saw his hazel eyes peering out from under the long, silvery blonde hair covering most of his face.

Concern filled those soft eyes, which made Bridget remember she wasn't alone in her pain. Killian and Vaughn had been best friends for decades. Vaughn had spent time in Ireland, where Killian was from and brought the silver wielder to the U.S. with him when he'd moved here. Vaughn trusted him more than anyone, except her, of course, but he was definitely inner circle. She gave him a soft smile that he returned. He was a kind man, who took Serena under his wing; befriending her and teaching her how to use her wielding properly, but she felt no one else truly knew him the way Vaughn did. She often worried about his solitude and feared he was lonely.

Circe spoke up, her musical voice with its odd cadence offering, "Yes, the likeness is strong, but when one tree is cut down, another can grow from the seed."

"Damn it, woman, this is not time for your witchy riddles!" growled Ivan impatiently. "My son, the father of my grandchildren, my daughter's *mate*, is missing."

"She means this is Baltrus' son," Jack said slowly as he stared at the older woman. "Don't you? Do you know him? Please, Circe, tell us all you know, we need to get Vaughn back."

The silver dragon elder nodded, swaying side to side as she often did, as if dancing to a tune only she could hear. "Yes, Baltrus kept him from most, but I knew. That is Cyrus, his son with a red wielder. Not a mate, he wouldn't bow to being chained like that. Cyrus is a red wielder like his mother, not a dragon, much to Baltrus' shame and dismay. It is why he kept him hidden from others. But the boy was devoted to his father and dedicated to his cause. He wouldn't have taken his father's death at the hands of the Council well and certainly would have blamed Vaughn for his part in it."

They all sat back in shock; this was news to everyone and raised their concerns to even higher levels.

"But Vaughn didn't have anything to do with that!" Bridget protested, her voice thin, an edge of panic coating her words, as she tightly gripped the edge of the table. She shook her head in denial and pounded her fist. "Baltrus betrayed his kind on his own, and it was the Council that executed him, not Vaughn!"

The others murmured their agreement and turned to Circe for more answers. "Tis true, light wielder," she agreed, "But Baltrus was afraid of your husband for years, decades even. You were there when he called for him to be thrown into the dungeon, to be imprisoned without consideration. He never wanted Vaughn to become what he is now; the most powerful dragon alive, and mated to the most powerful wielder. Together, you two are nigh unstoppable. Your children will be a force to be reckoned with." She nodded at the bump in Bridget's middle.

Bridget thought about it for a bit, covering her stomach with both hands in a protective gesture as old as time. She turned her troubled gaze at Jack, fear etched clearly across her drawn, pale face, needing her brother. He alone knew what she was going through. He moved behind her and squeezed her shoulders.

Davis spoke up, "So, you are saying, you think Cyrus is gaining his revenge on Vaughn by trying to achieve what his father could not?"

Circe waggled her head from side to side, "I fear it is possible. I cannot fathom another reason for him to have appeared thus."

"Revenge for a perceived wrong is an exceedingly strong motive," added Killian quietly, startling everyone again.

Davis sighed, "Then I think whoever was sneaking around Jorrie and Shepard's house last night, was possibly looking for Serena. She was captive of the Shadow Claw before, maybe they also want her back?" He looked around, the others nodding. He had filled everyone in on the mysterious visitor earlier. "I told Vaughn about it, and we were going to discuss it further, but he was taken before we got a chance. But shadows would explain how the person got away without us hearing or seeing them leave."

Liam stood and paced around the table, his expression still the hardened frown he'd worn since the attack. "But what of the shadow that opened for him? Surely, he's not a Shadow wielder? His parents were red, weren't they?" His eyebrows were pinched so tightly together they almost touched.

The silver dragon hummed and nodded in affirmation.

He continued, "Then, how is it possible a Shadow is still out there practicing, that we have somehow missed, and is helping this Cyrus now? And what is his last name?" His voice steadily rose as he barked out his questions until the last word was an angry shout.

Circe stood as well and glided over to Liam, who eyed her in distrust. He didn't have much faith in the old dragon.

"Let me see what you saw, young one," Circe said to Liam and reached for his head.

He leaned back. The last time she'd touched his head, she'd petted him like a purse chihuahua, and that was clearly not an experience he was keen to repeat.

"Relax, my green friend," she chided, "I need only a quick touch to make your memory available to all."

Liam reluctantly agreed, they needed this information to help find Vaughn. Circe put two fingers on his forehead and two fingers on his temple and closed her eyes, she muttered a few words in a language none of them knew. She frowned and opened her eyes, thrusting her chin at Killian, "You, help."

He stepped quietly over and put one hand on Liam's shoulder, the other hand on hers and focused.

Soon, a wavy, grainy image like an old, time-worn projection appeared in the middle of the room. They could see Vaughn's back moving away from them, the children skipping happily ahead as they hurried towards some swings. They saw Vaughn's head tilted back in laughter as he turned to look at Liam, the image capturing the warmth of his smile and the sparkle in his blue eyes. A strand of hair blew across his face as he laughed.

Bridget quietly approached, raising her hand as if to move the hair before remembering this was just an image. She pulled it back to her lips and shuddered. Jack wrapped his arms around her protectively. She dropped her head heavily on his shoulder, a small sob escaping. Davis joined the pair and whispered to Jack that he would do whatever it took to get Vaughn back for them.

The scene played out, showing the sudden appearance of a large shadow and the man they now knew was Cyrus, jumping out and zeroing in quickly on his target. They watched as he hit Vaughn from behind, with a bat or large stick of some kind. Knocking him out before the dragon had a moment to respond. Bridget gasped and covered her face at the sight of her strong, virile mate lying on the ground, blood dripping from his temple. The scene continued, showing Liam leaping towards the man, attacking, snarling, with his fangs and talons out. He was deadly, and after one vicious punch from Liam, Cyrus had changed tactics, reaching out and grabbing Celeste. The young girl had run to her father when he fell.

Liam hesitated, not wanting to hurt her. He managed to get her away, and they saw him turn and yell for the kids to run and hide, his first priority. While his back was turned, the man attacked him, and they saw him fall, too. Then they watched helplessly as Vaughn was dragged into the shadow portal before the man kicked Liam, and he blacked out.

A strangled cry from Bridget as she slumped in Jack's arms, then wept heart wrenchingly against his chest while he held her. He turned his tortured blue eyes to Davis, begging him for help. Not knowing what else to do, Davis took Bridget from Jack and wrapped her up, rumbling soothingly to her and whispering reassurances. He put his cheek on her hair and rocked her, then pulled Jack in close, holding them both again.

Chapter 7

AFTER A FEW MINUTES Bridget's sobs had turned to small sniffles, and Davis gave her back to Jack. His eyes were closed, and the desperate pain on his features squeezed Davis' heart into a tight, icy knot. They had to find Vaughn, there was no way around it. He turned back to the others and noticed Marco wearing a puzzled look on his face.

"Marco," he called, "What are you thinking? Come on, anything, we need a lead. You're the best tracker, what did you see?"

The red dragon nodded, unfurrowing his eyebrows, "*Gracias, amigo mio*, I was looking at the shadow, the way it formed, the way it snapped into place. That's not how the Shadow Claw worked. They would use an existing shadow and grow it, then shrink it back to the normal shadow. It didn't just appear full-size and flicker like that. Notice there were no shadows near Vaughn before it appeared? I don't think this was a true Shadow wielder."

Davis studied Marco consideringly, then grinned a decidedly feral smile. He was right, this was a good lead! "Circe," he snapped, "Show us again, but slow it down at that point, and freeze it."

She nodded and flicked her hand to the side. This motion rewound the image as if it were an old VHS tape.

Davis pursed his lips and moved closer, studying the shadows as Marco had done and shook his head in disbelief. The red dragon was correct. "You called it, Marco," he murmured. The shadow just popped into existence and then flickered before it firmed, and the attacker stepped out. This was not Shadow magic. It was someone trying to make it look like it was. Maybe someone who didn't know they'd all been eradicated? Almost as if they were trying to redirect their attention and send them on a wild goose chase. A low growl erupted from his chest, followed soon by the other dragons, and now the room was full of loud growls and snarling.

"Okay, stop!" shouted Jack. They fell silent and stared at him in astonishment. "Not that we don't appreciate the sentiment. But standing around growling isn't going to do a goddamn thing. So, get your dragony angst over with and get those scaly asses in gear, how do we find Cyrus?" he demanded.

Siobhan snorted out a laugh as she ran a hand over Liam's shoulder. She'd been doing it every few minutes as if reassuring herself again that her brother was okay.

Davis smiled at her, then grinned at Jack. He knew he shouldn't be turned on right now, but when Jack got all take-charge like that, it was pretty hot. He saw Jack smirk and wink at him. He'd somehow picked up on what Davis was feeling, which made Davis get a little warm in the face. Why on earth was he blushing? He looked around to see if anyone had noticed, but so far, he was in the clear.

Jack sat Bridget in her chair and stalked to the head of the table. He grabbed a notepad and pen and started writing furiously, "Okay, we know who, we have a possible why, now we need to focus on where and how we formulate our counterattack."

Ivan nodded approvingly; this was what he was good at. "Son, you would have made a fine red dragon."

As the only non-magical human in the room, Jack solemnly accepted the compliment. He knew it wasn't given lightly, and he agreed. He had secrets that the others, except Bridget, weren't aware of, but he didn't want to share them. He continued with his planning. "Circe, we need leads, where would Cyrus go? What's his last name? Who are his known associates? Who would help him with this? We need to know his end game and how he could pull this off. He's not working alone."

She considered a moment, "Sorry, I do not have a last name or know anything else about him. But where he came from?" She swayed slightly and closed her eyes. "Sand," she finally said.

"Well, that narrows it down a lot," drawled Davis, obviously irritated with her enigmatic response. He growled quickly and snapped, "Think you could narrow down what country this sand is in?"

She smiled indulgently at him, "Well, I need some of the sand to tell. But I saw when he stepped out, some sand came with him. Do you think…"

They heard the door slam and turned to see Marco was gone, presumably to find this sand. A few grains of sand, hours later, outside? The chances were slim. Liam sighed and shook his head.

Siobhan spoke quietly, "Marco's one of the best trackers around; so if anyone can find it, he will."

Davis turned a considering eye back to Circe, "Okay, so while the bloodhound is looking for that, what else can you tell us?"

She began to spin around in circles, one of her eccentric tendencies that usually led to another cryptic riddle. Suddenly, she stopped, "You are right blue one, this wasn't red magic; he could not have done that on his own.

This was a different kind all together. It's not silver or blue, neither green nor brown."

Killian suddenly appeared behind Siobhan. "This was black," he murmured thoughtfully.

"Stop doing that!" hissed Siobhan as he smirked at her.

"Black?" multiple voices echoed, in disbelief. There was no such thing as a black wielder. Of course, until Vaughn shifted the first time, there were no black dragons either.

"How Circe? How is that possible?" demanded Bridget, her fists were clenched, knuckles white as she leaned on them across the table. She had a wild look about her, and Jack was once again concerned about her and the baby; this was too much stress.

"Bridget," he started softly, and she whipped her head around, glaring at him furiously.

"What, Jack? What? Are you going to tell me to calm down? To take a nap? Not be involved in this? I can't, Jack! I can't lose him! Not again!" she shouted, then whimpered.

Jack reeled back, stunned. "No, Bridge," he whispered haltingly, "I was just going to offer to bring you something to drink and get you a stool to put your feet up. You should sit while we plan." His eyes dropped, masking the pain he felt at her harsh words.

She stared at him guiltily. They all knew Jack would never try to keep her back, she was just erratic in her emotions. She dropped her head in shame then sat quietly. "I would appreciate that, Jack, thank you."

Jack hurried to the kitchen to get Bridget some cold water. He leaned his forehead against the cabinet. He banged his head against it once, then slammed his fists down on the marble countertop. "Fuck!" he whispered, his shoulders shaking, fighting off the scream that wanted to come. He felt helpless. The same sense of desperation as when Brian died. But he needed to be strong for her. He couldn't let her down. He'd been there for her and Gabe then. He was here now.

He felt a pair of strong, comforting arms wrap around his waist from behind and a warm presence against his back. A rumbling purr resonated through his body. He smiled, the tightness in his chest loosening. He put his arms on top of Davis', squeezing to let him know he appreciated the gesture. He turned within the circle of those arms and wrapped himself around Davis, holding him close. Although Davis was a little taller than Jack, he was still the perfect height for laying his head on that broad shoulder.

Jack rolled his head side to side, then pushed his face into Davis' neck, taking in the water dragon's clean ocean breeze scent. He breathed in deeply and it settled him. His tight grip on Davis lessened, and he leaned back, smiling. "Thank you," he whispered before giving him a light kiss, "You center me, you know? Keep me balanced; from falling off the edge. You're my everything."

With his hand on Davis' chest, he felt the dragon's heart trip, stuttering a few beats. In the years they'd been together, Jack realized he didn't tell Davis that enough, and it probably meant the world to him. They both needed to work on their communication.

Davis kissed Jack back a little harder, "You mean everything to me, too, and this life wouldn't be worth living if I hadn't found you." He raked his fingers slowly through Jack's smooth blond hair. "Let's get back in there and find these assholes. Marco's back."

Back in the dining room, Circe was examining the small pile of sand Marco retrieved. It wasn't much. Just the smallest pinch. But hopefully, it would be enough for Circe to conduct her spell to trace its origin. She hummed over it until Davis mimicked clawing his eyes out. Jack looked ready to do the same; or maybe claw Circe's eyes out instead. Bridget had lapsed into a stupor, staring blankly at the table and not responding to anything going on around her.

Circe cleared her throat and waved her hands, satisfied that the sample was ready for her to test. She held her hands over the grains, pulsing silver waves into them. She said her spell, and her brow furrowed as she concentrated.

Just when the suspense became too much to bear, she finally nodded, "Florida, Miami, the South Beach area."

"That specific?" Ivan queried, seeming skeptical.

She nodded again, "Booze and sunscreen." They all looked incredulous at this announcement, but the old dragon laughed, "There's a lot of that, but the signature doesn't lie. This attack started in Miami. It is there you should begin your search."

As shared looks of anticipation circled the table, they all stood; it was time to assemble the others. Jack gritted his teeth, determined he was going to be right there, ready to be the first one to Florida.

Chapter 8

AT CLOUD WARRIOR GAMING'S headquarters, Liam and Marco stood at the front of the room. Marco looked composed, but Liam knew he was feeling particularly antsy and rather like an imposter, waiting to address the crowd of wielders and dragons assembled. He knew because he felt the same way. Lead filled his stomach, and bile etched the back of his throat, leaving a sour taste in his mouth. This was Vaughn's place; they usually stood to the side and backed him up. Now they were the center of attention as dozens of those who looked up to Vaughn, and depended on his guidance and protection, anxiously glanced around for their leader.

Vaughn wasn't an official ruler of any kind, but as the most powerful dragon in centuries, renowned for his kindness and beneficence, he was seen as the de facto leader of the North American dragon-wielder community. He was known worldwide for his strength, his wisdom, and his role in ending the Shadow Claw reign of terror.

An urgent meeting was called, but no Vaughn? The others were abuzz with nervous energy. The tension in the room was becoming palpable as fierce whispers turned to louder exclamations and speculations. Liam put his fingers between his lips and whistled a shrill, high-pitched tone that had everyone covering their ears and quieting down.

Marco stepped up to the front, his shoulders squared and his black wavy hair gleaming under the lights. "*Callate*!" he called, "I know you're wondering where Vaughn is, and why the urgent meeting. That's why we are here." He gestured to himself and Liam, before taking a deep breath. "Earlier this afternoon, Vaughn and his daughter Celeste were the victims of a targeted attack." The room grew loud again with gasps and worried voices. Liam whistled again. "*Escuchame,* listen up!" Marco roared.

The room once again fell quiet, and everyone leaned forward, rapt with attention and fear, as Marco continued, "Now, while we are happy to report that Celeste is okay thanks to the heroic efforts of Liam..." A burst of applause came while Liam waved it off, he was no hero. They were about to find out why. "Unfortunately, Vaughn was taken by the attacker. He is alive, but we were unable to stop them, we must get him back."

This time, the roar of concern was overwhelming, and no amount of shouting or calling for quiet was going to stop it.

Liam gazed uncertainly at the sea of anxious faces and wondered how they would ever get this crowd under control again. The panic and anxiety were ratcheting up and spiraling quickly out of control. Vaughn was the expert at these things, he would know what to do. Except Vaughn wasn't here, which was the reason for the unrest. Liam still held enormous guilt for allowing someone to get the drop on them and taking Vaughn. The man who had helped raise him and treated him like a son. He took a deep, ragged breath and was going to try his whistle once more when a hush fell at the sight of the person walking up the middle of the aisle.

It was Bridget. She was holding her stomach, one arm wrapped protectively around her son and holding onto Jack with the other. He helped her to the front, where she turned and faced the group. Even a person with normal human hearing could have heard a pin drop, it was so quiet. Only the sound of the building's air conditioning clicking on broke the heavy silence.

As Bridget stood in front of the crowd, she stared out over the group, her eyes passing over those assembled without truly seeing them. They watched her in concern, their faces melding into one blurry gaze of pity. She knew she wasn't looking her best. Her long, coppery hair, normally vibrant like a new penny, was dull and limp, her green eyes held no sparkle, dark circles filling the spaces underneath. Her skin was waxy and pale. It had only been hours, but she was feeling the loss of her mate keenly. Knowing he was still alive was the only thing keeping her going.

She spoke softly, she couldn't manage anything louder, barely above a whisper. Her earlier anger gone, only a deep pit of despair and desperation remained within her. When she tried to pull strength from it, it was like drawing water from a well with a bucket full of holes. It all ran out before reaching the top. She couldn't even call her magic she was so weak. She begged and pleaded with those assembled to listen to Liam and Marco, to help in any way they could. She needed everyone to do anything they could to return Vaughn to her. The father of her children and her life mate.

They all nodded solemnly in response. Bridget was the light wielder of prophecy who, five years before, had saved them all. She had drained the Shadow King of his dark magic, allowing Vaughn to finally end him. They would do anything for her and her family.

Marco began laying out the plan, outlining what was needed. Several teams were assigned and dispersed to gather intel. Soon, the groups were off and running like cheetahs on the hunt to find answers for the most urgent case they'd ever undertaken.

Vaughn had a network of dragons and wielders worldwide that kept a watch on everything. The intelligence hive was alive and buzzing now, information coming in from all over. They were able to start with the information that Cyrus was Baltrus' son and that he'd last been seen in Miami, Florida. It wasn't much, but it was all they had. Their intel indicated they were most likely going to find him mingling with a crowd of yacht owners that congregated around the Port of Miami and Biscayne Bay. They weren't able to narrow it down more at the moment. They suspected he was now using a false name.

Liam felt energized, this was what they needed, he was ready to stretch his wings and fly there now, razing the whole area with his fire if needed. He felt a small hand on his arm and turned to see Bridget holding onto him.

"Liam, I know you feel you have to be on the front line of this mission, but..." she trailed off quietly.

His heart lurched; she wanted him to stay. His dragon recoiled at the idea.

"Liam," she started again, "I need you. Here with me. I need you by my side, so I know you are safe and whole. I need you to be here to help protect Celeste and Serena. And Jorrie's babies. Please, Liam, don't leave me. I can't lose you, too." These last few words were whispered with a desperation he felt all the way to the bottom of his soul.

He knew there was no way he could deny her. He gave one short nod and put his arms around her, pulling her close to the safety of his embrace. She visibly relaxed, shuddering against his chest and giving a brief sob. He rumbled softly to help soothe her. He loved Bridget dearly and would do anything for her and Vaughn.

Marco gestured with his chin to Liam; he'd heard Bridget's plea. He understood. "Liam," he called softly, "I'm going, you're in charge of everything from here."

Liam gave an affirmative nod. He would manage operations from this end.

Davis sauntered up then. "So, rich party boy crowd of south Miami?" he asked.

Marco narrowed his eyes and nodded.

Davis broke into a grin, "I know the type." He pulled Jack close to him, "I know some people down there and have just the cover we need. Jack and I will fit in perfectly and can gain access with that crowd. Plus, Shepard taught me his ghosting trick, and I can shield my dragon from detection in human form now. With Jack being pure human, the two of us can get much closer."

Marco furrowed his brow in consideration, grumbling about their good looks and flirty behavior. "I see your point," he finally conceded.

"Good choice," agreed Liam, "You know they're both strong fighters as well."

"Fine, agreed," Marco said, "But I'm coming too. Ghosting or not, you may need an extra set of teeth. And we should take a wielder with us, a green or silver."

They tossed some ideas back and forth for a moment, but nobody wanted to point out the obvious choice.

Jack finally spoke up, "I don't think Serena's ready for missions yet, too many bad memories there." Everyone agreed.

Davis hesitated, then said, "Marco, I don't mean to make this uncomfortable, but how about Siobhan? She's the strongest green wielder around, and she's got extra tricks up her sleeve. She can heal, too, so if Vaughn's hurt..." He trailed off, looking uneasy about that thought. "I know you two used to date, but are you okay with that? Or we could take Killian?" he inquired gently.

Marco's eyes narrowed, and his jaw clenched, "*Sostén tu lengua*, I won't let anything distract from this mission. I'm fine."

Davis mimicked zipping his mouth, and went to find Siobhan, deciding to leave Killian in reserve. The silver wielder would protect Bridget with his life, as would Liam. No one would get past that pair.

Siobhan readily agreed, "I wanted to go on the last mission to capture the remaining Shadows, but Vaughn kept me back. I'm going this time, and *nobody* is stopping me!"

Davis arched an eyebrow. "Not even being on the mission with Marco?" He knew she claimed they ended things amicably. There wasn't any specific reason for their breakup other than neither of them wanted anything serious. Then Siobhan met Lorenzo, and they began dating. At least that was Siobhan's version. He suspected Marco had a different version of events. He saw the way the red dragon's dark eyes trailed her.

Everyone thought Siobhan and Lorenzo were going to be mated before long, but he was gone now, back to Italy. She refused to talk about it, and Davis knew she kept things very close to her heart. Liam swore she didn't have one, but he was an idiot in the way of all older brothers. Davis smirked, this was going to be entertaining and riveting to watch.

The four of them left to pack for the trip, while Liam made arrangements for the corporate jet and hotel accommodation.

Back at their house, Davis stared at his suitcase, thinking hard. Finally, he looked at Jack and inquired seriously, "Orange or blue?"

Jack glanced over in confusion, "Orange or blue, what?"

Grinning, Davis held up two pairs of swim trunks.

Jack rolled his eyes, "Take both, although you know this isn't a vacation, we have to find Vaughn."

Davis dropped them both into his bag and sauntered over to Jack, turning him to face him. "Darling, I know it's not, but we are going to be out on the water, hanging out with a bunch of yacht snobs. We must look and act the part that we don't care and are just down for surf and sand. If we go in all serious and angry, no one will talk to us. We need to be careful what we present to them. We can't go in demanding answers, and we can't afford to alienate anyone who might give us the lead we need to find Vaughn. That is my priority." He pulled Jack to his chest and made the rumbling sound that soothed him.

Relaxing in his arms, Jack kissed his forehead, saying, "I know, I do. I just want to get him back as soon as we can. I'm worried about Bridget."

Davis took Jack's chin firmly in his hand, "Look at me, Jack, I understand. We're all worried about her, and the baby. But we *are* going to get him back, and those that hurt our family, well, they're going to pay," he finished on a growl.

"God, I love you," Jack whispered as he gazed into Davis' eyes before he kissed him passionately.

Davis responded eagerly, and soon, they'd forgotten all about packing. They lay sprawled across their bed a little later, both working to control their breathing. Davis grabbed Jack's hand, "You know, you could wear that little yellow speedo. The one you got in Bermuda? It does amazing things for your —"

Jack smacked him in the face with a pillow and got up to finish packing.

They met at the private hangar where Bridget and Liam were waiting to say goodbye and go over some last-minute intel.

"Thanks to Davis' contacts," Liam nodded to the water dragon, "We were able to secure a private yacht for your use. It belongs to another blue dragon, Naomi. I guess she's down in Argentina right now but gave us full approval to use it."

Davis grinned. Naomi was a brat sometimes, but she'd really come through. He wasn't sure if she'd ever forgive him for that time she woke up alone in Ecuador the morning after. Jack nudged him, motioning to pay attention.

"The 'Blue Bayou' is all yours for as long as you need. She just asked Davis to please remember to leave the keys where he found them before he disappears again," Liam glanced at Davis with an arched eyebrow.

He feigned innocence and held up his hands.

Jack gave him some side-eye, obviously suspecting Davis and Naomi knew each other very well. He shook his head, it was time to go.

Chapter 9

"OH, MY GOD, THAT air! The salt, the ocean, the sand!" moaned Davis, his eyes closed as they got out of their rental car and stood in the valet area of their bayside hotel. It was a smaller hotel right on the water with sweeping views of the port and bay, while still being large enough to help them remain semi-anonymous. Being a water dragon made the proximity to the ocean akin to being a kid in a candy store. He was obviously in heaven. Siobhan laughed, amused as Davis opened his eyes to see Jack grinning at him in a salacious manner.

"Careful, my love, you don't want to sprout gills in front of everyone!" Jack teased in a sultry tone.

Davis frowned, "I don't have gills," he pouted.

Jack grabbed his arm and pulled him through the grand sliding front doors, both laughing.

Siobhan watched the pair with a small smile on her face. She adored the couple; they were so easy with each other, and she'd really taken a shine to Jack. She could be herself around him, he didn't expect her to be feminine and girly, he just let her be. Whether that was surly and prickly or soft and gentle.

He practiced martial arts with her and was very good at hand-to-hand combat. He'd never told her where he learned, but she had her suspicions. If Jack didn't want people to know, that was his business. She felt eyes on her and turned.

Marco was watching Siobhan. He loved the way the sun glinted off her red-gold hair. The way her green eyes sparkled. He still wanted her, prickly side, and all. He hadn't asked her to be in a serious formal relationship, but he hadn't wanted her to leave either. He definitely had some regrets where she was concerned.

He realized she'd caught him staring and grinned, his white teeth dazzling in his dark, tanned skin. His thick, wavy black hair and warm chocolate-brown eyes made him the poster child for a Latin Lover, and his abuela often told him he should be in her stories. Marco had no plans to star in telenovelas. He was built for fighting and flying, not wondering whose baby Carlita was carrying this time.

Siobhan rolled her eyes and stalked into the hotel, as Marco followed behind her, laughing, glad he'd gotten under that thick barbed skin of hers.

Once everyone was in their rooms and had taken some time to freshen up, Jack suggested they head down to the marina to check out the Blue Bayou and get familiar with her. It was early afternoon, so they had plenty of time to take her out for a spin before meeting up with Davis' friends for dinner. They found the yacht easily, and she started right up without a problem.

Naomi kept the boat well-maintained. Of course, being a water dragon, she spent a lot of time on it. Davis handled the boat with a familiarity that made Jack suspect he'd spent more than a little time on this boat.

He wasn't jealous, Davis was two hundred and forty-four years old, he'd had relationships with many others before. Okay, maybe he was a little jealous. He saw a picture of Naomi on one of the walls in the cabin below decks, she was beautiful and had obviously turned Davis' head at one time. Plus, she was a water dragon like him, they had a lot in common.

Jack shook his head; Davis proposed to him. He needed to stop being insecure about it and appreciate what he had in Davis. He grabbed some drinks and went back up on the main deck where Davis was piloting the boat. He was standing there in his swimsuit, his long, tanned legs braced against the seat behind him, his shirt unbuttoned and flapping in the breeze, his mahogany hair tousled by the wind. He glanced over at Jack and grinned, his sunglasses slipping down his nose as he winked one of his beautiful ocean-blue eyes at him.

Jack felt his heart skip a beat, that man was beyond delicious. He took a big sip of his cold beer, hoping it would cool him off. Between the hot Florida sun, and the dragon in front of him, that wasn't likely.

He handed the beers out to the guys and found Siobhan, who was getting some sun in her new bikini. She was lying with one arm thrown across her face, covering her eyes from the bright rays on the bow of the boat. Jack started to lower himself, then grinned at the intrusive thoughts that won out. He sat on her legs and put the cold can on her stomach instead.

She screeched and sat up, ready to fight. When she saw it was Jack, she laughed. "You stupid idiot, I almost clocked you!"

He laughed with her, "My sweet darling, would you really want to mess up this pretty face?" He pointed to his full lips and pouted at her.

She shook her head and wrapped him up, kissing him loudly and noisily on those lips. They were both chuckling in their amusement; Davis hollering protests from behind them.

Marco sat back, watching in silence. He didn't particularly care to see her kissing another man. Even though he knew Jack only had eyes for Davis, he still wanted her to kiss him and no one else.

Davis slowed the boat as they came around in the bay to an area where other yachts had dropped anchor. He drifted to the spot he wanted and lowered their own anchor. Once it was set, he slipped over to Marco and plopped down next to him. "You know, sitting over here pouting is not going to get her back."

Marco rolled his eyes, "Who said I wanted her back?" he growled.

He laughed and threw an arm around Marco's shoulder. "Oh brother, everything about you screams it. Look, come over and join the fun, you'll thank me later," he said, as he got up and went to join the others.

Marco grudgingly stood and followed.

Jack and Siobhan were spraying each other with beer and making a mess out of themselves. Davis grabbed one and dumped it over Jack, leaving him sputtering and laughing like a loon. They were just party kids having a good time. In reality, they were putting on a festive air to look harmless while they were secretly studying the occupants of the other boats nearby.

Marco grabbed another beer and took a few sips before he felt a cold rain down his spine as Siobhan sprayed him. He whirled and grinned at her, a feral smile that had her eyes twinkling in delight. He chased her around for a bit before finally tackling her and pinning her on the deck. They locked eyes for a moment, and he was seized with an overwhelming urge to kiss her.

He was instantly rock hard and felt himself throb against her thighs. Nope, this was not going to end well. He saw her eyes narrow, and to distract her, he poured cold beer all over her front while she gasped and wiggled. *Shit,* he thought, *that's not helping.* She arched her back, trying to throw him off her, which made him somehow impossibly harder as her hips rubbed against his. "*Basta!*" he gritted through his teeth.

Siobhan immediately stilled and stared at Marco. She could probably feel how badly he wanted her.

"Shi," he said gently, "I'm sorry, you know what you do to me, and having you pressed against me, it's getting beyond the limits of my control here. I'm going to get up and take a swim, okay?"

She nodded as he started to lever himself up. He studied her expression and was stunned that she seemed disappointed he stopped. But he might be mistaken. *Maybe I'm just seeing what I want to see.* Marco almost groaned with how painful his erection was. He hoped the cold ocean water would soothe some of that away so he could walk normally. The way she'd stared into his eyes, it was almost as if she wanted him to continue. He wasn't falling for that. If she wanted him back, she was going to have to start it.

"Marco," she called quietly.

When he turned and looked back, she ran and jumped on him, wrapping her long legs around his waist, her arms locking around his neck, and planted her mouth on his, hungrily taking what she apparently wanted.

Marco's brain froze. Siobhan was in his arms, kissing him. He was sunk; he'd thought she would have to make the first move, and as moves went, this was a hell of a starter. When they both came up for air, he whispered, "Are you sure?"

She nodded, "Now, Marco, please," and kissed him hungrily again.

He wrapped his fist in her red-gold waves and yanked her head back, biting her throat lightly and licking up the long, slender column. "You better be sure, because that cabin isn't soundproof, and I intend to make you scream so loud, everyone in this bay will know what I'm doing to you."

Her breathy cry was all the answer he needed. He saw Jack and Davis glancing their way, making shooing motions towards the cabins below. He managed to make it down the stairs with Siobhan wrapped around him like a jellyfish. He hurried into the first cabin he could find. He laid her down on the bed, grinding himself into the thin fabric of her swimsuit.

She moaned and squirmed, heat flushing her skin. "Marco!" she called plaintively, making it clear she was desperate to have him in her.

He grinned, *oh she wants it quick and hot*. Well, he was going to get more out of this first. He pulled her bottom off then yanked the top off as well. She was warm, naked, and sticky with beer beneath him. He began to lick her body from the neck down, cleaning her up, whispering about what a dirty girl she was. When he got to her breasts, she bucked wildly as he sucked and nipped on them, latching onto her nipple and pressing it to the roof of his mouth. She moaned and quivered, turning her head from side to side. He pressed a finger against her center and found her warm and wet.

She wasn't ready enough for him, though. He added another finger and delved deeper into her core, searching for that special place he knew drove her blind. He pressed there, and she began to pant his name. He leaned down and added his tongue to the little bundle of nerves at her opening. Her hips bucked, and she screamed his name as he laughed with a rumble between her thighs. Her breathy sounds drove him faster, and he licked and sucked right to the point where she shattered for him. He greedily lapped at her until she went limp and pliant. He stood and, catching her eye, slid his own suit down, groaning as he sprang free of its confines.

She watched him with greedy eyes. Seeing him full and hard made her call out for him, her voice thick with need.

With a deep growl that ended in a roar, he slammed himself into her and filled her completely. No soft, gentle glide for his bad girl.

She threw her head back and breathed his name, choking on it.

Marco stayed inside her for a moment, relishing how soft, warm, and wet she was. He'd missed feeling her body around him, her arms around his neck, her nails digging into his shoulders. He knew something she would have missed and flared out his brilliant red wings. She loved his wings. Loved stroking them and touching them. But she really loved them when he used them while they made love to give extra momentum. He was going to remind her of that now.

She was screaming his name again before he was anywhere close, and he grinned his feral smile before swallowing her screams with a kiss. She took his mouth and tongue like she was starving for them, and he felt her quiver as her latest release flooded him with warmth.

He decided that was enough, and now it was his turn. He stopped and pulled back, flipping her roughly over on her stomach.

She laughed and obligingly got on her knees; she knew what he wanted. He groaned as he entered her from behind, getting even deeper than before. She leaned down and angled herself up for him to get as deep as possible. She knew it was his favorite, and this time was no exception. He pulled her hard against his hips, taking her with a fierceness only a red dragon could match. He groaned as his rhythm faltered, becoming erratic and jagged.

She screamed his name one last time as the dam burst and she released long and hard. He roared his climax then and filled her with his own warmth, spasming deep inside her. She collapsed face down on the bed and he fell with her. They both lay there breathing hard and covered in sweat.

Siobhan stretched as Marco rolled to the side. He admired the way she looked, all rumpled and deliciously used.

"Mmm," she murmured and turned to find him looking at her softly. She gave him a wary, surprised look.

He stroked her arm, "I've missed you, *carina*," he whispered, the longing in his voice unavoidable.

She flashed him a halting smile, "Oh, um, yeah, missed you too," she said.

"That wasn't very convincing," he laughed then studied her guilty look. His gaze sharpened, "Shi," he said warningly, "What the hell? You just needed someone to get you off and I happened to be available? Are you just using me for sex? Screw how I might feel about it, huh?" He was pissed now. His anger surfaced as a low growl in his chest. He could feel flames in his eyes and tried to keep his fangs retracted.

Siobahn was startled; what did he think this was? She'd felt his desire earlier and was reminded of how much fun he was in bed. So yeah, she was just using him for sex. He was always good for a quick hot romp, and she'd been feeling tight and needy in her own skin since Lorenzo left. She didn't think Marco would mind. It wasn't like she wanted to get serious with him. Did he think she was rekindling things? She studied his anger and the betrayal clear in his expression. *Fuck,* she thought. That's exactly what it was.

He'd taken her interest as a desire to get back together with him and not just an opportunity to get a quick release from a hot man. There was hurt on his face and disgust as well, but she wasn't sure if it was with her or himself. Maybe both of them.

"Shi, that's..." he huffed out a disbelieving breath. "Damn, that's not okay." He backed up, his wings dragging the ground and his expression changing to one of defeat. "I'm not a toy you can just play with and then set aside when you're bored. I'm a person Siobhan, I have feelings. You can't play with my heart like that." He growled now, warningly. "Fuck that! Next time you just want a quick fuck without any strings, find someone else to do it. It won't be me, *al diablo con eso*." He pulled his trunks back on, pulled his wings in with a sharp snap, and left the cabin in a whirlwind of frustration. His anger radiated from him, scorching her like heat from a volcano.

She heard his feet heavily stomping up the stairs and then a splash as he jumped into the ocean, probably to cool off. Or wash the scent of her from his skin. Whatever it took to get away from her. She lay back on the bed, staring at the ceiling. She was an idiot. She covered her face, tears of embarrassment stinging her eyes like lava. *No wonder he's so pissed. He still has feelings for me*. Feelings she hadn't realized were there. Why hadn't she seen it? *Complete and utter idiot*. Did she want to start things back up with Marco or was she really just using him? Why was this so hard? "Since when do guys not want a quick bang and move on, no strings?" she whispered to the comforter under her head.

It didn't answer her, so she had to answer herself. *Apparently when they have emotions wrapped up in it*. She thought about how she would feel if Lorenzo just showed up, jumped her, and then left again. She'd be pissed too. She really owed Marco an apology. She decided to give him some time to cool off and then she would sit him down and they'd talk.

Really talk.

Chapter 10

WHEN SIOBHAN AND MARCO went downstairs, Jack and Davis exchanged concerned looks with each other. This wasn't going to end well. She was using him, and he wanted her back. It would be interesting to see how this played out, hopefully, it wouldn't distract from their mission. Now Davis was being a showoff, doing backflips off the top deck into the ocean below. Being a blue dragon, he had no fear of drowning. He could control the very waters around him. Another boat full of young ladies in bikinis sailed by and cheered as Davis executed another diving stunt.

Jack leaned over the rail and cat-called them, blowing kisses and calling out compliments. They ate it up and waved a reluctant goodbye as their boat continued on past, calling for them to come back tomorrow.

Davis climbed back onto the deck. He wrapped his arms around Jack from behind, his chilled body bringing goose flesh to Jack's smooth, tanned skin. A quick yelp from Jack made him chuckle.

"Mmm," Davis rumbled, "You wanton hussy, flirting with those girls while your fiancé was helpless in the water."

"Please," Jack laughed hard, "Who was showing off for them? And you are hardly helpless. Besides, you never have to worry about me leaving you for a woman."

Davis circled around to face Jack and traced his lips with a cool finger. "And you don't either!" he promised, giving him a soft kiss. "By the way, that thing Marco did with Siobhan's hair? That was pretty hot, I'll have to try that on you." He grinned as Jack's smile grew wider.

Just then they heard the door to the below decks slam and saw Marco stomping up, his face full of wrath, heat wafting from his body. He looked ready to murder someone as his talons were tucked into his fists and the tips of his fangs were struggling to stay under his lips.

He stared at Davis and Jack, embracing each other and nodded. "Women," he muttered before jumping over the rail and diving into the deep blue water below. The surface sizzled as the heat from his body made contact.

Jack and Davis stared at each other with wide eyes. They said nothing and waited for Marco to resurface. They were watching him swim hard laps around the boat when Siobhan also came up from below. Her expression was aloof as she lay back down on her towel. She studiously ignored the stares of her shipmates.

The men exchanged glances again, they were pretty sure they knew what had happened. The sounds drifting from below earlier made it no secret what the pair were doing. The ending was apparently not what either of them expected.

Davis sighed, "Well, time to head to the hotel and get ready for dinner with my friends. Hopefully, they will be our ticket in with this crowd."

Jack nodded and hailed Marco up to the boat. Once he'd dragged himself on board, chest heaving and expression studiously blank, they sailed back to the marina.

Once everyone was ready for dinner, they hopped in their rental and drove to meet Davis' friends at a restaurant nearby that served Cuban food. Jack was looking forward to it, it was one of his favorites. When they arrived, Davis found his friends waiting near the bar. He introduced them to a bubbly blonde who'd obviously spent some money on her appearance, and her equally blond husband who wasn't a slouch in the money-well-spent department himself.

Jack swore if their names were Barbie and Ken, he was going to leave. Fortunately, their names were Sissy and Dustin. Jack squinted, he suspected Sissy was a nickname and wasn't sure he wanted to know her real name.

Sissy and Dustin turned out to be very kind people and seemed genuinely excited about meeting Davis' friends. She greeted them enthusiastically, before exclaiming, "Oh Davis, darling, it's been too long! You'll never guess who we ran into today! She was so excited when we told her we were meeting you for dinner. I hope you don't mind, but we invited her!"

Davis studied her warily, seeming suddenly uncomfortable with the idea. His shoulders twitched in a way that Jack knew meant he was nervous.

Putting on a sweet innocent face with wide eyes, and his most charming smile, Jack purred, "Oh, do tell, Sissy, darling, I'm dying to meet more of Davis' friends."

Appearing even more nervous, Davis stretched his neck and rolled his shoulders. He opened his mouth, but before he could say anything, a squeal rocked the air and a woman with bright purple hair launched herself at him, shouting, "*Davy!*" She wrapped herself around him like an octopus and kissed him hard on his astonished mouth. He grabbed her to keep her from falling and abruptly ended the kiss.

"Oh, hey, Mandy!" he smiled quickly at her, "Ah... Nice to see you, I didn't know you were still around."

The woman laughed raucously as he set her on her feet. "Oh, come on Davy, you know I'm always here just waiting for you to come back and see me. I've simply been pining away without you." She rolled her eyes in delight and wiggled her hips. "It's been much too long lover! Where are you staying? Maybe I can come over after dinner and we can... catch up?" she said suggestively, walking her fingers up his chest and giggling.

Davis grabbed her hands firmly and yanked them off his chest, taking a step back. "Actually, Mandy, not a good idea. I have someone to introduce you to—"

"Oh, yes your friends!" she squealed. She seemed to do that a lot. "Hi everyone, I'm Mandy, I'm sure you can tell that Davy and I used to be hot and heavy," she grinned and giggled again.

Jack decided right then and there he hated this little hussy.

Davis cleared his throat, as he let go of her wrists. "Yes, well, Mandy, some things have changed since I last saw you. These are my friends, Marco, Siobhan, and Jack."

Mandy nodded to the first two, eyeing Marco for a moment until she caught sight of Siobhan's glare. Her gaze settled on Jack then she sidled over, looking him up and down with a lascivious smile that stretched her bright red lips even wider. "Mmm, Jack, what a hunk of delicious-looking man you are. You look like you could show a woman a great time. How do you feel about threesomes?" she purred at him as she ran her hands up his chest.

Jack was too startled by her blatant offer to respond.

Marco was trying to choke down a laugh, muttering, *"Madre de Dios."*

Siobhan was staring at her in open-mouthed wonder.

Davis looked like he could cheerfully die right now, melting into a large puddle in front of them all as his face turned bright red. "Mandy!" Davis called sharply, mortification apparent in his tone.

She whirled to face him, and Jack was able to recover enough to realize why he felt a wave of hurt rolling through him. Davis had introduced him as a friend to this woman who obviously planned to have more of 'Davy' later. Jack didn't want to cause a scene, so he decided to remove himself from the situation. He faked a smile and forced cheerfulness into his tone. "Hey, I'm going to grab a drink, anyone else?" and casually strolled to the other side of the bar, hands clenched in his pockets so no one would see how white his knuckles were at the moment.

"Jack!" Davis called after him, but Jack stiffened his shoulders and kept walking.

Mandy made to follow Jack, when Davis grabbed her arm firmly again. "Mandy," he hissed, his voice furious. His jaw was clenched and his hand trembled.

She turned to glance at him, a giant grin still planted across her wide-painted mouth, "Your friend is shy, huh? I can fix that," she moaned in exaggerated delight and licked her lips. "That is a whole lot of man. Good grief, he's even hotter than you! And that's saying something! Where did you find him? If he's not into threesomes, I'll take him on single-handed. Just delicious."

"No!" he told her firmly, giving her a slight shake. "There will be no *fixing* of that. You aren't listening. I told you; things have changed. Jack isn't just a friend, he's beyond that. He's my everything. My entire world, Mandy. I love him more than anything in existence and we are getting married. Jack is my fiancé. I'm not sharing him with anyone. He is *mine,*" Davis finished his statement with a slight growl in his voice.

Mandy's jaw dropped, as did Marco and Siobhan's. In the excitement over Vaughn's kidnapping, they hadn't told everyone the news. Sissy and Dustin offered their surprised congratulations as well.

Davis hadn't missed the hurt on Jack's face when he'd introduced him as a friend. Honestly, he'd just been so caught off guard by Mandy's whirlwind reentry into his life, he'd spluttered out introductions quickly as he regrouped. He realized his eyes were about to turn icy and a snarl was building in his chest. He took a few deep, steady breaths to regain his composure. "I love him," he repeated gently.

Mandy's eyes watered as she gazed at him in shock before sighing heavily and nodding, now meek and quiet. "Well shit, I'm so sorry Davis." She blew out a shaky breath. "I really put my foot in my mouth, again. Please, let me apologize to him. I promise I'll make this right."

Marco leaned over to Davis as she sauntered off to the bar, "You used to date Naomi and her?" he whistled, "I thought you were gay?"

Davis glared at the red dragon. "Not helping," he growled.

Jack was waiting for his drink at the counter. *Stupid bimbo,* he thought unkindly as he tapped his fingers distractedly on the marble bar top. He was sure she was a nice person, but she was throwing herself all over his fiancé, *oops, friend*. Not that Davis seemed to mind. He received his Old Fashioned and snorted into the glass, confusion ruining his appetite. He felt a hand on his shoulder and turned to see the purple-haired menace standing next to him.

"Jack," she started quietly, much more subdued than before. "I'm so incredibly sorry for my abominable behavior earlier. I had no idea. Davis told me in no uncertain terms that you two were engaged and to back off. He's been gushing about how much he loves you. I swear he even growled at me like an animal. Craziest thing. But I can see just how passionate he is about you. I'm sorry, really. I'm always sticking both of my feet in my big, fat mouth, so please forgive me, Jack. I can see why you caught his eye; you are quite the dish. Please, please, say we can be friends! I can tell you all the little things he is embarrassed about, and we can gossip about him, and he can't stop it." She was begging him now, batting her eyes at him and holding his arm gently.

Jack stared at this force of nature and decided maybe he liked her just fine after all. *If Davis really growled at her, maybe I overreacted*. Davis wasn't one to let his dragon off the leash in public. He leaned over and kissed her cheek lightly. "Forgiven, Mandy." He smiled, "But just so you know, I'm not attracted to women at all. So, there's not going to be a threesome, although I can see why any man would want one with you. And keep your claws off my fiancé, clear?" He grinned now.

She laughed then and crossed her heart. She wrapped her arm around his waist, hugging him tightly before she pulled him back over to the group. "All's well!" she declared.

Davis strode purposefully up to Jack, taking his face in both hands and kissing him hard. He ran his hands down Jack's body, settling them on his waist before pulling Jack hard against his own frame. Davis left no doubt he was publicly staking his claim.

Jack was a little flustered at the affectionate display but appreciated that Davis was trying to make it up to him. He took his hand, and they waited for their table to be called.

Dinner went on to be a fun, festive affair. The food was great, the company was excellent, and the drinks were cold. Although they appeared outwardly to be partying, the team took it easy as they wanted to keep a clear head.

Davis was gushing to his friends about life in Texas, his brother's new house, how he was an uncle of triplets now, and the escapades he and Jack got into. Sissy and Dustin, in turn, talked up the wonders of yacht life, the South Beach experience, and life down south in Florida. He asked them about newcomers to the area, how things had changed since he'd been around last. He hinted that he and Jack were thinking of buying a vacation home in the area but wanted to make sure it was still the right scene for them. As his friends rattled on, Davis and the others listened intently for any clues they possibly knew Cyrus.

Jack peppered in a few questions about men matching Cyrus' description, mentioning he had gone to college with him, and heard he'd relocated to the area. He was hopeful they could catch up. The fishing didn't get them an identity, but it did get them the other thing they needed.

The couple, as hoped, invited them to bring their yacht the next day to the cove, where they gathered with their friends to enjoy some of the lifestyle and party atmosphere so they could see for themselves. They graciously accepted, and the night drew to a close.

Chapter 11

BACK AT THE HOTEL, Siobhan tried to follow Marco to his room, saying she wanted to talk to him. He turned as he opened the door and stared at her, a hard, stony expression freezing his features. She called his name pleadingly, but he shook his head then shut the door in her face. "Fine!" she whispered. "Stupid ass dragon doesn't know what he's missing," were the final words on her lips as she stomped to her own room.

Marco leaned against his door, eyes closed. He winced when he heard her door slam. His sensitive ears had caught her last comment even through the thick wood slab. *She's wrong,* he thought, imagining exactly what he was missing, but also knowing it would be at the cost of his heart and pride. He pictured her stoic face any time he'd tried to talk to her; she shut down. Closed off to anything even remotely related to feelings or emotions. No, maybe one day he could tell her how he felt, but not today.

He dragged himself away from the door and threw himself face down on the comforter, groaning in frustration. Taking a few deep, ragged breaths, he thought about his abuela and how she would shake her finger at him, scolding him for mooning after such a stubborn, prickly woman. She would say Siobhan was just like his mother. He grinned, his abuela was just as ornery and feisty; all the women in her line were red dragons. He huffed out a wry laugh; they would love Siobhan. He rolled over on his back and stared at the ceiling before cursing under his breath. He stood and moved to the desk where his workstation was set up. He wasn't going to be able to sleep anytime soon. Might as well keep trying to figure out where Cyrus was.

In their own room, Jack and Davis were finally giving in to what had been building between them all day. Davis was sitting on the bed with Jack's silky hair brushing his thighs, begging him to do that thing with his tongue. Jack was happy to comply, and Davis groaned at the feeling of his lover's mouth, so warm and wet, wrapped around him. His head fell back, as Jack's tongue ran the length of him again. He cried out when Jack took all of him in and sucked harder. He started panting in time with the throbbing of his cock. The pressure was rising, and he couldn't tamp it down. He felt himself swelling and firming before he finally shuddered and roared in ecstasy as his fingers clenched in Jack's hair, the silky golden strands caressing his fingers like warm rays of sunshine. He fell back, gasping and shaking as Jack lay next to him.

Once he caught his breath, they kissed softly, and Davis' voice turned sultry, "My turn." He grinned as Jack quivered in anticipation. Jack always said Davis was a magician with his mouth, and he had him begging for mercy in no time at all.

Trying to catch his breath as Davis' mouth slid up and down him, Jack tangled Davis' hair in his fist and yanked his head back, grinning. "Are you going to make me scream your name loud enough that everyone knows what we're doing in here?"

Davis locked his eyes on Jack's and gave him a decidedly feral grin. Holding Jack's gaze, Davis dipped his head and dragged his tongue along the rigid length of his fiancé, a word he'd never tire of thinking. He used his magic to wrap an extra layer of steamy heat and wetness around Jack that intensified the sensation tenfold. Jack moaned and leaned back on his forearms, almost collapsing as he shuddered. Davis rumbled as Jack closed his eyes with pleasure. He laughed darkly when Jack came hard, convulsing from the intensity.

Afterwards, as they lay there, Davis, with his arms wrapped around Jack, dozing in bliss, he kissed Jack's temple, "I'm sorry for earlier with Mandy. She caught me off guard, I set her straight, though as soon as I was able." His voice was laced with sorrow for the pain he knew it had caused Jack.

Jack was quiet for a moment and then sighed, "It's okay, I guess we just haven't ever run into it before now, so we've never had to face this kind of situation. We've been so domestic, not really traveling together, so content to just be in our little sheltered world, it hasn't come up. I know better, I know you love me. I shouldn't be jealous of Naomi, she's not even here, and Mandy, she's — well — Mandy. I guess I just wasn't expecting it to be so blatant today. But I also realistically know you have a long history of lovers, men and women."

"Long history... you make me sound like a man-whore," Davis chuckled.

"Well, if the shoe fits, bitch," Jack murmured.

Davis roared in laughter, "You know I wouldn't be caught dead in heels, babe."

Jack made a questionable humming noise that had Davis pinning him on his back and sitting on his legs before leaning over and kissing him hard. "Himbo," Jack winked at him.

"Jack," he whispered with gentle admonishment, "You make it sound that way, but remember, I'm over two hundred years old. I've been biding my time, waiting for you. In all the years we've been together, why is this hitting you so hard now? I know we haven't run into any of my exes before, but there's no hard feelings anywhere. I've always been a love 'em and leave 'em kind of guy, and I was up front about it. I was too wild. The longest I've ever stayed with someone was a few months, at best. Until you. Because then I stopped searching. I settled down. I knew I finally found what I was looking for... you." Davis saw Jack's soft smile, and it made his chest warm and full. "I'm sure my history compared to yours would be much the same in perspective." He shrugged, then noted Jack was blushing, "Oh, what's that, my dear, are you actually admitting you have been a bit of a man-whore yourself?" he teased.

Jack's eyes filled with pain as he turned his head towards the corner of the room, trying to hide it. His hands slid from where they'd been resting on Davis' chest and landed limply on his thighs instead.

Davis was immediately concerned, leaning forward, a crease between his eyebrows. "Jack, what's wrong?"

Heaving a deep sigh, Jack murmured, "You'd think that, the way I act sometimes. But outside of you and Darren, there's only been one other." He continued to stare blankly at the wall, swallowing hard.

"I'm sorry to have brought up bad feelings," Davis whispered as he stroked Jack's hair and pulled him close, laying behind him.

Jack shuddered at the touch, and it broke Davis' heart just a little. Davis was always gentle and affectionate with him, sensing how much Jack seemed to need it. In the earliest days of their relationship, Jack admitted it was a big change from previous men he'd dated, and now it was one of the reasons he loved Davis so much. From the moment he met Jack, he wanted to make sure Jack's zest for living was never dulled. That he always felt loved. Davis hated seeing him sad or hurting. Jack was too vibrant and full of life to have his light dimmed this way.

"It's not bad feelings," Jack finally answered quietly. His voice trembled like he was afraid if he spoke too loudly, it would hurt more. "It's just that, well, growing up like I did, in the Bible Belt, there were a lot of mixed emotions and hard questions about me preferring men. My parents didn't understand. My brother was 'normal', so why couldn't I be like him? They didn't appreciate me coming out and being honest about who I am. Not Brian, he always supported me and loved me, but after he was gone…" he shook his head, "By the time I finally had the courage to be with someone, it didn't end well. It was the end of a career for me, and why I eventually ended up in corporate management with Vaughn." He shrugged and took a deep, fortifying breath, blowing it out shakily. "I figured this was going to come out one day. I guess I should have told you sooner."

Davis pulled him closer, deeply ashamed he'd never asked before. He'd known about Jack's parents not accepting him for coming out to them. He'd never met them but hated them for abandoning their first-born son. He always thought Jack had been in the corporate world because he was so good at it. He was ruthlessly organized and a skilled negotiator. It simply hadn't occurred to Davis there might be more to that story. "What career could you have been in that was ended by you having a boyfriend?" he asked quietly, confused.

Jack was quiet for a moment, then, "Don't ask, don't tell."

It clicked with Davis, then. Jack had been in some branch of the military, which explained his combat skills and great planning abilities. But being gay in the military, back when he would have been serving, would have been brutal. He held Jack tightly, whispering, "I'm so sorry, my love, that must have been horrible for you. I hate that you had to go through that, and my stupid ass never figured that out. You don't have to tell me if you don't want to right now. But I think we should talk about it at some point. I think it would help not keeping that bottled up."

Jack only nodded, before he took another deep shuddering breath.

Davis leaned over and pressed a kiss to Jack's cheek, "And then Darren and his sorry ass ultimatums," he growled with venom in his voice, thinking how grateful Darren should be that he'd never met Davis. Jack had begged him not to kill the other man.

Snorting in amusement at the growling dragon behind him, Jack's voice lost some of its shakiness, "Well, at least you were there to pick up those pieces."

Davis stroked his hand over Jack's firm stomach, "I wanted you from the first moment I saw you. So alive, so feisty and charming, you were and still are, the first thing I think of in the morning and the last on my mind at night. I love you so much, Jack." He pulled Jack's hips firmly against his own, nudging his now hard length against him so Jack could feel how much Davis was turned on by him, how much he was desired. He unfurled his wings and wrapped them around their bodies, nestling them in a soft cocoon.

Jack smiled, stretching against his chest. "I love you too, Davis, you really have saved me from myself. I'm sorry, I don't have super dragon recovery the way you do. I wish I did." He stroked the velvety soft skin of the wing nearest him and laughed at Davis' rumbling purr of pleasure.

"No, I'm glad you don't," Davis laughed, "We'd wear each other out. Especially with the way I need you."

Jack sighed in contentment and turned so Davis could gently enter him. After just a few thrusts, Davis had Jack moaning in pleasure. As usual, the feel of Jack's body wrapped around him drove Davis to a fever pitch. He reveled in the feeling of Jack arching into him, stroking his wings while he writhed underneath him. By the time Davis was panting his release, he chuckled as Jack learned he didn't need that special recovery to find his own anyway.

In the morning, it was obvious that Jack and Davis were well rested, and Marco was not. When Siobhan finally strolled down to breakfast, she acted as if nothing were amiss. Marco glared at her, still upset with the way she'd used him. Even more irritated that she seemed completely unbothered. He'd spent half the night tossing and turning, hearing her breathy moans in his head, replaying the way she'd locked her thighs around his waist. He grumbled into his coffee cup, trying to relax his grip so he didn't break it. She hesitated so slightly, he almost thought he imagined it, then she sat across from him.

She tossed her hair over her shoulder, then sighed, "So, what's the plan today? We lay around on a boat while you guys act like meat and let the ladies ogle you as you try to get info from them?"

Davis snorted into his cup, the strands of his mahogany hair falling fetchingly over his forehead. "Well, we aren't the only bait. If you can stow your cactus needles and act human for a bit, you can troll the guys, too."

Marco laughed at the accurate description and almost choked on his coffee. Jack patted him on the back with a grin while Siobhan glared daggers at Davis.

She flipped her middle finger at him, to which he politely replied, "No thanks, I like my dick firmly attached to my body. Besides, I'm already spoken for." He grabbed Jack's hand, kissing his fingers with a roguish smile.

Even she had to chuckle at that, which broke the tension. They grabbed their things for the day and met at the car to head back to the marina. This time instead of cruising around, they went straight to the cove area that Sissy and Dustin had invited them to the night before. After piloting past other boats full of mostly naked people baking in the hot Florida sun, they found their friends and tied up with them. Soon, the party atmosphere was in full swing, people moving from boat to boat, making new friends, drinking and generally acting like the day would never end. They had no idea they were secretly being interrogated.

Siobhan even managed to appear approachable, and soon, men were flocking around her, eager to meet the newest available woman in the group. Her red-gold hair lit up in the sun like streaks of molten metal. Her form was lithe and trim, with just the right curves. She trained hard with the dragons and was well-toned. She could hold her own in a fight. Not the typical beach bunny, she was a rarity that drew attention. Marco had to grit his teeth to not snap at one man who put his hand on her waist.

Marco was not without his own bevy of buxom admirers. He was living it up, smooth with the women flocking to him and turning a lot of heads. He was very well-muscled, and his short trunks didn't leave much to the imagination. They were running their fingers over his chest and through his thick, silky hair as it tumbled in the slight breeze. He smiled at them with his perfect white teeth and had them practically eating out of his hands. Jack might win in the game of charm, but even Jack couldn't smolder at them the way Marco could. His dark eyes burned intensely, and he held their hands as they spoke, making them feel they were the only ones in the world who could hold his attention.

He noticed Siobhan was watching them with an icy glare and tried not to let her see his satisfied smile. At one point, he went to grab a cold drink from the cooler, and she snapped, "Got a whole slew of girls to choose from over there, don't you?" with disdain coloring her voice.

Marco straightened, taking in her gorgeous curves and the surly temper coming off of her in waves. He sighed as his stupid heart thumped in longing. "Look, Shi, we had a good time, but that's all *you* wanted. Remember? I get to choose who uses me, and if one of these lovely señoritas wants a piece of me? Well, at least they are honest about it. If you can have fun without bringing your heart into it, why can't I? But Shi, do try to stop looking like you're sucking lemons; you're scaring away the people we need to question." He turned and wandered away, leaving her standing with her mouth open in shock.

"How dare you!" she gritted through her teeth.

He glanced back as she glared around, finally noticing the men had drifted away. Her face slowly turned a fetching shade of rose red as she blushed. A small, petty part of him cheered when she realized he was right, that she was very prickly and was being a complete ass to him. She stared down at her feet, and he could see a small look of contrition on her face. He hoped she was getting sick of the taste of crow.

Davis and Jack were on Dustin and Sissy's boat, chatting with the ever-present Mandy. She was currently sitting straddled on Jack's lap, rubbing sunscreen all over his chest and lamenting he wasn't available, "Cause I would just love to get a bite out of you!" she squealed.

Jack laughed and jumped to his feet, holding her so she didn't fall. He began to dance with her to the music coming from downstairs and dipped her over his arm before twirling her around. "See, I'm still fun!" he declared, breaking into a saucy Latin dance that was all hips.

She squealed again, "Oh, Jack, we simply *must* go dancing tomorrow night! There's a new place in town, it's all the rage. Anyone who is anyone will be there! You can meet some of the newest neighbors."

Davis casually glanced at Jack and gave a quick nod. This might be a good place to get some information as well.

Jack dipped her again and twirled her to Davis, who took over the dance moves. He, too, was moving his hips like a snake, and she was breathless by the time Jack came up behind her. He put his hips on hers, and the three of them danced a sexy number that got quite a few cheers from those passing by. Finally, they sat laughing, Mandy fanning herself and Sissy handing them all cold drinks.

"Whew, are you sure I can't convince you to do that threesome, Jack? Those hips are pure sin! Davy! I see why you are marrying that one for sure!" she laughed.

This time, Jack laughed with her; he knew she was teasing. "We'd love to go dancing, Mandy," Jack declared, which had her squealing again.

"Oh, Sissy, Dustin, you simply must come too!" Mandy insisted.

Dustin smiled, "Wouldn't miss it for anything!"

Sissy nodded in agreement, "That new place by the arena is amazing. The young man who opened it really knows his audience. He spent a lot of money fixing up the old building. Bringing in new talent, hot music, cold drinks. All the beautiful people go there. We've had a lot of fun the few times we've gone. I'll call Delilah and see if we can get on the list due to our friends being in town."

Davis arched an eyebrow, "So, is this place really exclusive? You have to know somebody to get in?"

"Yeah, if you don't want to wait in line forever, it helps to get on the list," Mandy chimed in.

"So," Davis grinned at Jack before continuing, "If someone were to drop that they were a booking agent for the band Still Waters, how would that go over?"

Mandy laughed, a loud, bawdy sound that captured the attention of passing boaters and was over the top. Everything about her was. "You'd probably get a VIP table. But come on, who would believe that?" She wandered off, calling out to Marco to refill her drink.

Davis reached for his wallet and pulled out a business card with his information, proving he truly was a booking agent for the band as he quietly handed it to Sissy.

Sissy gazed at him with awe and reverence. Her jaw slightly dropped, she grabbed her husband's hand in excitement and bounced on her seat. She exclaimed that she'd been telling Dustin that the drummer looked a lot like Davis.

Laughing, Davis explained, "That's because Shepard, the drummer, is my twin brother. That's who I was talking about last night. The singer, Jorrie, is my sister-in-law and his best friend." He pointed at Jack. "Jack's sister married a mutual friend of mine and my brother. Jorrie is her friend, too. That's actually how we met. The rest is history."

Sissy nodded, "Oh, we are so getting in!" After a few phone calls, Sissy announced they were on the VIP list and had a reserved table for the next night. She kissed Davis on the cheek. "Davis darling, who knew you were involved with so many interesting people! I'm sure the club manager is going to want to meet you, she's a huge Still Waters fan. Delilah was positively fainting with excitement!"

Davis grinned and winked at Jack. This was what they needed, an in with the super haute crowd.

Mandy bounced over, having just heard the news from Dustin, "This is fantastic! I'm going to have to get a new dress and shoes for the occasion. Oh Jack, please go shopping with me! You have impeccable taste, and you'll keep me from looking like a dried-up beach hag!" She threw her hand dramatically across her forehead as if such a thought was the worst thing she could imagine.

Jack's broad shoulders shook with laughter as he threw an arm around her, "I'd love to!"

"You don't want my help?" Davis looked put out, sticking his lower lip out like a pouting child.

Mandy laughed, "Davy, you are great at so many things, but really, Jack's the one with style!"

That night, they opted for a quiet dinner at the hotel. They had a long day tomorrow. Marco was going to run intelligence briefings with the Dallas team regarding the club and any possible connections to Cyrus. Jack was going shopping with Mandy; Davis was meeting with Dustin and some other friends for an early round of golf. He had promised to introduce Davis to the newest members of the club.

Siobhan didn't really have a job just yet, a fact that made her silent at dinner. Marco studied her downcast look and wondered if he wasn't being too hard on her. He sighed, they really didn't have time to talk before they jumped into it; perhaps she needed more time to say what was on her mind. Now he smirked, Siobhan didn't hold back opinions.

She must feel something, or she wouldn't have initiated anything. These days, women didn't need a man to get off if they wanted to, well, they never had, they were just more open about it. He shook his head, only problem with that theory, Siobhan didn't *do* feelings. *Maybe I'm deluding myself,* he thought. *I need to let her go, this isn't going to end well for either of us.* He lay awake most of the night again, remembering once more the feel of her thighs wrapped around him and her breathy gasps. He groaned into his pillow. He wasn't getting any sleep tonight, either.

Chapter 12

THE NEXT MORNING, THE team met for breakfast and rehashed their plans for the day. Siobhan quietly asked Marco if she could help with the intelligence briefings, she wanted to be useful. He hadn't slept much and was not in the mood to argue, so he agreed with a curt nod as he glared over the rim of his coffee cup. Her answering smile blew away some of the cobwebs the lack of sleep had created, and he was glad he'd gone along with it.

Jack and Davis had their heads together and were whispering in a way that Marco decided was personal, and he didn't want the details. He didn't care what they did in their free time, he just didn't want to know about other people's happiness while he was miserable and alone.

Davis left for his early tee-time, to avoid the worst heat of the day. Soon, Mandy arrived to collect Jack for an all-day shopping extravaganza, as she called it. Marco nodded at Siobhan, and she followed him to his room, where he had his communications base set up. He directed her to one of the laptops, and she quickly got to work perusing reports sent from their network.

Marco jumped on some calls, and before long they were working in tandem, passing details back and forth like a well-oiled machine. He missed this, working with her, being partners in crime, the smooth flow of their thoughts bouncing off each other. She had a mind that processed information so quickly, it was almost like a computer. He wondered if that was why she had trouble relating to humans or dragons sometimes.

"What?" she asked him quietly, without her usual venomous snap.

He realized he was staring at her, and she noticed. "Nothing," he yawned, with a weak smile, "I was just thinking, and my mind wandered. Didn't sleep much last night."

She gazed at him with an expression that seemed surprisingly like sympathy. "I totally understand that. Do you want to take a nap? I can monitor things for a while if you want to get some rest. We are going to be up late tonight; you'll need your strength."

He nodded, relieved, as that sounded great. "Are you sure you don't mind?" he asked, not wanting to take advantage of her help.

She shook her head quickly, "No, please get some rest. You are the Rumba King after all, you've got to show off those moves tonight," she smiled.

He laughed deeply, his shoulders relaxing. He said that once, as a joke when he took her dancing. He was pleased she remembered. Wandering towards the bathroom to change, he planted an absent kiss on the top of her head.

Siobhan turned her back quickly and flushed, the kiss had made her tingle unexpectedly. Things had been so relaxed and easy with Marco earlier, just the same as they had *before*. She was reminded again that they didn't have a reason to break up per se, she just drifted away and started seeing someone else. He hadn't objected, at least not to her. They'd never had anything formal in their relationship, so she wasn't even sure if it could be called one.

She heard the sheets rustling and noticed from the corner of her eye that he was under them now. She risked a glance and noticed he was still dressed. "You don't have to stay dressed for me," the words came out of her mouth before she'd even realized she'd said it.

Marco lifted his head and grinned at her, his smile devastating in its perfectness. "Oh really? You sure I won't be tempting you if I get undressed?"

She smiled nonchalantly even though her heart was pounding. "I'm sure I can contain myself; I just remember you prefer to sleep naked; you don't like clothes binding you up."

"I do," he nodded, "But I don't mind being more appropriate for you."

She laughed lightly, "It's fine, Marco, you be comfortable. You need to rest." She turned her back to show him she didn't mind.

She listened but didn't hear him moving. Then she heard his whispered, "Fuck it."

He stood next to the bed and slowly peeled his shirt over his head. He stretched, running a hand down his abdomen and shook out his limbs.

In the mirror, Siobhan watched Marco getting undressed behind her. She had tried not to look but not too hard as the man was built like Adonis and was twice as tasty. She felt her mouth watering at the thought of his hips and that little spot she used to bite that always made him groan. *Why is it so hot in here,* she thought to herself as she grabbed her water bottle and took a big cooling gulp.

She glanced at the thermostat and saw it was set at sixty-seven degrees. It wasn't hot, she was. She heard the slither of material as his pants followed his shirt and knew those muscular legs were now bare. She held her breath, was he going all the way nude? Parts of her throbbed at the thought, and she decided she had been an idiot for coming in here. She heard the bed creak as he got back in it and pulled the covers up.

She glanced in the mirror again and saw Marco lying back on the bed, his arms up behind his head. He was grinning. He obviously knew she'd watched him. *Wait, was that his revenge on me? Doing his little strip tease. No, I told him to do it, I didn't have to watch.* Besides, he'd left his underwear on, she could see the waistband peeking over the edge of the sheet pooled around his hips. She wasn't going to tempt herself anymore and resolved to ignore him.

He slid down and closed his eyes, but she was still too aware of him to focus. He tossed and turned a few times. Finally, he sighed, sounding frustrated. "Shi," he whispered.

She turned slowly and saw him staring at her with his dark, melted chocolate eyes full of something she was afraid to label.

"Marco?" she whispered back, her throat tight, her body tense with desire.

"Come here," he was holding his arms open to her.

She slowly stood and stared longingly but warily at him. Her thoughts were a jumbled mess. He lay there waiting. She slipped her shoes off and padded over to the bed, gently sitting on the edge. He pulled her closer. She slipped under the covers and pressed her body to his, her head on his chest and his arms wrapped around her.

"That's better," he whispered, nuzzling her hair, then after a few minutes, fell asleep.

Siobhan didn't think she'd sleep, but wrapped in the familiar comfort of his arms, she quickly succumbed to dreams as well. She'd had a pleasant one of her and Marco, riding down the highway on his motorcycle, her arms wrapped tightly around him as they went off to some small town to explore. It was soft and warm, the kind of dream that leaves you feeling refreshed and recharged.

She snuggled deeper into Marco's side and studied him. He was relaxed with a slight smile on his face. She loved the laugh-lines around his mouth. He was always ready with a quick grin or chuckle. She traced his cheek gently with her fingers and ran her thumb over his lower lip. She had good memories of biting it and shivered at the thought.

She gasped when Marco lightly bit her thumb as she passed it over his lips again. Her eyes flew to his and saw flames dancing in them. Her pulse quickened along with the rest of her body. She knew he didn't want to be used, but she really wanted him, Marco, not just his body. "I did miss you," she whispered, trying to convey what she was thinking.

Marco nodded and took her mouth tenderly with his own, giving her time to pull away. But she didn't. She met his increasing passion with fire of her own. He pulled her over onto his lap and stared longingly at her graceful form rising over him. She was so beautiful, it hurt him sometimes. Her red-gold hair tumbling around her, her piercing green eyes that saw everything. Her small, perfect breasts responded to his slightest touch. Her creamy, milky skin so soft under his own. God, he was torturing himself and felt his body hardening with need for her.

She leaned down and kissed him again softly, gently. He hoped that this wasn't just another itch to scratch. He wanted her to see him and not just what he could do for her.

Silently, they removed the rest of their clothing, and she resumed her spot on his lap, rubbing herself along his length and drawing a hiss from him in response. "Shi," he whispered, "You undo me, *preciosa*."

She nodded, "And you make me come undone." She reached between them and stroked her thumb over the tip of him, spreading the droplets there, before rubbing him against her own entrance. He jolted at the touch and clenched the sheets. She lowered herself onto him, inch by tortuous inch, until she was finally seated. She simply sat there for a long moment as their gazes locked on each other's.

"Please," he whispered, need thickening his voice and making it quaver.

She began to rock her hips, and he cursed under his breath, moaning in pleasure. He kneaded and squeezed her breasts, sitting up to take one in his mouth. It changed the angle, and her breathing became erratic. When he bit gently down on one nipple, she exploded around him, crying out in pleasure. She leaned back, pliant, and warm in his arms, a work of art come to life before his eyes.

He rumbled and purred, then flipped her on her back, putting her legs up around his waist before thrusting into her in with long, languid strokes. Her breathy moans and the feeling of her nails clenching into his back, drove him into a frenzy that made them both beg for mercy. When he finally roared in release, she smiled, and they went limp together. He wasn't sure which of them moved first, but they were back in each other's arms, her head on his chest, kissing along his collarbone.

"I meant it, Marco, I did miss you," she whispered intensely, her lips pressed to his skin, scorching him with her need.

He placed a finger under her chin and lifted her face as he leveled his gaze at her. He studied her expression, and his heart leapt a little with what he saw there. Finally, he couldn't hold back, he had to say what was in his head, his heart. "Shi, I don't know why you left me before." He rushed his words, wanting to get it all out before he lost his nerve. "I've tried so hard to think about what I could have done, or maybe didn't do, to push you away. I'm sorry for whatever it was, but please, tell me so I never do it again. I need you in my life, and I don't want to lose you. Not again."

Siobhan leaned back in shock, her eyes going wide and her mouth hanging open as she took in the tortured expression on his handsome face. He thought she had left him because he did something wrong. She didn't realize he ever felt there was anything to leave, "Marco, no, you didn't..." She sighed heavily, "I think we need to talk, really talk like we should have before," she said with a soft smile. Liam was never going to let her hear the end of this. He'd told her she'd broken Marco's heart; she didn't believe him. Now she was going to have to listen to him say, 'I told you so'. Studying the way Marco's silky hair fell across his forehead as he stared at her with his nervous gaze fixed firmly on her face, desperate for her to want him in return, she decided she didn't mind so much.

They spent the next hour talking through their feelings and how they both saw the relationship. Siobhan admitted she foolishly took him for granted, thinking it was just casual between them. He smiled ruefully and apologized for never telling her how he felt. He brushed her hair tenderly from her face and kissed her softly.

"I tried to keep it casual because I thought it was what you wanted, and, well, I just wanted to be with you any way I could." He ran his thumb over her jawline, caressing her skin.

Shaking her head, she huffed out a shaky breath, "Marco, I'm sorry. I don't know if I would have run away or not, then." She gave him a tentative smile. "But I won't run now." She lifted her palm to his face and cupped his cheek, as he looked at her hopefully.

"Does this mean we can try again, but this time, it's official? You and I are dating? Exclusive? We don't see others, and if you get tired of me, you'll actually tell me?" he whispered, his voice sounding strained.

She stared deep into his eyes, he looked so vulnerable then, as if his entire life depended on her answer. She couldn't believe she'd missed it before. Hating herself just a little more for the pain she'd blindly caused him, she nodded, vowing she would be more careful with his heart this time. "Marco, I'd like that very much."

He gathered her gently under him and kissed her again.

She gasped in surprise and then moaned in pleasure when he slid back into her, hard and ready for the next round. She noticed he was grinning roguishly a second before his ruby-red wings flared out, and he proceeded to remind her how well he knew her body.

Jack was having an amazing time with Mandy. She knew all the spots to hit for the best outfits, gossip, and lunch. They were laughing and talking, and he felt like he had known her forever. Mostly because she was an oversharer, and he knew her whole life story now. She'd been in some crazy escapades in her days, although he couldn't quite believe everything she said was true. She seemed to go from one harebrained antic to the next. He was utterly enthralled.

"Jack!" she squealed, rushing over to him waving a piece of clothing, "Darling, you simply *must* try these pants on. They would make that tush of yours so extra delicious. You have the cutest, tightest butt. Everyone is going to want a piece of you, and it will just make Davis wild with envy!" she declared.

He smiled indulgently and shook his head. "I don't want to make Davis wild with envy, though, darling."

She pouted, "Please, Jacky, do it for me?"

Rolling his eyes good-naturedly, he agreed to try them on while she clapped like a little girl getting a pony for her birthday. She bounced on her toes and bit her lip, so he hurried inside to keep from laughing at her enthusiasm.

In the dressing room, Jack admired his reflection, he had to admit, crazy Mandy was correct. They did wonders for his figure. He smiled, *why not?* "Okay, Mandy, you were right," he told her as he came out and modeled them, "Find me a shirt now."

She did a victory booty shake and ran to get him just the right top to compliment his coloring and the creamy off-white color of the slacks. She came back with a bright baby blue button-up with darker blue embroidered flowers down one side.

He eyed it skeptically but figured, when in Rome. He sighed; it did compliment his eyes. She had good taste in men's clothing, at least. They paid for their purchases, then stopped for a late lunch and a breather.

Mandy draped her hand over her forehead and declared she was wiped out and nothing would do to refresh her but a pitcher of mimosas on the patio at a nearby restaurant. They ate and laughed, and he tried to pump her for information about who else they could meet that might know Cyrus. She wouldn't be distracted from her own goal, though. She demanded Jack tell her how he met Davis. She knew of their mutual connections, but she just knew there had to have been a meet-cute. "Please, Jacky, tell me all the salacious details." She rolled her eyes as if tasting something delicious while she licked her lips.

Jack's mind went blank, and he thought frantically. He didn't know if Mandy knew about dragons and wasn't sure how much he could share. He finally rushed out, "We met at a work conference. We work for two different companies that the same man owns. We were both assigned to a project and went on a trip together."

She nodded, "Mmm, traveling for work and an illicit romance. Sounds steamy." She giggled and arched an eyebrow at him.

He choked on his mimosa, thinking of Davis blowing steam around his chest because he liked the way the vapor coated Jack's skin. "You have no idea," he murmured, winking at her.

"Jack," she moaned, "You are such a tease. You're every woman's dream. I was shocked you wouldn't look my way, and my heart was crushed. Then I found out you were with Davis, and it made sense. It's not fair! Davis obviously figured it out, so who hit on who first?"

Smirking, Jack said, "Oh, you know Davis, he was undressing me with his eyes when we were introduced. He has zero respect for corporate policies. We were off the clock when I returned the favor. I think he was just as surprised as you were."

She shrieked with laughter.

The man at the middle of their conversation appeared next to them and took Jack's mimosa, draining it. Davis was sweating and had definitely seen some sun today, his beautiful hair pulled back from his face, sticking up haphazardly. His toned forearms were more tan than usual.

Mandy tilted her head, shading her eyes, "How'd you find us, darling?"

"I could hear you down the street," he grinned, "That laugh of yours."

She demonstrated the braying laugh again, throwing her head back with her signature shriek.

Jack shook his head, she was fun, but he was beginning to see why Davis hadn't stayed with her long.

Davis leaned over and planted a hot, sweaty kiss on Jack's cheek. "My love, I'll have you know I'm an absolute failure at golf. Not a skill I've picked up over the years."

"Well, I'll tell you what you can do to get over it, take a shower! Phew!" Jack leaned back and laughed, waving his hand at the dragon.

Davis plopped down into a chair next to him, laughing as well, "Rude!" he declared with his dashing, impish grin.

"Darling," Jack smiled, "You know I love you, but before we go dancing, you are washing off the day." He reached across the table and took Davis' hand in his, rubbing his thumb across his knuckles, sighing in contentment at the gorgeous man that held his heart in his hands.

Mandy sighed dejectedly, "You guys are just so cute, I'm jealous."

Chapter 13

THEY DECIDED TO HAVE an early dinner before heading to the club with Dustin, Sissy, and Mandy. They lingered on the outdoor patio for a while, taking in the crowds and the fresh air. Being a Sunday, they also enjoyed the view of the enormous cruise ships leaving the port one after another, sailing off to tropical destinations. At the same time the passengers sipped Mai Tais and enjoyed all-you-can eat buffets.

Jack watched one giant ship sail by and shook his head in disbelief, "It's a floating city!" he exclaimed in amazement.

"Maybe we could go on a cruise for our honeymoon," Davis said softly, leaning his head on Jack's shoulder and twining their fingers together. "You think they'll let me dive off the top?"

"*No!* They would kick you off and it would cause a panic, and call to the Coast Guard!" Jack said sternly, then gazed at him tenderly. "Honeymoon. Davis, I wasn't sure at first you were serious about getting married. I still can't believe it sometimes." He shook his head. "I'm gonna marry the hell out of you!" He grinned and winked at Davis' devilish smile before pulling him back inside as their table was called.

During their meal, Davis watched Siobhan and Marco with interest. They were very at ease with each other, smiling and touching each other when they thought no one was looking. Whatever they'd done in the hotel while they were alone, seemed to have broken some barrier.

He was glad they'd apparently worked things out, so they weren't at each other's throats anymore. But it also seemed that Siobhan was over Lorenzo and was now with Marco again. Davis sighed softly, he really liked Marco and was glad for him. He also really liked Lorenzo and hoped Siobhan had been up front with him that she wasn't waiting for him to come back. He grimaced and shook his head, deciding that was a mess he didn't want to be involved in. He remembered how broken up Marco had been when she'd started dating Lorenzo. The normally fierce red dragon was a shell of himself, and it took months for him to get back to his normal training routine. Siobhan hadn't even noticed.

Davis changed his mind. He needed to know how this was going to affect their mission. "So, you two," he pointed at them with his fork, scrunching his eyebrows and adopting his most stern face. "What is this?"

Siobhan's face colored, and Marco beamed. She mumbled something unintelligible. Marco spoke up clearly, "What Siobhan was trying to say, is that the two of us are together. Officially, together this time." He was obviously very proud of this, his eyes bright and his smile stretching his mouth wide.

Davis' face softened, glad to see the elation on his friend's face. He turned a narrow glare on Siobhan, she had better treat Marco well, or he was going to have a word with her. Marco was a ruthless, skilled fighter, and they needed him at the top of his game when push came to shove. She seemed to sense his concern as she gave him a slow nod.

Jack leaned over and brought up the mission, getting them back on track. The four spoke in quick whispers discussing how to proceed. They needed to low-key interrogate as many people as possible, so they were going to divide and conquer to speak to as many others as they could. It was imperative that they quickly figured out who Cyrus was pretending to be now. They didn't know how long Vaughn had, and they were chafing at the delays already. There were too many and not enough hours in the day, all at the same time.

Back at the hotel, they were dressing for their night out. Jack sauntered out of the bathroom after putting his hair together. Contrary to popular belief, it took a lot of effort to get it to stay in its carefree-looking style.

Davis' mouth dropped open, and he leapt to his feet, breathing heavily.

"What?" Jack said innocently, with a cat who ate the canary grin.

A low whistle sounded, and Davis indicated Jack should spin around.

Jack did a fashion model strut and twirl while Davis gave him slow, appreciative applause.

"I got to give Mandy props on that. Jack, you look amazing. Damn, I don't want to take you out. I'll be beating the guys and girls off with a stick. The things those pants do to your ass. Mm," He bit his knuckle as he observed the area of Jack's body in question. "Hold on," he said, smacking Jack on his bottom, then unbuttoned the top two buttons of his shirt. "You wear it like this. But I better not see any hookers out there doing this," he leaned over and licked Jack's collarbone, then bit him gently. "You are mine!" he said with a growl and puff of steam from his nostrils.

Jack was ready to tell him they were staying in. Davis getting all territorial like that gave him shivery feelings deep in his stomach. And saying 'mine'? That did him in, melting him like butter. Any other time, he would have taken advantage of it, but he knew they had to get any lead they could on

Cyrus' whereabouts as soon as possible. He pictured Bridget's broken face in his mind, and it centered him quickly.

He cleared his throat, "Well, those hookers better keep their hands off you, too." He handed him a bag that contained an outfit he'd picked for him, with Mandy's help, of course.

Davis arched an eyebrow and grinned, "Oh, this should be fun."

As Davis was changing, Jack sat nervously on the bed, waiting. He knew the timing wasn't great. But the box had been burning a hole in his pocket, and he couldn't wait a day more. A few minutes later, Davis walked slowly out of the bathroom and stared at him. His eyes were shining, and his lips were trembling. "I think I found a little something extra in my clothes," as he held up his hand, showing Jack the ring that was now on his finger.

Jack smiled tentatively, then looked relieved as Davis grinned back.

"I love it, and I love you, and I'm so proud to wear this. It's perfect!" Davis announced happily.

"I love you, too, Davis. You can put it back in the box for the night, I understand," Jack said quietly as he let out a sharp breath, releasing the tension he'd been guarding as he waited for Davis' response.

The cheeky blue dragon shook his head, "Nope, it's on now, not coming off!" he grinned at Jack and waved his hand. "Mine, all mine, never coming off." He dropped to his knees in front of Jack as he sat on the edge of the bed. "Never," he whispered fiercely.

Jack felt his heart stumble and trip over how sincere Davis sounded, "I don't deserve you," he whispered, trying to keep himself together. Ridiculous to want to marry this man but not tell him why it meant so much for him to accept the ring. He bit his tongue to keep from blurting it out.

"Sure you do!" Davis said cheerfully, "And I absolutely deserve and cherish every wonderful part of you. Now let's go show these Miami bitches how we do heat over in Texas," he winked, wrapping his arms around Jack as he laughed. "We're perfect together."

When they made it to the lobby of the hotel, Sissy, Dustin, and Mandy were waiting for them there.

"Oh! EMM! GEE!" shrieked Mandy, "Look at you guys! Walking advertisements for hot sex, that's what you two are!" She was jumping up and down, seeing Davis and Jack dressed up for their night out. Then she caught sight of the ring on Davis' finger and squealed even louder. A feat which none of them had known was even possible. "Davis! It matches your eyes perfectly. Jack, you were right, it is an exact match! I could just cry! But I paid too much for these lashes to wash them off, so I'm going to settle for kissing you both!" She laid big smacking kisses on both men and twirled around, "Oh, love is wonderful!"

Siobhan and Marco, having just arrived, laughed in amusement at the theatrics on display. Siobhan smacked Jack on his behind and grinned, "Damn, Jack, looking good!"

Mandy caught sight of Siobhan. "Oh! Honey, no!" she gasped in horror, fluttering her hands in front of her mouth like frantic pigeons. "We can do better! You are a beautiful woman; you should look like one. Come on!" She grabbed Siobhan's hand and dragged her back upstairs, with the wielder looking helplessly over her shoulder, mouthing, *Help me.*

Marco tried and failed to hold back his laughter, while Jack and Davis grinned in delight.

Giggling, Sissy turned to Davis, "She won't take long, you said you had a car ready?"

He nodded, "Us big shots should arrive in style," he winked and took her arm, escorting her outside where a bright white limo had just pulled up, waiting to whisk them away. It had glowing, bright underlighting, which was currently painting the asphalt beneath the vehicle in a dizzying array of colors. Bass was thumping from the interior, and the driver held open the rear door, showing a disco ball churning away inside.

Jack stared at the car in abject horror, while Marco continued laughing until tears were rolling down his face. They had just begun to pile into the car when they heard shouting, "Wait for us!"

They turned to see Mandy hurrying towards them with a gorgeous woman in tow behind her. The woman had smokey bedroom eyes, full pouty lips begging to be kissed, and red-gold hair done up in a simple but elegant fashion that showed off the smooth column of her neck. Her blouse was hanging in a way that showed a hint of sun-kissed cleavage.

Jack's mouth dropped; whatever Mandy had done to Siobhan, it had been a miracle. He could tell the young wielder was nervous and uncomfortable with the changes, so he began applauding and whistling his appreciation.

She gave him a grateful, relieved glance as the others joined in. All except Marco, who looked like he had swallowed his tongue. She smiled at him shyly, and he staggered towards her as if he was being pulled by a magnet.

"Shi," he whispered, "You're always beautiful, but somehow, she performed the impossible and made you even more gorgeous." He put both hands on her waist and ran his thumbs up her sides, before slowly drawing her body possessively against his own. He was about to kiss her when Mandy slapped a neatly manicured hand over his mouth.

"Oh, no, you don't, lover boy. You're not messing up my work before anyone else sees it!" she laughed, "Get in the car, let's go!"

The others hurried to comply, and soon, they were on their way. In the car, Mandy demanded several selfies and spent a few minutes snapping just the right ones before posting a few with the caption 'Hot new faces alert!' Satisfied, she chattered non-stop the rest of the way to the club.

Once they arrived, Jack took a moment to appreciate and thank Sissy for getting them on the A- list in advance, because the line was around the building. He remembered a story Jorrie told him about her escapades in Russia. Their friend Franco pulled off an audacious stunt, pretending she was a celebrity, and the guys were her bodyguards. Somehow, the ruse worked. Franco was an incredibly gutsy man, his death a sore spot in their hearts. Jack was pretty sure that kind of trickery wouldn't fly here, not in Miami, where famous people were on every street corner.

A bouncer held the door for them and helped the ladies from the car, eyeing Siobhan in particular with open appreciation. She was followed by Sissy and Mandy, but the man's eyes returned to Siobhan.

Marco had to visibly check himself from growling. Jack squeezed his shoulder in reassurance and warning.

Jack and Davis exited the car, followed by Dustin. They glanced around and joined the other ladies.

After glaring at the bouncer, Marco hurried towards Siobhan and wrapped his arm possessively around her waist. "I wanted to burn his hands off for touching you," he gave a little rumble, and Siobhan grinned at him, her cheeks flushing at the attention.

Mandy sighed wistfully, "All the good ones are taken."

"Down, boy!" Siobhan whispered back, "I'll reward you for that later."

They made their way into the club and were immediately assaulted by strobing lights, loud music, and a crush of beautiful people writhing in time to the beat on the packed dance floor. It certainly seemed like the place to see and be seen. Jack narrowed his eyes and immediately began scanning the crowd for anyone looking even remotely like Cyrus. He glanced at Davis and Marco, noting they were doing the same.

After Sissy gave their names to the front desk, they were promptly escorted to a VIP booth. They ordered a round of drinks and settled in to do some crowd watching. Mandy had scampered away with the first man she made eye contact with. Dustin and Sissy were dancing nearby. The four friends leaned in and plotted in low tones about dividing up and working different sections of the club.

Before they could start their search, a woman with long black hair and hazel eyes wearing a skimpy red dress that screamed, 'Look at me', came over to greet them. Her thin spiked heels on the bright scarlet shoes seemed ready to snap under her at any moment. Her makeup was done with the heavy hand of someone trying to disguise the ravages of time and aging. "Hello," she purred in a voice that resonated with the grit of a pack-a-day smoker. "I'm Delilah, the manager, I understand one of you is Davis? The booking agent for Still Waters? Oh, and I know just which one you are, too. You look just like Shepard. Mmm, the most delicious set of twins I've ever seen."

She simpered at Davis as he stood in greeting, and coyly held out her hand, her fingers pointed down as if she expected him to kiss them. He reached to take her hand and purposefully held it in a way that showed his ring. Her face fell for a brief second, disappointment flashing across her features before she put on her mega-watt smile again. "So nice to meet you!"

She turned to Jack and appraised him hungrily. "And you must be Jack, I hear you and Jorrie have been friends for a long time. My, my, what handsome men they grow in Texas." She turned her eyes to his hands, obviously searching for a ring and smiled like a sly cat when she didn't find one.

Jack nodded as he also stood and took her hand. "She's my best girl. And she has great taste in men. So do I," he said with his usual charming grin as he brushed a hand over Davis' chest and took his hand.

Delilah's smile froze, and she looked helplessly around before settling on Marco, who was standing on the other side of the table. "Mmm, and who's this tasty treat?"

He made his way around the chairs and held her eyes as he kissed the back of her hand. His eyes smoldering and pinning her with his stare, he said in a sultry voice, "Lovely Delilah, my name is Marco, and I am delighted to be of... service, my dear." He'd laid on his Latin accent thickly and rolled his R's heavily as he flashed his dazzling white smile at her.

Jack stepped on Siobhan's foot to keep her from making any rude comments when he heard her sharp inhale.

Delilah's mouth fell open, and Jack could swear her knees quivered as she wobbled in her high heels. She recovered quickly, and she laid on some questionable charm, "Aren't you just gorgeous and smooth? And, who are you here with?" she asked Marco hopefully, wiggling her fingers at him.

"But senorita, I am so very alone, simply enjoying a night out with my good friends," he waved his hand to encompass the group before laying a hand over his heart.

She giggled and said, "Well, Marco, I hope to see more of you later," she winked and strutted away, completely ignoring Siobhan altogether.

The wielder burst into laughter as soon as Delilah was out of range and turned to Marco, "That was quite a fantastic display. I hope you know she expects you in her box office later."

He grinned back at her, "Well, she'll be disappointed then, won't she?" He turned to Jack and Davis and quietly said, "I thought we were going low-key and making ourselves available?"

Davis shrugged and flashed him the ring, "Sorry, but I put it on and made a promise, I can't take it off."

Marco stared at him consideringly, then nodded. He clapped them on their shoulders and, with a small smile, said, "Congrats you two, I'm really happy for you both, guess I'm taking one for the team." He raised his drink and called for a toast to the happy couple.

After a few rounds of 'cheers', it was time to hit the dance floor.

Chapter 14

JACK WAS TWIRLING SIOBHAN around the dance floor, whispering updates on his search in her ear. She had given hers to him already. He dipped her over his arm, to her surprise, then spun her again. She was laughing and having a great time. Marco cut in and took her off in his arms, hopefully, to pass along his intel, but more than likely, he just wanted to dance with his girlfriend after being pawed by Delilah again.

Jack smirked at them, then felt hands on his waist and a warm body close to his. He started to smile but faltered when he realized it felt off. These weren't hands he knew. He searched the crowd and noticed Davis was across the room dancing with Sissy and a group of her friends he was subtly interrogating. Jack's eyes widened, and he slowly glanced behind him. It was a man he'd never met before. The man was ruggedly handsome, although not nearly as gorgeous as Davis. Jack quickly caught Davis' eyes. He nodded once, indicating Jack should engage with the stranger. Jack fixed a large welcoming smile on his face, then whirled and danced with the man.

At the next song, the man introduced himself as Nathan and offered to buy him a drink. Jack declined the drink but agreed to another dance. After the song ended, he accepted the second offer and followed him to the bar.

Nathan smiled easily at Jack and asked him to tell him about himself. Jack talked a bit about who he was and where he was from, keeping the information vague and basic, claiming he was here for vacation with friends. He casually asked Nathan the same questions, trying to determine if he was someone who could possibly help them with their search. It turned out Nathan was not a local either. He claimed to be here on business, saying he was a photographer in town to shoot some ads for one of the cruise lines. "I'm always looking for models," he eyed Jack hungrily, "I have to say, Jack, you have a look. One I would love to capture. You have that guy next door meets Calvin Klein look that advertisers want. That I want." He brushed his knuckle over Jack's cheek.

Jack felt his cheeks heating up as he blushed, "Oh, I'm sure you say that to all the ladies," he laughed nervously. He was a little surprised at how upfront the man was. He would never have brazenly approached someone the way Nathan had done to him. He was solidly in love with Davis but appreciated the open admiration in the other man's stare, nonetheless.

Nathan tilted his head and studied him closely. He gave Jack a sultry smile before he handed him a card, "No, actually, I don't. Just something about you caught my eye, and I don't want to look away. I'm serious, though, Jack, please, give me a call." He placed a soft kiss on Jack's temple, saluted him with his drink and wandered away. Jack sat there in disbelief, no one had ever tried to pick him up so blatantly before. After a few minutes, a handsome man with eyes swirled blue like the ocean sat next to him.

"What was that about?" Davis asked.

Dumbfounded, Jack shook his head. "He's supposedly a photographer, and he asked me to model for him."

Davis blew air out of his lips in a rude noise and laughed. "Not that I don't believe you could, darling, but that's the oldest line in the book. I might have even used that before myself." He winked to show he was kidding. Davis picked up the card and idly studied it before grabbing Jack's wrist, "Wait, that was Nathan Wilde? He's, like, one of the top modeling photographers in the world!" Davis said in quiet awe. He pulled up a photo of the photographer on his phone and confirmed it, showing Jack a picture. "Okay, maybe that wasn't a line," he grinned, "You should call him!" His eyes swirled in delight, and he squeezed Jack's arm.

Jack tilted his head and stared at his fiancé like he was crazy, "I don't think he just wanted me to model," he snorted, "He made that abundantly clear. *You* didn't even hit on me that hard when we met."

"Maybe not, but I wasn't sure you'd be open to it," Davis shrugged, "But that's all he's getting!" They both laughed and ordered another round.

While they were waiting, Jack felt a different hand on his shoulder.

"Jack?" A voice came he never thought he'd hear again. He turned and stared disbelievingly at the man behind him, who was now staring back like he'd seen a ghost.

Finally pulling himself out of his shocked stupor, Jack spluttered, "Riley?" his voice rising incredulously.

The man, now identified as Riley, leaned in and gave Jack an awkward hug, ignoring the way Jack stiffened in the embrace. "Wow, of all the places to run into you, here you are."

Jack's face took on a stony, furious look, his eyes flashing with anger, and he grunted, "Here I am."

Davis could tell that whoever Riley was, he was not someone Jack was pleased to see. The two were still staring at each other. Jack in quiet, seething anger, Riley in hopeful wonder.

"So, um, how are you?" Riley asked, tapping his fingers on the bar rapidly.

"You really want to know?" came Jack's quiet response.

Davis recognized that tone, Jack's voice dropped to a deathly quiet when he was about to turn lethal; bad things soon followed. He needed to intervene, quickly. He leaned across and held out a hand, "Hi, I'm Davis. How do you know Jack?"

The other man took Davis' hand quickly and smiled politely, "Oh, Jack and I used to serve together. We, um, were friends, and uh, you know."

"Davis," Jack snapped before continuing in the same seething tone, "Meet Riley, my first boyfriend. A lot of firsts really. Including being the first man to break my heart by being the asshole who betrayed me and is the reason I'm no longer in the Marines." With that bombshell, he stood, knocking his chair over and stormed away.

Watching Jack's retreating form as it was lost in the crowd, Davis turned angry eyes on Riley, as he righted the bar stool. "So, you're *him*, I see," he said disdainfully with a slight growl. He clenched his teeth to keep his fangs from slipping out as they ached in his gums, ready to rip this man's throat out. He squeezed his hands into fists in his pockets in case his talons decided to make an appearance as well.

The man took a step back, obviously unsure what Davis was, but instinctively recognizing he was dangerous. He had a high and tight haircut that indicated he was possibly still serving. This made Davis even angrier, and fury practically radiated from his frame.

Riley seemed to gather a little courage before he smiled nervously at Davis, "Well, yeah, Jack and I dated, but it was before I was ready to come out and things didn't end so well," he stammered.

Glaring harder at him, Davis leaned in, "So, what, you see him sitting here after all these years and think you'll just pop over and say hey, as if nothing had changed in the meantime? Look man, I don't know all the details yet, but whatever you did, it had a major impact on his life, and he doesn't look on that as happy times. So kindly back the hell off and stay the *fuck* away from my fiancé." He stepped closer to the man, a growl in his chest, making it clear this was indeed a threat.

Riley stepped up to him, trying to puff out his own chest like he was the bigger danger in a show of misplaced bravado.

Davis simply laughed softly and let storms swirl into his eyes. "Oh, you clearly have no idea who you're fucking with right now." He snarled viciously, letting the warning rumble ripple over the other man, before repeating, "Stay. Away. From. Jack. He is *mine*."

Riley nodded and sat, completely cowed by Davis this time. His eyes were wide, and his mouth worked to make a sound without success.

Davis grinned malevolently and went looking for Jack. He wouldn't normally have made a scene like that, hinting at what he was, but Jack's happiness meant everything to him. He wasn't about to let that pansy-ass douche hurt Jack any more than he already had. He finally found Jack back at their table, having a drink with Siobhan who was taking a breather and rubbing her foot.

She'd not lacked for dance partners this evening, Marco claiming half of her time. Sissy and Dustin were still out on the floor and Mandy was dancing with Marco. Well, she seemed more interested in climbing in his pants but regardless, they were entertaining each other. Which meant she wasn't at the table bothering them.

Davis put a firm reassuring hand on Jack's arm and tenderly kissed his temple. "That piece of shit won't bother you anymore," he told him quietly.

Jack gave him a small thankful smile, "Thank you, my love, so fierce, you are too good to me."

Shaking his head, Davis told him, "Never, you are worth everything and more, my Jack." They kissed until Siobhan cleared her throat.

"Get a room you two," she said with an indulgent smile and envy in her tone.

Laughing, Davis grabbed Jack's hand, dragging him back to the dance floor where they both enjoyed the soothing slow song.

Jack sighed happily against Davis' neck as his fiancé's strong arms enveloped him, pulling him close and stroking his back. After the song ended, a strong Latin beat came on, and suddenly, Mandy squeezed herself between them, making a little sandwich. They laughed and shook their hips to the rhythm, a hot and close dance that soon caught the attention of the others in the group. Their friends joined in, and Davis and Jack were caught in a crush of warm bodies, swaying and pulsating to the music. Davis noticed that Jack was lost in the moment when he saw a hand on Jack's shoulder, smirking to see Nathan was behind him again. He grinned, relieved it wasn't another hard memory and turned Jack to engage the handsome photographer in the dance.

Nathan leaned into Jack's ear, "Have you given any thought to what I said earlier?" he asked hopefully.

Jack nodded and grinned as Davis discreetly poked him in the back repeatedly, encouraging him to accept. "I'm open to listening," he replied.

Nathan's eyes lit up and he smiled back, his full lips curving enticingly. "Call me tomorrow," he said before softly kissing Jack's lips then disappearing into the crowd.

Marco watched a blond man dancing with Siobhan in a way he felt was a little too familiar for his tastes. He was about to cut in, when Delilah, the manager, came up and ran her fingers through his hair.

"Hello Marco, so nice to see you having a good time," she tried to purr at him but sounded more like she was trying to dislodge phlegm.

He grinned at her, to cover how revolted he was. He thought, *the guys owe me big time for this.* "Well, the lovely Delilah, *hermosa*, you have returned to grace me with your beauty, *carina!*" She giggled in a way that someone had probably told her was cute and sexy but was actually grating on the nerves. Marco kept his smile anyway, he had a role to play.

"Oh, you are smooth, I'll give you that," she simpered, walking her fingers over his bicep.

He winked and let his gaze rove up and down her body like he was enjoying the view.

She inhaled sharply and lifted her breasts to make them look perkier. "So where are you staying?" she asked coyly.

Marco paused, "At the hotel with my friends, working, you know," he said, hoping she wouldn't ask the name or room number. He noticed Siobhan watching him flirt with Delilah and saw she was grinding her teeth.

He didn't blame Shi; Delilah was fawning all over him and it was shameless. He watched her take a calming breath and force herself to smile at the man she was dancing with. They agreed earlier, this was just for show, he wasn't going to go to bed with the brazen woman, just as Shi wasn't taking any of these men back to the hotel. Siobhan glanced back over just as Delilah leaned on him and began running her nails over his chest. His prickly woman flicked her wrist and the heel on the Delilah's shoe snapped like it had been threatening to do all evening.

She almost fell flat on her ample behind, but Marco caught her. Delilah made her embarrassed apologies and limped away to her office to change her shoes. Siobhan smirked then caught Marco grinning at her. He knew she had done it, and he bet she wasn't one bit sorry for it. She grinned back and winked as Marco came to claim her for the next dance.

"Shi." He shook his head. "That was a dirty trick, *mi amor*. She could have twisted an ankle or something," he murmured in her ear.

"Good, would serve her right," Siobhan snorted righteously in return.

"Shi, so angry! Over little me?" he whispered before he bit the delicate lobe of her ear gently, purring in a way he knew got her worked up.

"Mmm," she moaned, "All the time, I can't stand watching these tramps throwing themselves all over you. I just want to get back to the hotel and…" she leaned in and whispered in his ear what she wanted to do.

Marco's eyes went wide, and he swallowed hard. Siobhan had quite an imagination. He needed to sit for a minute and drink something cold, dancing was not going to be easy anymore. He dragged her back to the table, where he pulled her onto his lap and told her to sit and think about what she'd done to him. They shared a quiet, knowing laugh.

"I know you think I'm just letting them get handsy," he told her, "But I learned a little something about the owner of this place. It's actually a woman, and she's here from South Africa, where Baltrus was from. Maybe it's just a coincidence, but I think maybe not. Do we know who Cyrus' mother is? Or if there are any other siblings? We need to find out when we get back to the hotel."

Siobhan was quiet for a moment, chewing over this new information. "Should we get the others and call it a night?" she asked him.

They searched the large room, finally finding Davis and Jack in the crowd, dancing with each other and looking about as happy as could be.

"Nah," he laughed, "Let the newly engaged ones have a little more fun, I think Delilah was going to come back with more information anyway."

She grinned and nodded. "Oh yes, poor Delilah."

Jack and Davis were still dancing, they hadn't made any headway on finding Cyrus, so they were getting ready to call it a night. Marco popped over and gave them the heads up that he'd received some information from Delilah, and they were waiting for her to join them again.

A song made for holding your lover tightly began to play and Davis wrapped his arms around Jack from behind and danced closely with him. "I really love these pants, have I told you that?" he asked him.

Jack hummed merrily, "Only three times, but you can tell me again!"

Davis grinned, "Okay, I love these pants!" They were both chuckling now, Davis with his chin on Jack's shoulder as they swayed to the slower song.

Mandy ran over and grabbed Davis' arm, "Hey, Delilah said the owner was here and wanted to meet you. She's coming to our table! Come on!" she dragged them back.

They seated themselves around the table and Marco leaned over to share more about what he'd learned so far which clarified for Davis that the owner was indeed a woman. Not a man like they thought. But the fact that she was from the same area as Baltrus was certainly setting off alarm bells. Maybe this trip wasn't wasted after all.

Soon, Delilah returned in a pair of flats accompanied by an older woman with ebony skin and a dazzling smile. Davis had ghosted his and Marco's dragons so they wouldn't be caught if anyone was using any type of detection spells or indicators. They knew from past experience, that anyone working with the Shadows used stolen magic to sense when dragons were near. They sat at the table casually while Delilah introduced the exotic looking woman as Saharra.

She had a velvety voice that was low-pitched and sensual. It seemed as if the entire room quieted down to listen even though there was no discernable change in the volume. She simply exuded a command for a person's focus on her to the point they tuned everything else out. Many eyes turned her way when she walked through. She was an elegant, classic beauty not often seen in this area. Her hair was very short, cropped close to her head. She wore a sleek sheath of silvery material that fit her like a second skin. Her musical laugh and engaging warm brown eyes put everyone quickly at ease.

After some small talk, she got down to business and inquired with Davis about booking Still Waters. Fortunately, Davis was not bluffing when he said he was a booking agent. He pulled up their calendar and explained they would be going on a tour soon, and they weren't playing small clubs anymore, but if she was interested in a private booking, he could help her out. Turns out she was and didn't balk at the price that Davis quoted.

"My lovely friend, you seem very eager to have them play for you. What is the reason for the event, should we plan to play anything special? A birthday? An anniversary?" he inquired lightly, going for a casual sound.

Saharra gave a throaty laugh, "Oh, much better, a celebration of an achievement generations in the making! Something my family has been trying to accomplish for a long time."

Jack tightened his hand on Davis' leg under the table. That did not sound good at all, in fact, it was rather ominous. Davis gave an almost imperceptible nod, "I see, quite an achievement then."

She laughed again, "Oh yes, quite a coup." She stood, "Please, send me the contract, and we will talk soon, yes?" She nodded and walked away before they could ask anything further, melting into the crowd like a ghost in the fog that blanketed the port in the morning.

Chapter 15

BY THE TIME THEY got back to the hotel, everyone was tired but knew they needed to follow up on this new lead immediately. They hurried to Marco's room to make use of his computer setup with its multiple stations. They made their inquiries about Saharra and her family connections, while Jack called Bridget and gave her updates. She was understandably saddened they hadn't found Vaughn, but grateful they were trying. She knew Vaughn was still alive, she could feel him through their mating bond. It was the only thing keeping her together, but she couldn't reach him directly. He was too far away and possibly unconscious or drugged. Once they'd gathered all they could for the night, everyone dispersed to their separate rooms. At least, Jack and Davis tried to pretend they didn't see Marco follow Siobhan to her room.

The next morning, they decided to stick close and monitor the incoming information about their target. Answers were slowly beginning to trickle in about Saharra. Davis was pacing like a caged animal, his impatience for any small lead on Vaughn's whereabouts wearing upon their nerves like a heavy weight. His agitation was palpable and suffocating for the others. Finally, after the fourth time he'd muttered *fuck* under his breath, Jack shooed Davis out to run some errands. Anything to give them some room to focus and concentrate. The blue dragon was not one for sitting still, the delays chafing his short fuse. Unexpected rain fell around the bay, sending sunbathers scurrying for cover. After a few hours, Davis returned — calmer — with a small bag and a visitor.

Jack was startled to see Nathan Wilde enter his room behind Davis. "Um, hi, Nathan, good to see you again. Sorry, I wasn't expecting company, or I would have tidied up in here a bit." He glanced around the spotless room; he just didn't know what else to say in the awkward moment. Davis gave no clues, just grinned at Jack with a mischievous twinkle in his ocean-swirled eyes.

Nathan laughed in understanding, "It's quite alright, Jack, I'm sorry to drop in like this. Davis here called me and told me you agreed to pose for me. I mentioned that ad for the cruise line, I believe? You've got the look they are going for."

"Oh, he did, did he?" Jack said sweetly. His voice was syrupy and laced with a touch of venom that wiped the smirk from Davis' mouth. "Well, I would love to as soon as I finish up my job here."

"I also understand that some congratulations are in order?" Nathan grinned harder as he glanced back at Davis who had taken a step back. "Davis told me you two are engaged!"

Jack now stared at Davis lovingly, his earlier irritation vanishing in a blink. "Yes! Just happened, as a matter of fact. Thanks so much." He leaned forward and pulled Davis close, kissing his temple tenderly.

The handsome photographer smiled softly at the couple. "Which leads me to the other reason I'm here. I have a proposal for you." He grinned at Jack's raised eyebrows, "Not *that* kind, but related. I'm doing a spread on weddings for a magazine. In addition to how incredibly gorgeous you both are, given your connection to Still Waters, your wedding would be a great draw. I would be honored if you would let me shoot your wedding for my project. I get the pictures I need; you guys get a photographer. What do you say?"

Jack was speechless, as his mind raced. *What is even going on? This kind of thing just doesn't happen.* A world-renowned photographer wanted to use him as a model and offered to do their wedding for free in exchange for using their shots in a magazine. *Yes, I'm dreaming, that's it.*

"Jack," murmured Davis, nodding his head to indicate that Nathan was still waiting for an answer.

"I guess I say, sure, why not, yes!" Jack laughed.

Davis grinned, then knelt on one knee, holding up a box, "Since you're in a yes mood, and I didn't get to do this properly the first time, I want to correct something. I'm not one for flowery speeches, but Jack Ridgeway, I love you more than anything in this world, and I want nothing more than to spend my life making you happy. Will you please do me the honor of being my husband, my partner, my best friend for the rest of our lives?" He opened the box, and Jack saw the ring was almost an exact match of the one he gave Davis the day before. The stones were a slightly lighter shade of blue, just like his eyes.

Jack, who hated crying, couldn't hold back the tears and nodded an enthusiastic yes, as Davis slid the ring on his finger. The metal felt warm and alive on his finger, sending waves of happiness through his body.

Hearing a few camera clicks, Jack realized Nathan was still there and had captured the moment.

"Well, that was just beautiful and a fantastic start. You guys are just so inspiring, you give me hope. Now, go celebrate; I will be in touch, Jack," Nathan said before he quietly left the room.

Jack turned to Davis, his smile trembling. The night before, when they were lying in bed, Davis told Jack about finding the ring in the clothes.

He stopped dead in his tracks and stood there in surprise when he saw the small velvet box in the bag with the new clothes. At first, he thought Jack left it there on accident. Then he realized it was positioned right on top where he couldn't miss it. He correctly surmised that Jack was asking to make it official. Davis said he tried not to cry; he didn't want to give Jack the wrong idea. When he opened it and saw the titanium band with deep blue sapphires worked through it, he realized they were the same color as his wings. Davis' admitted his heart skipped a beat at how perfect it was.

Now Davis turned his stunning smile on Jack. "My happily ever after forever love," he murmured as he leapt to his feet and gathered Jack to him, kissing him deeply.

Jack stared at the ring now resting on his finger and twisted it around. It was just as gorgeous on his hand as it was on Davis'. Maybe more. He smiled at it, his heart feeling full, as Davis quietly slipped his hand into Jack's and their rings clinked together with a soft metallic chime. Jack sat suddenly, his knees feeling weak and wobbly, his stomach fluttering. "Davis, I can't tell you what this means to me. I never thought I'd see a ring there."

"Never?" asked Davis quietly as he sat and brushed his fingers through Jack's golden hair. "But... you... were engaged before," he gazed at him curiously, his words slow and halting, reflecting his confusion.

"I was," Jack agreed miserably, "But Darren didn't want to wear a ring, and he never wanted me to have one either. He said they were too feminine and just a symbol of ownership." He shook his head sadly. "It was just another thing he controlled and held back from me." He sighed, "It's why I was nervous about giving you one. I know you're not Darren, and you wouldn't do that to me, but it's hard to let go of the past sometimes."

Davis grabbed Jack and kissed him again, fiercely, and passionately, "That stupid ignorant ass! Complete idiot. I'm so sorry he hurt you, Jack,

I'm sorry he broke your heart. But my love, I'm not sorry he's gone because that meant you were available for me. You know I wanted to be with you from the moment I met you, and now we are going to be together forever," he whispered.

"I... I need to tell you something Davis," Jack said softly taking a deep breath, "I need to tell you why there's so much you don't know about me even now. There are huge parts of my life that I've never shared with anyone, because I've always been led to believe I should be ashamed of who I am. I'm not anymore. But my life until I met you was full of secrets and hiding. I don't want that between us. I have nothing to hide from you and I want you to know everything that I've never been able to tell anyone." His eyes locked onto Davis' the fear of baring his soul plain in them.

Nodding Davis pulled Jack down on the bed and wrapped him in his arms. "I'm here to listen Jack, give me your fears."

Jack shuddered in his arms as he used the words that Jack gave him in the night when he needed to be comforted. Slowly Jack shared with him the details of his family's rejection, Riley's betrayal, his miserable attempts at being 'normal' and finally Darren's controlling abusive behavior. Davis took it all in and simply encouraged Jack, letting him know he was safe and loved. When he was done, he turned his eyes to Davis, the need to be cherished clear within the bright blue, shining with unshed tears. Davis pulled him close and showed him how much he desired him. They made love, gently, tenderly holding on to one another, cherishing what they had in each other.

Chapter 16

THAT EVENING, THEY RECEIVED an invitation to come back to the club the following night. Their names would be on the list again. They were gathered in Marco's room, reviewing the information that had come in during the day. Try as they might, they could not link any information about Saharra to Cyrus. It seemed on paper as if this was a true coincidence. Davis grumbled that he still didn't trust it.

Jack spoke up, "What if you tell her you need to know for security purposes, and that it's a clause in their contract that there are certain events they won't be involved in, you know, like a rider, for political reasons?"

"Babe, that's brilliant!" Davis stared at him with pride.

"Yes!" Siobhan nodded, "They have to be careful what they attach themselves to these days. Celebrities getting canceled is all the rage."

Davis borrowed one of Marco's laptops and pulled up their standard booking contract, then adjusted some of the wording. He nodded when done, "I may just make this part of the standard contract from now on. Thank goodness Shepard negotiated that with the producer. Although, after this big tour starts, they probably won't be doing any more private bookings unless it's like, the President or something."

Jack slid behind Davis, put an arm around his chest, and kissed the top of his head. Davis put his hand on Jack's arm and squeezed it in acknowledgement. "Okay, contract is altered and ready to send over," a few more keystrokes, "And done! Now we wait!" He smiled around the room.

"Got it!" Marco said suddenly. They whipped around to face him, hope on their faces. "Cyrus is now going by the name Gavin Westwind, he's working as an art dealer and is collaborating with a local gallery here for a display of South African art that will open in two weeks. It's not the same time frame as Saharra's supposed generational accomplishment so that's interesting. I don't know why we can't find a link, but there has to be one!" He grimaced; irritation apparent in the set of his shoulders.

Normally, Marco could get any question answered quickly, but he just wasn't having any luck here, and it was obviously frustrating him.

Siobhan moved behind him and began rubbing his shoulders, murmuring soft encouragement. He relaxed a little and shook out his fingers, "Okay, so I'm working on a home address still, but I do have the address for the art gallery. What do you say we check it out tomorrow?" He glanced around at the others.

Solemn faces nodded back. They made their plans and went back to their rooms, ready to call it an early night for the long day ahead tomorrow.

Marco noticed that Siobhan was lingering behind him, clasping her hands in front of her in agitation. He tilted his head and made a soft humming noise of inquiry.

"Marco," she finally sighed, running her fingers through his silky hair. "Don't be so rough on yourself, this is a hard job, and you're doing amazing."

He rumbled in his chest and rubbed his face on her palm, "I know, it's just, this is *Vaughn*. And Vaughn, well, he's usually the one running this. I feel like an imposter, like I'm going through the motions but not really getting anywhere." He sighed heavily. "This is why Vaughn is the leader, and I'm the guy standing behind him."

She drew in a sharp breath and knelt in front of him. "Don't you dare say that!" she demanded. "You are by far one of the smartest, strongest, and bravest men I know! Vaughn couldn't do this on his own either, he always has you and Liam to help him. Don't do that, Marco. Don't you sell yourself short!"

Marco stared at the fierce and fiery woman in front of him. It was no wonder he'd fallen for her. She was all fire and passion; she should have been a red wielder, but she was born into a green family. He loved that about her. He stilled. *Loved?* He thought. He realized it was true, he did love her, and he'd been putting off admitting it. But he wasn't sure she was ready to hear it. Maybe he could show her, though.

He grabbed her and kissed her hungrily, pouring heat and his feelings into it. He thought maybe, just maybe, she had picked up on some of it, her expression dreamy and full of wonder. He laid his forehead on hers, "*Gracias, carina,*" he whispered, giving a soft chuckle, "Thank you for believing in me and for helping me pull my head out of my ass."

She laughed softly, "Any time."

He stood quickly and pulled her to her feet. "Come on," he said.

"Where are we going?" she asked, confused.

"Out," was all he replied.

"But what about the others?" She started towards Jack and Davis' room.

"No, this isn't about the mission, this is about us. Shh now. No more questions. Just… come with me, Shi. Please."

Finally, she silently nodded and followed him out the door.

The hotel was close to the beach, so they quickly made their way down to the sand. They slipped their shoes off and strolled along the shoreline, water rushing over their feet. Holding hands, they wandered farther from the lights of the city, enjoying the bioluminescence of the waves at night. With no moon, it was very dark.

Marco came to a sudden stop. "Stay there!" he instructed her gently, moving a short distance away. He glanced around, checking for other people, and seeing no one, stripped off his shirt. He let his wings unfurl and flapped them in the breeze a bit, enjoying the night air on his skin.

Siobhan started towards him, irresistibly drawn to those magnificent ruby-colored wings, but he held up a staying hand.

He undressed completely and stood there on the beach, fully nude, wings extended. *He's glorious*, Siobhan thought, *absolutely stunning*. He shimmered then, and her breath caught. *He's shifting? To full dragon?* She'd never seen his dragon up close before.

She'd only see glimpses of his form, and it was only in battle. She saw Lorenzo's dragon from a distance in the same battle but never close up, not one-on-one like this. It was something dragons didn't do unless they were with a mate, or they were carrying a wielder for a specific purpose.

Her mind shied away from the 'M' word. She didn't want to think about mating anyone. *It's because I'm a wielder*, she justified in her mind, a slight panic setting in. *He just wants some air and doesn't want to be alone.* Continuing to create justifications in her head, she reasoned, *I can put up a shield for him if needed*, ignoring the fact he had his own magic and perception filters.

She tilted her head back and looked up and up, studying the massive red dragon in front of her. He was enormous. Even larger than Vaughn's father Ivan, whom she had seen on their trip to Italy. She'd thought he was huge. She felt her heart swell suddenly with the knowledge she was seeing something he never showed anyone else. Try as she might, she knew her flimsy justifications weren't true, there was much more at the heart of this. They were definitely going to have to discuss the reasons later. For now, though, she decided to just enjoy the beauty in front of her. She slowly walked around him and tentatively ran her fingers along his scales. She'd felt dragon scales before. Her brother Liam used to take her flying all the time. But this wasn't her brother, and Marco far surpassed Liam in size.

His wings, outstretched now and catching the warm breeze coming from the ocean, were like the sails on a ship. His long tail was covered in spikes that grew exponentially larger as they continued up his back. His fangs slipped down past his lips in a deadly grimace even though he was relaxed. Their wicked curves followed the line of his hard jaw, vicious in their stillness. His talons, much like Ivan's, were razor-sharp scythes on the ends of his toes, gouging deep grooves in the sand under his paws. No doubt, if he were on pavement, he would make sparks when he walked. The deep fire engine red of his scales gleamed despite the lack of light. Siobhan applied more pressure to the hard scales under her hands, her awe at the beauty in front of her causing her breathing to become shallow and her smile ratcheted up even brighter. He was magnificent!

Marco purred and rumbled at her touch, letting her know she was welcome to keep doing it. She continued along his side, stroking her hands over his wings. He flopped down in the sand and leaned towards her, moaning and begging for more. She laughed then, her voice ringing out over the water, the sound echoing like music on the waves. He gave a small chuff, seeming to enjoy the sound. She made her way back up to his head and stared him full in the snout.

"You are gorgeous in this form, Marco. Thank you for sharing it with me, I'm honored."

He nodded his giant head and nudged her shoulder.

She laughed again, and he squeezed his eyes in contentment. She, of all people, would understand what this meant to him.

He sighed, a happy sound, and chuffed again. He motioned for her to get on.

Siobhan stared at Marco in shock. Was he inviting her to fly? It was one thing to show her his true form, it was quite another to let her ride. She'd only ever flown with Liam, and that was because they were family. She took a step back. He chuffed at her again and motioned.

He fluttered his wings and made a small sound that seemed to be the word, please.

She grinned then, "Oh, hell yeah!" she said. She ran and vaulted to his neck, settling gently between the spikes there.

He was definitely a lot more deadly than her teddy bear brother, but she'd been flying a long time and knew how to do this.

With a rumble and a snort, Marco launched himself straight out over the ocean.

Siobhan squealed a little. Okay, *that* was not something she was used to. Most dragons she knew took a running start to fly. She took a few deep breaths to try and calm her racing heart.

Marco was so powerful; he apparently didn't need that extra running room. He shot off the sand like a cannon, and she had to hold on for dear life.

She slapped his scales, "You jerk!" she shouted, "You could have warned me." She heard a low grumbling, and his neck rippled. He was laughing at her. The sound made it impossible to hang onto her anger, so she laughed with him and threw her arms out into the night sky. She loved this feeling!

She was lucky she grew up with a dragon brother who adored his little sister.

"Marco, this is... it's... I can't find the words. Just, thank you!" she called to him, her voice thick with emotion she didn't want to label, leaning down and kissing his neck.

He chuffed again and rumbled under her, letting her know he was enjoying it too. They flew high into the clouds, and she trailed her fingers through them; then, he glided lower over the water, dragging his claws through the waves. Some of the spray flew up and coated her in the salty brine, but she didn't care. This was her idea of heaven.

It was getting late; Marco reluctantly huffed, they needed to go back. He felt her lean down and wrap her arms around his neck. He smiled, and his body heated in response. He was sunk; he loved her with every fiber of his being. It warmed him in ways his internal fire never could. Now, he just needed to get her to realize she loved him, too. It had to be her idea, or she might run. He wanted her badly as his mate but knew she would balk if he even mentioned the word. Of course, he'd thought a lot of other things about her in the past, and because he hadn't talked to her about it, she'd drifted away.

Maybe this time would be different. They were talking now. He was hesitant, though; he didn't want to push too hard and too fast and push her away again. He didn't think he could take it this time.

"Mmm, I'd love to know what's going on in that big scaley head of yours," she whispered teasingly to him. Her tone was sultry and full of heat.

His ears twitched. He wasn't going there.

She laughed suddenly, "I know you can't tell me until you change back, which looks like it will be soon. I see our hotel and your tiny pile of clothes on the beach there."

He nodded and glided down to the edge of the water, landing gracefully near where they'd taken off.

Siobhan slid down to the sand and stepped back. He was about to change when she spoke quickly, "Wait! Before you shift back, come here!"

He obligingly put his head down next to her, curious what she wanted.

"Jorrie told me something about you guys, and I just have to try it. Tilt your head this way," she instructed, waving towards herself.

He did, and she hurried over to his side. She stood on her tiptoes, stretching to his ear and began to scratch behind it, sinking her fingers in the soft flesh there. He moaned, and his eyes rolled back in ecstasy. He purred so loud it sounded like a giant diesel truck warming up. He licked the back of her leg and rubbed his head on her so hard he almost knocked her over with his enthusiasm.

She laughed in sheer delight, her eyes lighting up in a way that made him quiver inside, he never wanted that look to leave her face.

"Oh yeah, you like that! Jorrie was right, after all!" She continued to chuckle as he whipped his head around and gave her his other ear. She scratched that one, too, and he continued to rumble.

Suddenly, he shimmered and wrapped his arms firmly around her back. When he shifted, he was naked, and now that body was hard and ready, pressed firmly against her, his length digging into her stomach.

He frantically pulled her clothes off, and they tumbled to the ground, waves gently lapping over their feet. "God, Shi," he gasped desperately as he wrapped her hair around his fist and pulled her head back, biting at her throat, the way he had on the boat. "You touching me like that, it's more than I can take," he growled, scraping his fangs over her shoulder before raising his gaze to hers.

He knew he had flames in his eyes, and smoke was pouring from his nostrils. He felt as wild and primal as if his dragon was still in charge. He hoped he wasn't scaring her or overwhelming her.

Siobhan arched up into him and caught his mouth with hers, nicking her lip on his fang but ignoring it. She bit his lip just hard enough to sting, then licked it to brush that away. She called his name, dug her nails into his neck, and ground her hips against him.

Marco gasped and responded with another growl before he yanked her thighs open and plunged into her. He still had his wings out and used them to drive into her as hard as he could, not even feeling the water rushing over and under them. The intensity and urgency he was experiencing pushed his movements, driving him with reckless abandon.

She was soon screaming his name and wrapping her legs around his waist, digging her heels into his backside, urging him deeper. Her hands flailed for something to grab onto, and she ran them up his back and over the arches of his wings.

He growled loudly, the feeling so intense he could barely stand it. He set a punishing pace that was wrecking them both. A few sparks flew from his mouth, and he tried to hold back the raging inferno building in him. He stared into her eyes and felt his fangs drop even further. God, he wanted to mark her so badly.

But she wasn't ready, so he dragged them along her throat again as she moaned and enjoyed the raspy breaths she was taking in between. He hoped she was close, the way she was writhing under him was dragging him to the brink.

Her thighs tightened around him like a vice, and she screamed his name, before he felt her warmth flooding him as she shattered underneath him.

Her eyes blazed with her magic, glowing in the night as waves of green burst from her skin and shimmered around him. He almost paused in his motion; it was so beautiful, and it had never happened before. Siobhan kept a tight hold on her magic, and for her to lose control… His own breathing became jagged, and he frantically fought to keep his rhythm, but the warm, wet, and beautiful woman wriggling under him was too much. He roared his release, filling her with his pleasure as the green waves sank into his skin. They slid through him like a caress and wrenched another groan and spasm from him.

He collapsed to the sand with her, gasping as the ocean waves now crashed over their bodies, cooling them. Steam rose from his back, where the water sizzled with the heat of his skin. He propped himself up on his elbows and grinned down at her, marveling at the sheen of green magic still shimmering softly on her skin. She looked like a goddess. A very soggy one as another wave wrapped around them and swirled through the molten metal color of her hair. He snorted, "Oh Shi, you're all wet!"

She smacked him with a handful of wet sand and their combined laughter carried over the water's edge into the night.

Chapter 17

THE FOLLOWING MORNING, THEY were all sitting in the hotel dining room, having breakfast. Marco leaned over and whispered something to Siobhan that had her face flaming, and she whispered back something that sounded like having sand in places sand shouldn't be. He snorted into his coffee cup.

Jack rolled his eyes, those two were certainly in a much better place.

Davis grinned at him and whispered, "Maybe we should see where we can get some sand later."

He almost choked on the bagel he was eating. He glared at his fiancé, who laughed at his thunderous expression. He swallowed the bite, and told him, "Only if the sand is in *your* places."

"You, my love, are not a morning person," Davis snorted as he rolled his eyes in an exasperated manner and scrunched his nose.

Jack blew a kiss at him and winked, eliciting laughter from the couple on the other side of the table.

They decided to take the boat out and enjoy some sun while they could, hoping to wrap up the mission soon. They really needed to find Vaughn. Bridget was not doing well, according to the reports from home. They spent some time talking to other boat owners and high rollers, receiving plenty of invitations for the next few days for dinners and other activities. They asked about art dealers and local galleries, mentioning an interest in acquiring some pieces but didn't receive many leads. After a few hours, they were ready to go to the art gallery Marco had located to see if they could find out more about Cyrus from there.

The interior of the gallery was bright, but cool. It took advantage of natural lighting through several skylights and high windows, angled and filtered to protect the delicate pieces within. The soft glow was welcoming, inviting and peaceful. The space was filled with beautiful pieces and a reverent, quiet hush. Only a few other guests strolled through the large open space, mumbling softly over the tasteful collection. A tall, strikingly pretty woman with neatly coiled dark brown hair, hazel eyes, and a willowy grace came from the back to greet them. She was wearing a neat business suit and pencil skirt. Her no-nonsense heels clicked sharply across the tile floor.

She stopped in front of them, smiling shyly, and greeted them before softly asking, "How may I help you?" Her voice was light and airy, pitched in a way that didn't echo in the space but conveyed warmth and comfort.

Jack smiled back genuinely, enchanted by her for some reason he couldn't understand. He suddenly felt a protective pull towards her. Shaking himself, he remembered their mission and gave her his signature disarming grin, placing a hand over his heart. "My goodness," he drawled, a hint of southern charm in his voice, "I'd heard the proprietress here was lovely, but I didn't know she would be such a stunning vision of beauty! I hope you can help me — us — I mean... us." He smiled coyly at his seeming slip-up. "We're here from the University of Texas, Austin. I have a few students with me, and we heard you were getting an exhibit from South Africa. I was hoping to show them while we are in town. Professor Simon Shelton." He held out a hand, kissing the back of her fingers when she took it.

She smiled brightly, responding to him as most people did. She blushed and giggled slightly, "Oh, Professor Shelton, how lovely to meet you! I'm so sorry, but I've only just received the pieces yesterday. I won't be showing them for two more weeks. Will you still be in town then?" she asked with hope sparkling in her eyes.

Jack's face fell, his expression suggesting he was devastated. "Oh dear, no, we must be back at the campus by then. These wonderful young minds are students from one of my advanced studies courses, and we came here to view some of the Haitian exhibits at the Perez Museum. I heard from a friend who had it on good authority that you have a new showing here. I was so looking forward to it." Disappointment pulled his lips down into a cute frown that had the woman biting her lip.

He turned to the others, doing their best to look like college students, and not a group of dragons and a magic wielder who aged unnaturally slowly. Jack was the only one who looked somewhat close to his real age, even though he looked at least a decade younger than he was, so he'd been elected 'Professor'.

The woman frowned, seeming sincerely distressed at letting him down. "I'm so sorry you've come all this way. The pieces really are magnificent, and I'm so fortunate my benefactor decided to display them here and not at one of the local museums."

Jack nodded slowly, "That's what captured my fancy," he gave her an appraising look as if that wasn't all that captured his attention. His gaze raked her from head to toe and back again, approval curling his lips, his expression showing a hint of lust. He took a small step closer to her. "I wonder, is there a chance the owner of the collection might consent to a private viewing? In the name of educational progress? These lovely young people are the future of the art world, and it would really be something to add to their CVs to study such pieces." He could tell she was going to give in. "Please, Marissa?" he cooed, glancing at her name tag. "It would mean... so much to me," he gave her his most dazzling smile, and she smiled back, clearly taken in by his plea.

"Of course, Professor Shelton," she started, her voice reflecting her eagerness to please.

He waved a hand negligently, "Please, a woman as beautiful as you, simply must call me Simon."

He winked, and she stifled another giggle, "Okay... Simon," she said as if she was being naughty, "I'll give Gavin a call and see if we can arrange a little something."

Jack clapped his hands, "Oh, that's lovely. Marissa, I must admit, I'm finding myself drawn to you. I hope you won't think me too forward in saying you are stunning. I didn't know Miami had such beauty hidden away. You are obviously as passionate about the arts as I am. I love what you've done here," he looked around in appreciation, "The use of the natural light, the composition of it all. I wonder, Marissa," he gently ran his fingers down her arm as he leaned in, "If I might call on you for lunch soon so we can discuss our common... interests?" He spoke softly, as if he didn't want the others to hear him.

She swallowed hard, then nodded silently as she wrote her number on the back of her card. Jack wrote his on another, and he kissed the back of her hand. "I look forward to hearing from you soon," he winked and then turned to leave, throwing a smoldering glance over his shoulder that seemed to make the woman's knees shake. The others were doing their best to look like they were bored with the whole thing.

Once they were around the corner and out of sight, Siobhan jumped on Jack's back like a rucksack and hugged him from behind. "Jack, daaaahling!" she drawled, "That was brilliant! You are the king of wooing women who don't know any better," she laughed as Jack made a pained face.

"Ugh, I feel so dirty!" he said, "I hate using her like that. She just seems so innocent. I mean, the poor dear was practically a puddle at my feet. Surely, other men have come on to her before." He shook his head in disgust.

Davis and Marco laughed, clapping him on the shoulder. "Come on, you dirty old man, let's go grab a drink to wash out that filthy mouth of yours," Davis cheered.

Jack rolled his eyes and smirked, "That's not what you said last night."

They all roared with laughter at Davis' indignant expression before he joined in on the merriment.

Siobhan leaned over and kissed Jack on the cheek, "Honey, I know you don't want to hurt anyone, but we need to find Vaughn. You're a very good-looking man, and you're really in tune with what people want. It's not like you walk around with a blinking neon sign that says you're gay or that you like men," she shrugged, "neither one of you do. So, most people don't realize it unless they see you two together." She gestured at both of them and shook her head.

Davis cleared his throat and held up Jack's right hand where he'd switched his ring so it wouldn't give away that he was engaged. "He doesn't like men, he loves me!" he huffed. He grinned when Jack leaned over and kissed his cheek, smiling.

Back at the hotel, they ran a double check on the owner of the gallery, Marissa, to be sure she wasn't involved. From all appearances, it seemed she was on the up and up. She was young, but it seemed her parents gifted her the gallery when they retired. Nothing was off in her background, Marco announced.

Stretching, Marco glanced up, "Hey, what time are we going tonight? I wanted to reach out to a friend in Prague about something, and I need to catch him at the right time."

They checked their watches and debated, deciding to get ready for dinner now, then pick up the others and head to the club to see if they could get more information from Saharra. They retreated to their rooms and began the process of prepping for their next sojourn into the world of Miami's nightlife.

They picked up Mandy only, Sissy and Dustin begging off for the evening. She was currently giving Siobhan some fashion advice and touching up her makeup. When they arrived, they were escorted straight to a table and offered a bottle of champagne, compliments of the owner. Davis nodded at the others; they were definitely being courted for something.

They were concerned that Saharra was on to them, who they were and why they were here. They needed to turn up the heat a bit before they lost the opportunity. Delilah approached with a simper for Marco and a side eye for Siobhan. She was picking up there was something there, and she had competition. Marco only smiled back as a courtesy.

Davis distracted the manager, "Delilah," he cooed, wrapping her name around his tongue in a sultry voice that made her shiver, "It's so wonderful to see you again. And thank you for inviting us back. It's an amazing place, and I've been telling my brother and sister-in-law all about it. They are very intrigued and looking forward to possibly playing here." He was so smooth she was nodding in agreement, but Jack knew it was a lie because they'd all agreed to leave Jorrie and Shepard alone during this. They would only bring them in if they were absolutely needed.

She gushed at Davis, still obviously attracted to him and remembering his connection to Still Waters, "Of course, of course. We are absolutely delighted to have you all back. Saharra should be along shortly; I know she was anxious to finalize the deal with you." She brushed a hand along Marco's shoulder as she slinked away in what she probably believed was a sexy strut, wiggling her hips. Mandy trotted off after, trying to get more information about the private event and wrangle an invite.

Siobhan glared daggers at the woman, "Trashy cougar," she grumbled.

Marco burst out laughing, "I think she would have to be older than me, *si*? I'm the one robbing the cradle here, does this make me the cougar?" he tapped a finger on his chin before winking and giving her an exaggerated growl.

She smiled, acknowledging it was true.

Davis chimed in, "Um, sorry, but if anyone is winning the age gap game over here, it's me!" He turned a smile on Jack and saw the light leave Jack's eyes. Apparently, Davis' comment made him sad. Davis was about to ask why, but Jack shook it off and finished the rest of his drink in one long swallow.

"Let's have some fun!" Jack declared as he jumped to his feet.

They made their way to the dance floor and started swaying to the beat. Jack moved away and began dancing with anyone and everyone. Davis watched Jack having fun flirting with others and felt a low growl building in his throat. He knew they were trying to get information about Cyrus, but Jack was acting strangely. *What the hell is going on with him?* This wasn't like Jack. He was loyal and steadfast. He'd stuck through thick and thin with Davis, even when he thought Davis was going to leave him, he'd held on. What on earth had triggered this? After everything Jack had shared the night before, Davis thought they were stronger than ever.

Davis retreated to the bar, holding on to the edge of the scarred wood surface like his world was caving in. *Jack isn't having second thoughts, is he?* The glass he was holding shattered in his clenched hand. He glanced down, startled. A couple of people stared, alarmed, and he shook his fingers. "Whoops, slipped," he said to the bartender, who hurried over to wipe up the mess.

Siobhan sidled up to him, quietly murmuring, "Calm down, I know what's wrong with Jack."

He frowned at her; she must have seen him break the glass. "Okay, so enlighten me," he ground through his clenched teeth. His voice was half anger, half pained sorrow.

She smiled softly, "It's the age difference. It just hit Jack all over again that you're over two hundred years older than him. He's not a wielder or a dragon, and since you think you can't mate bond him, he's going to continue to age and eventually die. He feels like you're not going to want him anymore when he's old and gray. He's more upset for you than himself, but he's trying to reconcile it in his head."

Davis stared at Siobhan, his eyes widening before he softly brushed her cheek with the back of his hand. "When did you get so wise, little one?" he whispered in her ear as he pulled her close and held her. "Wait," he said, straightening up, "What do you mean I *think* I can't mate bond him? It's not a *think*, it's a *know*. We can't breed, so we can't be mated."

Siobhan rolled her eyes and sighed ruefully, shaking her head and smiling. "That's not true, that's just something the old Council spread around to keep the family lines strong, or so they claimed. All that is needed for a mate bond is for two people to love each other, without reserve, beyond all reason, and it will happen automatically. You know I can read people's auras, right?"

He nodded slowly, in surprised shock at what he was hearing.

She shrugged, then squeezed his shoulder. "Davis, you're already there, you are open to the bond. It's Jack that's holding back, but he's almost there, too. He loves you so much, Davis. But he's worried about tying you to him when he doesn't know what it's going to be like for you. Get him past that, you'll be marking him in no time," she smiled gently at him.

Davis stared at Siobhan at first in disbelief, then tentatively in hope. If what she said was true, he was astonished. How had he not known this? He thought about where he had learned his concept of the mating bond, and his heart stuttered, realizing it had come from his parents. His same parents who wanted grandchildren and at first, hadn't understood that Davis was attracted to both men and women but had seemingly come to accept it. They said they loved Jack and loved that he made Davis happy, but they hadn't told him the truth about the mating bond. Was that possible? Maybe they hadn't known either. He was so conflicted about it, he was going to have to set it aside for now. He glanced over at Jack — he knew what he wasn't conflicted about.

Warmth and excitement filling his heart, he grabbed Siobhan and threw her over his arm, kissing her deeply. He stood her up, and she was smiling dreamily. "Thank you, Shi!" he told her, "I don't know how I can repay you."

She grabbed him and kissed him again, just as hard. She leaned back and said, "Teach Marco how to kiss like that," as she sighed and wandered away, swerving a little like she might be drunk.

Davis grinned after her, fully intending to fulfill her request, but first, he needed to find his fiancé and kiss him. He saw Jack's back retreating through the crowd and heading to the back patio area reserved for smokers.

He rumbled low in his chest and chased after him. His expression intense, his determination cleared a path for him as people hurried out of his way, the crowd parting in an unconscious awareness of a predator in their midst.

Chapter 18

JACK WAS OUT OF sorts. He watched as Davis broke the glass, and Siobhan comforted him. It hurt. Jack was the reason Davis was upset. Bitter tasting shame filled his mouth. He was out there flirting with everyone while Davis stood by watching. He saw Davis kiss Siobhan, looking excited about something. It was too much. He of all people knew what it was like to be betrayed by someone you loved. He felt awful about what he was doing to Davis, especially after everything he'd shared last night. How he'd confessed the years of hurt, betrayal and hiding himself away. He was a grown man, but for some reason, he was acting like a teenager.

He hurried outside to get some air. It was too close inside, and he needed to be away from people. He took in a few deep breaths of the thick, humid night air and tried to center himself, to release the pressure in his chest. "Fuck," he whispered, pounding his fist on the patio railing. Frustration and desperation crashed over him like a wave. It wasn't working, and he felt his breath clogging in his lungs. "Fuck!" he said again and closed his eyes, bracing his hands on the rail and leaning over, hanging his head in agony.

He felt arms come around him from behind, "Was that an invitation?" he heard a rumbly voice ask. It was Davis. Of course, it was; he always seemed to sense when Jack needed him the most. He sighed and turned, wrapping his arms around Davis and holding him close.

"I'm sorry," whispered Davis.

Jack leaned back and stared at him in surprise, "For what?" he asked warily.

"I'm sorry that you're feeling this way. That you're thinking about your mortality and what it means for us, our future." Davis watched him intensely.

"How…" Jack stuttered, his eyes going wide. He felt hot, stinging tears filling them and tried to hold them in. He didn't want to be a blubbering mess in the street, and he hated crying. After last night, Davis now knew why. Knew how Jack's father reacted to tears, often thinking a belt was the best cure to make his son 'man up'.

Brushing a gentle hand over Jack's cheek, his own blue eyes shining in the streetlight, Davis laughed softly, "Siobhan. She saw me break a glass when I was feeling jealous. You were having a great time without me, and I got a little growly. She clued me in."

Jack's eyes dropped, "I'm sorry, Davis. I was too deep in my own head. I'm embarrassed about the way I was acting. I saw you kiss her." He turned his face away, staring at the cars driving by.

Davis grabbed Jack's chin and forced him to look him in the eyes. "Jack, you don't understand, I was thanking her for a wonderful gift she gave me. I was overcome, Jack, it's amazing you won't believe it!" he said, almost jumping on his toes.

Shaking his head, Jack studied him cautiously. What could possibly be such wonderful news that he would kiss her like that?

"Jack, do you love me?" Davis asked.

"Of course, Davis, I love you with all of my heart," Jack responded automatically.

"I know you love me, but Jack," Davis replied and shook his head, seeming frustrated, "All of your heart, is it open to me? I mean, no reservations; you love me beyond all reason, beyond all else, and you want nothing more than to spend the rest of our lives together. Regardless of the age thing, regardless of your mortality. Jack, my heart, my love, do you truly want to spend forever with me?"

Davis squeezed his hands tightly around Jack's, intertwining their fingers and begging him with his gaze to understand something that Jack felt was just out of his grasp. He could tell Davis was asking him something beyond the actual question, but what, he couldn't quite decipher. The dragon fidgeted and bit his lip as he watched while Jack thought it through.

Jack stared deeply into Davis' eyes, the beautiful ocean colors swirling and mesmerizing him with their dancing hues, shifting the way they did when Davis was highly emotional or nervous. He could tell by the way Davis was watching him, so anxious for him to accept everything he was offering; this was a monumental moment. The dragon made a small chuffing sound, almost a whimper, and Jack smiled. His heart lurched suddenly, then settled, and he knew, without a doubt, that he wanted to spend the rest of his life looking into those eyes, no matter how short that life was compared to his dragon lover. "Yes, I do, I love you so much Davis. Beyond all else. Forever." He opened his heart, putting away the last of his reservations.

Davis inhaled sharply and tightened his grip on Jack's while a single tear rolled down his cheek. He lit up like a child on Christmas, and all his wishes had come true.

Reaching his hand to Davis' cheek, Jack made to wipe away the tear when a sudden dizziness came over him. He wobbled where he stood, almost falling. He grabbed his head as a snapping sensation ricocheted through his brain. "Ow, what the hell was that?" he groaned, bending down and dragging several ragged breaths through his mouth.

Jack! Came an excited voice that sounded directly in his mind.

He whipped his head around, looking for the voice, not wanting to acknowledge he was hearing things. His shoulders tensed as if under attack.

Davis gently put his hands on Jack's shoulders and pulled him up, beaming at him. *It was me, Jack, silly, quit looking around and look at me.*

Jack dared to look at him again. *Davis?* He thought carefully.

Yes! Well, technically, it's Lake, but it's both of us. That's confusing. Jack, meet Lake, my dragon. He's been dying to talk to you!

Jack stared at Davis, stunned. *How can this be? Only mates can do this.* He put his hand on Davis' chest and felt it thundering under his palm.

Davis nodded excitedly. *Jack, everything I thought I knew about the mating bond, was wrong. I didn't realize. That's what Siobhan told me. She told me she could see our auras and that I was ready to bond with you, but there was a small part of you holding back. You didn't want to burden me with your human mortality. All it took was you acccpting that and opening your heart all the way. Jack, we can be bonded mates. I can mark you, and you will receive part of my life force, and we will be together for the rest of our lives. You won't grow older; you'll be with me for centuries more.*

The sky above them opened up, and a warm spring-like shower drenched them. The refreshing kind of rain that wipes away the memories of the cold winter before, renewing the land. They smiled at each other, finally fully at peace. Davis grinned; *sorry about that. It's easier to call storms this close to the ocean.* He tousled Jack's now-soaked hair, making him laugh.

If it's because you're happy, I'm okay with it, Jack thought back.

Happier than I've ever been. Davis tossed his own dripping hair from his eyes as the small storm tapered off. *Jack, you don't ever have to worry again about me possibly meeting my mate because I've already found him. It's you. It was always only ever you. My Jack.* Davis put his forehead on Jack's and sighed happily. *My mate.*

Jack thought about Siobhan and the incredible gift she had given them. He was going to find her now and kiss her himself, and then he was taking Davis back to the hotel or to Alaska or to wherever they needed to go to do this. He wanted more than anything to have Davis mark him as his mate. The wedding wouldn't even matter; this was for life. "Davis," Jack whispered, his voice strained, thick with emotion. He didn't even need to explain what he wanted. Davis could feel it.

His mate nodded and grabbed Jack's hand, pulling him back into the club to let the others know they were leaving.

Saharra was at their table, chatting with the others when they returned. Skipping greetings and idle chit-chat, Davis told her, "I'm so sorry, but something's come up, and we have to leave right now. Marco and Siobhan, you're welcome to stay, but Jack and I have to go and, uh, dry off."

The others jumped to their feet, exclaiming in surprise at the two soaked men while Davis flippantly described the freak rainstorm. Saharra sent a server scurrying off to get them towels.

Siobhan grinned knowingly; she could tell from their auras what had actually happened.

Davis, love, a few more minutes won't hurt; we need to find Vaughn. That's the reason we're here, Jack reminded him gently.

Davis glanced at Jack and nodded; he was right. He gratefully accepted the towel the waitress offered. "I'm sorry to be so abrupt. I know you've gone out of your way to meet with us. Thank you for the towels. Now that we are a little drier, let's go ahead and discuss that contract."

Saharra nodded with a grateful smile, and they started talking shop.

Jack pulled Siobhan away from the table and took her to a quieter corner. He was shaking with his gratitude towards the green wielder who had changed his life for the better. Or maybe it was the chill from the rain. Either way, she was also willing to keep his secrets and let him be himself. For that alone, he adored her, but now... "Siobhan," he started, his voice once again thickening with emotion.

"Jack, it's okay." She put her hand on his cheek. "I'm so happy for you both!" Her eyes were shining with happiness as she chuckled, "I love you guys."

He put his forehead on hers and whispered, "You've made this possible."

She shook her head, "I may have jump-started it, but you two knuckleheads would have figured it out on your own sooner or later." She tapped him on the forehead, "You're too smart for that, Ridgeway."

Jack smiled at her. He loved this prickly woman. She was a good ally and friend. He took her face in his hands and pulled her against his body. "We love you, too. I almost forgot I'm supposed to thank you like this." He kissed her passionately, the same way Davis had. When he let her go, her eyes rolled up.

"Oh god, what is it with you two?" she muttered, "Please, teach Marco how to do that!" she begged.

The man in question stormed up then, "Teach Marco how to do what? Why are you kissing my woman?" he demanded, irritation in his tone, a small puff of smoke trickling from one nostril.

Jack grinned, "This!" he said before leaning Siobhan over and kissing her even more passionately than before. When he finally stood her up, she had to grab his arm for balance.

She smiled drunkenly, "Yes, that!" she slurred.

Marco was staring hard at Jack, "Dude!" he said. He seemed at a loss for any other words.

"I was thanking her," he grinned, "This incredible woman. She told Davis how we could actually be mated, and we broke the barrier. I can hear him now, and when we leave, he's going to mark me. Marco, we're mates! It's actually happening!" He wanted to jump up and down like a kid.

The red dragon relaxed and grinned back, excited for his friends. "That's awesome! I'm so happy for you guys!"

"Yes," Jack said excitedly, "Your woman is an amazing creature and if I weren't so incredibly in love with Davis, I'd steal her away from you!"

Marco scoffed, so Jack grabbed him and kissed him with just as much passion and heat as he could give.

Marco's eyes went completely blank for a moment, his expression indicating his brain was misfiring. When Jack let him go, he whispered. "Holy shit, that was hot. I've never kissed a man before and probably never will again, but…" He stood there and stared at Jack in shock, nodding, "*Madre de Dios, gracias*, I believe I understand now."

Siobhan roared with laughter and wrapped her arms around him. "Kiss me like that, Marco," she said, rolling the R in his name, "And I would do anything you asked of me!" she teased.

His eyes lit up, "Anything?"

They were still laughing, when Davis spun Marco around, kissing him just like Jack had.

Marco finally took two big steps back, "Holy shit, you guys, I got it, okay? My turn to kiss her!" He gave Siobhan an evil leer that had her running for the door.

Jack found Mandy and let her know they were leaving. She opted to stay, saying she'd catch an Uber later.

On the drive back to the hotel, Davis shared with the others that Saharra had disclosed the reason for the private event and the nature of the accomplishment. She'd been trying to start a girl's school back in her home country that had been championed by her grandmother but had always received pushback from the government. She finally had enough money and clout to make it happen. She was also donating money to dig wells so the people of her town could have better access to fresh water.

They were all silent. They felt bad suspecting this savvy woman who was trying to give back to her community.

"That's wonderful," Siobhan finally said quietly.

Davis nodded, "And because of that, I told her that Still Waters would play for free, and she could charge for tickets so the money could go to the charity. She cried," he said, rubbing his chest and looking sentimental.

"Well, it doesn't help us find Vaughn, but at least we aren't wasting time chasing down that false lead anymore," Marco said.

The others nodded; now they could focus on working the art gallery angle. Someone had to know Cyrus and how to get close to him.

In the lobby, Davis took Jack's hand and said to their friends, "If you don't mind, Jack and I have something we need to go do," he grinned at his soon-to-be bonded mate.

Jack nodded, as his heart sped up, feeling like it might pound right out of his chest.

The others smiled at the pair. Jack and Davis were so obviously in love with one another that it was hard not to be overjoyed for them.

Chapter 19

ON THE DESERTED BEACH, it was blissfully quiet, with only the slightest sliver of light from the nearby hotels to see by. The men stood there on the shore, the water rushing over their feet, professing their love to each other. Davis explained to Jack how the mating mark was placed. He warned him it would hurt like hell, but it would be worth it. "An exquisite pain," Davis whispered.

Jack gripped Davis' hips with his strong hands after they slowly undressed each other. Each item of clothing dropped heavily down to the sand like stones. In a sense, they were the boulders in a wall the two were tearing down. The one that had kept them from truly belonging to one another.

Hesitating, Jack whispered, "Davis, are you sure? This is the moment where everything changes for us."

Davis leaned into the gorgeous man in front of him, grinning his usual impish smile, and snorted, "Shut up and kiss me."

Jack laughed, and Davis took advantage, crushing his lips on Jack's full but firm mouth, moaning in delight as their tongues met. He stroked his hands up Jack's firm stomach and rested them on his chest.

Trembling, Jack stroked his large hands over Davis' skin, making the dragon rumble deep in his chest.

Davis then circled his arms around Jack's strong back and pulled him even closer, so their bodies touched completely. As their hips ground into each other, Jack gasped, as Davis' hard length was digging into him with an urgency he couldn't contain.

Davis thrilled at the way Jack's breathing became faster and thready as he continued to press closer. It turned him on even more, hearing his lover's sounds, knowing it was for him. He reached between them and took Jack in his hand, using his thumb to stroke him from base to tip in a slow, sweeping motion. Jack moaned softly, and Davis grinned into his mouth. That sound was a particular favorite of his.

Gripping Davis' hand with his own, Jack angled his hips so they could wrap their hands around both of their shafts and stroke themselves together.

Jack shook hard with a sharp intake of breath, and Davis knew he was close, so he was surprised when Jack backed up. "Not yet," Jack murmured and dropped to his knees. He took Davis into his mouth and hummed in satisfaction as the dragon groaned and tightened his hands in Jack's hair.

Davis began to thrust his hips forward in time to Jack's suckling and licking, flushing at the sight of the hollowing of his cheeks. The vision before him loosed a strangled cry from his tight throat, and his wings unfurled behind him, dragging in the sand. Moaning as the pressure kept building from that golden hair brushing his thighs and those bright blue eyes glinting lovingly up at him.

He knew Jack loved it when he watched him like this. He bit his lip, his own blue eyes swirling in a storm and holding back a whimper as Jack reached up to stroke his backside. His muscular thighs suddenly felt as weak as twigs as he trembled and tensed. Before he could think of taking another breath, it whooshed out of his heaving chest, and he shouted hoarsely as he spasmed down Jack's throat. He threw his head back, gasping, trying to drag in even the smallest amount of air he could. It was near impossible as Jack kept swallowing around him, taking in the hot pulses of Davis' pleasure. It left him panting and quivering above Jack's shoulders.

Davis' legs shook harder, and he dropped to his knees heavily, leaning his forehead against Jack's neck while he shivered. Even though Jack was human, he had always been a magician with his mouth. Davis wasn't sure if it was what was to come or just being on the water's edge but tonight was even more intense and erotic than usual. He huffed out a brief laugh, not knowing how much more he could take, but knowing he had to, he had to make Jack his.

He raised his hooded eyes and met Jack's gaze, showing him how undone he was. He loved that about Jack; he was never shy about the different ways they could make love, and they got very creative. His mind flashed briefly to a spicy encounter once in their kitchen, and he grinned. "Do you remember the incident with the strawberry cake?" Davis rumbled, still trying to catch his breath, his wings fluttering weakly.

Jack chuckled as he moved behind Davis. "One of my favorites. I'll never make that recipe again without thinking of you like this," he whispered as he shoved Davis down on his hands and knees and gripped his hips. "The places you had frosting." He leaned forward and nestled himself between Davis' thighs. "I had a hard time looking your mother in the face the next day." He slipped himself just inside and moaned quietly as Davis' body gripped him tightly.

Davis' head fell back in ecstasy; he loved it when Jack took him this way. He felt Jack's strong hands gripping him and stroking his back as he fully entered him. His breath shuddered out, and he thrilled at the sensation of Jack filling him. "Fuck, Jack," his voice wavered.

"Oh, I plan to," Jack called and gave a particularly powerful thrust. He began a hard pounding rhythm that left them both breathless. Finally, a strangled moan was ripped from Jack's throat as he came, and he stroked Davis' wings hard. It was so intense Davis couldn't stop himself from releasing his own climax on the sand in front of him.

Overcome, Davis dropped flat on the ground, feeling the warm stickiness coating his body, not caring that the gritty sand was now clinging to him. He turned as best as he could with his wings out and pulled Jack to his chest. Breathing in the spicy scent of his lover, his fiancé, the man he was about to mark as his mate. His Jack.

Jack clung tightly to him, aftershocks of his orgasm still wracking his body. "Davis," he whispered, "You got me all sandy."

They both laughed quietly and lay for a while catching their breath and watching the night sky deepen around them. Davis nodded at the stars and leapt to his feet. Jack's eyes widened as Davis yanked him up and threw him over his shoulder like he weighed nothing. He liked playfully showing off his dragon side, knowing it always cracked Jack up when he did things like this. They were not small men, both tall and well-muscled. So Jack knew it took a lot of strength to toss him around like a feather. What he didn't know, is Davis wasn't playing this time. Lake was burning in his veins, growling to take over.

Jack howled with laughter as the dragon began to march towards the water, the large man bouncing in his arms like a small child.

"Davis, I'm not some damsel in distress, what the fuck are you doing?" Jack shouted, amusement coloring his tone, just as Davis expected.

Setting Jack on his feet once they were waist deep, Davis leaned down and washed the sand from his body and did the same to Jack. The dragon's swirling eyes stilled and settled to a deep blue so dark it was almost black. He slowly pulled Jack back closer to the edge of the surf, where the sand met the ocean, right to the water's edge and smiled, his fangs peeking down from under his lips. "My turn, but this time, it's for keeps, and it's going to hurt some." He growled low in his chest. A warning. He watched as Jack's eyes darkened, now in understanding of how close Davis was to losing control.

He pulled Jack to the ground with him, the surge washing over their legs. Davis hovered over him, his wings arching high above him now. He stroked his hands up Jack's body, murmuring in appreciation. Fast as lightning, he grabbed Jack's arms and, with one hand, pinned his wrists above his head. He ran his nose down Jack's throat, inhaling deeply and rumbling in pleasure. He let his fangs drop just enough to scrape them over Jack's skin.

Jack stared at him in alarm, his eyes widening and his mouth dropping open slightly as he tried to move his arms. Davis tightened his grip and rumbled again in warning. For all his playing, Davis had never used his extra strength when they were intimate. He'd always been gentler with Jack, remembering his lover was human. Not many people could overpower the former Marine, but Davis had just done it with minimal effort. He wanted to remind Jack how lethal he was, making sure he knew what he was signing up for. "Last chance," he snarled, "This is what you want? Forever with this beast inside of me? Knowing that Lake and I will kill anyone who ever tries to harm you or get between us?"

As Jack nodded frantically, Davis laid his other arm across Jack's chest like an iron band. "Do you know, Jack, how incredibly fucking long I have wanted to do this?" He let the predator inside of him show in his gaze as he stared at Jack, his voice back to his rumbling purr. "How many times have I bitten my own lip to keep from sinking my fangs into your gorgeous neck?" His voice dropped deeper as his tone filled with gravel and desire.

"Jack," he growled, "My Jack." *My Jack,* Lake echoed in their heads. "You are mine, and now the whole fucking world will know. Nobody will ever come between us again. You. Are. My. Mate." He wedged his knees between Jack's legs and widened them as he settled between them. Jack moaned and lifted his hips so Davis could slowly push inside him. "Oh god, Jack, I have to mark you fast. I should have done it earlier over there, but I got caught up in you. I don't think I can hold out long here. You feel too damn good."

Jack nodded, "Do it. I can take it."

Growling, Davis began to thrust hard and let his fangs drop completely. Just as he felt himself tensing, he snarled and bit Jack over his collarbone, taking a couple of deep swallows of his blood. Jack jolted from the pain, but didn't cry out or push him away. Instead, he grabbed Davis' shoulders and held him close. Davis sent a wave of his magic through his mate's body, trying to ease him through it and could tell when the pain turned to ecstasy. Despite already being spent, the magic wrenched a climax from Jack, and they collapsed in a tangle. They lay there in the surf, gasping and holding each other tightly, the warm waves washing over them.

Jack began to laugh, breathlessly.

Davis glanced up at him, incredulously. They just experienced the most intense encounter either of them ever had, and Jack was laughing! "What?" he demanded, his own voice shaky with exhaustion.

"Sand, in interesting places," Jack grinned.

Jack lay back on the sand, still warm from the day's sun, and stared at the stars overhead. Lake was swimming in the dark ocean in full dragon form. No predators would dare attack him like that. Jack wasn't so sure about his own tender flesh, so he opted to wait on the shore. Sated, tired, and happy. He ran his fingers over his collarbone and looked down again at the blue dragon now tattooed on his shoulder.

It was gorgeous, similar to Jorrie's mark, but with a few differences. Her dragon had a longer tail and was circled in waves. Jack's dragon had its wings outstretched as if he was flying and water was bursting around him. Davis told him the dragon picked the mark. He loved it. He felt complete for the first time in his life, like he truly belonged somewhere, with unconditional love. He couldn't wait to show Jorrie and Bridget.

He thought about how rough Davis was earlier. He knew the dragon could easily break him, but Davis was always careful not to hurt Jack. Tonight, though, Davis had let himself off the leash and shown Jack more of what he was capable of. Jack shivered in surprised delight at the display of dominance. He rather liked the way Davis manhandled him.

Jaaaack, he heard and jolted up to see a giant blue water serpent dripping over him, grinning. If you could call that wicked display of deadly teeth a grin.

What? he thought back warily.

The enormous head lowered and nudged him in the chest. *Will you scratch behind my ears?*

Jack burst out laughing as the fierce beast in front of him gave him puppy eyes, batting eyelids the size of hubcaps at him in what was probably supposed to be a coy gesture. On a dragon, it was just plain menacing.

Shaking his head, he rose to his full height and smiled softly. Jorrie told him about how much dragons liked this, so he cheerfully obliged his mate. He sighed with pure happiness as those words rolled through his mind, his mate. There was no turning back now. They were linked forever. He kissed the love of his life on top of his scaly head and switched to the other ear.

Lake's tongue lolled out like a giant dog, and he rumbled as he flopped in the sand, wriggling closer. It was downright adorable, the opposite of how growly the dragon acted earlier. Jack wished he had his phone so he could take a picture. Suddenly, the dragon was a warm man wrapping him up in his arms and kissing him in a way Jack knew meant he wasn't getting dressed again anytime soon.

Chapter 20

JACK WOKE WITH A start, the sound of seagulls cawing and squawking above him. He gazed around, trying to place himself, and realized he and Davis had fallen asleep on the beach. The sun had just breached the horizon. Davis was back in his dragon form and had curled protectively around him. One paw wrapped like a barrier, his long neck and tail completing the circle. He looked like a giant blue bagel. Jack laughed at the mental image and stretched. For someone who slept outside propped against a dragon, he had been very comfortable and felt well-rested. He kissed Lake on the snout and saw an ear twitch. He began to run his hands over the crest of the dragon's head, and soon, Lake was rumbling like a bus.

I hate to wake you... but aren't you worried people will be able to see us? he thought to Lake.

No, came a sleepy reply, *perception filter, remember? Comes in handy when you don't want to be seen by humans. They don't see me this way. That's how Shepard was able to mate Jorrie in the ocean when she called the waterspout.*

A light snore came from the dragon. The mental image that came with the message he sent was more than Jack bargained for. He'd always known dragons were creative lovers, but, *holy shit*, that was spectacular. *Wait, how do you know that?* Jack asked his mate.

One large eye slowly peeled open. *Um, I don't suppose you'd be willing to forget what I just said?* Lake asked hopefully.

Jack snorted, "Oh no!" he said out loud, "I'll never get those images out of my head. Not without some serious brain bleach."

Lake rumbled what sounded suspiciously like a laugh as well and stood, stretching his wings and claws. He shimmered as he shifted back to human form and stretched again.

"Hi," Davis grinned. *My Mate!* Came the gleeful thought. *My mother will just have to get over herself. You're mine forever, and no one can take you away from me.* "I love you so, so much," he whispered.

Jack smiled tenderly, "Love you too. Now, let's get you dressed and get some breakfast."

Davis grinned, "Are you sure you want me to get dressed?"

"Oh, my dear depraved dragon," Jack laughed, "I love you naked, but right now, I think I'd love some coffee more. Besides, I don't want you to get a sunburn on your —"

The rest of his comment was stopped by Davis slapping his hand over Jack's mouth as he roared in laughter.

They were enjoying breakfast in the dining room when Siobhan and Marco joined them. Siobhan raised an eyebrow. "Still in last night's clothes? Are you guys doing the walk of shame?" she asked, amusement coloring her voice.

Jack laughed and pulled his shirt aside to proudly show his mark, "Is it still the walk of shame if you aren't ashamed?" He winked at Davis.

Davis grinned in his coffee. "So shameful," he whispered.

Siobhan squealed and came over to hug Jack before she took a closer look. "Oh, Davis," she sighed, "It's so beautiful; you chose well!" She hugged the dragon then and tousled his hair. She took her seat next to Marco as Davis grumbled about her messing up his 'do. It was already messy, which was the way he usually styled it, so they fell into a good-natured argument about whether or not she had improved it.

Jack glanced at the quiet man next to her. Marco was watching Siobhan's every move, the pure longing he was experiencing plain on his face if she only turned and looked. The red dragon so badly wanted to mark her, but he was afraid to say it. Jack caught Marco's eye and winked.

Marco nodded slightly as he schooled his features, huffing under his breath, and they all tucked into their food.

They were discussing what to do next to further their search for Vaughn when Jack's phone rang. He looked around, surprised; "I thought I left it upstairs."

Siobhan held it up. "Sorry! You actually left it in the car last night, so I thought I'd bring it to you. I got so excited about your news I forgot to give it to you."

He took it gratefully. It was a local number that looked vaguely familiar, so he gestured for them to be quiet. He answered with a short, cautious hello, listened for a moment. Then, his face underwent a change as he put on a different persona.

"Oh, hello, Marissa," he drawled in his 'professor' voice, "Of course, I remember you. How could I forget such a beautiful woman as yourself? You must have known you were on my mind. In fact, I was about to call you. Are you available today? I'd love to take you to lunch and get to know more about you." He listened again, "Oh, they will be thrilled!" More listening, "Wonderful, I'll come pick you up at the gallery at 12:30? And you know the area better than I do, so please pick a place you'd like to go. No, just us two for this; I want to get to know you without the kids around. Yes, darling, see you then," he practically purred into the phone.

The others were biting their lips, trying hard not to giggle and ruin his cover. Davis was rocking back and forth in his chair, clapping like a demented seal and when Jack finally hung up, they let it out. Their raucous laughter turned more than one head as they continued to laugh until they were gasping, Marco almost in tears, Siobhan also wiping her eyes.

"Yeah, yeah, yuck it up, chuckleheads, but I've got a lunch date with the lovely Marissa where we will discuss how my students are going to get a chance to view the items 'Gavin' is having displayed. Which means you all better brush up on your art history so you can sound halfway intelligent. I'm going to shower for my date, you philistines. I have sand in interesting places." He sniffed haughtily and strutted away with as much dignity as he could muster.

The others snickered until Marco announced, "Well, you heard Professor Shelton. Time to hit the books." They followed suit and went upstairs to brush up on their early African art studies.

Davis smoothed down Jack's collar. The man looked every bit the hot art professor that he would have loved to have in college. All three times he went. He grinned, "Mmhm, I am hot for teacher!" He laughed as Jack rolled his eyes.

His mate grinned back, "Do I look straight?"

"Jack," Davis rolled his own eyes, "You've always looked 'straight'. When I first met you, I thought you were with Jorrie. One of the best days of my life was realizing you were interested in me. Your problem is when you do that flamboyant act."

"Bitch!" Jack flounced around and sashayed his hips in exaggeration across the room to get his phone from the charger.

"Exactly," Davis chuckled, "Ugh, please don't do that, it's not you. Don't be a stereotype."

Grinning at him in the mirror, Jack turned back and resumed his normal walk. He gave Davis a grateful hug. "Okay, so I think I'm ready to go on my first date with a woman in, hmm, twenty-two years, I believe. I don't know if I remember how to do this."

"Just pretend she has a beard," Davis snorted.

"But I much prefer the clean-shaven look," Jack said as he darted in and lightly bit Davis on the jaw.

Davis' eyes turned the color of stormy seas as he stared intently at Jack. He watched his mate shiver under his stare. "Do that again, and you'll be late for your date," he said in a voice thick with desire.

Jack kept his eyes locked on his mate and slowly leaned in, inch by inch, and bit him again, this time licking his way up to his lips before he barely brushed his mouth across Davis'. He leaned back, with one golden eyebrow arched, "You were saying?"

A feral smile lit up Davis' face as his fangs slipped down. He remembered Jack's earlier thoughts that slipped through of how much he enjoyed being dominated by Davis the night before. Something Davis had never done with anyone else. With a low throaty rumble, he picked Jack up and threw him on the bed.

Jack, or Simon as she knew him, called Marissa from the car, apologizing for running behind, claiming he got turned around, but he was almost there. She laughed and told him it was fine; everyone was late in Miami.

He felt bad when he arrived and saw she'd dressed up in a loose, flowy dress that enhanced her small curves beautifully. She'd also let her hair down, and her makeup was fresher looking, less stern professional. She was trying to impress him, and she was very much not his type.

He nervously spun his engagement ring, which he'd moved to his opposite hand. He didn't want to take it off, but Davis reassured him it was okay. They were mated now, which was stronger than a wedding vow anyway.

He hopped out to open the door to the SUV for her. "Marissa, darling, I am so sorry I'm late, y'all's traffic 'round here is a lot different than I'm used to back home," he explained, thickly laying on the Texan drawl and southern charm.

She fluttered her lashes, "Oh, that's okay, Simon, I know our streets don't make much sense most of the time. Wow, this is a really nice car!" she exclaimed, looking around. "So much space."

Jack laughed, "Well, when you're dragging three surly college kids around, you need all the room you can get," he told her as he took her hand and assisted her into the vehicle.

She nodded as if she understood completely.

"So, where to ma'am?" he drawled after running around and sliding into the driver's seat.

She directed him to a little French bistro nearby, which wasn't crowded, thankfully, but did seem rather intimate. He cringed inside, hoping he didn't have to kiss her. He could absolutely do it, but he hated leading her on, she seemed so kind, a truly nice person. After they were seated, she asked him to tell her about his work. He babbled on in what he hoped was a convincing manner about how the three with him were his graduate students, and they were doing a research project with him about the history of different tribes of African descent and their impact on the art world.

She nodded along, fascinated. She waxed poetic about different artists and styles, and Jack was glad Davis had given him a crash course before he got there.

They ate their lunch, and Jack began to feel even worse. She was an incredibly sweet woman, and he hated this. If he were a single man who appreciated women, she would be quite a catch. She was smart, funny, and very engaging. She was so hopeful it was giving him pain in his stomach, aching with regret at leading her on like this.

"Are you okay, Simon?" she asked, worry evident in her tone.

He groaned internally; he must have sighed out loud. "Of course, I am," he smiled at her, pouring on the charm. "I was just thinking it's too bad I won't be in town much longer so I can spend more time with you. You are an incredible woman, and I'm enjoying getting to know you better. I hope you don't mind me talking business, but my students are anxiously awaiting word. They are planning some beach time. You know how they can be." He rolled his eyes as if they were exasperating.

She laughed, a light tinkling sound that tickled his mind. "Oh, I'm sure, but absolutely. I think I mentioned our benefactor is being very generous, loaning us these pieces to show. He may even have more to donate to the university in the future if that's something you may be interested in. But are you, and your students, of course," she blushed, "Available tomorrow around seven p.m.? He's agreed to come in and let your team study them, to see if they can add anything to what we already know about these pieces. He's excited to make a name for himself."

He nodded, "We are absolutely available, and even if we weren't," he dropped his voice, "I'd make time for you." He brushed his fingers over hers lightly and grinned.

She almost melted in her chair when he fixed his bright blue eyes on her.

Jack thanked the stars above he'd been born handsome. He wasn't always as confident as he seemed, so he'd relied on his looks often to help him out of jams. This was one of those times. They made their arrangements, and he picked up the check, "Only fitting for a gentleman enjoying the exquisite company of a lovely lady," he murmured to her. He drove her back to work, citing an important meeting he had to attend, and escorted her to the door of the gallery.

He hugged her and hoped it would be enough, but she looked at him so expectantly, he knew he would have to do it. He lightly brushed his lips across hers, lingering for a moment before he tenderly brushed her hair from her forehead. "Until later," he smoldered at her.

She simply nodded and gazed at him adoringly, flushed and breathing a little heavily.

As he drove away, Jack cursed himself in every language Jorrie had taught him swears in. He *hated* toying with her that way. Hopefully, when this was over, he could take her somewhere for a farewell dinner and leave her with fond memories of the sweet professor from Texas she'd never see again. She shouldn't get too tangled up in him anyway. He was much too old for her. In real life and pretend. She was just too young, regardless. He hoped she wouldn't think poorly of herself or take the blame in any way; she really was a delightful woman.

He brought the SUV to a sharp halt as he parked in the hotel lot, the seat belt digging hard into his chest in a painful reminder of his agitation. He banged his head on the seat back a couple of times in frustration. He loathed being deceitful and toying with Marissa's emotions. He'd been on the receiving end of it enough that it made his stomach churn to be on the giving end. Right now, he wanted nothing more than to have a cold beer and the comfort of his mate's arms. *I'm back, and I need you,* he thought desperately to Davis. He felt warmth in his mind and heard, *on my way.* He loved this connection with him, it was like coming home.

He dragged himself heavily from the vehicle and was trudging through the lot towards the lobby when he heard his name. He turned with dread, recognizing the voice. It was grating and painful on his already raw nerves, but he raised his eyes grudgingly and saw Riley standing there.

"Jack, hey, I've been looking for you, I heard one of your friends say you were staying here. Look, I don't want to bother you. I just... have something I needed to tell you." The man shifted nervously from foot to foot.

Jack stared quietly at him for a long time, debating internally before he finally decided what the hell and to hear what the man had to say. It didn't matter anymore now that he was mated with Davis. He nodded slowly.

Riley blew out a sharp breath. "Okay, thank you, Jack. I wanted to tell you I'm sorry for how things went down when we were together. I wasn't ready to come out yet, and when we got caught, I just panicked. I didn't want to admit anything, and you were so... God, you were so confident in it all." He shook his head, "I shouldn't have done what I did."

"So, you panicked and blamed me," Jack said calmly as he glared at him, "Told them I came on to you against your will. Got me pushed out of the Corps, something I was damn good at, and I loved; all because *you* were scared?" He seethed with anger, his chest rising and falling rapidly, the blood pounding in his ears. Now, fury colored his voice. "Fuck that, Riley! I wasn't confident. I was scared, too. Terrified! You were my first! I thought you loved me, and I finally felt I could be myself around another man. That there was nothing wrong with me. And the second there was any hint someone might know, you threw me away. You told them it was against your will, but you seemed pretty willing before you got caught." He was practically yelling at the man who had betrayed him when he was so vulnerable.

"Jack, I know." Riley shook his head, an expression of misery on his features. "I'm so sorry. You were my first, too. The thing is, you didn't deserve that, and I felt horrible about how you were treated." Riley's voice hitched, and he held up his hands, "I should have contacted you before now to tell you that, but I didn't think you'd want to talk to me."

Nodding, Jack clenched his teeth, "You thought right. I don't want to talk to you. Not ever again. I don't want to see you; I don't want to hear your name. Leave me the fuck alone!" Jack yelled at him.

Riley stepped towards him, his expression pinched and troubled, "Please, Jack, I'm sorry. I've never stopped thinking about you! I've missed you and seeing you again…" He grabbed Jack then and pressed his lips to his, kissing him with the desperation of a drowning man trying to get air.

Jack shoved him away and wiped his mouth in disgust. "What the fuck, Riley? I'm engaged. My fiancé is on his way down right now."

"Correction," Davis growled from behind Jack. An unearthly snarl ripped from his throat, "Your fiancé is here." Davis was watching Riley like a lion stalking his prey as he glided next to Jack. Everything about him screamed absolute menace and predator. Rage oozed from each inch of his body, and his muscles were taut like a snake about to strike.

Riley jolted visibly and noted all of this, but he apparently thought he would hold his own just fine. He took a step forward and puffed out his chest. "Oh yeah? Come on, pretty boy, what are you going to do, huh?"

Jack put a hand on Davis' chest and felt the furious rumbling there. "My love," he whispered, "Let me." Davis nodded once, and Jack turned to Riley. He smiled softly, watching Riley's eyes flicker in confusion, and then Jack hit him so fast that Riley never saw it coming. With one uppercut,

Jack laid him out on his back. Riley groaned and tried to sit up, but before he could, Jack was kneeling on his chest with a knife to his throat.

Davis grinned and stifled a laugh. He may not have known Jack was carrying that knife, but he was amused to see him pull it.

"Riley Fitzgerald," Jack said slowly in a conversational tone. "Let's see if I can make this, abundantly clear. Because I'm out of finger puppets and crayons, you dumb fuck. I will tell you this one time and one time only. I never want to see your face again. Do you understand me? Because if you think I've hurt you, it is nothing compared to what that man there will do to you. Are we clear?" He leaned back so Riley could see Davis. The dragon obliged by making his eyes swirl with storms. He flicked out his talons and ran his tongue over his fangs before he growled menacingly at the man while steam poured from his nostrils.

Jack had a moment to relish how beautiful Davis looked just then, before he smelled urine.

Riley had wet himself; terrified of the creature in front of him. "The fuck, the fuck," he whispered frantically, before he crawled backwards, blood dripping from his nose, his pants stained. He finally managed to gain his feet and ran through the parking lot. He threw himself into his Jeep before he drove off so fast he barreled over the curb, taking out a small bush along the way.

Jack stared after him for a moment, then threw his head back, laughing long and hard.

Davis squatted and wrapped his arms around Jack's shoulders, "You okay, my love?" he whispered.

"I am now," Jack replied softly and leaned his head against his mate.

When they entered the lobby, they stopped in front of Siobhan and Marco, who had been on standby in case they were needed. Siobhan leaned against Marco's chest and sighed, "That was beautiful."

Chapter 21

UPSTAIRS IN THEIR ROOM, Jack was in the shower. He had wearily followed Davis inside, claiming he wanted to wash off the feel of the day. Davis was now leaning against the counter in the bathroom, listening to Jack quietly recount his 'date' with Marissa. He was lamenting how rotten he felt for tricking her. Davis made sympathetic noises; he understood how Jack felt but reminded him of the importance of finding Vaughn.

Jack sighed heavily, "Yeah, I know, just first Marissa and then Riley. Two people kissing me today that I'm not enjoying."

Davis studied his mate's body through the shower glass. He couldn't see him well because of the steam, but he knew every inch of it. Every sculpted muscle and smooth piece of skin on the man was etched in Davis' brain. Even Jack's scar from their Shadow battle was clear when he closed his eyes.

Jack was just naturally beautiful — head to toe — and as a lover of beautiful things, Davis couldn't help but admire him. He wished there wasn't quite so much steam so he could appreciate him more right now. A devious smile tugged the corners of his lips, curling them wickedly as he remembered one important detail. He was a water dragon, and the steam was his to command. He grinned harder as he directed some of the steam to solidify and form a tendril, wrapping it around a certain part of Jack's body.

He smirked as the large man jumped before he wiped away part of the condensation on the shower door and stared warily at Davis. He grinned innocently at Jack. His gaze turned hungry as he took in the slicked-back golden hair and imagined water dripping down Jack's back and over the curve of his hips. He tightened the grip of the steam tendril and made it slide up and down the length of his mate. Jack groaned and braced his hands on the shower wall, the strength of his pleasure racing through their mating bond like lightning striking Davis' veins.

Davis himself was now incredibly turned on and quickly undressed. He kept the silky steam stroking faster while he moved closer. He closed his eyes as he heard Jack moan in the shower and whisper his name. He gritted his teeth; good God, he hadn't expected this to be so erotic, then wondered why he hadn't thought of it before. He got in the shower, and Jack turned to face him. He made the steam stroke Jack even faster and harder as he wrapped one hand around his mate's throat, forcing his chin up and pushing him against the wall, the other hand splayed low across Jack's stomach. Davis licked and bit along his jaw as he heard Jack's breathing go ragged, then captured his mouth with his own.

Jack's body spasmed a moment before Davis felt the warmth covering him, and Jack groaned in his mouth. Suddenly, Jack spun Davis around and yanked him against his broad chest, his muscles flexing like steel bands around his mate's shoulders. Wrapping his hand around Davis' throat, he pulled the dragon's back tighter against him. "Do you get to have all of the fun?" Jack murmured in Davis' ear, his voice low and husky. "Big, strong dragon, pushing me around. You figured out I like that. What about you? How do you like to be on the receiving end?" He squeezed Davis' throat tighter with one hand before taking the dragon's heavy length in his other, stroking and squeezing.

Davis rumbled deep in his chest, hearing it echo off the tiles as Jack's teeth scraped over his neck. Davis leaned hard back into his mate, "Oh fuck, yes, Jack." Now he understood why Jack had liked it so much. They had unlocked a whole new world of exploration of each other. Jack might not be a dragon, but he was no pushover either and he could easily best Davis if it weren't for his supernatural strength.

His abdomen straining, Davis tried to lean forward and turn in Jack's arms. He could break free by calling on his dragon strength, but he didn't want to. Not at all. The vise grip on his throat tightened more as a lethal voice crawled over his skin. "Where the fuck do you think you're going? Stay right there until I'm done with you." Jack's words slithered over him, leaving a trail of heat that wrenched a strangled shout from his lips. He convulsed with his release, and they both shuddered. Jack's face buried in Davis' hair, Davis panted heavily while warm water continued pouring over them both.

Jack spun Davis to face him again. "You are so dirty," he said breathlessly as he grinned.

"Me?" Davis blinked innocently but couldn't contain his laughter. "Well, at least we're getting clean now." His face lit up with his signature cheeky expression.

Lying in bed with Davis, Jack was resting his head on the dragon's smooth, warm chest. Davis idly ran his fingers through Jack's golden hair as he sighed deeply in contentment. Jack whispered, "I love you so much," before drifting blissfully off to sleep.

Davis smiled softly at his fiancé; he had been through a lot the last two days. It had been hard on Jack emotionally. The stress of finding Vaughn, and so much of his past coming back to haunt him out of nowhere.

Shoving it in his face to examine in the harsh light of day. Then their mating ritual and discovering this side of each other, that was darker than either of them expected. It was a lot to take in. Davis himself was still in awe of how much he had been able to let go with Jack. He'd never done that before and didn't realize just how much he liked it in return. Neither of them had.

Now, Davis was happy to let Jack take a little nap before waking him. He would lay still for hours, just holding him if that's what he needed. He loved the feeling of Jack's hard body pressed against him, so tight and warm. He snuggled in closer and just breathed him in. "Jack, you are the best thing that's ever happened to me. I love you so much," he whispered. His heart thumped, and he smiled. Life was almost perfect.

At dinner that evening, Jack filled in the others on the details for the next night. "Hope you all have been studying," Jack mumbled, staring down at his plate, not eating much. He'd woken up out of sorts and feeling down.

Davis figured it was residual from the emotional day, but he couldn't seem to shake off the heavy cloak of despair that had settled on his shoulders. He knew Jack was worried about Bridget, Vaughn, and their family. Progress was slow, and they were all chafing at the delays. Davis had done his best to cheer him up, but Jack quietly said he just wanted to go back to bed.

Davis squeezed his arm in sympathy, picking up on the storm of emotions swirling through his fiancé.

Jack gave him a weak smile. *I need to call Bridget with an update*, he sent to Davis, his tone suggesting he was not looking forward to it.

I'll do it, Davis offered gently. Jack tilted his head at Davis, who nodded slightly. *I'll call her and update her for you. Why don't you go ahead and go to bed, and I'll join you right after? You need the rest, my love.*

Nodding, Jack excused himself and went back to their room.

Davis was in Marco's room, making the promised call to Bridget and giving her the updates. He let her know about Jack's ex showing up, what a toll it had taken on him, and that Jack was resting now. He didn't share their mating news; he thought Jack would want that honor himself. He also didn't want to remind Bridget more keenly of what she was lacking, with her husband still missing.

As he hurried back to the room he shared with Jack, he picked up the direction of his mate's thoughts.

He sensed Jack tossing and turning and figured he had been for a while, not able to settle in. Jack was thinking about the shadows in the dark corner of the room and how they reminded him of the day of the battle with the Shadow King. Jack knew Davis still had dark nights when the battle tormented him, but he still didn't understand why. He was worried Davis might have another bad night and wasn't sure he had the energy to help Davis through it tonight.

On the rescue mission, Davis was the only one who wasn't seriously injured. Yet he'd suffered almost as badly as Shepard. Jack thought it was some twin thing and now decided he was finally going to ask Davis about it. They were mated; they shouldn't have any secrets from each other.

Crap, Davis thought. He knew Jack wasn't aware how loud his thoughts were, not being used to how much their mate bond let through. Davis shook his head, closing his eyes and quieting his own thoughts. He hoped he'd have a chance to talk to Shepard before this came up. Jack was smart, though; he would have figured it out sooner or later.

Shepard, he sent to his brother, hoping he could get him even halfway around the world, not sure of the time difference.

Yeah, bro, what's up? He heard a faint reply.

He sighed in relief. *Look, man, sorry to bug you on your trip, but I have a situation. See, Jack and I are mated, the bonding worked and —*

Shepard's excitement flooded the link, *DAVIS! Congratulations, that's excellent news! I can't wait until you announce it so I can act surprised with everyone else. I'm so happy for you, little brother!*

Davis chuckled quietly. *Thank you, Shep. It means the world to me. Problem is, now that Jack and I can link, he's worked some things out, and he has hard questions for me. Things I can't answer unless I let him in on our secret. I don't want to keep anything from him. Have you told Jorrie?*

There was silence on the link, and Davis was starting to think he'd lost him.

Finally, Shepard's reply came in, weary. *No, I haven't told her, but I agree, it's been hard not sharing everything with them. These are our mates; we should be honest with them. Let's tell them.*

Davis nodded, relieved he was on the same page. *Agreed, thank you, brother. I love you, Stream. Hope you're having a great time!*

Shepard laughed. *Love you, too, Pond, and yeah, we are having a great time.* An image of Jorrie came through that Davis could have done without. He sent him back one of Jack.

Shepard roared in laughter.

Davis grinned before cutting the link and entering the room. He saw Jack lying in bed, the sheets twisted around his legs, clearly restless. Davis climbed into the bed and straightened out the covers, pulling Jack close to him.

"My love, I have some things to tell you now that we are mated. Before I do, I spoke to Bridget. I didn't tell her about that part. She sends her love, by the way. So..." he paused. "I also spoke to my brother. The things I want to tell you about: I needed to be sure he was okay with me sharing our secrets before I let you in. Please know I'm telling you this because you are now my mate, and Shepard will be telling Jorrie, too. She didn't know before. This is super top secret. Only Vaughn, the two of us, and now you two as our mates, know. Not even our parents know this."

Jack nodded slowly in the silence that followed.

Davis took a deep, steadying breath, then continued, "Shepard and I can mind link. The way mates do, and other dragons do in their full form, but we can do it in human form as well. And it's not limited to being close in proximity either. We can do it from anywhere. I just talked to him a minute ago, even though he's in Australia."

Jack stared at him in amazement. He would understand what a big deal this was. Most mind links had to be within a few miles of each other. Halfway around the world? That was huge!

Davis swallowed thickly; this was the difficult part. "Jack, I need to tell you something else now that I hope you understand and forgive me for keeping from you. I love you, and I trust you, but I couldn't tell you before because it wasn't mine to share. Shepard and I have always been different from others because of our bond as twins. Our link isn't just of the mind. It's more. It's so, strong that when Shepard was hurt in the Shadow battle, I could feel his pain and his grief. It spilled into me, flooding me with what he was experiencing. Shepard almost died, and I'm fairly certain had he done so that day, I would have, too. You remember how much you and I leaned on each other afterwards, grieving and healing. I know you wondered why it hit me so hard."

Jack nodded quietly and took Davis' face in his hands, kissing him softly.

"It's because I was taking some of Shepard's suffering as my own. Jack, Shepard was so guilt-stricken over Dio's death, he blamed himself for a long time. At one point, he contemplated suicide, and it took everything in me to keep him alive. I was constantly siphoning some of his pain, blocking it in his mind. It took a major toll on me, but I was able to keep him with me.

When he started spending time with Jorrie after Liam left, trying to cheer her up, that finally healed him enough that I could back off some. I think he knew in the back of his mind even then, she was his mate. But I almost lost him, Jack. I almost lost a part of myself then, too. I want," he shook his head, "No, *need* you to know that your love and understanding is what got me through it. What helped me get my brother through it. Without you…" he stared at Jack, his eyes shining, willing him to understand.

Tears formed in Jack's eyes as well. Davis reeled, feeling the depth of Jack's response. The powerful, intense way he hurt so much for the dragon in front of him. Jack was awed by the incredible thing Davis had done. Taking on that suffering. It was a huge sacrifice, one that left him haunted by shadows still. It was a testament to their bond as brothers that he did it. Knowing that Davis credited Jack with helping him through, moved Jack's heart in a way nothing else could have.

Jack gathered Davis gently in his arms. He held him tightly, letting his awe and love continue to wash over their link so Davis would know how he was feeling.

Davis shuddered in relief and gripped Jack tightly. *It's been so hard, keeping this to myself, not able to tell you why I still have nightmares and anxiety.*

I'm glad you can now. Let me help you through it, give me your fears Davis, Jack replied.

Gazing at Jack with sad eyes, Davis sighed. *One more thing. Three years ago, when Shepard and Jorrie were in Australia. Do you remember that one day you couldn't reach me, and you were so worried? The day before I moved in with you?*

Jack nodded quickly.

Davis sighed, dropping his eyes to the sheets below as he idly twisted them with his fingers. *Shepard almost died then, too. That Shadow asshole shot him while Shep was in his human form. He was on the edge of death again, basically gone. Jorrie and Liam combined their magic to save his life. Jack, I felt like I had been shot, too. I was flat on the floor in my condo. Unable to move. I just felt this numbing cold all over, and I couldn't breathe. I don't know what would have happened if they hadn't brought him back. It made me realize I couldn't be without you. Once I recovered, it's why I was so adamant about living with you.* He lifted his eyes to meet Jack's once more.

A gentle smile crossed Jack's lips. *You sat me down, told me you loved me and never wanted to be apart from me again. You asked to move in with me and convinced me it was the right time. I haven't regretted that decision, ever. Not for a second, Davis, thank you.*

They talked a little longer about the little things and what the twins could do before Davis drifted off in the safety of Jack's arms. Jack soon followed him into dreams, and they held each other through the night. Any shadows flickering through the room went unnoticed by them both.

Chapter 22

THE FOLLOWING MORNING, JACK and Davis recommended they take the boat out and see if they could make any new contacts, just in case, while they prepared for their meeting with the man they suspected was Cyrus. Siobhan and Marco agreed readily, not wanting to be idle while they waited for their evening meeting. Out on the water, Marco was wandering the deck, looking a little lost. Jack teased him about not getting enough sleep due to extracurricular activities. The red dragon merely smirked and flopped down on one of the vinyl-covered benches, groaning as he stretched out. Whatever he was thinking about, gave his eyes a tired, hollow appearance.

Siobhan, on the other hand, was thinking she was pretty sure Marco was having doubts or second thoughts about being with her. He had tossed and turned all night, murmuring her name in his sleep at one point. It was not a happy sound. She could peek at his aura for some answers, but she was afraid to do so. *What if he wants to mate me instead? Am I ready for that?* Could she see herself with Marco for the rest of their lives? She gazed at him now, the daylight gleaming blue highlights on his hair as it blew in the wind. The sunshine kissing his skin, the relaxed smile on his full lips.

He turned his melted chocolate eyes on her, and she saw sparks in them when his gaze settled heavily on her, the twinkle mesmerizing. *Shit,* she thought. *I think I could do it. I could absolutely spend my life with that man. But only if he's honest with me about how he feels.* She smiled tentatively at him, and he smiled back as if she had rewarded him with a mighty bounty, placing his hand on his heart. She wondered if she should just ask him how he felt.

She knew from their previous experience that because they hadn't talked about emotions and feelings, it led to their breakup. They both agreed that they were going to be open with each other this time, but he still seemed to be holding back. She decided he was probably still wary from how things had ended before, so she needed to be the one to speak up this time. Not right now, though. She would do it in the privacy of their room tonight. Maybe.

They anchored their boat amidst the few others in the little cove and lie out on the deck, soaking up the warm sun while they waited for others to show up. Marco fell asleep and woke later to Siobhan shaking him.

"You'd better turn over before even your tan ass gets a sunburn," she told him laughingly.

He blinked at her drowsily, "Impossible. But I'd like it better if you were lying under me," he smiled wickedly.

She blinked at him and let out a deep belly laugh, the sound echoing over the water.

He jumped to his feet, pulling her up with him. He fused his mouth to hers and kissed her hard. His chest was heaving like he had run a marathon as he angled his head and took it deeper. Her arms tightened around his shoulders as she sagged against him. They heard catcalling from the other boaters, but she didn't care. He hitched her up around his waist and took her downstairs as her head dropped to the warm space between his neck and shoulder, biting on the spicy skin there as he rumbled in pleasure in her ear. The sound made her breathless with desire.

Jack and Davis laughed at the two as they went below for some alone time. "Young love, so cute!" Davis grinned at Jack.

"Yeah, but you're cuter, old man," Jack grinned back, winking at Davis as he put a hand over his heart and gasped in mock fury.

"Ahoy there, Blue Bayou!" came a cheerful hail. They waved as Dustin and Sissy pulled up alongside. They jumped to help them tie up with them and greeted their friends. Sissy studied the gorgeous men in front of her with open delight.

"Jack," she trilled, "What a beautiful tattoo that is! Why, that must have taken forever! And it looks so healed already. The artist must be quite talented."

Jack tilted his head coquettishly at her and simpered, "Well, not as long as you'd expect, but yes, it's quite magical, isn't it? The artist is so talented, you could say he's mythical."

Davis elbowed him in the ribs, and he grunted.

Sissy gave Jack a concerned look, "Are you alright, dear?"

"Never better," he wheezed.

Davis snorted, and Jack glared at him.

"You two are so adorable," Sissy laughed, "I expect a wedding invitation, you hear?"

They both nodded solemnly. Jack glanced around, "Where's Mandy today?" He didn't see the ever-present bubbly woman he'd come to adore.

"Oh, she stayed on shore, said she had a hair appointment and then needed to update her nails. Claimed they looked 'ratchet' and she was tired of purple," Dustin shrugged, "Whatever that means."

They had a good laugh and whiled away the hours laughing and talking. They hailed other boats trying to get updates but weren't having much luck. They'd almost decided to head back in when a large silver yacht sailed near.

"Who does that ostentatious thing belong to?" Jack asked Sissy, staring at it in awe.

She laughed, a pretty little sound so different from Mandy's bawdy laugh. Jack liked it better, but it tickled his brain, making him think of Marissa for some reason.

"Mm, that belongs to a couple that recently moved here. I haven't met the husband yet, but his wife is quite sweet. Art dealers, I understand." Sissy leaned in, "Didn't you just mention being interested in art, Davis?"

Davis' head whipped around. "Art, you say? Well, how interesting. Jack and I *have* been thinking of investing. Do you know her well? I'd love to meet them!"

Sissy waggled her head, "Somewhat. Her name is Esmerelda, so exotic sounding, don't you think? A lovely woman, though. I think her last name is Westin or Westwind? I don't remember."

Jack and Davis exchanged barely contained excitement in their shared glance. *Vaughn could be on that boat!* They had to get aboard.

Davis turned to Sissy, "Please," he grasped her hands in his, squeezing tightly, "Can you wave her over? I'm dying to meet her!" he urged.

She studied him, acknowledging he was acting strangely, but shrugged and obliged. She hailed the vessel, which obligingly pulled up alongside. "Yoohoo! Esme!" she called. A striking woman who did indeed look exotically lovely, waved back, and Dustin helped her tie up alongside.

"How are you, love?" Esme called down to them.

Sissy and Dustin assisted her onboard their boat. "Esme, please meet our dear friends Jack and Davis. They are visiting us from —"

"California, originally," Davis cut in, taking her hand and bowing.

Sissy glanced at Davis in confusion, and he winked. She shrugged and went along with whatever scheme Davis was cooking up.

Jack gave his most dashing smile, kissing the back of her hand as Davis handed her over, "Darling, please tell me all about yourself. An exotic beauty such as you cannot possibly be from this area. You outshine them all!" He had his charm on full blast, and it seemed to be working.

She giggled, "Oh, Mr. Jack, you are too kind, I can see that you are very desirable yourself. But of course, you are correct. I am not from the United States. I am from Seychelles. You are familiar with it?"

Jack nodded solemnly and worshipped her with his eyes, "*Oui, C'est magnifique*! A beautiful area, the islands, the culture," he said as he gazed adoringly at her.

She clapped excitedly, "Oh, *tres bien,* Jack," she exclaimed, "Even your accent, *merveilleux*!" She kissed him on both cheeks in delight.

Davis bowed over her hand again and murmured to her. "Well, that explains how a delicate beauty such as yourself can pilot that big boat all alone. You come from a nation of seafarers! But surely you are not out solo? Where is your husband? Boyfriend? Crew?" He raised his eyebrows in a hopeful arch, tucking his lower lip in as if he couldn't wait another second for her answer.

She laughed, fluttering her hands, "Oh, darling, it's just me today. This boat, she runs like a dream, no? Alas, I am alone. My husband has some business to attend to. He is the art dealer and is so busy, busy, all the time." She playfully pouted and smiled at him in a coy manner.

Davis pouted along in seeming disappointment. "An art dealer, how fascinating! Oh well, I'm sorry to have missed him, another time then. My dear lady, Jack and I have recently become engaged, and we are thinking of buying a yacht such as yours. This one," he waved negligently at their boat, "Belongs to a friend, but it's a little smaller than we'd like. Might you be willing to give us a tour? We would love to see this dream ship. Maybe we will get one just like it." He could see the hesitation on her face and hurried to reassure her. "Oh, I'm sorry, you only just met us. You don't want strangers trampling all over your yacht."

She shook her head slowly, "It is okay, I would be delighted to show you around Davis and you too, Jack," she smiled.

Sissy, seemingly understanding her discomfort and sensing that Davis was up to something, volunteered to come along. "We'd love to see it, too; Dustin and I have been thinking of upgrading."

Esme shook out her shoulders, apparently more comfortable with this, and escorted them to the large silver ship. They wandered the entire ship, looking around and vocally admiring it. Davis had already ghosted his and Marco's dragons, but while on board, he hung back as the others went from room to room. As soon as they were through a door, he ghosted himself completely, so that he could search the boat without detection. He finished quickly; there was no sign of Vaughn. Disappointed, he rejoined the others as if he'd been there the whole time, and they went back to their own yachts.

They thanked Esme effusively for the tour and complimented her on the beautiful ship. They reassured her they would let her know what they decided. They declined Sissy's dinner invitation, citing other engagements. On their way back to the marina, Jack wandered over to Davis as he piloted the boat with apparent ease. "You know, it would be nice to have one of these. Smaller, lake-sized, of course, but we could take it out whenever we wanted."

Davis grinned, his face lighting up in delight, "Darling, I would love that!" His tone was as enthusiastic as if he'd won the lottery.

Jack laughed with him, then sobered, "I know you didn't find Vaughn, but any sign of him?"

Slowly, Davis shook his head, "I didn't detect Vaughn on the boat, but I did smell magic. She's definitely a wielder of some kind." He thought for a moment. "Siobhan!" he called, and she sauntered over. "Hey, when we were with Esme, did you detect anything about her? Read her aura?"

She nodded, "Yeah, I was going to tell you, she's got a weird vibe going on for sure. I've never seen anything like it. She's got power, all right; I'm just not sure what kind. It wasn't any one color the way most wielders are. It was like an absence of color. If I had to guess, I think she's the black wielder Circe warned us about. But I didn't get any sense of menace from her, which was even stranger. I mean, I should have. Right?" She frowned and worried her lower lip between her teeth, a gesture that was foreign on her face.

The others nodded; it weirdly made sense. "What if she's helping him but doesn't know the truth of it? Maybe she's a pawn in all of this?" Davis proposed.

Marco chimed in, "Pawn or not, kidnapping a man in front of his child is not a sign of innocence. Don't let that fool you."

Siobhan started to protest, but Jack held up a hand. "Marco's right," he told them, a hardness creeping into his tone, "She's the enemy, a hostile until we prove otherwise, and we proceed with extreme caution. We have to take a logical and educated approach to this to ensure we investigate all of the targets before we eliminate anyone."

She studied him consideringly, "Jack, did I hear you say yesterday you were in the Corps? As in Marine Corps?"

He stared back at her sadly for a moment before he softly said, "Oorah." He shook his head, a dejected expression crossing his features, the sparkle gone from his eye. His normally broad and straight shoulders curled inward, and his head dropped.

Davis placed a warm hand on his mate's shoulder and squeezed.

Siobhan gently tilted Jack's chin up, "I'm so sorry for what happened, but thank you for your service and willingness to serve. It actually explains a lot. Like your fondness for knives," she grinned. "Remember the time you pulled the knife on Vaughn when you found out he mated Bridget without telling anyone? You scared the shit out of him!" They all laughed at that; it seemed so long ago.

Jack grinned with her, "Yeah, he always looks nervous when I reach in my pockets now."

Back at the hotel, they freshened up and went for an early dinner before driving to the gallery. Once there, Jack assumed his Professor Simon persona and sauntered in front of the others with an air of authority. "Come, come, children, mustn't keep the nice lady waiting," he chided them.

Marco flipped him off and rolled his eyes.

"I'm taking points off your thesis for that," Jack warned haughtily, tilting his nose in the air. The others laughed quietly as they entered the gallery. Siobhan had expressed worry on the car ride over that Esme might be there and remember them from the boat. Jack was confident he could play it off. Marissa hurried out to meet them, her face lit up, beaming at Jack.

He took her hands in his and kissed them to halt her enthusiastic greeting. She looked a little surprised but went with it. He jerked his head at the 'students' and winked. She grinned, understanding as he wanted her to that he was keeping it low-key in front of his charges.

"So nice to see you all again," she squeaked breathlessly, "Mr. Westwind is very excited to show our future art historians these new pieces and perhaps even learn a little more about their provenance."

"Ah yes, please, if you would tell us a little more about what you already know?" Jack asked her.

She shared the background that she was aware of, where the pieces were located, the suspected period, and the possible creators of the pieces.

Jack nodded along as if he was following all of it but was listening to Davis explain what she was really saying in his head. Thank goodness for their ability to mind link. Jack made a few seemingly intelligent comments as she beamed at him.

Davis coughed to cover a laugh. *I'm like Cyrano over here,* he told Jack.

Yeah, except that neither one of us is secretly in love with her, Jack replied in a snappy tone.

Just then, the man who they had seen in the recreation of Liam's memory strolled in, and Siobhan had to step on Marco's foot to stop the growl that was building in his throat. Cyrus was alone, thankfully. "So sorry to keep you waiting, Professor Shelton," he shook Jack's hand cordially.

"Please, call me Simon; Professor is so stuffy," Jack replied smoothly.

Cyrus, or Gavin as he claimed to be, beamed at him, "Then I must insist you call me Gavin. I am so pleased the University wants to study my modest collection."

Jack nodded enthusiastically. "As I was explaining to dear Marissa here, we were originally in Miami to enjoy part of the Haitian heritage festival, and we heard through the grapevine about this exciting exhibit. So curious that you chose to display it in a local gallery rather than a museum like the Perez, although I do understand supporting the amazing local economy," he said in a conspiratorial tone as he winked at Marissa.

Cyrus nodded excitedly as well, "Yes, Simon, I want the public to be able to see and experience it close up, not hidden away in some basement for years while they study and debate over it. The story needs to be told, here and now! And, of course, this gallery has such a fantastic reputation."

"With Marissa as its curator, I don't see how you can go wrong," Jack smiled; she blushed, and Cyrus nodded again, enthusiastically.

"Exactly! We are so excited. I wish you could stay for the official opening, but I know you have other students to return to. I'm glad to help further the education of our future minds! Please, let us commence!" he waved them on.

Chapter 23

THE GROUP WANDERED AROUND, looking at the pieces and discussing them in low voices. To disguise that they were merely pretending, they made copious notes on their tablets. Jack was trying not to notice that Marissa was following him around like a lost puppy as he spoke with Cyrus. "Please, tell me, Gavin, how did you become interested in this specific genre of collecting? This period or even art in general? What is your *why,* what was the first moment you said, 'Aha!' This is it!"

Cyrus stopped next to a table, "An excellent question, Simon. I will show you. It was this exact piece here," he pointed to a simple stone sculpture, a small, seated figure of a woman holding multiple babies. "The representation of Mother Earth. It was so primal. Simple but reverent. It spoke to me and told me; this is the heart of your people. Who am I to deny such a message? I must share this message with everyone!"

"Powerful, exhilarating, what a wonderful beginning to a beautiful career!" Jack gushed, then heard Davis trying not to laugh, cautioning that he was laying it on too thick. "Gavin, I understand you are new to the area? Marissa tells me you've recently moved to Miami. A beautiful place,

I'm sure, but why here? There are so many arts-centric locations in this country, in the world," Jack asked casually.

Cyrus laughed, "It may seem complicated, but it's actually quite simple. It's for my wife, Esmerelda. She wishes for the nightlife and the shopping, to be near the ocean. She is from a country of islands, and sailing is in her blood. We just bought a yacht, a beautiful work of art itself. You should come, meet her! She is a lover of the arts as well!"

"How wonderful to share such a passion." Jack nodded, "I am surprised she is not with you this evening!" he grinned.

Returning the smile, Cyrus shook his head, "Oh, she had other business to attend to this evening, but why do we not plan tomorrow for dinner, and you can meet her then? I'm sure she would love to meet you all and learn more about the program. She is dedicated to schooling and would love to, how do you say, pick the brains of the young ones?"

"We'd be delighted," Jack agreed quickly, "Please, let's exchange numbers, and we can coordinate tomorrow. I think dinner would be lovely." He hoped this would buy them more time to think of a cover story. "Have you purchased a home yet?" he asked Cyrus. "I love this area so much I was thinking of having a vacation home here," he smiled coyly at Marissa as he said this. She practically had hearts floating around her head.

Cyrus chuckled. "Oh, I think this area has quite a few points of attraction," he said. "We purchased a house just last week, in fact. We are planning to move in soon, for now, we stay in a rental off Biscayne Bay."

"Yes, a fantastic area; I have friends locally who love it as well. Is that where your home will be?" Jack asked innocently.

Cyrus nodded, "Yes, we want to be close to the marina."

Jack asked for the name of the realtor they used, citing the need for a good referral. The man was all too happy to share the information. He excused himself, then pulled Siobhan away from the group, and spoke to her in low tones. Jack pretended not to listen and focused as if he was studying the piece in front of him.

Davis wandered over, ostensibly sharing his notes with his professor.

Can you hear them? Jack asked.

Yes, shh, was his reply. At one point, Davis' nostrils flared in alarm, but he held up a cautionary hand and pointed at some random words in his notes.

Jack nodded like he was following along. "Looks good there, Davis, nicely done, I like the angle you are thinking of here," he pointed at a random spot on the page.

After a few minutes, Cyrus shook Siobhan's hand and strolled around by himself, observing his treasures like a proud father. Another anxious twenty minutes passed, and they were able to reasonably wrap it up and leave, promising once they compiled their notes, they would be delighted to send them to 'Gavin'. Jack lingered to whisper flirtatiously with Marissa and promised to take her to dinner before he left. He also promised to call Cyrus tomorrow to confirm dinner plans.

They retreated to their SUV, and as soon as they were down the street, everyone started talking at once.

Finally, Marco snarled, and silence filled the vehicle. He pointed at Siobhan, "You first, what did he say to you?"

Siobhan smirked, "First, he was asking me about my name, the origin, where my parents are from and all that. I lied about most of it. I didn't want him to link me since the name is unusual for an American. Then he asked how I liked my program at school, and if Jack, sorry, Professor Shelton, is a good instructor. I gave a glowing review."

Davis snorted.

"Okay, so I may have said you were a hard ass sometimes, but otherwise you were fair." She glared at Davis, who grinned back at her. She continued, "Anyway, then he asked me what color my power was."

The others gasped. "What did you say?" Jack whispered as if he was watching a horror movie.

Siobhan rolled her eyes, "I told him I was a green wielder bent on killing his ass, and he'd better watch himself."

There was shocked silence in the car again, then Davis snickered. He knew that wasn't true, but he was enjoying the startled faces of the others. Finally, it registered that she wasn't serious, and everyone enjoyed a good laugh, the tension leaving the vehicle.

She continued, "I asked him what he meant about color and power. I played dumb. He seemed like he didn't believe me at first, but I'm pretty good at looking at people like they're stupid, so I asked him if he was feeling okay. He let it drop."

Marco nodded, "I can confirm that look part." He winced as she punched his arm. "Okay, but this is good, he can sense wielding power, but he didn't sense us as dragons. And Jack is normal. No offense, Jack."

Behind the wheel, Jack rolled his eyes. "Yes, because it's insulting to be 'normal'," he retorted with a hint of snark.

With a sheepish smile, Marco replied, "Well, you know what I meant."

"Lucky for you, I did!" Jack grinned at Marco in the mirror, "My turn now! I found out that Cyrus and Esmerelda have been renting a house in the Biscayne Bay area. *And,*" he drawled, "They just closed on a house in the same area last week *and* he gave me the name of his realtor, the house is in his *wife's* name Esmerelda Payet, which is why we couldn't find it before. Cha-ching!" he laughed, pumping his fist in victory.

The others cheered; this was excellent information. They'd have the location of the house in no time, and they could sweep it for Vaughn. Excitement filled the car, they were getting so close, it was almost palpable.

Jack told them about the dinner invitation as well, and they realized it would be the perfect time to do their search. Jack and Davis could go to dinner with a cover story about how they knew Esmerelda, and say Marco and Siobhan weren't feeling up to it. Then, the others could search the homes while Jack kept them entertained and unsuspecting. It was crude, but it would have to work, they didn't have much time.

Back at the hotel, they reconvened in Marco's room, utilizing his equipment to run their new leads. In no time at all, they had the location of both the rental property and the new house. They decided they would start with the rental and, if Vaughn wasn't there, move to the new house. If he wasn't at either, they would just take the pair hostage in return and interrogate them until they got the answers. Bridget was getting worse by the day, and Celeste was nearly inconsolable, crying for her daddy.

Jack and Davis went to their room, where Jack began fretting over little things. Straightening a painting. Moving the chair an inch to the left. Then, back to the right. Finally, Davis demanded he tell him what was wrong.

"I feel like we should let Shepard and Jorrie know," Jack blurted, "I mean, I know we were trying to be respectful of their time, but Jorrie is Bridget's best friend, besides me, and she needs her there. And maybe Shepard could come here, and you two can use your Wonder Twin powers to really help seal this deal." Jack stared at Davis for a moment, hoping he wasn't crazy for suggesting it.

Davis gazed at him thoughtfully, then nodded, "Jack, my love, I think you're right!"

Blowing out a relieved breath, Jack whirled and grabbed his cell.

Waving his hand and grinning, Davis stopped him. "Oh darling, that's too basic, prepare to have your mind blown." He sat on the bed holding Jack's hands and indicated he should close his eyes. *Ready?* Davis asked Jack.

Jack nodded, then remembered their eyes were closed and felt his face flush with embarrassment, his cheeks warming like the sunburn he'd attained the first day on the boat. He was glad Davis couldn't see him.

It's okay, Davis sent, *it takes some getting used to. I can feel your emotions, and you were thinking about it pretty hard.* He laughed, and Jack grinned back, knowing Davis couldn't see it, but loving that he could feel it.

He pushed a wave of love towards Davis but didn't say anything. He felt Davis smiling through their bond; *I love you too,* he heard. Jack was awed; imagine you didn't have to say it, and your partner would know.

It's still nice to hear, Davis reminded him. *Now, on to business.*

Jack felt like his head was being stretched, it wasn't unpleasant, it was just strange and foreign. *Shepard,* he heard. *Calling Shepard, come in, nerd.* Jack smothered a laugh.

Why do you always have to be such a jackass? Shepard replied.

Jack's eyes flew open. *How the hell?* He closed them again quickly and focused.

Davis sent his brother a mental image of a middle finger and then thought, *I've brought Jack into our little chat room here, can you bring Jorrie in?*

Jack heard Shepard grunt in agreement, then, a moment later, he felt the stretching again, and as it subsided, he heard Jorrie as well.

Okay, that was weird, what the hell was that? Jorrie said in wonder.

Hi Jorrie! Jack said excitedly.

She squealed, *Oh my god, hi Jack! This is so cool! How is this even a thing? Oh, right, the Wonder Twins.*

Jack sensed her smirk through the link and returned it.

Davis smothered a chuckle. *Is that what you call us behind our backs? Jack just said that, too.* They all laughed.

Wow, Davis, hi! It's so cool to talk to you this way. And congratulations on your mating, you two! I'm so excited! When's the wedding? Jorrie was thinking even faster than she spoke, which was impressive.

Jack grinned as Davis shook his head. *Darling, I promise, you and Bridget will be the first to know, but in the meantime, that's not why we are calling, linking, whatever mind-meld thing this is. There's an urgent problem, and before you get mad at us for not telling you sooner, Jorrie, we were trying to keep it on the downlow and let you guys enjoy your alone time.* Jack rushed through the last part, knowing Jorrie was about to be royally pissed.

Jack. She somehow managed to make his name about twelve letters long.

Davis? He begged helplessly.

Quickly, Davis gave them the rundown. The attack on Vaughn and subsequent kidnapping. Liam being attacked trying to save Celeste. Bridget's condition and their mission to find him. Where they were and what they were doing.

Jorrie was seething. Her children were endangered, her best friend's husband was taken, her niece nearly kidnapped, and Liam was hurt.

Jack shook his head at the furious heat coming through the line. She was packing now. Cursing in between throwing things.

Shepard seemed amused by her behavior but was understandably concerned as well. *Don't worry, brother, we are on our way. See you tomorrow morning.*

Jack blinked at Davis. How in the world could he possibly get here from Australia that quickly?

Davis arched an eyebrow and gave him a wry smile.

Jack's mouth dropped; *Shepard's going to fly that far?*

Davis nodded slowly.

Shepard chimed in, *I'm taking Jorrie to the airport right now, and she's going to fly to Dallas to be with Bridget. I'm coming straight to Miami. Where should I go?*

Davis gave Shepard the name of the marina and the boat. *Let me know when you get here, we'll come get you. Thank you, brother,* he told him, relief evident in his voice.

Love you, Jorrie, I'm sorry! Jack called to her.

Love you too, she said softly.

When the connection closed, Jack fell back on the bed, overwhelmed, exhausted and in awe. "That was intense," he declared.

Davis seemed worried, raking his lower lip between his teeth.

Jack sensed it was the thought of his brother flying so far in dragon form, but that used to be their main mode of transportation anyway, so he should be fine. Jack pulled Davis to him and then stifled a big yawn.

"Bedtime, love?" Davis said.

Jack hummed yes, already feeling his eyes getting heavy. He fell asleep in the comfort of Davis' arms, finally starting to feel everything was going to be alright. They'd have Vaughn back soon.

The next morning, Siobhan and Marco were brought up to speed on the updated plan. They nodded their approval; glad Shepard would be joining them. An extra dragon with his fighting skills and magical abilities would be most helpful since Davis would be with Jack in the distraction portion of events. They planned out their routes and gathered the gear they would need. It wouldn't be difficult; they were mostly worried about getting caught.

Fortunately, with Shepard joining them, his ghosting would lower the chances. They felt they were as ready as they were going to be and spent the day resting and waiting. Saving their energy for tonight's operation.

It was late morning when Davis finally received word that Shepard was in Miami. He was in the bay now, letting the water soothe his sore wings. He'd flown as fast as he could and was exhausted. Davis drove out to the marina to pick him up and bring him back. He took him to Siobhan's room since she was now staying in Marco's, and they let him catch a few hours of sleep. By the time they were ready to leave to meet Cyrus and his wife, Shepard was refreshed and ready to go. He hugged everyone and congratulated Davis and Jack again on their mating.

Siobhan whispered something in his ear that had him grinning wickedly at Marco. The red dragon stared at her questioningly, but she refused to tell. With that settled, Davis and Jack were off.

Chapter 24

JACK SPUN HIS GLASS of wine nervously at the bar where he and Davis were waiting for Cyrus and Esme to show up. Davis took the glass, whispering, "Shh, you'll spill that, and you don't want him to wonder why you're so nervous. We've got this." He smiled at Jack's apologetic grimace.

Davis had ghosted his dragon side in the parking lot to make himself undetectable in case they were scanned with spells. He tensed when he saw Cyrus enter the restaurant, followed by Esme and whispered to Jack, "Showtime!"

They stood to greet their hosts, and Jack feigned surprise, "Esme? You're Esmerelda? Oh, my goodness, I didn't connect the two! How amazing is this? Gavin, your lovely wife was so kind to us just yesterday, we apparently have mutual friends! This is wonderful. You know, I mentioned wanting to get a vacation home here. We've also been thinking of a yacht, and she was kind enough to give us a tour of your silver lady. You two have just been the best hosts in this city. Next to Sissy and Dustin, of course!" Jack beamed at them.

"They're the ones who told us about the exhibit at the Perez Museum," Davis added, "Which is what brought us down in the first place."

Cyrus narrowed his eyes in suspicion. "I see, and where are the other two?" he asked sternly.

Jack grimaced, "Too much sun and alcohol, I'm afraid. They are sleeping off the last day of our trip. We are flying home tomorrow, so I gave them the day to do what they wanted." He rolled his eyes.

Cyrus smiled then, murmuring that he understood the follies of youth.

Esme was watching them through narrowed eyes, as well. "You, I remember as Davis," she pointed at him, then turned her venomous gaze on Jack, "But you; weren't called Simon."

Jack blushed and grimaced in a deprecating manner. "I can certainly see why that would be confusing. Simon is my middle name, and I go by that in formal situations. Can you imagine, Professor Jack? Simon sounds more professional. And, well, it's frowned upon for professors and students to have a relationship. Then, on top of it, with us both being men. But," he took Davis' hand, "The heart wants what it wants. I'm sure you can imagine, being part of a same sex couple in Texas is still somewhat frowned upon, even somewhere as liberal as Austin. California was much easier," he shrugged. "The others, they've been my students for long enough, I know I can trust them not to say anything about our relationship." He smiled shyly at Davis.

With those words, the tension eased somewhat at the table. Cyrus nodded, "I understand, being of color in America is not always easy, no? Add to that being foreign, it raises the suspicion."

Jack gave them a sympathetic smile and raised his glass, "To the outsiders, banding together!" he toasted.

"Hear, hear," Cyrus grinned.

Esme was quiet, still studying Davis, who smiled at her.

"So, tell me, Esme, have you been to the Perez Museum yet?"

She nodded slowly; her eyes glued to him in suspicion.

"Oh, isn't it lovely?" Jack gushed, "We really enjoyed the Haitian heritage festival; the exhibits were marvelous."

She seemed to ease up a bit, as they fell into a discussion about their favorite exhibits. Jack sent Davis his thanks they'd taken the time to check out what was in the exhibit that morning so he could speak intelligently about it.

Davis sent a link to his brother that they were clear to go. Shepard kept him up to date on their progress with a running commentary. They were searching the rental home now, so Davis watched the two wielders in front of him.

Shepard sent him a message; *heads up, they have some sort of magical wards on their attic. Siobhan just broke through them, but it might have alerted them.*

Thanking Shepard, Davis worked to control his smirk when he noticed that Esme's nostrils flared and her eyes pinched. *So, they were her wards*, and she'd felt them break. "Are you alright, Esme?" Davis asked, concern lacing his voice, leaning forward, his eyes crinkled, showing he was eager to lend her aid.

She glanced at him, her own eyes flashing in anger before she schooled her features, "Yes," she replied, "Just a little, um, you call it indigestion? The food... is spicy," she smiled.

He nodded knowingly, "Yes, I know what you mean. Shall we ask our server for some milk? Or maybe a pina colada to cool you down?" he winked.

Cyrus laughed, "So thoughtful, my friend. So, Simon, or is it, Jack?"

"Well, I think we are friends enough now you can call me Jack, but please, in front of my other students or professional settings, it's Simon." Jack smiled conspiratorially.

"Jack then," Cyrus nodded, "Esme tells me you have an interesting tattoo above your collarbone there." He tapped his own to indicate where Jack's mating mark was.

"A blue dragon," she added sternly and stared at him, suspicion filling her eyes again.

"Ah yes, yikes," Jack laughed in self-deprecation as he pulled his shirt aside to flash a quick peek. He leaned back, shaking his head. "Sad to say I lost a bet. You should see my best friend's tattoo. She has a matching one. She got to select the tattoo. She's fascinated with fantasy shows and books, especially dragons. What's that show?" He glanced at Davis, then snapped his fingers, "Game of Thrones, whew! Too bloody for me. But I picked blue to match my eyes. Hurt like hell, too! Never again! I am not good at football statistics, and she was my partner in our fantasy league." He rolled his eyes dramatically and grimaced cutely; his charm turned to maximum. "Oh, hang on, I have a picture of hers," he said, scrolling through the pictures on his phone. "Here's a good one. She was not happy with me for taking this picture," he huffed a laugh, showing a photo of Jorrie wearing a swimsuit, with a good view of her mark, making sure not to show her face in case they recognized her.

Esme nodded and smiled in seeming relief at his explanation.

Davis smirked. Jack was right, she'd suspected it was a dragon mark, but Jorrie having a similar one due to them mating twins helped his story's credibility.

Shepard updated Davis; *rental home clear, moving to the new property. Stall more.* Davis passed it along to Jack.

Jack acknowledged the thought and dialed up the charm even higher. He gushed over Esme's dress and her hair, waxed poetic about her accent and spoke a little French with her playfully.

Davis peppered Cyrus with technical questions about various artists, and they kept the conversation going well into dessert. Davis heard Shepard's excited voice, *wards are much stronger at this house. Siobhan's working on them now. I'm pretty sure Vaughn's here. I can feel it! We just need a little more time.*

Davis had to concentrate hard to keep still.

Wards are down, we're moving in.

Suddenly, Esme gasped and slumped in her chair. They all focused on her, with Cyrus patting her hands urgently, "Dear, please, what's wrong?"

Jack rushed around the table and offered her water. "Do you need a doctor? Shall I call for help?"

She reeled away from him with a hiss. "The wards, they're down, first one set, now the new ones."

Staring at her, a bewildered expression across his features, Jack feigned innocence. "I'm sorry, I don't know what that means." He glanced at Cyrus helplessly.

Cyrus glared at the pair, "Who are you?" he demanded.

Exhibiting even more confusion, Jack scrunched his eyebrows and stared at him, his expression turning to alarmed. "Gavin? What's going on? I'm Jack, remember? Art professor? We met yesterday at the gallery. Are you alright, should we call for a doctor?"

Gritting his teeth, Cyrus snapped at him, "A pretty story, but tell me what you are!" He whipped his gaze to Esme, "Scan them," he ordered her.

She focused her attention on Jack first, "He's human," she said slowly, disbelievingly, obviously not expecting that to be the case.

Jack stared at them wide-eyed, "Well, of course, I am! What else would I be? I think you two have had too much sun," he declared, hurt coloring his tone.

Esme turned her glare on Davis. She smiled smugly, as she obviously felt she was about to catch them.

Davis stared back at her, defiantly.

She finally sat back dumbfounded. "He's human, too!"

Shepard came through, almost yelling in his excitement. *We've got him! We've got Vaughn! We're clear, taking him to the boat for now. Meet us there quickly.*

A brief silence fraught with tension.

It's not good.

Davis surged to his feet and grabbed Jack's arm, pulling him roughly against his side. "Look, I don't know what the hell game you two are playing, but I think we've had enough," he snapped. "How… just, how dare you! I can't believe this! We came to meet you in the hopes of friendship and understanding in shared interests and hardships. I can see that was a grave mistake. I'm not sure what this is about, but if it's because we are gay, I will *not* tolerate this hostility towards my fiancé." He huffed out a breath laced with anguish and betrayal. "Thank you for showing us your collection, but your bigotry is unbelievable. How dare you insinuate that because we are both men, we are less than human! Disgusting! Absolutely disgusting. It's sickening, and I won't allow my love to be subjected to another second of this! And you can rest assured the University wants nothing further to do with you or your potential donations."

He threw some money on the table for their portion, staring haughtily down his nose. He threw his broad shoulders back and took Jack's hand. He spun and stormed off, his fury snapping about him, palpable in the air. He pulled Jack behind him as if the man were merely a sheet in the wind.

No easy feat at Jack's size, being a tall, solidly built man in his own right, but Davis made it look effortless. Of course, for him, it was, but onlookers didn't know that.

The second they were in the car, Jack turned to him, giddy and barely able to contain his excitement. "Davis, that was brilliant! I really felt offended on your behalf, of being offended on my behalf!" He placed a hand over his heart, his eyes flashing, his lips curled into a giant smile.

Laughing, Davis shook his head, "I think I follow that, but Jack," his expression turned serious, "We got Vaughn; Shepard is taking him to the boat now. Call Bridget," he urged, "We did it."

Nodded frantically, his eyes wide, Jack called her immediately.

Davis could hear sobs of relief across the line. He could also hear Jorrie in the background, cheering and shouting her excitement as well. He was glad she'd made it there so quickly.

Jack promised he was on his way to Vaughn, and as soon as he was there, he would call her. After hanging up, Jack reached for Davis' hand and squeezed it, "We did it," he whispered, his voice thick with emotion and triumph.

At the marina, they bolted to the boat and found the team below deck, Vaughn sprawled out on a bed, lost in deep sleep. There were lines etched into his face that weren't there before. Lash marks covered his chest and back. His wrists bore ugly purple raw patches where he'd been bound. The circles under his eyes were deep and dark. He was also covered in festering burns. It was obvious Vaughn had been tortured.

Marco stood watch, nearly breathing fire, he was so angry. Small sparks escaped his lips when he snarled. Siobhan perched next to Vaughn, a worried expression stamped on her face. She was holding her hands over him and chanting under her breath, examining the extent of his injuries. Shepard leaned against the opposite wall, his teeth clenched and his eyes the color of the sky just before a hurricane hit, his chest heaving in his agitation.

Davis skidded to a stop, in disbelief at seeing their leader in such a state. They'd rescued him just in time, it appeared.

Siobhan glanced up with tears gathering in her eyes. She gave a watery smile, "I can heal him, but it will take time, they really did a number... They used black magic to hold him, to hurt him. These wounds are immune to his natural dragon healing. He will be okay in the long run, though." Her breath hitched as she choked back a sob. "What do we tell Bridget?" she asked worriedly.

Jack spoke in a whisper, seething in anger at seeing this man he considered a brother reduced to this state, "I already let her know we had him. I don't want her to know how bad he is right now. It will only make her fear for him and with the baby..." he trailed off, shaking his head, the worry clear on his features.

Vaughn stirred, "Bridget," he whispered achingly, his voice strained. His startlingly blue eyes cracked open, and he searched the room frantically. He smiled weakly, "Thank you, all of you. I knew you'd find me. Please, Bridget, I need to hear her voice. Jack," he held out a trembling hand to him.

Jack quickly called Bridget and put her on speaker as Vaughn was too weak to hold the phone. "Vaughn!" she cried as he made soothing, hushing noises, reassuring her he was okay, even though he clearly wasn't. The others left the room to give him some privacy.

Davis watched as Jack noted the tears on Vaughn's face before Jack closed the door and bit his lip to keep his own in check until there was a barrier between them. Davis knew Jack hated crying, but he gathered his mate in his arms and held him while the normally strong, tough man, fell apart against his neck. He rocked him while Jack sobbed against his chest, his own heart breaking.

Chapter 25

A FEW HOURS LATER, while Vaughn was still deeply asleep, Siobhan quietly shared with Davis and Jack that they'd found him tied with magic bonds to a post in the attic so he couldn't stand or lie down. He hadn't been able to rest at all since he was taken. They were on the upper deck to give Vaughn the quiet he needed, although they suspected nothing short of a hurricane would wake him.

They urgently needed to get the black dragon home and the rest of his family to safety. Shepard, Davis, and Jack were going to carry Vaughn, leaving in just a few hours. Killian had already collected Gabe from his school in Austin, knowing he needed to be guarded as well. Once there, the whole family would be taken elsewhere to keep them secure.

Davis was deeply troubled about his brother flying from Florida to Texas on so little rest, but Shepard waved it off. It was only about three hours by plane, and they could do it much faster. Also, they wouldn't have to wait for Vaughn's plane to get to them first. Getting Vaughn home was top priority. Shepard had flown without a rider on his journey from Australia to Florida; he was going to ensure Davis made it home with two. Vaughn was in no shape to fly or ride on his own.

Siobhan performed several healing sessions on Vaughn already, so he physically looked better, but was still weak and exhausted. He needed much more sleep, and just being with his mate would do wonders to restore him.

Marco and Siobhan stayed behind to monitor the movements of Cyrus and Esme. They still needed to be punished for what they'd done; nobody attacked the Drake family and got away with it. They needed to be stopped before they tried again. Under the cover of night, the team made their way to the deserted beach. There, Shepard carried Vaughn to shore in his arms, his wings churning the water below as they strained to support the two large men.

Davis dove into the water and shifted, then flew up so Jack could jump on his back from the yacht. Once on shore, Shepard handed Vaughn up to Jack. No easy feat as he was much bigger than all of them, but Shepard used his supernatural strength to give the extra push. Once Vaughn was secured, he stepped away to shift to his full dragon form as well.

Vaughn chuckled softly. He glanced back at Jack, "All my years of being a dragon, I've never ridden one myself."

Jack laughed at the incongruity of it and hugged him, "Well, there's a first time for everything. Rest easy, brother, I've got you."

The black dragon nodded gratefully and leaned back into the strength of Jack's arms, his broad frame trembling in exhaustion.

Lake and River launched into the sky and flew away from the sun that would be rising in a few hours, heading deeper into the star-filled night. They flew over the Gulf of Mexico, cutting their travel time by not following the curve of the coastland. Even if they needed to go down, it was safe. They were water dragons, and no one was more deadly in the middle of the ocean.

Jack studied Shepard's dragon, River, in a new light now that he was mated to his twin. Although they did look very similar, Jack could see the subtle nuances. There were even more differences in their dragon forms than in their human. Suddenly remembering something, Jack thought to Lake, *hey, can you ask River what Siobhan said to him when he first got there?*

Lake snorted and was quiet for a moment. Suddenly, both dragons were chuffing, and Lake's neck rippled in laughter.

Jack raised an eyebrow, *okay, so what was that about?* He felt Lake's laughter still echoing in his mind.

Oh, it's good; she wanted to know if Shepard was as good of a kisser as we are and wondered if he would kiss Marco for her so he could pick up some more pointers. I guess our initial lesson went well.

Jack had to slap a hand over his mouth to keep from laughing loudly and disturbing Vaughn.

Apparently, he wasn't quiet enough because Vaughn spoke up, "Please don't hold back on my account. I haven't heard laughter in a while; I could use something fun to think about."

Jack obliged, telling Vaughn the whole story of Jack seeing Davis kiss Siobhan and her telling him to teach Marco. Then Jack kissed Siobhan, and she said the same thing, so they had both kissed Marco. Davis without realizing Jack had already done it.

Vaughn was laughing heartily by the time Jack was done telling the story. He'd regained some color and looked much better, leaving Jack to ponder the old saying that laughter was the best medicine.

Leaning back against Jack, Vaughn murmured, "Jack, my dear brother, I'm so happy for you and Davis. I always hated that you two weren't able to be mated because of that stupid bloodlines thing. I'm glad that we were wrong about that part. It's obvious you were meant for each other." He made a happy rumbling sound and fell asleep again.

As they neared the rooftop terrace of Vaughn's building, they could make out Jorrie and Bridget standing there. Killian was there too, leaning against the wall, his expression as always cloaked by the silvery waterfall of his hair. Lake landed first, while River circled. Jack slid down and then helped Vaughn to the ground.

The weary dragon took a few steps before Bridget threw herself at him. "Careful," cautioned Vaughn, "I'm still a little unsteady, my love. But so much better now that I'm with you." He breathed her in, and Jack could see the tension leaving both of their faces.

He wiped his eyes and felt arms around his waist as Davis moved up behind him after shifting back.

That's what the mate bond does. That's what we have now, Davis told him, watching as both Bridget and Vaughn healed and bloomed right before their eyes.

A soft whoomph sounded as River came in behind him for a landing.

"Shepard," cried Jorrie as he stumbled towards her.

"I'm alright, darling!" he said, "Just a little tired from all the flying. Never going to laugh at Mom talking about flying up a mountain both ways in the snow again, though."

They all laughed, and when it was quiet, Bridget ran to Jack and Davis, hugging each of them tearfully. Thanking them for returning Vaughn to her. She moved back to her husband's side and wrapped her arms around him.

"Celeste?" Vaughn asked with an exhausted rasp in his voice.

Bridget nodded, "Asleep in our bed, waiting on her daddy," she smiled tearfully.

"Liam?" he asked, worried for his godson.

Killian laughed, "You know Liam, he's fine. His hard head kept him from being too injured; more's the pity. He's downstairs, keeping Gabe occupied." His Irish brogue came out thick and strong, betraying the worry and anxiety he'd felt for his best friend. He hugged Vaughn tightly before slapping him on the shoulder and grinning.

Vaughn smiled gratefully, and they all went downstairs. Everyone needed a good night's sleep.

Late the following morning, Jack woke and stared at the ceiling, trying to remember where the hell he was. He turned and saw Davis still asleep, his mouth open, snoring slightly. Jack stifled a laugh, then quietly got up and pulled on his pants. He wandered to the kitchen to see if there was coffee. They stayed at Vaughn's place overnight, everyone too tired to do anything else. Jack found Liam in the kitchen, putting together a brunch for the group. It was his thing as the chef in the family, although apparently Shepard had some hidden talents he wasn't fond of sharing, mostly because he didn't want to get roped into cooking for large groups.

Jack leaned against the counter, letting the soothing aroma of the coffee reach into his soul and wake him up. Davis was right; he wasn't a morning person. Jack felt eyes on him and turned towards Liam. The tall, handsome man with the same red-gold hair as Siobhan was grinning at him. He grunted at Liam, which the latter understood to mean, *what?*

Liam laughed heartily, "Congrats, Jack, if that's what I think it is," nodding at Jack's dragon mark.

Jack studied it, and a slow, warm smile spread across his face. He shared that smile with Liam, "Thanks, man, we didn't even realize it was possible. Not until your sister set us straight. She's a wonderful human being!" Jack sighed happily.

"*My* sister?" Liam snorted in disbelief, "Siobhan? Are you sure we're talking about the same person?"

Nodding, Jack confirmed, "Yep, I'm forever in her debt, and so is Davis. And by the way, she thinks Davis and I are great kissers. She tried both of us, then declared we were even better than Marco. So, we both had to kiss him and teach him some things. I think they're having fun out there." He winked and slurped his coffee, then left, carrying a cup for Davis. He chuckled at the last sight of Liam's face as the green dragon was gaping like a fish behind Jack's retreating back.

Davis rumbled and opened an eye. "I smell heaven," he muttered. He sat up and took the coffee from Jack, drinking it right away. Dragons didn't need to wait for pesky things like hot liquids to cool. "Oh God, you do love me!" he moaned to Jack, who laughed and told him about what he'd just said to Liam.

Davis' mischief-filled eyes twinkled, and Jack almost felt a little sorry for Liam and what he was about to endure. Almost. Not enough to warn him, though. Jack grinned at Davis; he loved him so much. He brushed a stray piece of hair from his forehead and stared at him lovingly.

"I know, I love you, too," Davis smiled in return, giving him a soft kiss. Then his impish, trouble-starting grin returned, "Shower?"

By the time they returned to the kitchen, Jorrie and Shepard had joined them. Shepard looked much better today after a full night's sleep. Vaughn and Bridget were also now in the room, his arm around her shoulders for comfort instead of support. They didn't seem to be able to be apart for more than a few seconds at a time. Jack heard screeching, the joyful kind, and Serena's light tinkling laughter coming from the pool room. The kids must be swimming. Family. This felt normal.

Liam was glaring at Jack and Davis from across the table, a small stream of smoke trickling from his nostrils. Jorrie noticed and elbowed him with a 'what the hell' look. He smiled sheepishly and tucked into his breakfast.

Shepard, grinning evilly, ran up behind Liam, dragged him out of his chair and planted a noisy kiss on his cheek. "My darling, I'd forgotten to tell you how much I missed you; please tell me you missed me too!" he exclaimed dramatically.

Liam groaned as peals of laughter surrounded them. "For fuck's sake, Shepard, you don't have to kiss me every time you see me!" He wiped his face in exaggerated disgust.

Finally having mercy on Liam, Jack distracted them by telling the story of how Siobhan had read their auras and revealed to Davis they could be mates. Jack showed his mark, and Jorrie stood next to him to compare. Cheers, and congratulatory calls filled the room for a moment until Davis noticed Liam was frowning.

"Liam, dude, it was a sweet kiss, a thank you, heat of the moment, one at a time. It's not like we were having an orgy with her," Davis rolled his eyes.

Liam looked startled, his eyes widening and his head jerking back. "No," he shook his head, his long hair flying, "It's not that, it's just, well, Siobhan and Marco? They're back together?"

"Pretty hot and heavy if you ask me," Jack confirmed.

Jorrie looked sad, and Liam sighed heavily.

"What am I missing here?" Jack asked curiously.

Liam muttered something about family idiocy.

Jorrie rolled her eyes, "Well, she's moved on to Marco with Lorenzo only gone a month, and he was planning to come back. I mean... I'm happy for her and Marco. I thought they were going to be mates before she even met Lorenzo, but she seemed so taken by Lo. I just worry about poor Lorenzo. I don't know if he knows it's over. Doesn't seem very kind to him."

Nodding miserably, Liam explained that he really liked Lorenzo; they had bonded on their mission that resulted in rescuing Serena. Jorrie and Shepard were also very fond of him as well. Often having him over for 'guys' night.

Bridget spoke up, "She's young and maybe doesn't know her heart well. If she decides Marco is the one for her, then I will make sure she talks to Lorenzo." Everyone nodded, it was all they could do.

Clearing his throat, Shepard spoke up, "Speaking of those two, they're still in Miami, keeping surveillance on our villains. I think we need to get an update from them and from Vaughn about what he remembers so we can plan from there." The others nodded, and he called Siobhan, putting her on speaker before he turned to Vaughn. "Man, I'm sorry to ask. I know it was hell for you, but can you tell us anything about them? What do we need to know?"

Vaughn took a deep breath and, grim-faced, said, "I'll tell you what I know so we can end this." He spoke quietly of his captors, how they'd tormented him, blaming him for Baltrus' death despite his protestations that it was the Council and nothing to do with him. He explained haltingly how Esme's black magic worked, and the kinds of things she was able to do. Of the two, she was certainly the more powerful one. Cyrus' red wielding was more of the torturing, fire-related kind, thus the burns and the binding marks on his wrists and ankles. The lashes that marred his skin, fading reluctantly, were from Esme and her dark wielding. Somehow, the wounds inflicted by the black magic were immune to his natural dragon healing.

Angry glances bounced around the room. On the phone, Marco and Siobhan were silent for a moment. Then Siobhan quietly told them how she'd set up a minor ward to monitor the comings and goings of Cyrus and Esme. She gave a dark chuckle when she recounted watching and hearing the shrieks of anger when the captors returned to find their prisoner gone. Bolts of dark magic had flown through the house, crashing noises and the sounds of glass breaking echoed through the night. Marco reported the pair went to the rental house after that, and the process repeated itself. They had witnessed Esme performing magic that seemed to be a locator spell. No doubt, looking for the identities of the intruders, but Shepard's ghosting had been effective.

The two evil wielders had quietly discussed whether or not Jack and Davis had anything to do with it, but their tests had shown them powerless, and someone with strong powers had done this. Only Marco's sharp hearing caught that conversation.

Marco chuckled, "They weren't counting on someone like Shi, attacking those wards." His pride in her was only too obvious in his tone.

Liam glared at the red dragon's voice as if he could wither it with his stare.

Jorrie kicked him under the table. He gave her a dirty look in return but leaned back in his chair.

They fell silent for a minute, each contemplating the seriousness of the situation, before Marco finally asked, "Vaughn, you're the most affected here. I know what I would recommend, but this is your decision. Please, what next for these two?"

Without hesitation, Vaughn growled, "Now, they die."

Chapter 26

GIVEN HOW POWERFUL THIS unhinged wielder was, knowing her magic was not the normal variety, a larger contingent of dragons and wielders was needed to bolster the original team. Vaughn called for a community meeting. When he strode in, everyone stood and cheered, thunderous applause booming through the room. He stopped, rooted to the spot. He gazed around in shock, not realizing until now how much of an impact his absence caused. His throat tightened when he saw the sheer relief on so many faces around him.

"You mean a great deal to everyone here. You keep them safe, employed, and happy. Your actions have a ripple effect on us all," Bridget whispered to him, rubbing his back gently.

He nodded, overcome by emotion. He cleared his throat and made his way down the aisle. He locked eyes with Killian, and the quiet silver wielder gave a nod in return, indicating the assembly was ready. Once Vaughn reached the front, the group immediately became silent, rapt with attention. "Thank you all so much for your warm welcome back. I had no idea you all liked me that much." Laughter rippled through the room. "I need to tell you about who was holding me and to ask for volunteers to go to Miami to end this threat."

Every hand in the room immediately shot in the air.

Vaughn was astounded all over again. "Before you volunteer," he cleared his throat, a thick lump forming from the emotion building. "You need to know one of these wielders is a black wielder with very powerful raw magic. It's like nothing we've ever seen before. Their magic can overcome our healing abilities, and they fight to win." He hesitated and slowly took off his shirt. Gasps resonated through the room at the sight of the angry lash marks on his torso. He turned, and more cries of alarm sounded as they saw his still-raw back.

He stared at the floor, feeling weak and ashamed. He was supposed to be the strong one, and the enemy had been able to hurt him like this. He was afraid to turn around and see the pity on the faces of his brethren.

Killian appeared silently next to him and hugged him tightly. He was quickly followed by Liam, Davis, Shepard, and Jack joining them, all murmuring reassurances to Vaughn. Applause sounded throughout the room again. Vaughn slowly turned to see everyone on their feet again. Shouts of pride in him for withstanding what had obviously been horrendous pain. Their conversations indicated they knew for something to still be this visible, it must have been awful.

Liam held up a hand, calling for silence, "You know my sister and her healing abilities; she's already done four sessions on these wounds, and it's been three days since the last one was inflicted. This is a dangerous mission. We are going in with a plan to kill. They must be stopped. So now, knowing this, who volunteers?"

Vaughn was struck speechless. Every hand once again shot high in the air. He glanced at Liam, "You pick," he murmured, unable to speak further past the emotion choking him. He pulled his shirt back on while Liam called out to the strongest fighters and wielders.

Quickly, Liam divided the teams into two groups. One to go to Miami, one to stay here and guard the families. Either assignment was an honor and one they were proud to accept.

Killian tapped Liam on the shoulder, his long hair tucked behind his ears so the green dragon could see how deadly determined he was. "Miami," he murmured, his usual musical lilt flat in his anger.

Liam nodded. "Yes, we'll need you on this mission."

Vaughn patted his friend on the shoulder. He knew Killian wanted revenge for the atrocities committed against him. He was the closest thing Vaughn ever had to a brother, and the wielder was fiercely loyal. Killian turned to him and nodded once, communicating everything he needed in that one look.

The team traveling to Miami went to Vaughn's house to prepare. For their safety, since Vaughn's home was obviously known to the black wielder, his family and Jorrie's were being moved for the time being. Vaughn was torn between his need for vengeance and not wanting to be separated from his family again.

Bridget solved it for him by simply asking him to stay. "My love, I cannot bear to be parted from you again. Although they hurt you the most, they've hurt us all. They've attacked the very foundation of our family, and for that, I believe our family can take care of this for us. I can't risk losing you again, not while you are still healing."

He quietly acquiesced; he would have flown to the sun if she asked him to. He kissed her softly, appreciating her more than he could voice.

They gathered the children and packed them up to go to the safe house. The team assigned guard duty, escorting them out, surrounding them in a wall of protection.

Vaughn pulled Jack and Killian aside before they left with their assigned guards. "Guys, I need you to do something for me," he told them, nervously running his hands over his arms as he crossed them on his chest. He shivered slightly. "I need you to find out if Cyrus owns a gallery or is buying one. I heard something that I just remembered when I was with the kids. One night, I heard the sound of children's voices and then something about keeping them in a gallery. It was a boy and a girl, I think; they sounded very young. Killian, Jack, I'm afraid they've taken some children and might be holding them, too. I can't bear the thought of them keeping little ones the way Serena was kept. Please, please, find out and save them?"

Jack swallowed heavily. "Of course," he whispered, horrified.

Killian simply met his gaze and nodded.

Sighing in relief, Vaughn hung his head. He knew they would take care of it.

The men turned to leave when Vaughn called out, "Jack, wait." He put his hand on his brother-in-law's shoulder. "Jack, this whole thing has taught me something else. I need to think more about my future, with another child on the way. I was going to do this anyway, but recent events have moved my timeline up. I'm stepping down as CEO of Chesapeake. I'm going to focus on the gaming company. It's more than enough, anyway. That being said, Chesapeake needs a leader, someone I can trust. Who has proven strength and loyalty. It needs you. When you get back, we will make it official."

Jack's jaw dropped. "Vaughn," his mouth worked a bit more before he finally found the words. "I'm honored. I'll be happy to run the company for you. I appreciate your trust in me."

Vaughn laughed tiredly. "Oh, Jack, you're going to do more than that. I'm giving you the company. Think of it as a wedding present. I owe you so much for all the ways you've saved my life. Introducing me to Bridget, and then, of course, actually rescuing me." He grinned.

Spluttering, Jack's eyes were wide, and he held up his hands.

The large dragon laughed heartily now and wrapped his strong arms around Jack. "I love you, and you won't change my mind on this."

Killian nodded at Jack over Vaughn's shoulder, his wry smile indicating Jack should just say thanks and move on.

After Vaughn's family was packed and gone, Davis directed the rest of the team to the cars out front so they could head to the airport. A company of five additional dragons and six wielders would be joining them. Liam was staying in Dallas to manage operations here since Vaughn was in what Liam called the Dragon Witness Protection program.

Jack only knew some of the team members vaguely. Liam and Davis reassured him they were hand-selected for their stealth, courage, cunning, and strength.

Shepard was coming back with them as well, and although Jorrie was terrified of him being hurt, she felt better knowing that Jack and Davis would be there. She knew they wouldn't let anything happen to him.

Once the flight was in the air, Killian and Jack called the group together and revealed what Vaughn had shared with them about his suspicions of kidnapped children. Shocked cries of anger filled the cabin before the team fell into stunned silence. How depraved *were* these monsters? They would have to change their approach. They needed to rescue the children before they executed the dark pair. They didn't want to risk the possibility of not finding the innocents first. With grim determination they discussed the ways they could neutralize the wielders without killing them.

Two of the wielders, one red and one silver, revealed that they had been using Siobhan's methods and combined their skills to make some magical restraints. It was similar to what was done to Vaughn except it didn't hurt the person with brute force. Instead, it simply put a damper on their power, much like a Faraday cage, and the person was unable to push their magic outward from their body. It sounded promising but needed to be tested. The other wielders agreed to be guinea pigs once they reached Miami.

Davis whispered to Jack that he and Shepard had been working on expanding their ghosting technique and could do some trials on that as well.

Jack stared at him in concern, wrinkling his nose. *Are you sure you and Shepard are ready to share that knowledge with everyone here? Knowledge is power.*

Nodding seriously, Davis replied, *we talked, and you're right; knowledge is power. We intend that power to be used to our advantage. If we can keep everyone safe, then it's worth it for a few more to know about us. Maybe our enemies need to fear us instead of us fearing them. I'm ready for people to leave us alone and just let us live our lives without the constant fear of someone trying to harm us. Cyrus and Esmerelda brought this upon themselves by attacking our family. Otherwise, we might have never been aware of them.*

Jack pondered for a few moments. It made a certain amount of sense. *But there's always a bigger fish,* he reminded him, *if you put it out there that you're the biggest badass around, someone will always want to take you down.*

Davis' lips curled in laughter as his eyes danced with glee. *Darling, I AM the biggest badass around.* He winked, and Jack laughed.

"Yes, you are," Jack told him and kissed the tip of his nose.

Shepard laughed as he sat next to them. "You two are so adorable." He snatched Davis' phone and opened it.

"Hey, what are you doing, jerk face?" Davis griped as he tried to grab it back.

"Shut your hole, pipsqueak," Shepard told him with the kind of love only a brother could give while putting his hand on Davis' face and pushing him away.

Jack grinned. It reminded him of how he and Brian used to squabble as kids and call each other similar names. Shepard and Davis were centuries old and still did it.

"You're jealous because I'm older."

"And you're jealous because I'm better looking, and Mom likes me more. I'm the favorite, and you know it."

"Not anymore! I'm the favorite now, although that might change shortly."

Jack laughed, *siblings*. He missed his own brother deeply at times like this.

"There," Shepard said and threw the phone back to Davis.

Davis quickly looked through it and stopped. Horrified. "What did you do? I hate you!" he whispered in terror.

"Something you should have already done, idiot," Shepard grinned, rumpling Davis' hair. He stood and hugged Jack. "Welcome to the family, brother," he said as he strolled back to the others and took a new seat.

Jack's curiosity was peaked about what was going on, "Davis?" He moved to sit next to his fiancé.

"He's dead," Davis whispered, his eyes wide, his face paling rapidly under his golden tan.

Leaning over to see what had Davis so fired up, Jack glimpsed a picture of them on the boat. Siobhan took it for them in Miami. Apparently, Shepard sent it to someone.

Davis' phone rang then. He let out a strangled groan as he pinched the bridge of his nose. Glancing at Jack, he muttered, "I'm going to kill Shepard. Kill him and stomp on his corpse and kill him some more." He sighed, "I do not need this right now." Shaking his head and hunching his shoulders, he shot a furious glare at Shepard.

His cocky twin called out, "You might as well answer, she'll just keep calling until you do."

"Hi, Mom," Davis grimaced as he answered, locking eyes with Jack and taking his hand.

Jack heard excited squealing. He realized who Shepard sent the picture to and why. It clearly showed Jack's mating mark and their rings. He bit his lip to stop the laugh that was building as Davis nodded slowly.

Davis had planned on telling his mother. He'd promised Jack, after all. He just wanted to do it on his terms, when there wasn't danger hanging over them all. Then his asshole brother pulled this stunt. Shepard reminded him that Barbara would be persistent, so he might as well answer. He flipped Shepard off as he clicked accept, then squeezed Jack's hand, keeping him nearby for moral support. Hurricane Barbara was making landfall.

"Darling! I just got that picture of you two! It's so lovely, and you both look so happy! Oh, baby of mine, you did such a good job with your mark. I'm just so proud! Your father is here, he's proud, too!" Barbara gushed.

Davis was so stunned he dropped Jack's hand. He pulled the phone away from his ear and stared at the screen to make sure this was his actual mother calling. Yep, right number. He put the phone up to his ear, and she was still talking.

"Love Jack so much, and oh, you two will be so handsome in your tuxedos! Have you set a wedding date yet? You should definitely accent with blue; both of you have such gorgeous blue eyes."

"Uh, Mom?" Davis said, puzzled, scratching his head.

"Davis?" she said back, sounding amused.

"Don't take this wrong because I'm happy that you're happy, but I thought you wanted me to mate with a woman so we could carry on the bloodline and more grandchildren blah, blah, blah. Now you're thrilled I'm mated with Jack even though you always told me that wasn't possible. I don't get it," he said sternly, some of his anger leaking into his tone. "All you've done is push me away from him."

Even Jack could hear Barbara laughing loudly through the phone.

"My sweet Davis, I admit, I didn't know it was possible for you actually to be mates. We believed the Council story for so long because we didn't think they would lie to us. Obviously, we know now how twisted they were. But honey, I can see how much you love Jack. A blind dragon would know. We adore him as well, and we wanted you to marry him so he could be our son, too! But I knew you wouldn't do it because you didn't realize how much he meant to you. So, I've been pushing you in the opposite direction. You're so stubborn, and you never do what I want you to. I'm so sorry for the subterfuge, but it was time you stopped playing around and cherished what was right in front of you all along. Jack is your mate, Davis, and I'm so glad you finally realized it."

Davis stared blankly out the window of the plane. All of it was just his mother's manipulations. Because she knew if she pushed him to Jack, he'd resist. That wonderfully evil woman. He threw his head back and laughed hard.

"Davis? Davis honey?" Jack could hear Barbara calling out. He wasn't sure exactly what was going on. "Jack, darling, are you there?" he heard. He gingerly took the phone from Davis, who was now lying on the floor of the plane, laughing and rolling around.

Shepard was grinning at them and gave a thumbs up.

"Hi Barbara? It's Jack," he said cautiously into the phone.

"Oh, Jack, my love! Thank goodness I can talk to the saner of you two. What is that crazy boy doing? Oh, never mind," she sighed, "Jack, I need you to know I've always been on your side. We've all loved you since the moment we met you. We knew you were the one for Davis. I'm so excited you completed the mating bond and will be together for such a long time. That silly playboy child of mine just needed the right push. After two hundred years of watching him work, I knew just the way to do it. I'm so sorry if I ever hurt your feelings. It wasn't what I wanted, and I do hope you'll forgive an old woman's meddling. You are just what he needs. You keep him grounded and happy, and that's all I've ever wanted for you both. Welcome to the family, officially, my darling son. Please say you'll forgive me. And let me help with planning the wedding?"

Jack smiled, "Of course, Barbara," he replied, his voice thick with emotion, swallowing back the lump in his throat.

After a few more minutes of her congratulating them both, Davis finally disconnected the call. He glared at his brother and flipped him off again.

Shepard blew a kiss back at him, where he still sat on the floor.

"You knew, didn't you," Davis snapped accusingly to Shepard as he strolled over.

His brother shrugged, "I suspected, but you know she's right. You couldn't get your own head out of your ass to realize this amazing man here," he shook Jack's shoulder, "was perfect for you. Hell, we all knew you two were in love before you did!" he laughed.

Davis just stared at him; then he jumped up and hugged his brother as tight as he could.

Shepard hugged him back, just as hard. "Love you, asshole," he whispered.

"Love you too, dumbass."

Jack joined the hug, "I love you both, idiots."

Chapter 27

"THANKS FOR MAKING LIAM stay," Siobhan whispered to Jack after he told her of her brother's reaction to the news that she and Marco were dating. She got a kick out of how Jack messed with him. She wasn't thrilled with the idea of calling Lorenzo but promised she would. She also wasn't looking forward to Liam's badgering when they got home. Jack smirked at her and winked. "That wasn't me, thank Bridget when we get home."

"Stupid brothers," she grumbled, kicking the legs of the bar stool at their rental house.

Siblings, grinned Jack.

Did you page us? asked Davis as he and Shepard wandered over.

Jack laughed. "No, but since you're here, you can explain to her this wielding melding thing they are going to be testing on each other. I think she should stand by as a paramedic." His eyebrow arched and he jutted his chin towards two wielders shooting bolts of magic at each other while Killian watched quietly.

Shepard nodded, "Good idea, new magic and experiments can get out of hand quickly, but in a controlled environment, we can get a better idea of how this will work."

Marco joined them, "Nice job on this house, Davis, it's a much better set-up than constantly running to each other's rooms. Although I guess we will all have to be a little quieter from here on out," he grinned at Siobhan who glared back at him.

She turned to Shepard with a wicked smile.

The blue dragon chuckled and nodded. He grabbed Marco, just like Davis and Jack described, threw him back and kissed him as soundly as if he was Jorrie.

Everyone else in the house stopped and stared. Most knew of the joke by now, so they were cat-calling and cheering. When Shepard let Marco go, he roared with laughter while the other man's cheeks colored and flamed.

"*Madre de Dios*, when are you going to run out of guys to make kiss me? I feel like I should be insulted you think I need this much help," Marco glared at Siobhan.

Davis and Jack stood next to Shepard. "Okay," asked Davis, "Now which of us is the better kisser?"

Marco rolled his eyes. "No way, not happening."

"Do you need a refresher?" Davis advanced on him.

"No!" Marco yelled, backing up and raising his hands in defense. The others were laughing and chanting for him to choose.

Jack circled behind him and held him still.

"Pick, or I'm going to do it!" Davis taunted.

Marco laughed, "Okay, *si, si*, I'll choose! *Cretino!*"

They stood in a line again, and Marco paced back and forth like a judge at a beauty pageant. He adopted a serious pose, his arms behind his back. He stopped in front of each of them and gave them a considering look before nodding and moving to the next. "In third place," he intoned with his nose pinched, which set off another round of giggles, "Shepard."

Shepard threw his hands in the air in disgust, "My wife likes me best!" he challenged.

"Sore loser," called Davis, "Also, I've never kissed your wife; I didn't want to steal her from you."

Rolling his eyes, Shepard went to stand with the others and received encouraging pats on the back.

Marco rubbed his jaw, "It's the stubble man. You need to shave." More roars of laughter filled the house.

Turning to Davis, Jack took his hands. They faced each other as the last two participants in the pageant. "Shepard, I've never kissed your wife either; she's not my type. Davis, no matter who wins, you know I love you," Jack said.

Marco stepped up to them, "And the winner is..." The others began a drumroll on the counters and tables. Marco held up a hand for silence, "Jack!"

Cheers erupted, and Jack pumped a fist into the air. "Victory!"

Davis hung his head in defeat while his brother gave him a hug of conciliation. Jack leaned over to Davis and kissed him, and he laughed then, showing he wasn't really upset.

Waving again for everyone to be quiet, Shepard asked, "Marco, man, what is it about Jack's lips that drove you wild about him?"

"I gotta tell you man," Marco grinned, "It's that thing with the tongue. I'm straight as an arrow and even I thought that was hot!"

A chorus of whoops went around the room, and Davis cackled. "Amen!" he shouted, "That's what I've been telling you!" Another round of laughter.

Marco strode determinedly to Siobhan, backing her against a wall. He yanked her body to his and kissed her the way Jack had kissed him. When he let her go, she had a goofy dreamy smile as she murmured, "Definitely that way!" A final round of applause and the group gradually dispersed.

Shepard stared at Jack consideringly and started towards him.

"Oh no!" Jack raised his hands, laughing, "Not going there!"

Davis got between them, "Back. Off. My. Mate," he growled.

Jack stared at him in alarm, surely, he didn't think his own brother... he rolled his eyes as the two laughed and fist-bumped.

Turning towards him quickly, Davis demanded, "I need a demonstration of just how you kissed Marco, I want to be sure he didn't get something you haven't given me!"

Shepard snorted and grumbled, "Get a room."

That evening, Shepard was in the kitchen, grumbling again, complaining about being no better than a mess hall cook. Since Liam wasn't there, Shepard was assigned dinner duty.

Jack felt bad and offered to help him. "I'm a good kitchen bitch; just order me around. I've been doing it for Bridget for years," he volunteered.

"Sold," Shepard grinned. Together they worked well, and in no time, the meal was simmering away, filling the kitchen with delicious smells.

Grabbing two beers from the fridge and popping the tops, Shepard handed one to Jack. "So, brother," he started.

"I like the sound of that," Jack offered quietly.

Shepard studied him consideringly, nodding. "I don't know if I ever told you, but I'm very sorry for your own brother's passing. It was a terrible thing, finding out that truth. If there is any silver lining, though, it's that we came to be together because of him. Bridget and Vaughn, me and Jorrie, you and Davis. So, here's to Brian Ridgeway who gave his life that we would become family."

Jack stared at Shepard, then nodded as tears rolled silently down his face. He clinked his bottle to his new brother's, and they drank in solidarity. Jack felt warmth behind him and leaned back against Davis' chest. He always knew when he was needed. Jack sighed as Davis glared at his brother.

"Why are you making my mate cry? He hates crying," Davis growled.

"Stop it," Jack slapped Davis' arm. "He was welcoming me to the family in the most beautiful way possible, and I won't have you ruin it with your growly, dragony angst."

Shepard snorted and almost spit out his beer, laughing.

"I'll have you know; I grew out of my emo, dragony angst stage years ago," Davis said stiffly.

"Yeah," Shepard nodded encouragingly, "You only had it like age thirty-five to what, age two hundred forty-three?"

Davis threw a tomato at his brother, who dodged, and it hit Marco instead as he came around the corner.

"Dude," he groaned, wiping seeds and juice off his face. "What the hell, man?"

Grinning at him, Davis simpered, "C'mere Marco, let me apologize to you the best way I know how."

"*Que no suceda*!" Marco shouted, running for the exit, his black hair fluttering behind him like a startled crow's wings.

The brothers laughed, and Davis offered to set the table while Jack and Shepard finished up.

Shepard turned to Jack again. "What I meant to say earlier was that I'm really glad my brother got his head out of his ass. I knew from the moment I saw you two together that you were the one for him. Call it a gut feeling, I don't know. I've always been able to feel things like that where he's concerned. Maybe because I'm the older one, I feel like I have to be his protector. But now he has you, and I couldn't be happier, Jack. I love you, and I'm so glad you are my brother now, too. Normally, this is where I should say if you ever hurt my brother, but instead, I'll say, if he ever hurts you, let me know and I'll kick his ass. Also, I hope you'll forgive Mom for her shenanigans. She loves you so much, sometimes I think more than she loves us, and she didn't want Davis to get in his own way and screw this up." He hugged Jack.

"Water under the bridge," Jack nodded.

Shepard chuckled, "I hope you know that phrase means the equivalent of swearing on your life in this family."

Jack thought about it. Then he smacked his forehead, "Water dragons," he laughed under his breath. Shepard nodded, and Jack smiled in return. "I do mean it. I didn't understand how she could profess to love me so much then keep nudging Davis to go another way. It makes more sense now. He can be so damn stubborn, so tell him to do the opposite of what you want him to do so he goes the way you wanted in the first place."

"Yep, you've got him figured out," Shepard grinned.

Jack smiled, "I do love your parents and how accepting they've been of me. It's nice to be loved for who I am and how I am, without any strings attached."

Considering Jack quietly, Shepard added, "I'm sorry. I guess I didn't think about how your family might react to you being, you know, you."

"Gay. It's okay, Shepard, you can say it. I'm gay. I've made my peace with it," Jack told him gently. "It took a while, too long, honestly, to admit what I've always known, but I'm no longer ashamed of it, and I'm not hiding it."

Shepard shook his head, "No, not that, I mean, yeah, you're gay so what? I meant it's part of who you are and the way you were born; you don't have control over that. So, I hate that they treated you differently because of it.

You deserved just as much love and affection as your brother, maybe more to help you through a difficult life. I hope you don't mind; Davis shared some of what you've been through. He told me about Riley and gave me a mental picture of him, so if he does ever show his sorry ass around us again, I can kill him." Steam wafted from Shepard's nostrils.

Jack stared at him in open-mouthed astonishment. He'd never felt such unconditional acceptance from family before. Brian was the only one who stuck with him, loving him, even though he didn't fully understand what Jack was going through. Until Bridget and Jorrie came into his life, then they became his family. He thought about his parents. He hadn't spoken with them much since his brother died. They stayed in contact with Bridget more, mostly because of Gabriel, her son with Brian. Now that she was remarried with new children, and Gabe was an adult finishing up his last year of college, they barely spoke.

Jack had debated not inviting them to the wedding, then sighed. He knew he would. Whether they came or not, well, that was up to them, but it wasn't going to make or break his day. He had a family that loved him just the way he was. He hugged Shepard tightly, silently thanking him.

Shepard hugged him back and picked him up, swinging him around easily like a child before plopping a noisy, wet kiss on his cheek. "Love you, jerk face," he said.

Dinner was a hit, and everyone unanimously voted that Shepard was in charge of meals. He threw up his hands and groaned. "Fine, but I'm not a short-order cook. You get breakfast and dinner. You eat what I make, or you figure it out yourself. And since I'm cooking, I'm not cleaning or taking out the trash. You guys are on your own for that." He stomped off to the living room and turned on the television to some sporting event from the sound of it.

Jack raised his hand and pointed at himself, "Sous chef, I'm out too!" He joined Shepard on the couch. The others laughed; it was a good deal. Once everything was cleaned up, they returned to the dining room to plan their next steps.

Marco and Siobhan reported that Cyrus and Esme were in their newly purchased home. The rental was vacant, so they moved in as planned. Their wards were back in place but significantly stronger than before.

Siobhan was confident that she could break them, maybe with a little help from the others. Warding was her main strength. "She's using brute force to make her wards, just gathering raw power and shaping it into a shield. It's not uniform, so there are weak spots I can manipulate to drop them. But now they know we are on to them and will be ready with backup. They won't be fooled again." The team nodded in understanding.

Jack's phone rang, startling everyone in the silence that had fallen. He studied the number and groaned. It was Marissa. He motioned to Davis and ran to the bedroom. Once there, he answered it on speaker. "Hello?" he said cheerfully.

"Simon?" her voice wavered.

"Marissa, hello darling! I'm so glad to hear from you!"

"Is Simon really your name? Or is it Jack?" she asked quietly.

He sighed, already hating this. "Marissa, I'm sorry. I lied to you. I'm guessing you've been talking to Gavin. Please, just listen. I need to see you and talk to you. You are in danger from him, and I don't want you to get hurt," he pleaded, fingers crossed.

"Too late for that, Simon, or Jack or whatever your name is. Don't talk to me ever again!" she cried and hung up.

Jack hung his head; he felt awful. She was so sweet and innocent in all of this, and now she was possibly in danger as well. He gazed at Davis with sadness in his eyes. He felt an inky cold numbing his body as the thought of her pain filled his soul.

Davis firmed his lips and grabbed the car keys from the dresser. "Come on."

They sped to the gallery and pulled up just as Marissa was locking up to leave for the night. She turned and saw Jack and Davis, then shook her head, quickly hurrying away.

"Marissa, please just wait, could you please hear me out? I promise. I just want to talk to you, and if you still want nothing to do with me afterwards, then you can leave. We can go somewhere public, a coffee shop, a bar, anywhere you choose. Please," Jack begged. He saw her shoulders drop and heaved a sigh of relief. She was listening.

She whirled and snapped at him, "Gavin told me you were going to try to cover up your lies with more lies. I don't know why I should believe you when I've only known Gavin to be honest with me. All you've done is lie. I looked up Simon Shelton, he doesn't exist. You were never interested in *me*, were you? Gavin even told me you're with him," she waved her hand in Davis' direction.

Jack's chagrined expression had a frustrated groan huffing from her lips.

Davis stepped forward, his deep voice calm and soothing. "Marissa, please, it's my fault. Jack is my fiancé, that's correct, but I'm the one who put him up to it. I promise we have a valid reason for the subterfuge, and I'm glad to explain it to you. I'm so sorry you were caught up in this and were hurt. Jack's felt awful and miserable about deceiving you. I swear, and although that may not mean much to you, he really did want to protect you tonight. If we didn't care about you, we wouldn't be here right now."

She visibly wavered.

"Please," he pleaded and held out a hand, "Aren't you a little curious about it all? The subterfuge, the intrigue? Don't you want to know why?"

Finally, she slowly held out her own hand and took his. She nodded to a coffee shop across the street. "Let's go," she agreed.

Chapter 28

ONCE THEY WERE SEATED and had their beverages, they stared at one another. Not sure where to begin or how much to say, Jack gazed at Davis, and Davis stared at Marissa, who was watching Jack. "I don't know where to start," Jack admitted, holding his hands up slightly.

She nodded, "I've always found the beginning, and the truth works well."

Davis glanced at Jack and sighed. *Tell her.*

Startled, Jack replied, *all of it?*

He nodded. *She may know something about the other gallery or could help us find it. She needs to know why this is so important and doesn't tell Cyrus we are back, looking for him.*

Jack nodded this time.

"See, that!" She pointed at them. "Somehow, you two just had a whole conversation without saying a word. Start talking now, or I'm gone, and I will tell Gavin you were here," she snapped, temper lacing her words.

Davis simply reacted, and he admitted later it was poorly. He growled at her, and his eyes turned stormy gray. Steam trickled from his nostrils and down his neck.

Marissa's eyes flew open wider, and she lurched back from the table, the metal chair legs screeching on the worn linoleum floor. The sudden noise made heads turn in irritation. Her earlier feisty veneer was replaced by shock and fear. Her hands trembled as a small whimper escaped her lips. She rolled them in as if she were trying not to scream.

Jack laughed to cover it up. "Sorry! Didn't mean to startle you!" He grinned and waved around. Not wanting to be involved anyway, the other patrons were reassured and went back to their own cups. He leaned across and grabbed her hand. "Marissa," he spoke quickly, "Please just calm down. I'm going to tell you everything, and some of it you're going to find hard to believe but I'm begging you. Please just listen. We are not going to hurt you, okay? Look at me, look at my eyes, breathe. Not going to hurt you."

Her breathing slowed, and her expression turned from one of fear to one of fascination. "What are you?" she whispered to Davis.

He tilted his head, taking in her now eager eyes and lips parted in anticipation. With a grin and a rumble in his voice, asked, "Are you sure you want to know, little one?"

She shivered in obvious delight, no longer afraid as if his words wrapped around her like a physical caress. She pointed at him, "Talk. Now."

Davis laughed, and she shivered again at the rich delicious sound. "Okay, my dear. You look like a dreamer — so tell me — do you ever fantasize about there being more to life than just your normal day-to-day? More than just... humans," he said in a low voice, and she nodded as if mesmerized. He smiled wickedly as the tips of his fangs came down, and storms flashed through his eyes. He glanced around and confirmed no one was watching as he poured water from her glass on the table and rolled it into a ball. He solidified it, then handed it to her.

She held it cradled in her palms like it was a precious gem. Her eyes were shining with unshed tears. She gazed at them and smiled as if the entire world had just been handed to her, "I knew it! Finally," she breathed, her voice shaking.

Jack and Davis exchanged a confused glance. Davis shook his head and pulled his dragon features back in, his face returning to human. He took some of his coffee and made it into a bracelet that he floated across the table. It slid over her outstretched hand before settling on her dainty wrist.

She twisted it around, staring at it and grinning, her face lighting up with pure joy. "That is so freaking cool. So, are you some sort of vampire or wizard? What is this?"

Davis studied her in awe, like a scientist observing a new life form. "You know this is not the usual reaction I get nor one I expected," he told her, "But vampire? Seriously? That's insulting."

She shrugged, "Well, fangs, magic. So, tell me. Werewolf?"

He laughed, "Marissa, I'll have you know I am something much cooler, scarier, and badass than all that. I, my dear, am a dragon." He rumbled low in his chest to emphasize his point.

"No shit!" she squealed loudly, causing more glares. Marissa slapped her hands over her mouth and offered a muffled, "Sorry!" to everyone.

Jack was trying to control his laughter. "Marissa, look, there's a lot to tell and it's going to take a while. At the risk of sounding creepy, do you want to come back to our place so we can talk freely without being overheard? You can meet the rest of the dragons and wielders. They're like wizards. We are on a mission, and we need your help, as crazy as it sounds, to stop the bad guys and rescue some kidnapped children."

Her mouth dropped, "A quest? Oh, I am so totally in."

By the time they arrived at the beach house, they had given her the rundown. Who they really were and where they were from, what Gavin or Cyrus had done to instigate their wrath, and how they had rescued Vaughn.

"So, let me get this right," she said from the passenger seat. Jack was driving, Davis sitting behind him. "You mean there is a straight-up dragon and wizard, good versus evil, duel about to take place, and I'm caught in the middle?"

Jack shrugged, "More off to the side, adjacent, than middle, but there's a good chance you would have been caught in the crossfire, and we didn't want to risk you getting hurt. You can stay here while we go in. You'll be safer."

She made a noncommittal noise.

"Marissa, this is big; you don't know how dangerous this is yet. Please come meet the team, and let's go from there," Davis pleaded.

They got out of the car, and Jack paused. "Let me go give them a heads-up first. Dragons are very private about who they share their identities with. As you can probably imagine, the chaos it would cause if this went public."

She nodded, and he went in to talk to the others. She turned to Davis. "So, you're a dragon, he's a human, you're mates, engaged, whatever. So, do you just have those things you already showed me, plus power over water? Or can you go full dragon?"

He laughed, "I can do partial with my wings in this form, or I can go full dragon, *and don't,*" he held up a hand to stave off the next question he saw on her lips, "Ever ask me or any other dragon to go full dragon for you. It's not a party trick, and it's very private. We only do it in times of battle and for our mates."

She nodded and mimed locking her lips and throwing a key over her shoulder.

Davis gave a rumbly chuckle that made her shiver despite the warm air.

She tilted her head. He sighed, "What else?"

She grinned, "Can I see your wings at least?"

Davis laughed again and deepened his rumble into a purr. He removed his shirt, and her eyes glazed over with desire. He shook his shoulders a little and ran a hand through his hair. Her eyes locked on his biceps and then his chest. "Marissa," he called softly with a grin at the effect he was having on her.

She glanced at him absently, "Hmm?"

He grinned even wider, showing a little fang. "My wings are back there." He unfurled them, and she gasped as she stumbled back.

"Holy shit!" she whispered reverently. She beamed at him as if he had just made all of her wildest dreams come true. Her mouth formed a small O at the sight of the beautiful blue wings and scales attached to the incredibly sexy man in front of her.

Jack sauntered over and rolled his eyes. "Davis, my love, if you're done dazzling the fair maiden, everyone's ready."

Davis threw his head back and roared with laughter, the sound making Marissa swallow heavily. Davis grabbed Jack and kissed him soundly, making sure she got the hint he was not available.

Marissa sighed, "Damn, I was hoping that part wasn't true. Jack, I have to hand it to you. I didn't think you were gay. You are very convincing as straight. You too, Davis." She shook her head. "All the hot ones."

Jack laughed and hurried into the house, motioning for her to follow.

Inside, she took in the large group of people gathered there. All at ease, engaged in various normal household things. She almost felt disappointed, like she'd expected them all to be walking around with their wings out and doing spells.

Jack smiled at her expression. "Everyone, this is Marissa. She's the person who helped us find Cyrus." There was a round of applause then and some cheers. "As I mentioned, she's just learned the truth tonight, so take it easy on her, okay? Now, introduce yourselves!" he called out.

Siobhan went first. "We've already met; my name really is Siobhan. I'm not an art student, I'm a wielder, green magic, which is wards, shields, plants and some healing."

Marco followed her, "I'm really Marco, also, not an art student." He winked. "Better, I'm a red dragon. Known for our speed and fighting skills. I'm actually the mission leader, although Jack is doing a fine job as well," he said.

Shepard went next, and she whipped her head around, staring at Davis and then back at Shepard, narrowing her eyes.

"You're…" she started.

"Twins, yes, we are."

She shook her head, "Well yeah, I can see that, but it just hit me why I felt like I knew you, Davis. You're Shepard, drummer for Still Waters."

He grinned and nodded. "That I am. And like my younger brother —"

"By two minutes," Davis interjected.

Shepard laughed, "Still older. Anyway, like him, I'm a water dragon too." He pulled some water from a nearby glass and shaped it into a rose, froze it and handed it to her.

She gasped in delight.

"Show off," Davis grunted.

Shepard winked at him.

Marissa studied him openly. "So, are you…" she jerked her chin towards Jack and Davis.

He roared with laughter, "No, I'm not, but don't get your hopes up. I'm happily married."

She snapped, "To Jorrie, that's right."

Davis cleared his throat, "Technically speaking, I'm not gay either. I think the term is bi-sexual — I could go either way. But since I met Jack, I just prefer his way." He grinned at Jack and blew a kiss to him.

Jack rolled his eyes, "Okay, great, now that we've established I'm the only gay one here."

One of the women in the back raised her hand, "No, you're not the only one!" They all laughed, and she introduced herself to Marissa. "I'm Sarah, and I'm a red dragon. Kinda like Xena, badass warrior chick."

The introductions continued, the other dragons and wielders sharing their names and what they were. Marissa shook her head, "I'll never be able to keep this straight. So, if I call you the wrong name, I apologize. So, what's next?" she asked.

The silver wielder in the back, who'd introduced himself quietly as Killian, spoke up with a beautiful lilting accent. "We find out what color wielder ye are, an' why ye don't seem to know it, lass." He eased closer, the group silently making a path for him to reach her. The one eye she could see through his hair flared silver for a moment, as he studied her, nodding.

Marissa laughed uneasily as he stopped in front of her, and his gaze took her in, from her hair to her toes and back again.

He was by far the most stunning man there, with hazel eyes and hair that was a soft blond so pale, it was almost silvery white. It was shorter towards the back but longer in the front and brushed just below his chin, covering most of his face. She almost hadn't seen him before, as he'd been standing in the back, quietly watching everything. He had a soft smile and broad shoulders. He looked like he could pick her up with one hand, but his eyes were kind. She felt a warm current running through her whenever she looked at him. Something in his voice made her heart quiver and her body flush. As gorgeous as he was, she just knew he was taken, too.

The others were now staring at them intently. Siobhan leaned in and seemed to be sniffing her. She nodded, "Ki's right. I can't believe I missed it before, but it's there. Just really faint for some reason. Almost like static."

Marissa glanced around, startled. "Okay, not funny, don't tease the newbie," she said.

Jack slowly shook his head, "They wouldn't tease about this. Marissa, tell us about your family."

"I don't know anything about them. I was adopted." She shrugged.

Killian reached out and stroked her cheek gently with the back of his hand, lingering near her jaw, and she felt an electric tingle coursing over her skin. Tossing his hair back so his whole face was visible for a moment, he grinned. "Welcome, sister of silver," he told her as her breath caught in her throat.

Siobhan nodded, "Of course, Ki, that explains why you picked up on it before the rest of us."

Marissa was floored, "Are you saying I'm like you?" she whispered. They all smiled and crowded around her. Calls of welcome and sister came to her like soft velvet over her skin. It felt right and normal. She suddenly realized this was what she'd been missing all her life, and these were her people. Her eyes grew moist, and she grinned.

Killian took Marissa with him to a quiet corner to talk to her about wielders, their history, and the nature of her latent magic. He suspected because she'd never had instruction, it hadn't ever manifested, although she'd often felt like a misfit or that she didn't fit in with others. She'd felt off in some way, different. She was fascinated by magic, dragons, and fantasy. She figured this was just normal nerdy behavior. She was absorbing everything she could find out about who she was and what she could possibly do in the future. As she listened to the cadence and lilt in his voice, which he explained was because he was Irish, she felt herself even more drawn to Killian. Marissa felt sure she was drooling and was doing her steady best not to make a fool of herself.

In the dining room, Marco, Jack, Davis, and Siobhan were sitting with Shepard, quietly discussing the fact that Marissa being a wielder was no coincidence. "She may not have known, but Esme and Cyrus must have," Siobhan insisted. The others agreed.

"They were planning to use her in the future, I bet," Shepard added grimly. His expression thunderous, no doubt remembering what had been done to Serena.

Jack shuddered, "We got to her just in time." They heard Marissa's light laugh then as she entered the room. Jack felt a tingle in his mind, like there was something he was supposed to remember but couldn't.

"Look!" Marissa said excitedly, "Look what I can do!" She held out her hand, and a small silver flame danced in it. "I can do it, it's real, you were right!" She hugged Siobhan, tears streaming down her face, and she laughed again, the sound like tinkling bells.

Siobhan suddenly jerked back from her and gasped. She held her out at arm's length. "Son of a... no! I can't believe I didn't see it before!" She smacked herself in the forehead.

Shepard leapt to his feet, his face pale. "The dreams," he whispered.

Marissa was confused, "Siobhan, I don't understand, what's wrong?" Her lips trembled.

"Hang on to your hat, girlfriend. This is about to get wild." Siobhan sat Marissa down and ran to Killian, whispering something in his ear. His nostrils flared, and he nodded. The dragons, who all had excellent hearing, stood there with their mouths open.

Jack glanced at Davis and spread his hands in a what gesture. Davis pointed at the women and mouthed 'watch'.

Siobhan put her fingertips on Marissa's temples, and Killian began to wave his hands over her like he was weaving something. They began to pulse their magic together, and soon, a large shimmer blew outwards from Marissa like a pressure wave and shook the house. Siobhan and Killian were both flat on their backs on the floor.

Jack helped Siobhan to her feet but almost dropped her as he saw Marissa. She was staring back at him with eyes of silver. But that wasn't the most startling fact.

Her hair was no longer brown. It was a light blonde so pale it was silvery white. With her hair and eyes like this, it hit Jack suddenly what the elusive thought had been. "Serena," he whispered, shock coursing through his body. The others nodded as well.

Marissa's eyes returned to normal, and she noticed her hair. "What the hell just happened?" she shrieked.

Davis dropped to his knees in front of her, taking her trembling hands in his own and squeezing them reassuringly. "Shh, little one, it's okay," he told her in a soothing soft voice. "What happened is that it you've had a spell cast over you. Probably most of your life to conceal who and what you are. Someone was hiding your identity, but Siobhan and Killian were able to remove it."

She shook her head, breathing quickly. She turned to Jack, "But you said Serena. Is that my name?"

"No," he said gently. "There is something else we know, and I'm so delighted to tell you this, but Marissa, you have a sister. Her name is Serena, and she lives with Shepard. Shit!" he said as Marissa's eyes rolled back and she fainted.

The group watched in surprise as Killian scooped her up in his arms and carried her away silently.

Chapter 29

MORNING BROKE, AND SUNLIGHT filtered between the curtains in the strange bedroom. Marissa opened her eyes to a cloud of silvery white. *Oh, right*, that was her hair now. She paused to do a reality check. She'd stayed the night with a group of people she'd just met, who were all either dragons or magic wielders. Not only that, but they'd figured out she was one of them just by removing a spell cast over her, revealing her identity and releasing her powers. It was why she'd felt off her whole life. Why she was often described as flighty and weird; her magic was suppressed and had been trying to fight its way free.

Now, her true appearance had emerged, and she had a sister. A sister! She blew out her breath and heard a rustle. She glanced over and saw Killian next to her. He'd stayed with her after she'd fainted and then carried her to his room. They talked quietly when she came to, and he asked her to stay so he could look after her. Letting her sleep in his bed. He'd slept next to her, fully clothed.

She smiled ruefully at that. She studied the long line of his legs in his jeans and the soft rise and fall of his broad chest. His shirt was slightly pulled up, and she flushed at the bare skin she could see of his abdomen.

She swallowed heavily at the trail of fine silvery hair running below his navel as it disappeared beyond the waistband of those jeans. She noted the well-defined muscles that announced he obviously spent time in the gym. She remembered the tingling feeling she had, speaking to him last night and hoped she hadn't made too big of a fool of herself.

After years of feeling off and inadequate, she was hoping it was the spell that had kept men away, but he'd been almost brotherly to her. She thought things couldn't get any stranger, but today, she was supposed to help them locate a gallery that Gavin, no, Cyrus, might have bought or rented. He was rumored to possibly be holding children, hostage. It was a lot to take in, but one thing she knew for certain; she was going back to Dallas with them to meet her sister and find out what the hell was going on. The team hoped that they could crack her adoption records, despite them being sealed, to find out more about her birth parents.

Wow, from being an adopted weirdo to having a sister and magic powers in one day. She was anxious to get started. She leapt out of bed, forgetting for a moment that Killian was still sleeping.

He jumped up, startled, then laughed when he saw her. "Eager to get going on the day then, dear Marissa?" he asked softly.

She nodded sheepishly. "Uh, sorry about waking you up like that," she said, blushing.

He smiled and ran a hand through his own silvery white hair, which was identical to hers. He brushed it away from his face, and she noticed he had a small silver ring in the corner of his lower lip. His hazel eyes sparkled, and she bit her own lip, wishing it was his. He caught the look on her face and slowly moved to her, taking her face in his hands and kissing her forehead tenderly, his lips burning hot on her skin. "And you're quite beautiful and tempting, lass, but there's still so much to do right now. Let's get through this challenge and help you meet your family. If you are still after being interested in me, then I'd be delighted to see where this might go."

She stared at him, surprised at his bold honesty. Most guys weren't so open like that. Add that dreamy Irish accent, and she almost melted. She sighed. He was right; it made sense. Just because she was a loner, it didn't mean she had to jump into bed with the first single guy who was the least bit interested in her.

He smiled, "I think, though, I'm making sure you remember me fondly, perhaps, just a wee taste." He slid his hands through her hair and pulled her firmly to him, her soft body pressed against his very hard, muscular frame. He placed his lips on hers, and she felt fire burn all the way down to her toes. He angled his head to deepen the kiss, and she moaned a little. He grinned against her mouth and finally pulled back.

Her eyes fluttered, and she felt lightheaded. *Holy shit, that was a taste?*

He tapped her nose. "Just remember that later. Don't go forgetting me. I'll step out so you can freshen up if you like. Sarah brought in some extra clothes she thought might fit you."

He left the room, and Marissa swallowed heavily, sitting down with an "oof," followed by, "I'm screwed." She touched her lips, remembering how soft they were and that cute little ring rubbing on her mouth.

After a shower and getting dressed in borrowed clothes, she ventured into the front of the house. She saw Shepard and Jack in the kitchen, singing along and dancing to some pop song, while they made enough food for an army. Siobhan and Marco were playing poker with Sarah and Killian. Davis was setting the table, and the others were lounging around the TV, watching highlights of some sports news show. She grinned, family. And they were her family now.

"Marissa!" Jack waved her over.

She turned and wandered into the kitchen amidst a chorus of good mornings from everyone. Jack grinned at her, kissing her on the cheek as she blushed. He was so sweet, and she found she still had a bit of a crush on him. Which was fine because she knew it couldn't go anywhere. She grinned back.

"Good morning, darling," he said, "I hope you slept well?"

She nodded, "I did, Professor Shelton, thank you."

Jack laughed hard, "Careful, I'll report you to the Dean," he teased. His face took on a sad smile, and he eased around the counter towards her. He brushed her hair from her face and put his palm on her cheek. "Marissa, please believe me when I say I'm so sorry for the deception before. I hated every second of it. It made me feel physically ill. Not the spending time with you part — that I enjoyed — but the lying to you. Ask Davis; he was tired of my moping. I hope you'll forgive me, and we can be friends?" he said hopefully.

She smiled, "Of course, Jack, I understand now, and besides, look what I gained from it. A family!"

"I know that feeling," he told her. He pulled her into his arms and hugged her.

She sighed and snuggled into him. Suddenly, she felt arms around her back as well and now warm bodies fully surrounded her. Shepard and Davis had joined the hug, rumbling. She stood there enjoying the feeling, then waved her hands. "Too much hotness that's off limits!" she laughed.

They joined her in laughter and then called in the horde for breakfast. Jack let Marissa go first. She didn't take much, being too excited to eat. She noticed you could tell who the dragons were by the amount of food on their plates. She felt eyes on her and noticed Killian was quietly watching her. He winked, and she swallowed hard, it was going to be a long day.

After breakfast, they adjourned to a different room that Marco called his headquarters. It was supposed to be an office, so it was fitting. He had lots of electronics set up.

She was surprised to see so much modern equipment around dragons and magic wielders.

He laughed, "Even dragons have to modernize, dear."

Siobhan strolled in and brushed his shoulder as she passed by.

He grabbed her hand and pulled her back into his lap, kissing her hard, then laughing when she punched his shoulder and called him a pervert.

She smiled as she jumped up and continued past him.

Marissa smirked. Interesting dynamic those two had.

Marco turned back to her, "Okay, Marissa, your turn. Tell me everything you know about Cyrus and Esmerelda Westwind."

She nodded sharply, and they got down to business. They quizzed her about other galleries and anything else they may not have thought of related to the trade. She gave them the name of his import company, which was not linked to him personally but rather through several shell corporations they discovered. They finally had it narrowed down to three possible locations. They debated in what order to hit them but decided they would need to do them all at once. Otherwise, the pair might catch on and move the children.

With their plan in place, they went back to the others and divided into teams. Marco and Jack were acting as commanding officers, and as Marissa watched Jack, she got the feeling that he'd been in the military before. Once again, she was sad that Simon wasn't real. She realized as she studied the groups she hadn't been included in one.

She approached Jack. "I know I'm new to all of this, but I want to help!" she told him, determination in her voice.

He sighed. "I know, love, but right now, we'd be so worried about you getting hurt. It could be a distraction. We know from experience those can be fatal. We've lost people before in what we do. I'd hate to lose you when we just found you." Jack hugged her, seeming to sense her frustration. Then he quirked his lips. "Siobhan, why don't you, Killian, and Marissa go pre-scout the locations, check out the wards, and show her what to look for. Since she knows Cyrus and Esme, she can help be on the lookout for them to show up?"

Siobhan nodded; she liked this plan. She motioned with her chin to Killian to gear up, and soon, they were on their way.

As they closed in on the first location, Siobhan explained to Marissa how close they could get and what she was looking for. Killian described how her particular flavor of magic, as she liked to think of it, would be of help to her. They circled the building and continued getting closer until they were able to walk right up to it and touch the brick walls.

Shaking her head at Killian, Siobhan sighed, "Dang it, Jack is too smart. There are no wards on this building. There's no point in us even coming here. They wouldn't waste time warding a location with nothing to protect. This was a dead end. On to the next one." Back in the car, Siobhan called in her findings to Marco.

He was quiet for a moment. "I should have thought of that; scouting in advance is a basic thing," he said, sighing at missing something so obvious.

She smiled softly even though he couldn't see it. "Marco, there's a lot of moving pieces at play. Jack's been trained for this, Marine remember? Let him help you."

Marissa checked a mental box. Jack had been a Marine. It made perfect sense.

At the second location, they stopped further back. The building they were circling was very heavily warded. Siobhan nodded, "Yes, now *this* location absolutely has potential."

Marissa stepped a little closer and felt the magic prickling on her skin. She realized she'd sensed it before but never knew what it was. Her mouth dropped open. She shared her discovery with Killian, and he smiled at her.

"No doubt it was your powers trying to break through. Your heritage was fighting to make itself known." His smile was encouraging, and she was grateful again to the group for welcoming her so thoroughly.

Killian taught her how to illuminate the wards just for them, and she was able to do it briefly before she was exhausted.

"Slow down lass; it's hard to control how much power you need to do these things when you first learn. You set the channel. Think of a small trickle, not a fire hose. You can add more gradually, but if you open the hydrant wide to start, it's harder to close it back."

She nodded in understanding. He made it easy to comprehend and follow. He was a great teacher.

He showed her again, doing it with ease and no visible strain.

She was in awe. "How long did it take you to learn that?" she asked him.

"Years," he answered, "But I was very young when I started. It's much harder when you are a wee child and have no patience. You must learn control as well."

She thought about it and wondered aloud, "Then why not teach you when you are older?"

He laughed, "To keep us from setting the farm on fire, from flooding the house, from creating portals to alternate dimensions, the usual," he grinned.

She laughed with him. She could only imagine having children with uncontrolled magic. Children. Not something she'd ever thought about.

"If I were to have children someday, would they inherit my powers too?" she asked Killian.

"Aye, it's passed down from generation to generation, depending on the kind, the color, and the level of power," he nodded.

"What kind?" she asked, confused.

He shrugged. "Depends on the partner," he explained, "If you mate with a dragon, then your first child will be a dragon. Any after that would be a wielder. They follow the color of the dragon or stronger wielder. So, if you, for example, mated with a silver wielder," he grinned at her, and her body went tight and hot, clenching her thighs, "Then any children would also be silver wielders. Or take Siobhan and Marco; their babes would be a red dragon first and then a red or green wielder after. Maybe one of each, the way those two are always at it."

Siobhan gave him serious side-eye; she obviously wasn't interested in this discussion. "Shut up, Lucky Charms. I like you better when you don't talk as much," she barked at him.

He snorted, "Calm down, Shi. I'm not after marrying you off to him yet. Just an example." He winked at Marissa, and she chuckled in return.

Marissa noticed that Killian seemed to be very quiet and soft-spoken most of the time. The others always seemed surprised to see him or hear him speak. She idly wondered what that was about.

Siobhan stood from where she was kneeling, "Okay, I have what I need. Let's check out the third location," she announced.

Once there, Siobhan groaned, "This location is warded, the same as the other. Looks like we have to hit them both." She waved them closer to help evaluate it fully in case there were any subtle differences they needed to know.

Marissa tried her wielding again and, this time, focused on a trickle of power the way Killian instructed. He stood closely behind her and put his arms alongside hers, making spot corrections to her hand positions. She was having trouble concentrating on what she was doing, focusing more on the feel of his warm body pressed against her back. Her hands began to shake as she lost control of the channel. Her arms dropped, and she turned to him. "I'm sorry, I was having trouble focusing," she said breathlessly.

He smiled, his lips curving sinuously as if he could guess why and wasn't the least bit sorry about it. In fact, it almost seemed as if he'd done it on purpose. He leaned in closer, "Trouble? Whatever could you have been focusing on besides the wards? What's… distracting ye, lass?" His voice had dropped to a whisper, his eyes sparking with silver as they connected with hers.

She was about to make a smart remark when her eyes went wide, and she grabbed Siobhan's and Killian's wrists, dragging them into the nearest building. It was a credit to their training that they immediately went along and didn't question it or balk. She realized she'd dragged them into a laundromat, and none of them had clothing to wash. The grumpy old man in the corner was eyeing them suspiciously.

"Quarters," whispered Killian. Marissa dug in her purse and grabbed a few, handing them to him as he rushed over, stripped off his shirt, and threw it in the washing machine, starting it. The old man frowned, but they were now paying customers.

Marissa stared at Killian. His upper body was a thing of beauty. She'd suspected as much, but he always had clothes on. Now she could see the intricate tattoo winding around his left bicep that looked like a band of silvery flames, and the large Celtic knot over his heart. Her eyes roamed the washboard abs and that intriguing line of fine silvery hair leading to the waistband of his jeans that she'd been admiring just this morning. She swallowed hard and noted he was watching her with undisguised enjoyment at her appraisal. She flushed what she was sure was a completely unattractive shade of red as her stomach fluttered. It felt like a pack of butterflies was rampaging through it, and her lips trembled. She raised her hand halfway to check her hair, then dropped it, flustered.

"If you're done ogling the incredibly yummy wielder, can we please know why we are in here with a now shirtless Killian?" Siobhan asked, amusement clear in her voice. "Not that I'm complaining, Ki," she fanned herself, rolling her eyes in an exaggerated fashion.

He rolled his eyes back and grinned at them both.

Marissa whipped around, remembering why they were here in the first place. "Sorry, I saw Cyrus and Esme!" she squeaked. She cleared her throat and tried again, "They were driving down the street. But on the other side. They weren't looking our way. They are coming over here, though, so I thought it best we hid."

Siobhan nodded, pride evident on her face. "Well done, Marissa! You just saved our asses and gave us a big lead. Let's watch!"

Chapter 30

"SHE WAS BRILLIANT!" Siobhan bragged on Marissa, whose face brightened at the praise. "She was able to identify wards, light them up, and she saw the wielders before we did. If not for her, we most definitely would've been caught!"

So, it's the third location?" called one of the dragons.

Marco shook his head, "Just because they were there, doesn't mean there wasn't some other reason. I think we hit up both of the warded places. Siobhan was right; if there's no wards, they don't have something worth hiding." The others murmured agreement.

Killian strolled back into the room. He'd thrown his sopping wet shirt in the dryer and gone to get a clean one from his room. He was pulling it down over his stomach and grinned at Marissa when he walked in, tossing his hair back just long enough for the light to spark on the little ring shining in his lower lip.

Smirking, Jack watched her bite her own lip without seeming to realize it. He could understand her interest. Killian was a very handsome man. Jack smothered a laugh as she sighed in longing. He nudged her to pay attention, grinning when she refocused on the task at hand. He was glad she had gotten over her heartache, even if she did still have a little crush on him. He wasn't worried about that. He just hoped Killian was kind to her. He glared a little at the wielder, cut his gaze at Marissa, then back at him menacingly.

Killian dipped his head; he'd received the message. Jack had declared himself her protector and would not take lightly to anyone hurting her.

Davis grinned at his mate. *Jack, you're such a softie; you would make a great father.* Davis lost his grin.

Jack's heart clenched in pain. Davis would, too; he just knew it. He thought about suggesting adoption, so they could have their own family. But he didn't know how kindly courts in Texas took to allowing same-sex couples to adopt. They'd barely allowed them to marry.

Davis squeezed his arm. *Everything okay, Jack?*

Jack smiled gently. *Just thinking.*

Stop thinking so hard, then, it's making you sad. I don't like it when you're sad. How can I make you happy again?

He felt Davis' love filling him. He smiled brighter; *you just did. Thank you!*

The team broke into two groups as planned, with Davis and Shepard each on separate teams so they could ghost their squads. Marissa was asking tons of questions, fascinated with the concept of ghosting and couldn't wait to experience it. They decided to bring her along with them after all, Killian being her assigned guardian. A hardship neither of them was unhappy about. They would be relying on the twins to coordinate the go time with their mind link.

Jack was going with Davis, Marco with Shepard. They were each designated their squadron commander. Davis was beaming with pride at how well-respected his mate was. It was unheard of outside of their group: a human leading dragons and wielders. He watched Jack strap knives all over his body and raised an eyebrow. *Okay, that is unexpectedly hot!* He sent and was rewarded with a grin before Jack's whole demeanor shifted.

Davis watched the change settle over Jack's face as he strapped on his protective gear. Jack became a different person when going into battle. Gone was the softness and the playboy smile. The sparkle in his eyes hardened into diamond, and his expression set into a much sterner mask. Davis didn't think Jack was even aware he did it, but whatever specialized training he received, had stuck with him. The man was lethal, and he disguised it well most of the time. Few people got to see this side of Jack, and those who were on the receiving end wished they weren't. Davis smiled, remembering his confrontation with Riley in front of the hotel. He didn't need Davis' help; it just drove the threat home. At heart, Jack was still a soldier.

The plan was for the wielders to break down the barriers and bind anyone if needed, while the dragons would go in for the search and rescue portion. In dragon form, they were fire and bulletproof, so they could take a hit if they were attacked. They hoped they wouldn't have to go full shift, but they could if needed. They'd all dressed in loose, expendable clothes in case they needed to shift fast.

Jack's group gathered outside of their designated building and waited for Marco's group to signal they were ready. Marissa watched in awe as Davis stood in front of the group and began breathing deeply. He started puffing out clouds of shimmering steam and blew them around each person. They disappeared before her eyes. When he 'ghosted' her, she felt a cool tickling sensation on her skin, much like walking through thick fog, then suddenly, she could see her team again. They could see each other as ghosts, but no one else could. *This is so cool,* she squealed in her head, not wanting to embarrass herself by geeking out where others could hear.

Finally, they received the signal that Shepard was done ghosting his team, and they were ready to move. The wielders got into position, and on Davis' mark, they began their strategic attack on the wards. Marissa joined the others, not directly attacking, but lending her magic for them to draw on. She was pleased to be able to help this way, or in any way, really. She felt the wards tingling on her skin and grimaced at a nagging sensation. Something didn't feel right. She tried to ignore it, but it got worse and stronger until she couldn't take it. "*Stop!*" she shouted.

Jack signaled, and they all cut off their attack.

"Something's not right. It's different! In the ward! Something's changed from earlier," she told them, feeling as if she was babbling and stumbling over her words. Hoping she was right and not delaying the rescue of the kids.

Killian concentrated, then his eyes went wide, "She's right! Tell the other team to stop, quick!" he demanded. The urgent command booming from him was so different from his normal soft tones that Davis jumped to comply.

The message was relayed, and they waited for several agonizing moments until they confirmed the other team stopped as well.

Marissa sighed in relief, waiting on pins and needles again. Siobhan was with Shepard and Marco's team, so she rechecked those wards while Killian investigated the ones in front of them. When he was done, Siobhan and Killian confirmed through Davis and Shepard that their wards had been altered as well, and both groups were walking into a neat trap.

Marco was furious. If Jack hadn't suggested checking the wards in advance earlier, they would never have known. And it took a novice wielder to notice. With some back and forth, they figured out how to defuse the trap and took the wards down quickly.

Marissa stood by, still feeling on edge but not knowing why.

The dragons hurried into the building but soon came out empty-handed. There was no one there. The building was completely vacant, storing only large piles of dust and leaves. They were confused and frustrated about why such heavy warding had been placed on empty buildings.

"Something's about to…" Marissa trailed off when they heard the first siren. Moments later, the area was swarming with police officers and flashing lights.

Everyone was ordered to stand still. They couldn't be seen, thanks to Davis' ghosting. He was able to confirm with Shepard that the same was happening at their end. It was a second trap. If the wards didn't take them out, they were to be arrested for breaking and entering. Clever. But their enemy didn't know about the ghosting skills of the twins.

The teams slowly made their way quietly out of the area and proceeded to a rendezvous point they'd agreed upon in case of emergency. Marissa agreed, this qualified as one. She was terrified, shaking while thinking about how close they'd come to getting killed or caught. She realized she'd underestimated what Jack meant earlier when he told her how dangerous this was. Killian wrapped a comforting arm around her and softly rubbed her back. She sent him a small smile that he returned with one of his own.

Once safely away and joined up with the other team, they dropped the ghosting and exchanged looks of deep concern. Not only had they failed to rescue the children, but they'd come very close to having some serious questions asked or even more serious injuries. How had Cyrus and Esme gotten so ahead of them? Siobhan suspected they must have realized they were poking around earlier that day.

Marissa was still troubled by a small niggling feeling in her mind and wandered away a bit to pace while the others argued. Killian and Jack followed her.

"What's going on, Risa?" Jack asked quietly.

She smiled at the nickname. No one had ever given her one before. "Something is sticking at my mind again, and I can't figure out what it is." She cringed at how whiny she sounded, but it was important to discover what it was. The last two feelings like this proved to be insightful, and she wanted to help in any way she could.

Jack studied her, "Risa, you won't remember by thinking directly about it so hard. You need to stop focusing on it, and it will come to you when you least expect it."

She nodded. "Think of something else, think of something else," she chanted. "Ugh," she groaned, frustrated. She was pacing faster, and now everyone was staring at her. She put her fists to her temples. "Something else," she said again, angry at herself.

Without warning, Killian stepped into her, threaded his fingers into her hair and crushed his lips to hers. She fluttered her hands for a moment before settling them on his chest. He kissed her like he wanted to devour her. She felt warmth against her back a moment before another pair of arms went around her and pressed her even closer to Killian. Her eyes rolled back in her head, and she went limp in their arms. Suddenly, she gasped, "Basement!" The hard bodies that were surrounding her eased back slowly. Apparently, the distraction had worked.

"The basement! In my gallery. I've felt that same warding there. I thought it seemed familiar. There's a room off the workshop that I haven't been inside of in a while. I think the warding was warning me off. We need to get there. Now! Right now!" she said frantically.

Jack chuckled, "Good job, Risa, I knew you could do it!" He hugged her from behind, letting her know it was him who had helped distract her.

"You helped a lot," she whispered in his ear.

He laughed and pushed her back into Killian's arms, "But his lips did more."

Killian grinned and kissed her again, the little ring on his lip pressing into hers in a surprisingly erotic way.

She was pretty sure her heart stopped. The man was pure sin, and his lips were sending heat straight from her mouth to between her thighs. She had to agree with Jack; Killian was much better. She stood there in a daze before he grabbed her hand and dragged her along.

They all piled into the cars but soon realized they couldn't get through because of the police activity. "Fuck!" Jack shouted, pounding the steering wheel. He looked over at Davis, frantically.

"Everyone out," Davis ordered. He jumped out and began billowing steam, he waved them through, and soon Shepard joined him in ghosting the team. The dragons began spreading out and shucking clothing.

Marissa was standing there dumbfounded. They urgently had to go, but now everyone needed to get naked? She saw a shimmer, and there was now a massive blue dragon where Davis once stood, then another blue, and a red, and another red, then a silver and a green. She got dizzy and almost dropped to the ground, stunned at the sight of so many dragons in front of her. It was a rainbow fantasy come to life, the sheer size and magnitude of what she was witnessing threatened to overwhelm her.

Killian caught her arms as she trembled. "Apologies, dear lass, no time to be overcome with fascination," he said with a chuckle as he picked her up and carried her over to the nearest dragon.

He sat her down gently and vaulted to the beast's back in practiced ease before holding out a hand.

She grinned as she took it, and he pulled her up in front of him in an effortless maneuver that left her breathless. He hooked one arm around her waist as she looked around and saw the others mounted similarly. She caught Jack's eye as he sat astride one of the blue dragons, knowing it was probably Davis. He smirked at her amazement. She noted Siobhan was seated on a monstrously large red dragon that looked especially vicious, easily towering over the others. She guessed it was Marco. One by one, the dragons started running, and then they were airborne. Killian put his free hand over her mouth an instant before she screamed, anticipating her, and she swallowed it down. She understood they needed to be silent.

Once they were on their way, Killian dropped his hand from her face, murmuring an apology. She laughed, shaking her head, this was amazing! She threw her arms out and reveled in the feeling of the air on her skin, her hair fluttering in the wind.

Killian wrapped both arms around her and chuckled in her ear. "Exhilarating, isn't it?"

She nodded, not trusting herself, shivering at the timbre of his voice as it rolled over her body.

The dragons banked hard and flew towards the gallery on the other side of town. The trip was short, as they covered the distance quickly, but it was worth every second. They landed a couple at a time, the riders dismounting quickly, with the dragons shifting back the second they were clear, making room for the next wave.

Each rider threw clothes to their dragons that were quickly donned. Everyone regrouped together a few blocks from the gallery. Marissa watched in awe at the seemingly well-oiled maneuver. She blushed as she realized the dragons shifted back into naked humans, and the men were exceptionally well endowed. She averted her gaze and hated how red she knew her face was.

Killian leaned down to her ear. "Just so you know, some wielders are just as... gifted," he chuckled as he gently ran his fingers down her neck.

She felt warmth shoot all the way down her body yet again. She whirled to face him, hands on her hips, eyes flashing. "Okay, enough teasing me. Either we're waiting until all is done, or you are putting your... gifts, where your mouth is. Or my mouth. I mean..." she stuttered to a stop, horrified at what she'd implied.

His own eyes flashed silver for a moment before he lowered his voice, "My sweet Risa," he pulled her against his body, "Be sure I plan to follow up on my promises. I'm finding you — very — hard to resist," he laughed at her surprised expression and gently let her go.

She shivered in longing, then turned back around before she gave in to her impulse to jump in his arms naked right then and there.

All the dragons were dressed and ready, so they took off on foot to the gallery. Marissa was glad she was wearing tennis shoes. Finally, they were within a block of the building, and the formation broke to surround the property from all sides.

Chapter 31

DAVIS AND MARCO FLANKED Marissa as she ran forward to unlock the doors. Siobhan was on her back to watch for wards or traps. They made it inside. All was quiet. The rest of the team flooded the building, taking up defensive positions. Jack, Davis, Marissa, and Siobhan all hurried to the basement, Marco hot on their heels.

Marissa nearly stumbled backwards when she hit the edges of the wards. Davis steadied her, and Siobhan surged forward to blast the barrier.

Siobhan gritted her teeth, shouting it was stronger than she'd ever seen. She motioned Marissa over to put her hands on Siobhan's back, pushing her magic into her. It wasn't enough. Soon, all the wielders were in the basement, all pulsing their power into Siobhan's spell.

The wards visibly wavered a moment before contracting inward then exploding out like a supernova. There was a brief window where they saw what was about to happen, and everyone screamed. A second before the wards blew, there was a giant shimmer as both Marco and Davis shifted, creating a barrier of scales between the explosion and the wielders. Their large bodies were squeezed into the small space, leaving little room for the debris. The building trembled around them.

When the fireworks finally settled, and Marissa could move, her ears were ringing. She noticed everything was muffled, as if a cannon had fired right next to her head. The room was filled with smoke, dust, and all manner of rubble. The building shook in warning around them.

Jack was patting a large blue dragon that was hunched down, barely fitting in the cramped space, relief on his face.

Siobhan was on the ground, with a large red dragon's head on her lap. She looked like she was screaming. The others were just getting to their feet.

Not stopping to think, Marissa grabbed Jack's hand and ran towards the now-open door. Inside, safe from the explosion, they found two small children. A young boy barely old enough to walk and a small girl. Both filthy, scared, and certainly too little to be alone. Marissa stood there and stared, how was it possible they'd been here, and no one had known better? Jack pushed past her, grabbing both babies and calling reassurances to them. Soon, he was turning to run. Marissa came back to herself as the building tremored again. They needed to get the hell out of here! She ran out behind Jack and came upon a scene of mass confusion.

Davis was human again, and everyone else was on their feet except for Siobhan. She was leaning over the body of Marco, now back in human form, unnaturally still. Marissa couldn't tell if he was alive but noticed a distressingly large pool of blood around him. She moved closer and saw a piece of metal the size of her foot was wedged in his neck. It must have struck him right when he shifted, trying to protect them. Squatting next to Siobhan, Marissa saw he was very pale and gasping shallowly. His eyes fluttered, they were losing him.

He coughed, and blood pooled around his lips. He focused sorrowfully on Siobhan, "Love... you, sorry," he wheezed before his eyes sank closed and his body went limp.

Siobhan had her hands over him, trying to heal him, but she was so gassed from the wards, she had little left to give. She began to wail, "No, No, No, NO!"

Marissa gritted her teeth, she didn't have much, but she would give what she could. She put her hands on Siobhan's, and concentrated, pouring her strength into it.

Killian joined her, and one by one, all the wielders added their powers as well. The other dragons circled around, holding hands, and pushed their power into her, too.

Before their eyes, the metal piece wiggled out, and the wound healed itself. Marco's chest shuddered and fell, then shuddered again. He was breathing on his own. He groaned, and his eyes slowly came open, fixing on Siobhan's face as her tears fell on his cheeks.

"You idiot," she whispered as her body was wracked with sobs.

At the beach house, Jack and Davis bathed the children. Davis used his water magic to make them laugh. Jack was instantly the hero they trusted. He'd rescued them, so they clung to him like little magnets. Marco was recovering in bed, Siobhan not leaving his side. The others were milling about. Restless. Wondering what to do next.

They sat around for a long time before Davis and Jack came back in with the little ones. Both children were wearing the smallest shirts the team could find, which were still too large, but better than the filthy clothes they'd been wearing.

"Everyone," Jack called softly into the silence, "Meet Lily and Jonathan."

The team members gently smiled and waved hello to the children. They received a tentative smile from the little girl and a burbly wave from the little boy. Jack squatted down next to Lily, "All of these people are our friends. They helped rescue you and want to keep you safe. We're going to get you something to eat. Would you like that?"

She nodded quietly and smiled at him.

Jack swallowed hard; the simple beauty on her small face made his chest ache, and he rubbed it. He cleared his throat when Davis put a steadying hand on his shoulder.

Shepard went to the kitchen with them to find something suitable for the kids, and soon, laughter filled the air. The twins were doing tricks with their magic, using water to float things across the counter and making little marbles for the children to play with. No one was more stunned than the two dragons when Lily picked up a marble and made it float above her little brother's head. At their gasp, she dropped it, and it splashed on the boy. He laughed and giggled, and soon they all joined in.

They praised her, and Shepard asked if she knew why she could do that. She shook her head.

Davis squatted in front of her, he slowly blew steam from his nostrils, "Can you do that?" he asked her.

She concentrated, and a small trickle of steam came from her little nose.

Jack was stunned, *is she a water dragon?*

Davis nodded slowly, and a huge grin stretched across his face. "Lily, dear, you are so precious. You are a blue dragon like me. Does that make sense to you?" he asked her gently.

She thought, then nodded, "My mommy has blue wings," she finally said.

Davis smiled again, softly, "That's good, that's very good. Do you remember your mommy's name? Her real name?"

The little girl's eyes filled. She nodded and sniffed, obviously trying hard to be brave, but the tears began to fall.

"What's wrong, sweetheart?" Davis asked, his voice trembling, as if afraid to hear the answer.

"The bad man," she whispered, "He made mommy sleep forever."

Jack and Shepard both gasped, Davis' eyes filled with tears. He gently hugged her to him, rocking her. "I'm so sorry, sweet baby. We are going to punish the bad man for what he did to your mommy. Lily darling, I'm sorry to ask this, but what about your daddy? Did the bad man hurt him, too?"

The little girl stared at him with liquid blue eyes as bright as the ocean and wailed, then buried her face in his shoulder.

He sat down in the middle of the kitchen, pulling her into his lap and holding her while she sobbed.

Shepard and Jack joined them on the floor. Shepard began to sing a soothing song his mother used to sing to them about water dragons when they were little. Davis joined in, and Jack listened in awe. He knew Shepard could sing but he'd never actually heard Davis do it. His voice was like warm honey. The two men continued their song, and the children soon calmed.

"Don't you worry, baby," Jack whispered, "No one is ever going to hurt you again. I will make sure of that," he promised her.

Chapter 32

IN THE OTHER ROOM, the dragons were quietly weeping. With their superior hearing, they'd heard the exchange with the children. They whispered what they'd learned to the wielders, and Marissa thought her heart was going to break. She sat nervously on the edge of a chair, clenching her hands and relaxing them. She felt uncomfortable and didn't know what to do now. Her skin was prickling and burning, like something was settling over her, but she couldn't touch it.

Killian sat by her and took her hands in his. He smiled gently at her and pulled her to his chest, just holding her.

She sighed and melted into him; it helped a little.

Then she was angry. She shot to her feet, her thoughts racing. *How dare Cyrus and Esme use me and my gallery to hide such a depraved act? Was I just a pawn to them? Someone else they were going to take and use for whatever their evil plan was? No! They need to pay, dearly.*

For the first time in her life, Marissa felt like she could kill someone. Her eyes flared silver, and little sparks flew from her fingers. The others watched her in silence, expressions sympathetic. She felt like she was overheating and couldn't breathe. Her chest tightened in panic. She was losing control and didn't know what to do.

Killian took her hand and quickly pulled her outside. He tugged her down the path to the beach right to the ocean's edge. He ignored her questions and kept walking. He finally turned to her. "Scream."

She stared at him questioningly, feeling like she was suffocating, unsure.

"Scream, let it out." He scrunched his nose and waved his hand. "Your anger has called your magic, and it needs a release. If you don't, it will overwhelm you, and you'll pass out. It could drain your life force. Here, by the water, it won't be hurting anyone. So, scream, yell, shout, do something and get it out of your system," he explained.

She nodded and yelled.

"Louder."

She tried again and yelled louder, like she was cheering at a concert.

He shook his head and moved behind her. He leaned in, putting his hands on her waist. "Think about what they did. Think about your anger, your fury, pull it all together in your mind. Now, roar, little one!" he whispered in her ear.

She felt it then, that bubbling anger and finally knew what he meant. She threw her head back and screamed at the stars with all the fury she had.

Killian leapt back and watched as her eyes silvered and flames shot from her fingertips. Waves of rage poured off her and floated harmlessly out over the water. She was beautiful, ethereal in that moment. Her hair floating around her, the strands taking on a metallic gleam, and he knew. Killian knew then he had to have her. He'd talked about waiting. About not getting distracted from the mission. How she should get to know their world first. He'd thought she wouldn't want him anyway once she met others, so why bother? He avoided complications like a plague so he wouldn't get hurt. He didn't want things. But he didn't care anymore. Everything else be damned. He wanted her. He wanted the complications that came with it. For the first time in decades, he wanted.

He strode over as her scream tapered off and pulled her body roughly to his. The hard evidence of his desire was digging into her hip, and she had to be aware of it. "Risa, I'm done teasing you," he said, reminding her of her earlier statement. "I know it's bad timing. I know we've only just met and you're not knowing your place in our world yet. But I'm wanting you badly, and I want you now." He watched her face closely to see how disgusted she might be by his words. He knew he was very forward, but that's who he was.

She grinned at his blunt honesty and nodded, "Oh, thank God," she whimpered. She jumped and wrapped herself around him.

His surprise was short-lived as relief coursed through him while he held onto her. It was replaced by hunger, desire, and a primal need to take. He devoured her lips with his as he kissed her with wild abandon. Minutes later, he dropped to his knees and laid her back on the sand. He nipped and licked her throat, which she exposed for him and moaned.

"Killian," she panted, writhing with her need for more.

He called some of his magic and lightly stroked it down her body, making her shudder and buck under him, in turn making him groan with barely restrained pleasure. He needed this woman with a fierceness he could barely stand. His skin felt like it was on fire, and he knew she was the only one who could quench it. He didn't know who he was at the moment. Private Killian. The quiet one. The man who faded into the walls. The man no one saw or really knew, was about to take this woman out in the open, and he didn't care who saw them. He flexed his hand and threw a shield around them, knowing that though he might not care, she would. "Marissa," he called, his throat tight with his desire, overwhelming his senses. Her answering gaze nearly undid him.

She looked up and moved his hair from his face so she could stare into his hazel eyes with their impossible depths. She saw tenderness and desire in them. She'd never seen that look on a man's face for her before, and it almost undid her. She put her hands in his soft silvery hair, so like her own, pulling him to her again.

He gently undressed her as she undressed him. She swallowed hard as she saw the rest of this gorgeous man who seemed to need her with a desire bordering on madness. She was pretty sure he wanted to devour her, and she couldn't wait for him to begin. He nuzzled her small breasts and ran his tongue all over them, gently pulling her nipples into his delicious mouth. She felt her thighs quake as he settled against them and felt his hard length pressing against her again, this time without their clothes between them. She whimpered and squirmed at how velvety soft his skin was in contrast to how firm and rigid he was. She'd never wanted anything more than to have him deep inside her right now.

He chuckled then, a low sound that made her tingle. "So anxious, little one," he whispered. "Let's see if you're ready, though." He trailed his fingers down her body, lightly stroking her ribs and her stomach. Swirling them around her belly button, then down to her thighs, nudging them apart.

She was going to die if he didn't touch her soon, she was sure of it. Finally, her wish was granted, and he ran his finger up the center of her. She swore he made a purring sound then.

"Oh, Risa, you're a good girl aren't you? I appreciate the efforts here."

She blushed at his reference to her clean-shaven approach.

"Oh no, don't be embarrassed, I like it," he grinned. He spread her thighs wider and gently stroked her a few more times with his fingers. "I see you, already hot and wet for me, so I'll give you what you want this time," he whispered in her ear as he dipped his fingers inside her. He curled them slightly and applied a slight pressure that arched her back off the sand. He pulled them out and licked them, "But next time, I'm after a better taste of you."

She was about to explode, and he wasn't even in her yet. His wanton promises tormented her overheated skin. Moaning, she angled her hips in invitation. She sighed in pleasure as she felt the tip of him probing her entrance. The delicious burn as he pushed his way inside ignited her body and filled her veins with liquid fire. She arched again instinctively as he continued his slow slide. He groaned her name and panted. He was stretching her to the limits of her body. She wasn't sure how much more of him she could take, gasping in surprise as he was finally fully seated in her. Turns out she had just enough room after all.

He was still for a moment, giving her time to adjust to him. He had been murmuring to her soothingly since her moment of panic as he filled her. He leaned back down and whispered, "I warned you dragons weren't the only ones," as he trailed hungry silky kisses down her neck again, "I wasn't after exaggerating. Are you alright then? Am I hurting you?"

She whimpered, then shook her head no.

"Well, which is it, darling Marissa, no, you aren't alright or no, I'm not hurting you? What do you want, my silver goddess? Tell me what you need, and I will make the world end if that's what you desire."

Speechless, she pushed her hips up towards him.

"Oh, you want more?" he asked before he pulled back a little and pushed slowly into her again.

"Killian," she said breathlessly, "Please! Take me. I want more, all of you," she begged.

His eyes flashed silver, and she felt his warm magic rush over her skin before he began to thrust into her over and over.

Her own magic came to the surface in answer, warming her up as it had before, this time gentler, less fury and more ecstasy.

He laughed in pure delight then and took her mouth, his tongue mating with hers.

She lost herself in the sensations and reveled in the glorious pressure building inside of her like a tidal wave rushing towards the shore. Suddenly, she ripped her mouth from his and screamed as the wave crashed inside her, and she shuddered with the hardest release she'd ever had, her body lifting from the ground. She collapsed back to the sand, spent.

Killian smiled at her and slowed his thrusts to give her time to recover. She gasped as he took one of her breasts in his mouth, worshipping her with his tongue.

She stilled and called his name softly, putting her hands on his broad chest. She wasn't sure if she should tell him what she wanted, or if he would be willing. She decided since he was upfront and honest with her, maybe he'd appreciate it in return. "Killian, will you, can we stop for a minute? I want..." she lost her nerve.

"Risa?" he questioned warily as he complied with her request. Nervous now, he hoped she wasn't regretting her decision as he took in her uncertain gaze. He nearly groaned as he left the warm caress of her body, his own aching at the loss of her touch.

"I want to be on top," she finally said with a wicked smile.

His heart stuttered a few beats before he grinned and opened his arms, the invitation clear.

She quickly jumped at him, and he fell back into a sitting position. She lowered herself into his lap, sliding down his shaft.

"Fuck me," he whispered, his voice strained, his accent thick. He moaned a second before his eyes closed and his shoulders shook, barely bracing his arms behind him in time.

She nodded, "Oh, I plan to."

His head spun at her response, and he huffed out a laugh filled with pleasure.

"It's my turn, Killian, of the silver eyes and tongue. Let's see how pretty those words are now," she whispered, her voice like satin over his skin.

He locked eyes with her, and they slowly filled with silver as she started to move her hips and rock in his lap. His head fell back again as he gasped; this woman was much more than he'd expected or bargained for.

She began to lick and bite his neck then, and he moaned louder, encouraging her to continue. She obliged and worked her way back to his mouth, where she used her tongue to toy with the piercing on his lip. She continued to rock in his lap, gyrating her hips in a way that had them both on edge.

He shuddered at the sensations, and soon she felt his legs tense and his breathing went ragged. Now, he was the one begging her. "God, Risa, I need, I'm... don't stop... I, I can't," he panted. He wrapped a fist in her hair and dug his fingers into her waist in a bruising grip. "Please..." he moaned, nearly whimpering and not the least bit ashamed.

She was making breathy sounds that were driving him crazy. Her thighs were quaking, and he knew she was close. She cried out then, clenching his shoulders hard as she came. It was too much, finally enough, and his hips jerked. He shouted his pure ecstasy, spasming as he filled her with his release.

He fell back on his elbows, struggling to hold himself up. His chest was heaving like he'd run a marathon, and a fine sheen of sweat covered them both. He sighed in delight at the way her skin glistened in the moonlight.

She sat there warm and sated, grinning like a pleased cat as they both struggled to catch their breath.

"Risa, God, that was…" He was at a loss for words. He never had many as it was, always being the quietest of his friends, but now, when he needed them, they weren't there.

"Incredible, amazing, so much better than I expected," she suggested as she rocked her hips one more time.

He groaned in pleasure, agreeing, "Aye, all of that and more." He dropped flat to his back on the sand, his long, silvery hair trailing behind him. He laughed as he sat back up and wrapped his arms around her, kissing her deeply, then laying his forehead against hers. "You are full of surprises and delights. I'm looking forward to discovering more." He leaned back and smiled, "I take back all that I said about meeting others. I know we've only just met. I know it seems sudden, but there is something about you that pulls me in. Like a siren calling sailors to the rocks. I'm being drawn to you in a way I cannot describe. You belong to me, lass, and I'm not caring if you're luring me to my death. I want you too much to walk away now." He gripped her tighter.

She shook her head, no, and he frowned, sucking in a sharp breath, saddened. "Risa?" he whispered, wondering how much heartache one man could survive.

She smiled. "Oh, Killian, darling, you belong to *me*," she whispered and bit his lip gently.

A slow feral smile stretched his lips, "I've no problem with that at all, *mo stor*."

They brushed off the sand and got dressed. They strolled back to the beach house, holding hands. When they went inside, smiling, it was obvious by their appearance they'd been up to something.

Marissa blushed and hid her face at the round of cheers and applause they received.

"Wait, Killian?" Sarah, the red dragon, gasped incredulously. "I didn't know you, you know, *liked*, people." She grinned at him.

Killian bowed and thanked them like he was receiving an award. "An' just so it's crystal clear, this is me, staking my claim," he dragged Marissa to him and kissed her so deeply she drooped in his arms like her bones had melted.

Chapter 33

JACK AND DAVIS HAD the children tucked into bed, and they were sleeping now. Shepard was on a supply run to get things they'd need for two small children. Especially one Jonathan's age. As the only father in the group, he knew what was essential. Jack was on a video call with Vaughn, showing him that the children were safe, but sharing the awful news that their parents had been murdered. He was hoping Vaughn could use his vast network of intelligence to find out who they were and if they had any other family they could go to. He also updated them about Marco's injuries. Thankfully he was going to make it. They talked about Marissa and what a valuable asset she'd become. She was going to come back to Dallas with them to meet her sister.

Vaughn listened with a soft smile on his face. He thanked Jack and told him his heart was lightened with the news the children were safe, although he was sorry to hear the little girl had witnessed her parent's death. The boy was too young to understand, fortunately. He agreed to see what they could find out about their family and ensure they were placed in a good home. He was concerned about Marco but knew Siobhan would take good care of him.

The news about Marissa was most interesting. The mystery about her being Serena's sister and her magic being bound? Quite intriguing. They hadn't told Serena yet. They didn't want her to be anxious about it, waiting until Marissa arrived. Once they settled things with Cyrus and the children, he was going to put someone on that case. They now knew that the dreams Serena was having were true memories, not just wishful thinking.

After they disconnected, Jack updated the others know that Vaughn was on the case. Nods all around. Everyone was appalled at the cruelty the two dark wielders had shown.

Jack smirked as he saw Marissa watching in fascination as several of the dragons were pluming smoke or steam and flicking talons in and out to express their anger.

Siobhan stormed into the room. "Jack," she announced flatly, "Marco is asking for you," her tone devoid of any emotion.

He nodded and joined her, hurrying to the back room where Marco was in bed recovering.

Marco was sitting up, the wound on his neck looking much better. A dark pink now instead of the angry red when it first happened. They suspected the residual dark magic of the wards etched the metal that cut him, hindering his natural healing. Siobhan's magic was slowly winning the battle, but what she couldn't do was replace the blood he'd lost. That needed to happen on its own, so he was much paler than his usual darkly tanned countenance.

Jack casually strolled in and leaned against the wall. "Hey, man," he called softly.

He smiled weakly at Jack, "Hey back, man. I'm glad to see you. I heard you and Marissa got the kids out."

His voice was a little raspy, and Jack wondered if the wound had damaged his vocal cords. He spared a glance at Siobhan and saw her watching Marco with hollow eyes that were somehow still burning into him. Jack nodded at Marco, giving him a small smile. "It was a group effort, thanks to you blocking us from the blast. Otherwise, we'd all be gone."

The red dragon grimaced and waved him off, "Davis did too; he was just faster on the shift than me. Guess that's something that comes with age."

Jack stepped over to the bed and sat next to reluctant patient. "Don't downplay this, Marco, you're a hero. You saved our lives, almost at the cost of your own. If it hadn't been for a room full of wielders, grateful to you for their existence, and, of course Siobhan's determination, you wouldn't be here right now. Thank you!" He took the man's hand and squeezed it encouragingly.

Marco smiled gratefully at him, then continued, "Jack, I need your help. You'll have to take full command of the team and close out this mission. Kill those fuckers for me. You know I wouldn't ask if I could do it, but your insight and command have been on point. I know you can handle it. Someone won't let me out of bed." He glared at Siobhan, and she growled at him. Considering she wasn't a dragon, it was quite impressive.

"Marco, she's right," Jack laughed, "You're in no shape to be leading this campaign right now. You know I got you, and I'm honored, truly. We will succeed. Don't worry." He stood and saluted him.

"I know you will," the red dragon smiled as he reached up to Jack, shook his hand, then grasped his forearm, "Watch your six."

Jack grinned, "Oorah." He glanced over at Siobhan, "Shi, can I talk to you for a minute? Outside?"

She nodded silently and left the room, stomping out loudly.

Jack stared at Marco. "Do you know why she's acting like that?" nodding his head towards her back.

Marco looked at him quizzically. "Because I keep trying to get out of bed?" he asked warily.

"Do you remember what you said to Siobhan right before you practically died in her arms?"

His eyes went wide, "N-No, what did I say?" he stammered, now terrified.

Jack grinned, "You told her you loved her. Have you told her since?"

Marco was struck mute for a moment. He shook his head slowly, "I don't remember much after the blast other than a few seconds on the floor, then waking up in the beach house. I... I guess I realized I was dying and didn't want to leave without telling her how I felt," he grimaced as he twisted the edge of the blanket in his fists. "*Madre de Dios*. How did she take it?" He stared at Jack, his eyes wide and frantic.

Jack winked, "You're alive, aren't you? Don't worry, brother, I got you." He hurried out and grabbed Siobhan's arm, dragging her into the backyard.

"What the hell, Jack?" she tried to yank her arm out of his grip.

"Stop it, unless you want all of those dragons in there to know what I'm about to say," he snapped at her. His tone was so different from his usual friendly, lighthearted voice, that she immediately stopped arguing and stared at him until they came to a stop outside. His expression softened, "Shi, listen to me. You did me a huge favor, now I'm going to do the same for you. Let me ask you something, and don't lie. Did you honestly not realize how Marco felt about you?"

She slowly shook her head, then whispered, "No."

Jack sighed, "Girl, that man has been in love with you for *years*. Why do you think he was so upset when he felt you were using him?"

She gritted her teeth. "Well, he didn't tell me!" she spat out, "Why does it take him dying in my arms to tell me loves me?" Her lips quivered, and hot, bitter tears filled her eyes.

He could tell it was a mixture of anger, fear, and anguish as each of the emotions flitted across her expression before she settled on one emotion that crumpled her face as it hit her.

"Jack," she whispered, pain thick in her voice now, "I almost lost him tonight."

Taking her in his arms, he pulled her against the warmth of his body. He put his chin on her head and stroked his hand down her hair. "Shh, let it out, darling," he comforted her.

Siobhan sobbed against Jack's shirt, her breath coming in rapid, jagged bursts. Drenching him with tears full of so many emotions, he was sure they felt like acid to this strong woman who didn't like to admit she had feelings.

"Shi," he cooed, "It's okay, baby. You sweet girl. I'm going to give you some real facts, and I want you to listen to me. You're not going to like what I'm about to say, but I love you, and I need you to hear this, okay?"

She nodded and stayed there, leaning against him.

"Okay," he sighed, feeling he was taking his own life in his hands here. "Shi, you have to accept that you are not the easiest person to know or talk to."

She sighed as well and nodded once, agreeing.

She'd been described as prickly, ornery, stubborn, and caustic. She was aware of that, as it was usually said to her face, but it didn't make it easier to hear so in Jack's gentle voice. It helped that outside of Liam, Jack was the only other person who knew about her relationship with her father. Knew how much his aloofness and seeming disinterest in her growing up had shaped her this way. How the chip on her shoulder that Liam was a dragon, and she would never have wings had affected her outlook on life. He knew these deepest secrets of hers and gentled his voice further to soften the blow.

"Honey, I'm sure he would have told you eventually. But he was scared to tell you. Scared, he was going to push you away. Scared you wouldn't take it well and leave. He didn't want you to hurt him. That huge, strong, red dragon, one of the fiercest warriors alive. Also, one of the bravest men I know, and he's scared of *you* hurting him. But he showed you his dragon, he took you flying. He put himself in danger to save you. What does that tell you?"

She shuddered, whispering, "Yeah, it's clear in hindsight. And you're right; I've been awful to him." She wiped her eyes and sniffed. "He deserves better than me," she muttered.

Jack laughed and pulled her away to look at her. He tapped her nose. "I'm sure he does, but for some reason, his heart wants you. Sometimes bonds don't make sense, but when two people care about each other like that, it's all that matters. You two make sense. Shi, be honest with me now. No evading or changing the subject. Look me in the eye and tell me. Do you love him?"

She shuddered, then nodded, "I do." She cleared her throat. "I love Marco," she declared, saying it out loud for the first time, and her face underwent a drastic transformation. A spark came back into her eyes. "Jack," she whispered, her fingers curling in his shirt, "When I thought he was dying, it was like my world stopped. He told me he loved me, and I was just so angry that he didn't tell me sooner so we could have had more time to enjoy that. Jack, I love him. And I'm going to marry him!"

He leaned back, startled, "Well, maybe we just start with you telling him you love him? Put him out of his misery?"

She laughed and nodded, "Okay, fine, I'll go tell him that right now, but Jack, he has three months to propose, or I'm going to do it myself!" she declared.

"Okay, but Shi," he grinned at her, "Keep in mind he's wounded, don't try to mate him tonight."

She flipped him off, giggled, and ran back inside.

Jack eventually wandered back inside to the main living area and noticed Davis smiling softly at him from the sofa.

You did a good thing there, my love, Davis told him.

They deserve to be happy, and now we've repaid her for helping us.

Davis chuckled, *yeah, but you're still a good person. It's reason 3,255 why I love you.*

Jack laughed as well. *Are you going to tell me the rest of those reasons?* He leaned down to kiss his mate, and Shepard groaned.

"Get a room, you two!" he said playfully.

Winking at Davis, Jack jumped over the back of the chair into Shepard's lap then kissed him. "Oh, sorry! Thought you were Davis!" he exclaimed in mock surprise, "You're just so pretty. But I agree with Marco, you need to shave." He rubbed his chin and grimaced.

Davis burst into laughter as his brother dropped Jack on the floor. "Idiots," Shepard grumbled, wiping his mouth with a grin on his face.

Siobhan ran back to the bedroom where Marco was, then stopped and put her forehead on the door. Everything was about to change, and she needed a moment to reconcile that. No, she needed to get out of her own head. She opened the door and stepped inside. Closing it behind her, she leaned against it and stared at the man lying in the bed. He was looking at her with an expression of extreme caution. "You big dummy," she whispered, "You absolute idiot."

He looked startled, then laughed, "Of all the things I thought you might say, it wasn't that."

She laughed with him and climbed on the bed before she laid a soft kiss on his lips. "Marco, when you were…" she trailed off.

"Dying, it's alright, *carina*, I was dying. Jack told me what I said," he told her, looking her in the eyes.

"Did you mean it?" she demanded, then held her breath, scared he would say yes and even more terrified he would say no.

He studied her face, took his own deep breath and finally shared what he had been unable to tell her before. "I did, and I do. Siobhan, *te amo*, I do love you. So very much. I've been scared to admit that to you because I didn't want you to have the ability to hurt me. But you've always had it. You've always held my heart in your hands. It's only ever belonged to you, and I love you. *Te necesito*. More than the air I breathe, I need you."

She let out her pent-up breath and bit her lip. She knew it cost him a lot to tell her, and now she needed to pay the same price. She took his face in her hands and kissed him again, gently. "I wish you'd told me sooner, but I understand why you didn't. I know I'm not the easiest person to know. No, I know it's true," she added when he tried to protest. "Marco, please, I'm like a cross between a cactus and a honey badger sometimes. Yet somehow, I'm lucky enough to have a man as strong, wonderful and brave as you to love me. I don't understand why, but I can tell you, I'm happy about it. Marco, you make me so very happy. And I'm an idiot. I wish I'd realized it before tonight. I wish it hadn't taken you dying in my arms for me to figure myself out." She put her forehead on his and let out a small whimper.

"Siobhan," he pushed her back, "What are you saying? Be plain. I need to hear you say it."

She smiled, "I love you, too, Marco. I do; I love you so very much! *Te amo.*"

He grinned, "That hurt, didn't it, Von-Von? You admitted you have a heart and emotions all in one night. Poor thing. Ow!" he yelped as she slapped his shoulder.

"I told you don't ever call me that!" she growled playfully and slapped him again.

"Wounded, almost died!" he pointed at himself as he tried to dodge her.

She laughed, "Dramatic, baby. You never used to be this soft."

Marco snorted a short laugh, "Well, I also never told you I loved you before. I guess it's a night for firsts. Siobhan, I'm sorry I didn't tell you sooner. I truly wish I had. But I've loved you for years, and I always hoped someday you would come back to me. Now you're here, and I'm not letting you go again. I will fight for you, to keep you by my side. Siobhan, I want to be more than just your boyfriend, or lover. I need more." He searched her eyes, hoping she knew what he meant.

Nodding, to indicate she understood, she opened her heart to him and felt it then, the telltale tingle that she knew meant he was her mate, her soulmate and the one she was destined to be with forever. There was no snap or pain like others had described. She was too stubborn to let it hurt and too sure of herself to accept anything less. *Marco,* she tested, gently with her mind.

His eyes widened and locked on hers. *My love, it's Incendium, by the way,* came a growly voice.

Hello, Incendium, she softly spoke to his dragon, *that's a great name.* Her eyes softened, and he smiled tenderly.

Siobhan, I, does this mean, do you agree? Are we? Can I? His heart sped up as he eagerly waited for her answer.

She nodded quickly and trembled as his lips curved into that gorgeous smile she loved so much. The one that caught her eye the day they met at a job for Vaughn. He'd given her that sensual smile and offered to take her for a ride on his motorcycle. She'd accepted with alacrity and been fascinated by his toughness, his devil-may-care style, and his sultry accent. He trained her in hand-to-hand combat, taught her multiple styles of weaponry. And helped her piss off her brother whenever she wanted. They'd had a lot of fun for a couple of years, before she'd wandered away, never realizing that Marco felt so strongly about her. She also refused to admit how much she missed him. Lorenzo was wonderful in every way, but she knew there was one thing they didn't have. She knew she wasn't his mate. Because it was Marco, it was always Marco. Now, she was back in his arms, and she knew it was for the last time as just a lover.

She was giving him her approval to mark her as his and only his. *Mates. Forever.* She kissed him fiercely.

He kissed her back just as passionately and started to pull her in his lap before he gasped and fell back against the headboard. "Well, maybe not tonight after all," he said glumly, disappointed in his weakness.

She grinned, "What can we not do tonight? Mate? There are still other things we can do."

Laughing, he said, "Bad girl, I need to be at full strength to handle you. Just let me hold you tonight and bask in the glow of your love and affection. My sweet cuddly Von-Von." He flashed his devilishly handsome smile as she rolled her eyes.

She decided not to punch him for that and lay down, putting her head on his chest while he wrapped his arms around her.

He rumbled in satisfaction, listening contentedly while she talked to his dragon.

Chapter 34

IN THE DINING ROOM, everyone else was gathered around the table debating. Most wanted to wait until the next day to attack Cyrus and Esme, in the daylight. A few were with Jack, who argued that the longer they waited, the more prepared the enemy would be. "That's the problem with waiting," he told them, "That's a typical dragon-wielder pattern. You draw back and prepare, draw back, and prepare. They know and expect it from us. If we strike now, they'll be unprepared. Breaking three of their wards in one night? That had to put a strain on Esme. When we rescued Vaughn, she blew a lot of energy out in frustration, and Siobhan was able to confirm it drained her. We broke through two of their traps, didn't get caught, and broke a third ward, found the kids, and liberated them. She's seething. We have the element of surprise on our side." He slapped his hand on the table in emphasis.

The others thought about it, realized Jack was right and began murmuring their agreement. Davis beamed, his pride in his mate evident. "Jack is in charge now. Marco assigned him, we're going with his plan," he announced.

Jack began designating teams in a way that was different to anything they'd done before. It was more strategic, less brute-force dragon tactic, and they soon realized that was the point. It would keep their enemy off balance, and they wouldn't know how to combat it. He nodded; this was going to work.

Shepard voiced it as well, "Jack, this is brilliant, they'll never see this coming."

He grinned at them, glad to have their support in the absence of their regular team leader. Taking into consideration that he was the only pure human, he was especially pleased. He absently pulled a knife from the strap on his leg that he hadn't removed yet and started twirling it between his fingers. He hadn't fallen into that pattern in years and didn't even realize he was doing it until he noticed it was silent and everyone was watching him. He glanced at his hand. "Oh, sorry, an old habit I thought I had broken. I guess all this strategizing is bringing back some memories," he said, his face coloring.

Sarah grinned at him, "Jack, you are one scary man, my friend."

Davis laughed, "And it's hot!" he added.

The remarks embarrassed him even more, and Jack blushed harder. He stood and turned like he was leaving, when one of the other dragons called out, "Oh, come on Jack, don't be ashamed of those tiny little blades. I'm sure they can do some damage. Just maybe not as much as our claws."

Jack paused, then whipped around and threw the first knife across the room so fast his movement was a blur. It slammed into the wall right next to Killian's ear. The tip was buried in the plaster with the handle quivering slightly. Before anyone registered what happened, a second blade whistled through the air and plunged into the wall just below the first. No one even saw him pull the second one.

Silence filled the room faster than a finger snap. Jack sauntered over to Killian and yanked the knives from the wall. "Still got it," he grinned, tousling the wielder's hair, "Nothing personal, Ki, I just knew you wouldn't move."

Applause broke the silence and Killian's deep, loud laughter surprised those around him who were used to his quiet, soft-spoken nature.

Davis spun Jack around and kissed him hard. "So hot," he repeated when he came up for air.

"Okay, that's enough, everyone, time to go," Shepard announced.

Marissa stood, then asked, "Wait, who's staying with the kids? I mean, I know they're asleep, but someone should be here in case they wake up."

"I've got it," came a raspy voice. They turned to see Marco slowly easing into the room, supported by Siobhan. The group cheered to see him up and about. He sat on the couch with a sigh of relief. "I may not be able to fight, but I can babysit. My nieces and nephews back home will vouch for that," he said softly as he grinned.

Siobhan was smiling tenderly at him. She turned and glanced at Jack; her smile widened, and a silent thank you formed on her lips.

He placed his hand over his heart and smiled back. He realized belatedly he still held the knives in his hand, and she narrowed her eyes.

She looked over his shoulder and saw the holes in the wall. "Jack," she chided, "Were you playing with your knives again? Didn't we discuss this? Not in the house!"

Shrugging, he gave her a sheepish smile.

Davis stared at him consideringly, then at her. "You knew?" he asked her, "You knew he could do the…" He mimicked throwing the knives while making a whistling noise.

She rolled her eyes. "Who do you think he practices with? He doesn't want to mess up your pretty face," she smirked.

A round of "oohs" went around the room, and Davis burst into laughter. "Oh, my dear mate, we need to talk about this later," he grinned at Jack, who grinned back innocently as he twirled one of the blades before sliding it back into its sheath, and the other disappeared who knew where.

"Let's do this," Jack said sternly.

The group was hunkered down, two blocks from the residence, waiting for the recon team to return. Siobhan, Marissa, and Killian, being the most familiar with the type of wards Esme used, went ahead to scout the home. They were accompanied by Shepard in his ghosted dragon form, River, in case they needed his teeth and claws. The wielders crept around the house, gently feeling and checking the barriers. River crouched on the street nearby, nervously puffing steam and clicking his talons. Marissa kissed his snout and told him not to worry. He grinned at her, his toothy smile making her pale as Killian pulled her away, laughing under his breath.

Once they were done scouting, they moved back towards the dragons and conferred in whispers. They felt they had a handle on it this time. These were the same wards that were on the warehouse decoys. Both Cyrus and Esme were home, they were certain of that. Siobhan's mouth curved into a feral smile that made Marissa shiver. Then, she remembered all the atrocities committed by those inside. She answered Siobhan's smile with a wicked one of her own.

Killian nodded; it was time to return. "River," he called quietly. He heard a quiet chuff and turned.

The giant blue dragon appeared in front of him, and the three wielders climbed up. River padded down the street, quickly making his way back to the rest of the force as his long tail rippled behind him.

Marissa had to stifle a giggle at the thought of a giant invisible dragon running down the road.

Once they reached the rest of the team, they slid down and relayed their intelligence while River stood by, not changing back yet. The other dragons were already in their full forms, shifting restlessly on their paws.

Marissa wandered over to the other blue dragon she knew must be Davis. "I know you said it was a rare thing, but I just wanted to let you know that regardless of the reason, I'm glad I got to see your dragon form. You are gorgeous!"

He lowered his head and nudged her with his snout, then snaked his tongue out and licked her ankle.

Jack rolled his eyes, "He's a sucker for compliments. Also, Lake wants you to scratch his ears," he told her. "All dragons are kind of sluts for that."

The dragon puffed out some vapor around Jack, grumbling at him like he was offended.

Marissa held out a hand timidly. She was delighted when the enormous beast in front of her bumped his ear on her hand, and she excitedly sank her fingers into the soft skin there. She scratched, and he started purring and rumbling in a way that made her whoop in joy.

He turned his head and presented the other ear, and she scratched that one, too. Suddenly, another blue head shoved that one out of the way, and she now had River's ear in front of her. Grinning, she obliged him, too.

Lake snorted in disgust and snapped at River's paws. Everyone laughed— it did a lot to lighten the mood.

"If you two are done?" Jack asked dryly.

River nudged Marissa again as she started to drop her hands.

Jack snapped, "River, do I need to call your wife?"

The dragon dropped to the ground and rumbled something that sounded suspiciously like sorry, as he whipped his tail back and forth across the road, skittering over the concrete with a dry rattling noise. The sound made the others shiver.

Lake was laughing, a strange wheezing noise that made his long neck quiver.

"Oh no, honey, you still have to answer to me later," Jack reminded him sternly.

That dragon dropped down, too and mumbled an apologetic sound, but one giant eye winked. He wasn't the least bit sorry, and Jack knew it.

Jack rolled his eyes. "Okay, are we ready?" he called out, and everyone nodded. The dragons were all puffing steam and smoke in their eagerness to get moving. "Alright, mount up, and we go on my signal." They all ran to their assigned groups, and the wielders climbed up on the dragons according to their combined tasks.

He surveyed the group with his arm raised. Once he confirmed all were ready, he pointed to Team Alpha and dropped his arm. They silently moved towards the target. Once they were in place, their dragons signaled Davis, who relayed it to Jack. He pointed to Team Bravo and repeated the procedure. They, too, quietly got into place. Finally, it was time for Team Charlie to move in. Once they were set, everyone assumed their stance and waited for the signal.

Jack studied the area, assessing for any additional man-made threats or possible collateral damage. If this worked the way he had planned, there shouldn't be any innocents harmed, but it was always a risk. His goal was to take out the enemy and ensure all his team made it out. They were not leaving anyone behind. He knew Davis and Shepard couldn't go through that again. The sight of Marco going down earlier almost paralyzed them both with fear.

Thankfully, the quick thinking of Marissa helped save him. That's what gave him the idea. Dragons and wielders had always worked together, but they'd used their powers only within their color spectrum or individually. They hadn't combined their forces with other types of magics to enhance each other until recently. Bridget and Vaughn did it first. No one had thought much of it, though, because their magic was so unique. Then Liam, Jorrie, and Lorenzo had done it to save Shepard's life.

This was the way it was supposed to be. Jack could feel it. They were never supposed to be so siloed in their affinities. So much of their history had been lost thousands of years ago when the Gods had stripped magic from the land. They were still discovering new things they hadn't known were possible since the return of the magic.

Jack completed his survey and smiled grimly. It was time. He leaned down over Lake's neck. *You ready?* He asked him.

The dragon rumbled; *I was born ready.*

Let's do this! Jack grinned. Dragons really were violent creatures in contrast to how silly and soft their human sides could be. It's what they needed now. *Send the signal to Alpha.*

Lake sent the prearranged signal to Team Alpha, which consisted of those skilled in shields, to begin erecting a new warding, one designed to keep the wielders inside from escaping. They constructed it against the backside of the existing wards, supported by the dragons that best complimented them. It was up in no time, faster than they'd ever done before.

Bravo, go! sent Jack. The second team brought Esmerelda's wards crashing down, in a mere blink of an eye. They heard shrieks from the house and knew they had the enemy's attention. Jack grinned, *any minute now.* The screams soon turned to anger as they realized the new wards were trapping them within what had been their own barriers.

Charlie, go! he called. The third team used their combined powers to lay a field of dampening down as planned, effectively binding the evil wielders' powers so they couldn't use them. Outrage continued to build inside the house.

Jack laughed; he was right. They weren't expecting this tonight and severely underestimated them. The usual tactics would have all the wielders taking down the wards, and the dragons would attack with brute force. By holding the teams together in a layered attack, and suppressing the offense of the enemy, they didn't allow them time to strike back.

Now came the justice part. Where they paid for their crimes. Jack's gaze hardened. *Team Delta... burn it to the ground,* he called.

I still think D should stand for Dragon, Lake muttered.

Soon, a ring of intense magical fire circled the house. The dragons and red wielders razed the house with flames. Burning the place where these evil bastards once tortured Vaughn and took childhood away from two innocent babies. The wards the Bravo team erected kept the fire in check so it wouldn't spread to the neighboring homes. The other wielders added their magic to enhance the dragons' powers, sending the inferno blazing into the night sky. Soon, Cyrus and Esme would either have to come out and surrender or burn.

As if on cue, Esme stumbled out. Coughing. Soot streaking her face. She screamed at Cyrus to get out.

Cyrus stood silhouetted in the doorway, his face grim. The flames crawled higher and stronger behind him, looking like the very mouth of Hell. The heat was unbearable, but there was nothing his wielding could do to stop it. He surveyed the dragons and wielders gathered in front of them and bared his teeth. "No! I would rather die here! With honor like my father!" He turned and ran back inside.

Esme was crying, screaming, and calling for him. Her knees buckled beneath her as she crumbled to the ground, a low, keening wail coming from her throat. Her world was ending.

It was heart-wrenching and Jack found a small moment of pity. But Cyrus made his choice. He'd rather die in the fire than be captured. That was fine with Jack. "Esme," he called to her.

She turned wild eyes on him and screamed in wordless rage, her tears drying in the heat from the blaze.

Jack maintained his blank visage, turning off his feelings. He moved to the edge of the wards, Lake hovering over his shoulder.

She seethed at him, "I knew that was a dragon mark. I don't know how you fooled my tests, but I knew you were rotten. Cyrus was an idiot; he wanted to believe you. All that nonsense about outsiders, bonding together, fighting the good fight." She spat at Jack, "What are you? You're not a dragon, not a wielder. What are you?" she demanded, rage causing her words to rise in octaves until she was screaming.

"Human. And, I may not be active anymore," he said, "But once a Marine, always a Marine."

Her eyes widened, and she began to laugh. It held an edge of hysteria to it. She lunged at Jack, but the wards slapped her back.

He simply stared at her in contempt and shook his head.

She gritted her teeth. "I surrender," she whispered.

Jack nodded and called Siobhan, Killian, and Sarah's dragon Blaze over. Wanting a fire-breather nearby in case Esme tried something.

Lake stuck his head through a hole in the ward Siobhan created and picked the dark wielder up by the back of her shirt using his teeth. She screamed as he swung her through and dropped her on the ground in front of them. He probably could've set her down gently, but he wasn't feeling too kindly towards her at the moment. He lowered his head and snarled at her, his meaning clear. Move and die. Dragons didn't eat people, but they sure didn't mind biting you in half if you threatened their homes or family. Jack watched Vaughn do it to the Shadow King. Shepard did it to a man who put a gun to Jorrie's head and knew Davis wouldn't hesitate if she even breathed at him wrong.

Esmerelda, the black wielder, now widow of Cyrus, simply sat there, and laughed again. Unhinged and cackling. "You think you're so clever. Cyrus was blinded by his revenge, but that wasn't our true cause, not the main goal. You'll see, you can kill me, but it won't stop the darkness that's coming." She slowly gained her feet, standing tall and proud, jutting her chin in the air.

"That may be, but at least we get to see Vaughn kill your bitch ass," Siobhan told her. They'd agreed that if the wielders surrendered, they'd take them back for Vaughn and Bridget to determine their fate.

Esme smiled coldly at Siobhan, "Yes, how is poor Vaughn doing? Hmm? Is he still screaming from the pain I inflicted on him? Are those marks still open? Weeping? Bleeding? Causing him delicious agony? I had to beat him so hard, over, and over. He refused to make any noise for Cyrus, but I finally broke him. He screamed so loud then. It was wonderful, delightful music to my ears." She licked her lips and rolled her eyes in grotesque delight. "I adored every moment of it. I fed on his agony. I lived in his torment." She smirked. "Is that bitch he married still having nightmares? Filth, breeding with animals, making more animals," she spat at the green wielder.

Siobhan lost her temper and launched herself at Esme, whose evil smile widened. Killian lunged towards Siobhan trying to hold her back.

Jack realized it was exactly what Esme wanted; she wanted Siobhan to get close and cause a distraction. He saw her hand go towards her back and knew she had a weapon hidden. *Stupid*, he should have checked her. They were all so proud of their magic, he just didn't think wielders used human weapons. Jack's hands moved on their own, and a split second before Esme raised the gun, he flung his knife and buried it in her throat. He hit her with such force it slammed her backwards to the ground. As close as he was, he heard the rattling gasp as she realized what happened.

The gun she grabbed now fell from her limp fingers as she hit the ground. She lay there in disbelief, blood dripping from her neck and bubbling from her mouth. Her eyes wide open in shock, she took her last breath. Bested by a human.

Siobhan dropped to her knees, as Killian released her, staring at Jack in awe, while she trembled at her close call.

They all watched in silence as he calmly kicked the gun away and leaned over Esme's form. "Enjoy Hell, bitch," he said, yanking his knife from her throat and wiped the blood on her shirt.

"Scary," repeated Killian.

Chapter 35

DAVIS AND SHEPARD STAYED behind to help put out the fire with their water magic just in case the fire department couldn't get it done quickly and safely. There was to be no more death today. They were in ghost mode, so no one would see them. Davis snuck into the house to ensure Cyrus was truly dead and to add Esme's remains to the fire. Let the authorities figure it out. He was still grumbling about a scorch mark on his chin where a particularly nasty flame snuck through his water barrier. He went in human form since his dragon form wouldn't fit through the door.

Shepard laughed. *Should've studied harder, little brother,* he chided.

Suck pond scum asshole, Davis replied.

And you kiss your mate with that mouth, his brother grunted good-naturedly, shaking his head.

Davis grinned, *that's not all I do to him with this mouth.*

Shepard groaned. *You're terrible.*

Davis laughed, "But you love me, Stream," calling him by his childhood nickname.

Shepard threw his arm around his twin, smiling as the burn healed before his eyes, "That I do, Pond, that I do." He glanced around. The fire department seemed to have things under control, they should get moving. Before they did, he wanted to say one last thing while it was just the two of them.

"Davis, I was thinking about something. Jack hasn't killed anyone in a long time. Be gentle with him tonight. He didn't want to kill Esme; I saw it on his face. He wanted to take her back to Vaughn, but he couldn't let her hurt anyone."

Nodding, Davis sighed, a weary expression on his face, "I know, I'm a little worried about him. He's been forced to tap into a side of himself he's kept very private and to confront some feelings he'd buried. But Jack is resilient, and I'm not leaving his side. He'll be okay." His tone was determined, with his normally grinning lips set in a firm line.

Shepard smiled softly. He knew his brother was right and would be everything for his mate. "Another thing," he began.

"Dude, what are you, Dad, now?" Davis laughed.

"No," Shepard grinned at him, "Dad wouldn't be able to get in this many words uninterrupted."

They shared a chuckle, thinking about how their mother did all the talking for her husband and herself. Joseph was content to let Barbara run things, though. He adored her.

Shepard continued, "I was thinking about Lily and Jonathan. They're going to need someone, and I have a feeling we aren't going to find they have any family out there. I think that's why they were targeted; no one to miss them. Just like Serena was. Maybe Marissa. They're orphans now. They can't just go anywhere; they need to be with a family that understands their magic and the challenges of being different. Of losing someone dear to them."

Davis thought about what his brother was saying and agreed, Lily would need to be around a blue dragon family, around someone she could trust.

Where they'd also have access to a blue wielder when Jonathan was old enough. He thought about who he knew, and it hit him like a lightning bolt. He looked sharply at Shepard with tears in his eyes.

Smiling softly, Shepard saw the moment Davis realized what he meant. Further confirmed when Davis threw his arms around him and hugged him as tight as he could, knocking them both over. Shoulders shaking hard, Davis sobbed into his twin's chest. Shepard lay there on the grass, the house behind them collapsing in flames, and held his brother close. He rocked him, comforting him by singing the song they shared when they were little, and one of them was scared or upset.

Soon, Davis joined in and got himself under control. He put his hands on his brother's cheeks and rested his forehead against Shepard's, "Best brother ever in the whole world," he whispered.

Shepard grinned, "Damn right!"

At the house, there was a full-on party underway. Someone made a run for pizzas, and others grabbed beer and champagne. Siobhan warded the children's room so the noisy crew wouldn't wake them up. Everyone was feeling euphoric. Except for the man of the hour.

Marissa noticed Jack was nowhere to be seen. He should be here celebrating. It was his strategy that worked, and he'd dealt the final blow. She wandered off to find him, finally locating him in the backyard. He stood there, quietly staring at the moon. She slowly approached him and put her arm through his before leaning her head on his shoulder. She didn't say anything, he would talk if he wanted to.

Finally, he sighed. "I guess you want to know why I'm not in there?" he asked.

"Only if you want to tell me," she shrugged.

He chuckled lightly. "I just don't feel like celebrating that I was responsible for two people's deaths. No matter how evil they were, no matter how justified the kill was. I still took their lives, and that shouldn't be a reason for a party."

"Fair enough," she nodded, "But they aren't celebrating that people died, they're celebrating that people lived. Because of you and everyone else here, those two children now have a shot at a happy life. Your friend Vaughn gets to live the rest of his life, his wife will go on to deliver their baby. Yes, lives ended, but how many were saved that those evil people would have otherwise killed? And what you did for me? I'll get to meet family that I didn't even know existed. You gave me back my sister. You opened the door to my true self and pushed me through it. You changed my life in a way that I can never repay you for," she finished quietly and turned to face him.

He studied her face, full of sincerity. He threw his arms around her, holding her tight. "You're so smart, little one," he said, kissing her forehead gently.

She snorted, "Why does everyone call me that?"

He stared at her in confusion. "Little one?" He laughed then, "Because to us you are. Marissa, how old do you think I am?"

"Thirty? Thirty-one?" she shrugged.

He smiled, "Darling, I'm forty-three. And Siobhan? She's twenty-eight, Marco is seventy-eight, and Davis is —"

"Two hundred and forty-four," came a rumble from behind her.

She whirled around, her mouth open. There stood the twins, both shirtless and oozing sex appeal, their wings fluttering behind them. "You're," she pointed at them both, "two hundred and forty-four years old?" Shepard laughed, and she locked her eyes on the gorgeous tattoo on his chest, her fingers itching to touch it. She slid her eyes over to Davis and his devil-may-care grin. "No way," she shook her head.

Davis laughed, "Aww. Don't believe me? Wielders and dragons age slowly, even more, when they mate. Go ask Killian how old he is." He winked at her as she slowly backed away and ran inside.

"Poor thing," Jack laughed, shaking his head.

Shepard waved at Davis, he was going in as well. He pulled on his shirt and hurried off.

Taking Jack's hands in his own, Davis smiled at him. "Hey, you," he said softly.

Jack smiled back, "Hey," he replied just as softly.

"Jack, I know this wasn't easy for you. Bringing up those memories you've been avoiding and having to end Esme that way. But I want you to know that I'm incredibly proud of you. You were amazing, and you saved so many other lives tonight. So, if you want to talk or just need silence, I'm here for you."

Jack grabbed Davis and kissed him so passionately that he could swear hearts floated around them. "Thank you, my love. Surprisingly, I'm doing okay now. That little silver wielder is smart beyond her years."

Chuckling, Davis replied, "Then I guess I better go repair any damage I might have done to her and Killian's little romance." He pulled Jack towards him again and wrapped his arms around his waist. "Jack, before we go in, I have something to ask you. When we get home, we're going to try hard to find Lily and Jonathan's family. Shepard said he felt like it's unlikely there'll be any family to find. That's why they were chosen, just like Serena, no one would miss them. Those babies are orphans, and with Lily being a water dragon and Jonathan probably being a wielder, they're going to need a special family. One that understands their magic and struggles. One that knows how to help them cope with their loss." He gazed longingly into Jack's eyes. "One with people they trust and feel safe with. What if — we — provided that home?"

Lips trembling, Jack's knees almost buckled as his heart went into overdrive. He reached up and cupped Davis' face in his hands. "Davis, do you mean it? We could adopt them as our children? Have a family of our own?"

Davis nodded, "Yes, our own family."

"I would love nothing more, but we are not getting a dog."

When Davis and Jack went back inside, the Celebration of Life Saved, as Jack had decided it was called, was still going strong. Jack was almost knocked over by a strong female ball of energy clouded with red-gold hair. Siobhan was wrapped around him like an octopus.

"I love you so much!" she shouted in his ear.

He laughed; she was a little tipsy. He set her back on her feet.

She stared into his eyes then poked him in the chest. "You saved my life. That skank was gonna shoot me and mess up this pretty face!" She waved her hand in front of her face. "But you!" here she poked him in the chest again and swayed on her feet, "You hot assed man, you saved me. I love you!" She kissed him hard and was squeezing his butt with both hands.

Still laughing, he had to peel her away while Davis cackled behind him.

Marco slowly made his way over, also laughing. "Come on, Shi, quit making out with Jack, his fiancé might get jealous."

She wailed, "But I love him!" and turned to Marco. Her eyes lit up. "But you! I love you even more! C'mere, my Latin lover!" She plastered herself against him and began kissing him in a way that was getting decidedly X-rated. Cheers echoed as Marco dragged her to their room to calm her down. Well, that was the theory, there might be a newly mated couple before the night was through.

Davis noticed Marissa talking in earnest to Killian, her eyes wide. He skipped over and put a hand on Killian's shoulder. "Sorry, man, I didn't realize y'all hadn't had that conversation yet."

Killian grinned. "Well," he drawled, "the little lady doesn't quite believe me that I'm ninety-eight. Hang on." He turned, "Hey, Sarah," he shouted. When she turned, he called out, "Tell Marissa how old I am?"

"Ninety-eight," she grinned, "And I'm one-hundred-fifty this year, baby!"

One by one, the other dragons and wielders started calling out their ages. Although none were as old as the twins, they were all significantly older than she expected. She and Siobhan were the youngest there.

Marissa laughed then, "Okay, this is crazy, but if I can believe in dragons and magic, I guess I can believe that, too."

They laughed with her, and Killian smirked. He leaned over and stage whispered, "And at my age, there's a lot I can teach you." He grinned suggestively at her.

Her face heated up as she hid it against his neck while he chuckled quietly.

Shepard strode in, "Hey everyone! Listen up! Thank you for what you've accomplished. We all learned a lot in this process. Vaughn is sending his plane now for us to fly home in the morning. Have fun, but don't forget to go to the airport tomorrow." Cheers and whoops of joy filled the room.

An hour later, Killian grabbed Marissa's hand and pulled her to his room, where he promptly took her in his arms and kissed her until she was gasping with need. They tore at each other's clothes, and soon, he had her pinned on the bed, taking her hard and fast while she begged for more. By the time they wore each other out, they'd somehow ended up on the floor, her sprawled over his chest. He was running his fingers through the silky strands of her hair.

"Mm, not that I'm complaining, but what brought that on?" she asked him, still panting slightly.

He slowly sat up, cradling her in his lap, then kissed her again, gently this time. His soft, lilting voice was hesitant this time. "Risa, tomorrow, your life is going to change yet again. You're going to meet your sister, and you're going to want and need to spend time with her. And there's nothing wrong with that, I want you to do it. You're also going to be immersed in our lore and culture so you can learn more about your own history. Plus, the search for your family to see who they were." He was toying absently with her hair again.

She sat up and ran her fingers through his hair, mingling them together so it was hard to tell which was hers and which was his. She brought her lips to his and whispered against them, "I won't forget you. I promise. How could I? You showed me what was in me. You recognized me for what I was and made this possible. Then, you showed me tenderness and patience. I couldn't do this without you, Killian. So, whatever you're thinking that makes you worry you won't see me again, just stop. I want, no, that's not right," she smiled softly, "I *need* to see where this goes. Besides, you belong to me, remember? You had better be there by my side. I don't want anyone else to teach me how to use my power. Plus, the sex is pretty good," she grinned and kissed his shoulder.

He laughed, "Just pretty good?"

She waggled her hand, "Eh, it's okay."

His eyes flashed silver, and he whispered something she didn't understand. He jumped up and threw her face down on the bed before he pulled her to her hands and knees.

She looked over her shoulder to ask what he was doing when he thrust into her again, recovered, hard, and stroked her deep inside. He sent a wave of magic sizzling through her, and she shattered around him. "Killian!" she cried in shock and pleasure.

He slowly pulled back, "Just okay?" he teased.

She tried to lean into him, wanting more.

He held himself away from her, "Just okay?" he asked again. He reached between her thighs and stroked her with one finger, causing her to tremble and shake. "Tell me, Marissa," his deep, quiet voice echoing in her veins somehow, "How is it when I'm inside you?"

"It's amazing," she called, her voice strained with need.

He thrust back into her hard and pulled back again. "One more time?" he purred to her, his tone laced with desire.

"Amazing, it's fucking amazing! Killian!" she cried, begging him to take her.

"That's what I thought you said," he laughed. "And who do you belong to, little one?" he whispered as he began to move again.

"You, only you," she moaned in relief. He filled her so completely she almost couldn't take it. It was like nothing she'd ever felt before. His breathing became ragged, so she leaned down and changed the angle, letting him delve deeper. His breath caught, and she felt him spasm in her.

He collapsed over her back, "Oh God, Risa."

She slowly lowered and slid him down next to her on the bed. Now, he lay on her chest, nuzzling her in contentment, and she stroked his hair. "No, Killian, I'm not forgetting you," she whispered.

Chapter 36

"RISA, YOU OKAY?" SHE heard Jack say as the plane crew was preparing for their landing in Dallas. Today would hold a lot more firsts. She'd never been to Texas, and she was going to meet a woman they claimed was her sister. She also had a serious lover for the first time in her life. She glanced over at Killian, where he dozed in his seat; they didn't sleep much last night. She was about to learn about her past and her future. As Killian predicted, it was going to be a lot to take in. She was grateful to him; he seemed to be dedicated to sticking by her side and was eager to teach her. She smiled at Jack and nodded, "Just nervous."

He smiled gently at her in return and took her hand. "You got this, babe," he reassured her.

The plane landed, and the group was met with a convoy of large SUVs to whisk them away to Vaughn's house. The littlest travelers were especially excited to see a new place as well. Lily bounced in her car seat, and Jonathan did, too. They were just about the most adorable things ever, and Marissa was so glad that Jack and Davis were petitioning to take them in. The two children would be so loved.

Right now, Davis was pointing out various things of interest as they drove by, telling them about their new home for the time being, or maybe forever, depending on how the search for their family went.

Shepard was on the phone with his wife, asking her about something called the triple threat. Marissa wasn't sure she wanted to know what that was.

Soon, they were right in the heart of downtown Dallas. She was amazed that it was just as hectic as Miami. They pulled up to the front door of one skyscraper, and she got dizzy looking up to see the top.

Killian took her hand and pulled her to the door. "Don't look up there, dragons like caves, too," he chuckled. They made their way down to Vaughn's floor, which was apparently under the building.

It took several trips, but finally the whole group was gathered in Vaughn's 'lair' as Jack called it.

It was a huge space, and Marissa suspected this Vaughn person must have a lot of money. Killian told her that Vaughn was his closest friend. The black dragon was even older than Shepard and Davis and the most powerful dragon in thousands of years. His wife was said to be the strongest wielder of them all. "Great, the proverbial power couple and me without my petticoat," she grumbled.

A gorgeous woman with beautiful coppery red hair, kind green eyes, and the cutest baby bump ever ran up and hugged her. "We don't make the peasants bow anymore," she smiled at her.

Marissa flushed. *Great, I just insulted the lady of the manor.*

Bridget laughed and introduced herself, thanking her for her part in saving the children and getting justice for her family.

Davis called over, "Dang, Bridge, how many gummy bears did you eat while we were gone?"

She glared at him, then sent a quick jolt of light across the room and zapped him on the arm.

"Ow!" he yelped, rubbing his bicep while everyone else laughed.

Marissa stared at her in awe, "I want to be you when I grow up."

Bridget laughed again, "We will get you there, my dear. Please come have a seat, there's some people that want to meet you." She brought Marissa over to meet the second most handsome man she'd ever seen in her life. Tall with shiny black hair like a raven's wings, crystal blue eyes that absolutely sparkled and a mouth made to sin. A small trail of smoke trickled from one nostril as he gazed at Bridget and brushed loose hair from her forehead. This had to be Vaughn, she decided.

She was correct, and he turned out to also be one of the kindest men she'd ever met. He asked about her well-being and offered to set her up in Dallas now that her life in Miami was chaos. Her jaw dropped; she'd completely forgotten about the gallery. It was destroyed in the explosion. She'd been so enthralled with everything else; that she forgot about responsibilities like jobs and rent. Instead, she flew halfway across the country with veritable strangers.

A warm hand took hers as Killian smiled at her. She relaxed and smiled back. He was here with her, she'd be ok.

Vaughn noted the look the two exchanged and smiled fondly at Killian. He told her, "We'll talk later, but I don't want you to worry about that. Everyone here is family, and that includes you now, too." They heard the door open, and he looked over her shoulder. "Speaking of family, Marissa, I'd like you to meet your sister, Serena."

Marissa froze; the moment was here, and she didn't know if she could do it. She took a few deep, calming breaths and turned. She studied the young woman in front of her, who looked eerily similar to her, only younger. The pretty girl gasped and spoke in a voice that rang like bells, "Marissa?"

Suddenly, her mind cleared, and she remembered her younger sister. They were separated when Serena was only six years old. But she was spelled somehow into forgetting her.

She trembled, and her heart almost burst with a heady combination of relief and love. "*Serena!*" she shouted, and they flew into each other's arms, sobbing in joy and pain over their lost years.

Bridget wiped her own eyes at the sight, and Shepard wrapped his arms around his wife, who brought Serena over and was now sniffling as well. They didn't tell Serena why they were here, wanting it to be a surprise. Davis held Jack closely, and they hugged the children who were shyly sitting with them.

Killian took the two women's hands and led them to the dining room so they could sit and talk in privacy.

The attention then turned to the little ones as Vaughn squatted down in front of them. "Hello, Lily and Jonathan, welcome to my home. I'm so glad to meet you."

"Mommy?" they heard as Celeste wandered into the room, making a beeline for Bridget. She skidded to a stop when she saw Lily on the couch and skipped over. "Hi, I'm Celeste! I'm a black dragon, we think. That's my dad," she pointed at Vaughn, "What's your name?"

Lily looked nervously at Celeste and then gazed up at Jack. He smiled and nodded, encouraging her. She quietly answered, "I'm Lily, I'm a blue dragon, that's my little brother Jonathan."

Celeste lit up and waved hi to the little boy. "I have an older brother; his name is Gabriel, and he's in college. I have a little brother, too, but he's still in mommy's belly." She nodded, as if she were an expert on these things. She studied Lily, then suddenly, she grinned and bounced on her toes. "Yes, you're going to be my best friend. I know it! Let's go swimming! Mommy, can Lily borrow one of my suits?" she pleaded.

Bridget laughed and said, "Of course, dear, if Lily wants to go?" she asked the little girl.

Lily's face beamed, and she chirped, "I love to swim!" and, giggling, the two girls ran off to change into swimsuits.

Jack set Jonathan down so he could toddle around a little bit, and everyone cooed about how adorable he was.

Vaughn stood and sighed, "Well, I have some bad news. We found out who their parents were, and unfortunately, they don't have any living relatives. They were the last in their line, and after Michael and Kelley were murdered, it turned those poor babies into orphans. I'm guessing that's exactly why they were targeted. They thought no one would look for them. Like Serena and Marissa, we expect."

Jack squeezed Davis' hand and looked at him, hope blooming in his eyes.

Davis nodded and brushed a hand across his cheek. "Vaughn," Davis began, "If it's okay with you all, Jack and I were discussing it, and we'd very much like to take in Lily and Jonathan and adopt them as our own. You know we can't have our own children, so adoption is our only opportunity. We can help them better than any human family. I'm a water dragon, Shepard and I can train Lily, and Jorrie can train Jonathan if he's a wielder. Jack and I have been through so much, we can help them cope with their loss, and make sure they never forget their parents. My parents would be glad to help too. We just have so much love to give to them, and really, they already love Jack so much, they trust us, and are comfortable with us. We just love them so much already, too. Please, I know if you think about it, and you'll see it's the best solution. I hope you'll agree, we just really have so much to offer," he finished in a rush and held his breath, realizing he'd been babbling.

Vaughn laughed, "Davis, Jack, take a breath, it's okay. I happen to agree with everything you said. I think you two are perfectly suited for the task, and I can see how taken they are with you."

Jonathan was holding up his arms to Davis, "Up, up!" he babbled. Davis picked up the little boy and put him in his lap, cuddling him and holding him close, sheer delight on his face.

Jack sat in stunned silence; they would have everything they wanted. A family, each other, and their friends, safe. He felt soft arms around him and found that Bridget and Jorrie were both hugging him. They pulled Davis in, too.

"Still one of my favorites," Bridget whispered and kissed Davis on the forehead.

Chapter 37

THE FRONT DOOR BANGED open suddenly, and Davis groaned. It was his mother. He glared at Shepard, knowing this was his fault. She kissed Shepard's cheek hugged him, then made a beeline for Jack. "Jack! My favorite son!" she cried, laughing.

He stood and hugged her as she threw her arms around him and rocked him side to side in her exuberance. "Mother," he kissed her cheek. "I'd like you to meet someone," he told her, pointing at his mate.

She turned to Davis, who stood, the little boy in his arms.

"Mom," Davis said with a soft smile, "This is Jonathan. Jack and I are adopting him and his sister, Lily. Jonathan here we suspect is a blue wielder and Lily is a dragon like us. They're orphans, and they need a loving family, the special kind that we have."

The little girl in question ran into the room hand in hand with Celeste then but skidded to a stop at the gasp from the older woman.

Barbara burst into tears and dropped into a chair. She held out her arms for the baby, and Davis handed him over. She cuddled him, tears running down her face. The twin's father cleared his throat, and she wailed, "Joseph! Look! Davis and Jack gave me grandchildren, after all!"

The stoic man grinned in a way the boys had seldom seen and shook Davis' hand. "Son, I'm so proud of you! And Jack, you as well. I love you both, you're going to be wonderful parents." He enveloped them both in a tight hug and sniffled, emotion overcoming him.

Davis was shocked, and Jack laughed. It might have been the longest sentence he'd ever heard the man utter.

Lily stomped over to Barbara and put her hands on her hips before saying, "Why are you hugging my brother and calling him your grandchild? I don't know you."

Barbara laughed, "Oh, Davis, she is definitely like you. Hello, Lily, it is a pleasure to meet you. I'm Barbara, I'm Davis and Shepard's mommy."

Lily squinted, turning to Davis, "She's a blue dragon like us."

He nodded in pride, "She is." He squatted next to her, and Jack followed suit.

"Lily, honey," Jack said softly, "We looked for your family, but there isn't anyone else. I'm sorry, sweetie, but your mommy and daddy were the last ones. Do you understand that?"

She nodded, sadness clouding her eyes. "What happens to me and Jonathan now?" she whispered.

Davis smiled. "Lily, Jack and I would like for you and your brother to come live with us. We will take care of you, we'll love you, and teach you about being a water dragon. We could be a family together, the four of us."

She thought about it. "So," she said slowly, working it out, "If we do that, we'd have two daddies?"

Jack blinked, and Davis grinned. "Yes, is that okay?"

She thought a little more and then asked, "So, he would be family?" she pointed at Shepard, who nodded and bowed. "And her? We would have a grandmama?" she gestured at Barbara.

Barbara sniffled and nodded, pointing at her husband, "And he would be your grandpapa."

Lily looked at them all consideringly and walked to Jack, taking his hand. She looked up at him. "Will you keep us safe from the bad man?" she asked in a very small voice.

Jack's heart almost broke as he scooped her up and held her close, "That bad man can never hurt you again, I punished him for you and your family. No one is ever going to take you away from us," he promised her softly.

She looked over to Davis, whose eyes flashed ice blue as he nodded in reassurance, "We will make sure no one ever forgets your mommy and daddy. And Lily, no one will ever hurt either of you again," he vowed, a faint growl in his voice and a trickle of steam from his nostrils.

Lily smiled, "I think me and Jonathan would like that a lot." They quietly cheered, and Barbara squeezed the little boy, who gurgled happily.

Celeste cheered the loudest, her new best friend was now part of her family.

Bridget smiled at the giggling and shrieking coming from the pool room. The girls were having a great time, the little boy was happily splashing on one of the ledges, and his new grandparents playing with him. Her heart was full. Her family just kept getting bigger and bigger. It was everything she'd always wanted. Davis strolled in, and she patted the seat next to her, holding out her arms. He obliged, and she snuggled up to him, whispering, "Thank you."

"For what?" he grinned at her, "Jack's the one who brings the gummy bears."

She laughed, "But you're the one that loves Jack and makes him the happiest I've ever seen him. You know how important he is to me. And now, you're family. It's wonderful." She leaned up and kissed his cheek. "Davis, I love you. I hope you know that."

He nodded solemnly, struck by her words, "Love you, too, Bridget."

Jorrie leaned over the back of the couch and kissed his other cheek. "Hey, dork, I hope you know I love you as well, and now that you've finally got your head out of your ass and mate bonded Jack, I love you even more."

"Eh, I don't know about you," he gave her a roguish smile.

She pinched his back and twisted, making him yelp.

"Okay, okay, I love you too, you crazy wench! Ow! Shepard, get your woman under control!"

His brother laughed, "Nope, I'm staying out of this," he declared. Jorrie blew her husband a kiss.

Davis glared at him, muttering, "Traitor."

Marissa and Serena came into the room, holding hands and smiling at each other. Killian jumped up from where he'd been sitting quietly in the corner, making a beeline for Marissa.

Most everyone in the room was startled. Killian was so quiet they often didn't even register he was there. This time was no exception.

Vaughn smiled. Relieved that his friend was obviously smitten with Marissa already. He knew Bridget worried about Killian's loneliness, too. Vaughn was the only one who knew it was self-imposed. He sincerely hoped those days were over.

Marissa spoke then. "Rena and I started piecing together some of our background. We're worried, we… well," she paused, glancing at Serena, who picked up the thought.

"We have another sister. An older one. She's a dragon."

A collective gasp echoed around the room. It made sense if one of their parents was a dragon. Glances were exchanged, and Vaughn nodded, they would find her.

Vaughn asked, "Have you been able to remember your sister's name? Or anything else about your parents? Who spelled you?"

Marissa shook her head. "Sadly, no. The only thing that sounds familiar is Isabella. We think that's her name. But we're going to keep trying. Killian and Siobhan offered to help us counter the remaining effects of the spells."

Vaughn nodded. The more information they had, the better. They needed to find the girls' family and discover why this happened in the first place. It sounded like what would have happened to Lily and Jonathan had they stayed captives of Cyrus and Esme.

Killian spoke up quietly, "I wonder what Esme meant, when she said this wasn't over and that more darkness was coming. What is that about?"

Vaughn sighed, he didn't know, but his network was already working on it. He was tired of the threats to his family, and as it grew, so did his concern for their safety. He studied his friend, who was giving him a look full of worry, something out of character for his quiet, reserved personality. "Killian," he nodded softly, letting him know he agreed and would follow up on it. Louder to everyone, he said, "In the meantime, we need to find Isabella."

The front door opened, and Liam strolled in. He had a grin on his face. "I found it!" he announced, pride in his voice at his success at finding whatever 'it' was.

Vaughn grinned, too, "Liam! Welcome back, have you met Marissa? Serena's sister?"

Liam immediately went to greet her, delighted that Serena had finally found her family. He adored Serena like a little sister and was the one who carried her to safety when they found her. "Hi, Marissa, so nice to meet you! Welcome to Dallas. I'm Liam, as you probably heard."

Killian put a hand on Marissa's leg, eyeing the green dragon. Liam's outgoing personality, playboy good looks, and long red-gold hair were usually magnets to women. They adored the cocky man. "Dragon," he greeted Liam.

Liam grinned at Killian and nodded, "Hey Ki, loud and clear!" He acknowledged a claim was made and would keep his distance.

Vaughn rolled his eyes. His godson used to be quite the ladies' man, although not so much since Jorrie married Shepard. He hoped Liam would find a woman that would love him back soon, he was worried Liam was getting reckless in his relative youth as a dragon. Vaughn decided to assign Liam to lead the search for the missing Isabella. To keep him out of trouble. He would also assign Siobhan and Marco. It would be a good, gentle task to ease Marco back into things. His recovery was going well.

Killian would want to be involved; he was sure. He nodded to himself; this would help solve several things at once and keep Liam grounded since he would have other people relying on him again. Vaughn laid out the plan, and they agreed, they needed a break from the bad guys.

Once again, the door opened, and Siobhan strolled in, arm in arm with Marco. Liam nodded at her and glared at Marco.

Marco grinned back at him. "Liam, so good to see you, *mi hermano*," Marco told him. He looked much better than the previous two days. The wound on his neck was almost completely healed, and he was moving normally. He was very close to full strength.

"Brother?" Liam asked, with a low growl in his voice.

Marco took Siobhan's hand and kissed it.

Liam's face paled. "Shi, tell me you didn't."

She smirked back and pulled her shirt collar down, a bright red dragon on her shoulder, surrounded by flames.

Gasps filled the room. Everyone turned to stare at Liam, anxious to see how he was going to handle it. He stalked to Marco, growling, his eyes hard.

Vaughn stood, ready to intervene if needed.

Liam stood toe to toe with the red dragon.

Bridget bit her lip, thinking, as they all were that Liam would be crazy to go against Marco. Even injured, he was a strong, lethal warrior.

Marco snarled at Liam, then stopped. Puzzled. He glanced down and saw Liam had his hand out. He looked back up, and now Liam was grinning. Marco barked out a short laugh and shook Liam's hand.

"Marco, I am so glad she's your problem now, man," Liam laughed.

Everyone relaxed then as Siobhan punched Liam in the shoulder. "Asshole," she hissed.

He rolled his eyes, "Hey, if he wants to put up with your snarky ass, he deserves you. Now I don't have to worry about you anymore." He held out his arms then, and she leaned into him. "I'm happy for you, sister," he murmured. "Love you," he kissed her temple. "Mom and Dad would be so excited," he added quietly.

"I love you too, Liam," she replied, "Thank you."

Killian kissed Risa's hand as she wiped a tear away. He promised her, "Now, we find the rest of your family. And stop this darkness coming for us."

Thank you for reading

The Waters Edge.

(I hope you enjoyed reading it as much as I loved writing it.)
Love this book? Don't forget to leave a review!

Every review matters, and it matters a *lot!*
Head over to Amazon, Goodreads, or wherever you purchased this book
to leave a review for me.
The Dragons and I thank you endlessly.

Read More!

If you're like me, you get invested in characters and want to know what happens after the last page. Head over to my website to subscribe to my newsletter to be the first to know when the next book in the series will be released. Who knows, I may give you a sneak peek at it!

www.tristaricketts.com
Book 1: Lahaina Noon
Book 2: Circles in the Sand
Book 3: The Waters Edge
Book 4: Silver Belles (Coming August 2025)

Made in the USA
Monee, IL
24 April 2025

16280226R00198

The Blood Red Moon Rose

SUBMERGED

I Felt Dried Up
Nothing Left to Give
Nothing Left to Feel
Nothing Left to Create
On My Way Home
Through *Plaka*
Under *The Acropolis*
The Blood Red Moon
Rose
Her Illuminating Rays
Reaching Out
To Me
Through the Columns
Of
The Parthenon
A Mother Seeking
Her Child's Touch
My Sedated Passion
Stirs
Submerging
My Inner Caverns
Like A Sudden Summer Storm
Flooding
The Earth

After She Has Been
Scorched
By
The August Sun

{HER}e

You Are
{HER}e
Feeling
Moving
Breathing
You Are
The Sublime Itself

TURN THE OTHER CHEEK

Look
To The Horizon
Let
The Sunrise
Pale
In
The Presence
Of
Your Glowing Smile
Turn
The Other Cheek

DISTILLED

Your Song
Enters Me
Before
Your Body
Touches Me
Love Comes
On
Waves of Air
I Breathe It
In

A Heaven Sent Distillation

CHERUBIM

In
My Next Life
I Will Come Back
As
A Dragonfly
Skimming
The Surface
Of
The Sea
With
My Iridescent Wings
A Cherubim
Perched
On
A Watery Cloud

I yearn to be longed for—
Too much is just enough

INTERVENTIONS

You Came
To Me
With
An Angel
At
Your Back
His Wings
Breaking Through
Your Skin
His Words
Spilling Out
Of
Your Mouth
Am I
Falling
For *You*
Or
Divine Intervention
In
Human Form?
Rilke Tells Us
Angels
Can Be Terrifying

But
All
I Want
To Do
Is Melt Into
The One
That Breathes
Through You

AGAIN

Your Name
Is
An Ancient Mystery
Resurrected
Hearing
It
Makes
Me
Old and New
Again

40 WAVES

Somewhere
In Between
Moonrise and Sunset
I Crash
Through
40 Waves
To Swim
With
10,000 Angels

IOANNA MALANDRENIAS

LIGHTEN UP

No Matter
How Heavy
Your Grief
Send
It
Up
To Heaven
The Stars
Will Lighten
Your Load

INHALE ~ EXHALE

SING TO ME

Sing to Me

ORPHEUS I

Your Voice
Holds
The Power of Transformation
I Feel
IT
When You Sing
To Me
I Live
Within
An Eternity
Fly Through
So Many Worlds
Just So
I Can Come Back
To
This Moment
And
Lose Myself
In
The Slightest Drop
Of
Ecstasy
Don't Look Back

When
You Exhale
That Final Note
I Fear
I Will Never Have
The Strength
To Follow
You
I Will Always Be
There
Your Shadow
Dancing
On the Wall

ONCE AGAIN

The Aegean
Speaks
To Me
As
I Swim
In
Her Waters
SHE
Feels
My Fathomless Pain
Embraces
My Boundless Joy
Together
We Sculpt
The New Land
On Which
I Will
Once Again
Stand

INHALE ~ EXHALE

SYNAXIS I

Last Night
I Dreamt
I Was Invited
To
The Assembly of The Archangels
Welcome to The Synaxis
Their Whispers
An Ocean of Wings
Beating
They Gave
Me
An Elixir
To Drink
As
The Liquid Rippled
Through
My Veins
I Felt
The Eons
Pass Through
Me
All
I Could See

Was
You
My Ever-Ready Protector
Eyes Blazing
You Gave Me
Sword and Shield
Side by Side
We Fought
As
Soldiers
Lovers
Creators
We Are
A Symphony
Of
Light and Dark
Beauty and Chaos
Gold and Silver
When
I Wake
I Can Still Hear
That Sea of Wings
Breathing
Around Me
Ever Expanding
Ever Protecting
Ever Rejoicing

An Ocean of Wings Beating

A PRAYER

The Angel
Asked
Me
For
A Prayer

So
I Danced

A MESSAGE

I Whisper
To You
A Nymph
Unfurling
On the Ocean Floor
I Know
You
Can Hear Me
The Waves
Will Make Sure
Of
That

SYSTEMS

Your Voice
Has
A Way
Of
Dripping Down
My Spine
Planting
Its Own
Nervous System
Next To
Mine

EUREKA

I Looked
Everywhere
For
LOVE
I Found
IT
In
The Music

INHALE ~ EXHALE

SERENADE

The Sound
Of
Your Heartbeat
Is
My Own
Private Concerto

My Own Private Concerto

IOANNA MALANDRENIAS

BEFORE THE SILENCE

Peonies Blossom
So Quickly
Eager
To Start
The Conversation
I Lean In
Listen
Anticipating
A Platonic Dialogue
Before
Their Petals
Go Silent

MY ELVIS

You Swore
To
Love Me Tender
So
I Became
Black Velvet

CLEARING

You Speak
Your Feelings
About Us
So Quickly
Is It
ME
You Love
Or
Hearing
The Sound
Of
Your Own Voice
In This Lofty Monologue
About Your Ever-Changing Emotions?
AM I
Another Supporting Character
In
The Play of Your Fabricated Life?
Your Words
Are
Smoke and Mirrors
Delicate Fibers
Holding

The Visage
Of
Prophet
In Place
If
I Shattered
The Mirrors
Cleared
The Smoke
Asked You
To Sit
In The Silence
Of
Your Own Company
What Would
Your View
Be Like?

BUTTONS

You Call
Me Selfish
For
Not Sacrificing
My Vision
For You
I Almost
Bend
Almost
Then
I Remember
I Didn't Spend
The Last Decade
Of
My Life
Shut Away
In
The Prison
Of
My Own Mind
Fearing
The Brilliance
Of
My Own Gifts

To Smother
Myself
Again
For Another Person
WHO FEARS
My Ascent
Would Render
Them
Insignificant
You Installed
My Buttons
Knew
When
How
Where
To Push
Them
Now
It Is
My Turn
To Push
You
AWAY

BEAUTIFUL CRUCIFIXIONS

People
With
Incredible Creative Genius
Enthralled Me
Once
Now
I Bow To
The Ones
That Have Learned
To Navigate
Their Inner Demons
The Ones
Who Bear
Their Cross
With Grace
Who Use It
To Bring About
Their Own Resurrection
Every Single Day
They Are
The Ones

With
Open Minds
Open Hearts
Open Souls
No Amount
Of
Creative Genius
Will Ever Buy
That

ORPHEUS II

I AM
Drawn Down
Into
That Space
Where
Our Heartstrings
Are
Threaded Together
That Magnificent
Voluptuous
Frame of Your Musical Flesh
You Hold
Me
There
Strum
Those First Notes
I AM
But Air
Around You
Endlessly Orbiting
With Every Single
Vibration

That Magnificent Voluptuous Frame of your Musical Flesh

IOANNA MALANDRENIAS

DECLARATIONS

Your Voice
Makes
Every Statement
A Sonnet

DREAMY

I Emerge
From
The Dreamy Sea
My Hair
A Sleek Stream of Strands
Down
My Back
I Feel
Your Warmth
Locking Me In
Breaking On Me
A Rogue Wave
You Are
My Apollo
I AM
Your Lyre

Make
Me
SING

EVERY TIME

Part of Me
Falls Apart
Every Time
I Look
At
You
I Still
Can't Believe
You're
Real

AURAL

God Composes
The Music
We Must Hear
The Melody

INHALE ~ EXHALE

Dance with Me

DEVOTION

I Belong
To
A Religion
That
Dictates
I Dance
To
The Gospel
Of
My Soul

HONEY

Meeting
My Soul Mate
Would Never Be
Enough
I Want
Us
To Dance
With
The Universe
Our Ecstasy
Overflowing
Like
Honey
From
The Hive

MISSIONARIES

I Run
Through
The City Streets
The Smell of White Jasmine
Wraps Itself
Around Me
An Erotic Mist
A Lover's Breath
When
I
Find
You
I
{RE}Member
The Stones
{RE}Member
Two Souls
From
Another Lifetime
Now Meet
In
This Alley of Ancient Aromas
Our Mission
Has Only
Begun

UPON RISING

My Soul
Rises
Before
I Do
She Beckons
Me
To Dance

I Obey

HOLY COMMUNION

This Theater
Is
A Vessel
Lacing
Us
Together
I DANCE
You Feel Me
I Feel You
A Sacred Communion
We Transform
Each Other

We Transform Each Other

POURING

Notes and Lyrics
Saturate
From
The Inside
Out
Countless Fragments
Of
A Broken Heart
Float To
The Surface
Ecstasy
Pours Out
Of
My Cells
I Become
Living Music

INHALE ~ EXHALE

YOUR PERSEPHONE

Eating Pomegranates
Always
Makes Me
Think of You
All That Red
Dripping Down
My Chin
Like
Virginal Caviar
You Brought
Me Down
Into
The Underworld
Your Persephone
In
The Darkest Corners
Of
Hell
I Found
My Light
Before

I Reached
The Surface
Again
Illuminated
By
My Own Rebirth

Thank You

SECRETS

I Share
My Secrets
In
The Simplest of Gestures
You
Only Need
To See
Them

HORIZONS

Our Enraptured Bodies
Entwine
Themselves
Into
Their Own Horizon
The Sun and Stars
Rise
Over Us
But
Our Light
Outshines
Them
All

ROSE PETALS

Your Ocean
Makes
My Earth
Blossom
Rose Petals
Fall
From
My Lips
Into
Your Mouth
All
We Taste
Is
The Flavor
Of
Our Own Private Universe

FAÇADE

With Scissors
In
Your Hands
You Whisper
You Are
The Angel of My Life
I Thought
You Were
My Prince Charming
You Were
My Bluebeard

SHE

I Have Heard
Men Say
AD NAUSEAM
How
They Desire
A Woman
Gorgeous
Intelligent
Magical
But
When
She Appears
They Realize
Their Deepest Fears
In
The Presence
Of
True Beauty
They Want
HER
To Expand
Only
Up
To
Their Own Limitations

Do NOT Wish
For
A Lover
You Have
Neither
The Courage
Nor Character
To HONOR

The Only Thing
You
Can Do
Is
Pray
To Hold
HER
FREQUENCIES

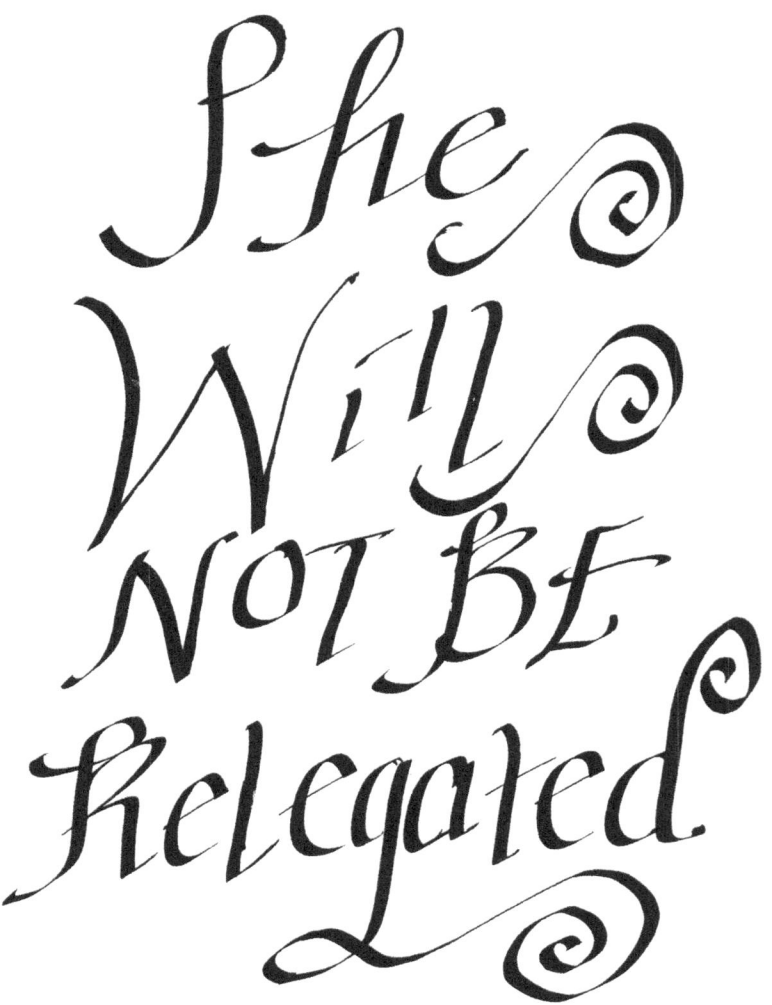

FINGERTIPS

I Do Not
Look Up
At
The Sky
To Find
My God
I Feel Him
Crawl Up
From
The Earth
Slip Under
My Nails
Into
My Skin
He Raises
My Fingertips
To
The Goddess
Who Carries
You
To
Me

CONSTELLATIONS I

When
You're
Inside
Me
I Say
Your Name
You Say
Mine
Together
We Speak
Entire Constellations
Into
Existence

SEAHORSES

Your Body
Stands
Next To
The Temple of Poseidon
Your Soul
Is
A Tribe of Seahorses
Swimming Through
The Abyss
Of
The Atlantic
Seeking
To Wrap
A Million Tiny Slivers
Of
Itself
Around
Mine

YOURS

You Said
You Fell
For Me
When
You First Saw
Me Dance
Now
I AM
Yours
And
You Want
To Cut
Me
Off
At the Knees

INHALE ~ EXHALE

THE LAST SPARTAN

We Fight
You Leave
My War-Torn Heart
Feels
As If
It Beats
In
The Chest
Of
The Last Spartan
Slowly Bleeding
Out
On
The Ravaged Hills of Thermopylae

IOANNA MALANDRENIAS

HOW WE FLY

We Both Fell
In Falling
We Soared

FREEDOM

There Were Times
In My Life
I Thought
I Only Existed
If
You
Saw Me
One Day
I Realized
You Couldn't Even
See Yourself...

....and I Was Free

INCENSE

I Cannot Dance

On

A Single Prayer

I Need

The Mysteries

To Infiltrate

Every

Single

Gesture

So

They Can Rise

Out

Of

My Pores

Like

The Sweetest Incense

In

The Darkest Temple

IOANNA MALANDRENIAS

RETROGRADE

We Are
Two Planets
In Retrograde
Always
In Each Other's View
Never
Close Enough
To Intersect
To Lock
To Meld
Our Heavenly Rings
Together
Always Going Backwards
We Have
So Much Baggage
To Unload
Karmic Debts
Must Be Paid
Before
We Can Touch
Maybe
In
The Next Lifetime

We Will Spin
Into
Each Other
In
This One
I Can Only
Feel
You
In
The Air
Around
Me

SECRET WORLDS

I Knew
You Were
Mine
When
I Looked
Into
Your Eyes
Dissolved
Into
Those Worlds
No One Else
Knew
Existed

CONSTELLATIONS II

Your Touch
Feels Like
The Glow
Of
A Thousand Constellations
A Protective Veil
Woven From
The Divine Rays
Of
The Gaze
Of
The Smiling *Theotokos**
You and I
Have Been Here
Before
It Took
Countless Lifetimes
To Eat
Their Own Tails
Complete
Infinite Revolutions
So We Can
Finally

Lose Ourselves
To Each Other
In This One

Greek for Mother Mary, The God-Birther

BEFORE

When
I Dance
I AM
Aphrodite Rising
From
The Waves
I Move
For
The Gods on High
Before
Anyone Else
Knows
I Exist
Divinity
Will Always Love
Its Own Creation
Wonder
At
It
Before
Mortals
Even Begin
To Open
Their Eyes

IN LOVE AND WAR

Loving You
Made Me
A Warrioress
Battles
Were
Inevitable

GUARDIAN

The Prophetess
Spoke
Of
My Twin Soul
My Protector
She
Did Not Speak
Of
The Catch
I Need
To Wield
My Own Sword
Before
I Meet
The One
Who Guards
Me
With His

INHALE ~ EXHALE

STARDANCER

The Dust
Descended
From
That Stellar Nursery
Sits Patiently
Under
My Soles
Waiting
For
My Soul
To Awaken
I AM
Moved
So
I Move
The Stars
Call Back
Their Interdimensional Flesh
Leaving Me
As
Nothing More

Than
An Earthly Form
Immaculately Animated
By
Their
Unrelenting Fire

THE CHASM

When You Left
I Felt
The Chasm
Take Root
Inside
Spill Out
Of
Me
Molding Itself
Into
My Stage

The Show Must Go On

INHALE~EXHALE

We Are What We Make

We Are What We Make

LAST NIGHT

I Thought
I Needed
Your Love
To Create
Last Night
I Realized
I AM
Love...

...Unbridled

DAWN

You
Ask
Me
Why
I Raise
My Hands
To
The Heavens
I Say
I AM
Opening
The Curtain
For
The Dawn
You
Leave
Again
You Always Preferred
The Darkness of Night
Where
Rebirth
Remains at Bay

New Beginnings
Fill
Your Heart
With Fear
It Is
NOW
I See
Through
Your Sage's Mask
Into
The Coward's Heart
Beneath
I Forgive You
I Release You
I Have
New Worlds
To Build
I Will Paint
Them
All The Colors
Of
The Freshly Born Sky

I have New Worlds to Build

INHALE ~ EXHALE

MAGNIFICENCE

We Strive
So Hard
For Perfection
We Forget
Our Own Wholeness
BEAUTY
Is
In
The Ever Fluid Journey
The Ultimate Balance
Of
Being Shattered
By Life
And
Putting Ourselves
Back Together Again
IT
Is
In
The Grace
Of
These Transitions
We Are Reborn
We Forget This

But
Oh
When
We Remember
How Magnificent
We Are...

RHAPSODY I

I Writhe
In
The Dissonance
Of
The Life
I Have Created
I Feel
See
Hear
The Rhapsody
Still Stirring
Inside
Me
Disharmony
Propels
Me
Forward

UNCHAINED

I Chain
Myself
To
The Melody
And
Become
An Unchained Melody

VESSEL

I Feel
Your Invisible Hands
Reaching Out
To Me
Through
The Music
Sculpting
Me
Into
The Holiest of Vessels

SUBMISSION

I Submit
To
The Birth of My Desires
In
This Submission
I Find
Freedom

SCULPTRESS

With
Shaking Hands
I Shaped
The Sand
Into
Your Face
As
The Priest
Did
In
Those Dark Moments
In
The Name of the Archangel
As
I Wept
From
My Unceasing
Heartbreak
The Ocean
Washed
Your Form
Away

As
Her Waves
Receded
SHE
Whispered
To Me
You Have Greater Love
To Sculpt
And
Be Sculpted
By
In This Lifetime

RADIANCE

Create
SO MUCH BEAUTY
In
A Day
That
The Sun
Refuses
To Set
For Fear
He Will Lose
A Part
Of
His Radiance
To
The Pieces of Earth
That Flourished
Under
Your Touch

EMPRESS

They Told You
To Find
A Prince
To Marry
They
Can't See
That
Even When
Everything
Turns
To Ashes
You
Have
Enough Magic
Flowing Through
Your Soul
To Raise
An Entire Empire
Inside
You

You have
Enough
Magic flowing
Through
Your Soul
to Raise
An Entire
Empire

SYNERGY

I AM
Not Worthy
Of
A Significant Other
I AM
Only Worthy
Of
A Co-Creator

SYNAXIS II

An Army of Saints
Fills
The Silence
With
Ethereal Whispers
An Entire Cosmos
Radiating
Above
My Every Step
They Follow
Me
Into
The Studio
To
The Barre
They Speak
To
The Countless Fluttering Angels
In
My Solar Plexus
I Arch

,

Onto
The Floor
Into
The Well of Your Blessings
My Limbs
Float
In
Boundless Wonder

This
Is
Bliss

WHY OUR LOVE WAS FATED

After
The Primordial Goddess
Wove
The Entire Universe
Into Existence
She
Gazed Lovingly
At
The Last Two Pieces
Of
Glistening Thread
Braided
Them
With Her
Delicate Fingers
Chanting
Blessing
Invoking
Those Threads
Into
The Prayer Rope
Infinitely Wrapped
Around
Her Wrists

Chanting
Blessing
Invoking

PILLAR SISTERS

Whenever
My Heart
Sits
Shattered
In
My Chest
I Go
To
The Caryatids
Sit Beside
My Athenian Stone Sisters
If
They
Can Hold
This Ancient City
Up
For Eons
I Can Hold
Myself
Up
For This Entire Mortal Experience

SWEET REVENGE

When
The Veil
Lifted
Revealing
My Wounds
You Became
One of Them
I Took
Them All
Wove Them
Into
The Memories
Of
My Insides
Strung Them
Into
A New Lyre

Transcendent Music Is The Best Revenge

IT'S GREEK TO ME VOL. 2

The Greek Word
For
Choreography
Means
Write
The Dance
Write
In Space
I Will Spend
Every Breath
I Have
In Me
Writing
Rewriting
This Epic Poem of My Life
Upon
My Last Exhale
I Will Surrender
It
All
To
The Gods

COWARDS

We
Destroyed
Each Other
Because
We Wouldn't
Risk
Love
Destroying
Us
First

PERCHED

I Want
To Disintegrate
Our Unforgettable Moments
Together
Into
Thousands of Fireflies
No Matter
Where
I AM
There Will Always Be
One
Guiding
My Path
Perched
On
My Fingertips
Filling Up
The Darkest Forest
With
The Brightest Light

YOU ARE THE DELTA

BEAUTY
Doesn't Come
To You
It
Flows
Through You

AUTHENTIC

A True Artist
Makes
The Tragic Beautiful
And
The Beautiful Tragic

INHALE ~ EXHALE

WAVES

A Woman's Body
Holds
The Secrets
To Creating
New Life
She
Is
Divinity
With
Curves
Every
Rise and Fall
Of
Her Luscious Waves
An Odyssey
Bringing You Back
To
Where
You First Fell
For
HER
Just So You Could
Be Born
Again

Divinity With Curves

IOANNA MALANDRENIAS

TRUTH

After
The Passion and High
Wear Off
Your Weaknesses and Faults
Pierce Through
That Perfect Illusion
Shredding
It
All
To
Pieces
I Stand
Next to
Those Remnants
Of
That Imaginary World
We
Had Built
Together
Excavating
The Essence
From Underneath
It All

I Live
In
Every Shard of Your Truth
See
Breathe
Touch
This Unadulterated Vision
Of
You
Your Reality
Answers
My Fantasy
It's Better
Than
Either of Us
Could Have Ever
Dreamed

SMOKED OUT*

I Watch
The Shoreline
Turn
To Cinders
As
I Sail Away
The Ocean's Watery Rhythms
My Only Solace
I Smell
The Salt
The Charred Remains
Of
My Former Life
My Old Dreams
Skewered
A Lost Feral Animal
Caught
By
A Starving Bird of Prey
Life
Has A Way
Of
Burning Away

Both
The Hunted
And
The Hunter
We Will Come Back
To
This Place
Build
On
Her Ashes
Our Freshly Formed World
Will Reach
Olympic Peaks
Here
Where
The Gods
Now Weep
They Will
Once Again
Lose Themselves
In
The Ecstasy of Their New Creation

written during the catastrophic Greek Wild Fires of Summer 2021

Lose Themselves in the Ecstasy of their New Creation

INHALE~EXHALE

PLACE OF WORSHIP

My Tides
Forever
Lap
At
Your Altar
Eternally Worshipping
Where
We Create
A New Breath
A Place
Where
Fluidity Saturates Form
My Psyche
Entangled
In
Your Eros
Where
The Horizon
Between
Heaven and Earth
Keeps
The Balance
We Are Suspended
There

A Love Story of Our Ancestors
Continued
Two Beings
Sustaining
The Gravitational Force
Of
The Entire Universe

PORTALS

I Asked
The Goddess
To Open
The Noetic Eyes of My Heart
Those
All-Dreaming
All-Seeking
All-Seeing
Portals
I Felt
The Opening
I Saw
The Beauty
What I Felt
What I Saw

I Became

I asked the Goddess to open the Noetic Eyes of my Heart

HOW TO BECOME THE 10TH MUSE

It Doesn't Matter
How Broken
Your Spirit
How Heavy
Your Heart
How Invisible
You Feel
1. Work on Your Art
2. Work on Your Art
3. Work on Your Art
4. Work on Your Art
5. Work on Your Art
6. Work on Your Art
7. Work on Your Art
8. Work on Your Art
9. Work on Your Art
10. Work on Your Art
THIS
IS
YOUR
BECOMING

INHALE~EXHALE

RHAPSODY II

The Music
Is
My Philosopher's Stone
We Smolder Together
Until
We Both
Catch Fire
I AM
Incinerated
Into
A Living Rhapsody

I AM
Incinerated
Into A
Living
Rhapsody

BOTH

Beauty
Is
The Most Powerful Force
In
The Universe
When
We Surrender
To
It
We Become
Both
Beautiful
And
Powerful

We become both beautiful & powerful

LIFE

I Live
As
I Love
Graceful
Ferocity
Unleashed
Through
A Female Form

ANOINTED

You
Are
An Original
Your Ascent
Is
Imminent

HEROINE

Whirlpools
Mercilessly
Draw Me
Under
Like The Wrath of an Archaic God
There is a Loveliness
In Their Spiral Violence
They Wash Away
The Parts of Me
That Died
Long Ago
But Still Clung to Me
Like Wet Silk
The Ones
That Sat
Festering
When You Left
I've Disinfected
Those Wounds
Since
You've Been Gone
I Was Never Meant
To Remain
Your Amputee

My New Limbs
Bloom
Like the Freshly Sprouted Points
Of a Starfish
Buried In
The Sand
Teeming
With Life
Yet Hidden
Gently Feeling
Their Way Up
Waiting to Surface
Their Luster
Undulates Out
Revealing My Path
For
A Long-Awaited Homecoming
I Sail
To
My New Ithaca
Like
That Hero
Who Burned a City
To Return
To His Own

MICHAEL

My Tears.
An Ocean
Of
Sorrow and Bliss.
I Sail
Upon
Her.
Arrive
At Your Harbor.
Every Wave
That Swells
A Chant.
A Divine Whisper
Driving Me
To
Your Mysterious Sanctuary.
My Airy Footsteps
Sprout Roots
On
Your Holy Ground.
Your Wings
Walls of Electrifying Grace.
Your Bodiless Power
Flows

Through Me.
A Celestial Ocean
Seeking
Mortal Shores.
My Hands
Reaching
Searching
Your Glistening Form.
A Silver Universe.
Your Unshaken Gaze.
A Formidable Serenity.
I Kneel
Enraptured By
The Scent of Invisible Rose Petals
Sent From
Our Sweet Breathed Lady.
The Unfading Blossom.
The Ever Present Priestess.
They Lay Strewn
At My Feet.
A Myriad
Of
Ethereal Touches.
All Consuming.

The Unceasing Whispers
Streaming
Like Nectar
Dripping Down
The Archangels' Backs.
Your Voice
Pierces Through
The Spell.
Worthy.

UNION

Marry Yourself
Marry Your Art
Marry the Divine
Unite
Heaven and Earth
Sea and Sky
This
Is
The Ultimate
{RE}Membering
Of
Soul

Marry yourself
Marry your Art
Marry The Divine

MIRACLES

Any Woman
Who
Has Ever
Made a Meal
Held You
While You Wept
Made You Smile
Inspired Kindness in You
Found
The Sublime
In
The Mundane
Is
A Living Vessel
For
Immaculate Conception
In Every Moment
We Are
Miracles
Made
For
Miracles

EMERGENCE

DRAGON RIDER

If Fire Be My Breath
And Breath Be My Fire
Let The Love of The Mother
Awaken My Every Dormant Desire
May My Ashes
Be My Birthing Pool
The Sound of My Soul Unbound
My Dragon Rider's Warrior Cry
When All Is Said and Done
I Outshine the Sun
As I Fly

						Cosmos

				Love

			Exhale

		Inhale

	Heartbreak

Chaos

INHALE ~ EXHALE

FINAL THOUGHTS FROM THE AUTHOR

Composing this poetry collection has been one of the most powerful experiences of my life as a writer and creator. My main goal for this and all future publications is to move and be moved by my audience.

If you felt affected after flowing through these poems, it would be an honor to hear your reactions, thoughts or feedback in the review section on Amazon.com.

This would help me gain priceless insight into the inner worlds of my beautiful readers as I am currently at work on my second collection. Even just a few words or short sentences would mean SO MUCH to me.

~Scan the QR Code above to leave a quick review!~

Sending you waves and waves of gratitude, Dear Reader, for purchasing this collection and supporting my work.

Warmly,

Ioanna

A Prayer

What gives me the most joy is sharing my passion for the Divine with others. I have felt The Divine Mother's presence many moments in my life and have written a prayer for Her. Scan the QR code below and you will receive my own original prayer written in honor of this incredible presence in our lives. May we all be continuously filled with Inspiration from Her and Gratitude to Her.

Blessings

GRATITUDE

Here, now, I arrive at the beginning again and acknowledge all the individual forces, souls, and occurrences that brought this work into its fullest fruition in this particular timeline:

To the Angels, Guides, Ascended Masters who woke up my long dormant instincts that these words had to come out. The Muse's fierce grip never let up the whole time I was writing this. I honor her chaining me down with the most divine leash.

To My Family who put me in the most sacred of containers for many years so that I can be molded into the woman I am today. All our Souls truly were in contract together. My Mother, who swam in the Aegean with me when I was in utero and brought me into the folds of Orthodoxy along with my Godmother Georgia. Orthodoxy, to me, has always been another link in the chain and the closest path to the Ancient Mysteries. One real glance behind the veil and one will find all those rites waiting to be truly seen and performed.

To my Father who began taking me to the ancient sites from a very young age so I could feel those stones beneath my hands and feet. To my brothers, Manos and Alexandros, who watched me go through many a journey on this path to finding who I AM and have supported me patiently. To Michelle who has co-created a new branch on the family tree with Manos. I look forward to watching it blossom and grow.

To my Theia Aggeliki who profoundly discusses and analyzes the links between the Mysteries of Orthodoxy and of the Ancient Greek religions. Who relentlessly tests me by making me dissect the Ancient Greek origins of words. Child of 11/11, our family Astrologer and Scorpio Mystic, always going deeper and deeper. You have been my Muse on more than one occasion.

To Kyria Mina who brought me into the church choir to chant the original hymns and live the Orthodox liturgy every Sunday. To all my Greek school teachers who helped me learn how to read and write the mother tongue.

To my cousin Jimmy who let me type and write while working the night shift at The Diner. Your Greek Fire will always be blazin'. Writing mystical poetic incantations while hearing to the cooks yell *Chicken Fingers para Niño* and *Linguini con Bolas* was the ultimate manifestation of the sublime meeting the mundane. I am forever grateful for it. Gotta keep it real.

To Antonia, who helped me understand the messages of the Guides and Angels. I will always remember Archangels Michael and Raphael watching over us while we opened the portal together for the first time. Divine Oracle that you are, you helped me see that I really wasn't losing my mind and that the Gospel of My Soul was truly calling me.

To Jeanne Bresciani, High Priestess of Tempio Di Danza and Director of the Isadora Duncan International Institute. Many moons ago, you initiated me into the Revolutionary Legacy of Isadora Duncan. Your teachings and presence shifted and molded me into the Artist and Dancer I am today, but the greatest lesson I ever learned from you was how to live a Mythopoetic Life. Thank you for activating and nurturing the gift of Wild Centeredness within me.

To Pamela. I came to you hoping for some guidance on how to reorganize and upgrade my life. I came out with the first steps of healing my ancestral trauma. Talk about getting more than you bargained for. Thank you for that unexpected and profound initiation. You are an exquisite Metaphysician and Healer.

To Ruth Rose for bringing Antonia into my life. You were the first one who ever called me *Priestess* before I even knew what the hell was going on. I will never forget it.

To my teachers of Danse Orientale, Rhea and Kaeshi. Rhea, who initiated me into the tradition of Bellydance in her apartment under the Acropolis many years ago. Kaeshi, who helped me expand and refine the craft in NYC under her tutelage of the BellyQueen School. You are a brilliant holder of space and builder of communities for women. May your journey and continued evolution in the Bellydance realm always be Blessed.

To Meggan Watterson for falling in love with the Orthodox Hesychasts and sharing her feminist theology with the world. Your books *Reveal* and *Mary Magdalene Revealed* had me crying puddles countless times and have become gospel to me. It was an honor meeting you at Omega and experiencing your Soul Voice Meditation and sermons live. We will always have the true meaning of *hamartia*.

To Marin Bach-Antonson, Founder and Guide of The Priestess Rising Mystery School and Sublime Space Holder for Women. You were my first luminary on the Rose Path when I began to realize my calling. Your Angel Walk on Mount Shasta was one of the most powerful experiences with a group of women that I have ever had. Thank you for bringing us to the Isis Pyramid and letting us soak up those energies. When the words *"I AM a Stardancer"* fell out of your mouth during ceremony, I knew I had found another piece for this collection. You were one of the first readers and supporters of this work and I am forever grateful. May your sacred ministry continue to open the hearts of women who also feel the call.

To Omaran for building the Isis Pyramid with his twin flame, Antera. That last day on the Mountain, in complete silence and darkness, I experienced an indescribable surge of energy flowing up my spine. Isis did speak. I look forward to returning and chatting with her again.

To Diana DuBrow, Priestess of Anointing at the Emerald Temple. I used your oils several times while I was writing this, especially the Vision and Priestess oils. Thank you for creating and blessing such high vibrational unguents.

To Beth who guided me in finding the perfect rose quartz crystal skull. I'm eager to see what consciousness she awakens.

To Shona Keeli Rose, Founder and High Priestess of the Rose Lineage Mystery School. Your Rose Womb Heart Teaching on Grandmother Kauai was the first time I began to viscerally experience the healing of ancestral trauma from within my womb. The healing touches of Sophia and Rhea will never be forgotten. Thank you for inspiring me to acquire my own Templar Sword to honor my inner Divine Masculine.

To Dr. David Pollio, my first mentor in the Ancient Greek Language at TCNJ. I had no idea I would be here after declining *tous bous* all those years ago. I feel like my philological journey is now only just beginning. Thank you for all your steadfast guidance in the Classics. I'm hoping by the time I'm 80, I might be able to translate Aeschylus at the level worthy of his work.

To Dr. Vangelis Calotychos and Dr. Karen Van Dyck who initiated me into the tradition of Modern Greek Poetry at Columbia. To this day, I still go back and read passages from Seferis, Sikelianos, Gatsos, Angelaki-Rooke and of course, Kazantzakis, to keep inspiring my work.

To Dr. Nancy Worman at Columbia who gave me the opportunity to play the role of Clytemnestra in *Iphigenia in Aulis* and actually speak out Euripides in the original classical Greek language.

To Dr. Lee Ann Riccardi, my first Archaeology Mentor at TCNJ who opened my eyes to the physical layout of the all sites of the Ancient Greek Mysteries.

To Dr. Jo Carney, my English Lit Mentor at TCNJ, who introduced me to the life and writings of the Venetian Courtesan and Poetess Veronica Franco and *The Bloody Chamber* by Angela Carter all those years ago. *Dangerous Beauty* has always been and will continue to be one of my greatest archetypal inspirations.

To Dr. John Camp, Director of the American School's Excavations of the Athenian Agora. You granted me the opportunity to actually put my hands into the Greek earth and pull out the layers of the ancient past. I'm eternally grateful for that rarest of experiences.

To Matt and Justin, my audio engineers and guides in the narration realm over these last few years. You make sure that I sound sublime to all my listeners. Always grateful for your guidance to create audiobooks of the highest caliber.

To everyone on the Publishing Services Team who were willing to update, redo, and perfect the format of this book so the words and images could flow seamlessly over the pages. Your eternal patience and willingness to accommodate my artistic vision will not be forgotten.

To Christa at Paper and Sage Designs who created such a BREATH-taking cover for this book.

To the incredible Hot Yoga Revolution Teacher Training Family. I'm especially grateful for Max's yoga sermons, one of which inspired the poem *Buttons*. I spent many a class mentally anointing myself in front Chia's gorgeous Ganesh mural. All of you helped me find my Breath of Victory. Namaste.

To Rosie, my Reiki Master. Thank you for working with the Guides so that my Solar Plexus can begin to fully expand. Every time I Dance, I think of the Angels at my crown and feet.

To Gina, my Pilates mentor, who relentlessly reminds me to BREATHE. You help us remember that sacred airy technology nestled in our rib cage. Thank you.

To Kerry and Betsy, my first vocal teachers who helped me build my breath and sing out all those years ago. I'm so happy we found each other again. *L'amour est un oiseau rebelle.*

To my dear friend, Nektaria, who shared her desire to go to Symi with me and light a candle to Archangel Michael at His Panormitis Monastery. I bring his icon from your shop everywhere I travel. Our paths were truly meant to cross in this way.

To Sofiana for letting me stay at her apartment in Glyfada, Athens while I was working on some of the final pieces of this collection. Writing a prayer to Archangel Michael while hearing my neighbors make wild, passionate love was only further confirmation that the spiritual can never be separated from the sensual. Both are pathways to ascension and are meant to be interwoven.

To Marco for letting me stay on his beautiful grounds on Amorgos. I wrote *Dragon Rider*, the very last piece of this collection, to honor my own alchemical transformation. The words came to me as I was driving past the baby dragon's wing on my way back to the Aloni after another unforgettable sunset.

A HUGE Final Thank You to all my early readers and reviewers. I did not expect such a powerful reaction to my words. Giving your time and energy to receiving this work has meant the world to me and I will never forget it.

ABOUT THE AUTHOR

Ioanna Malandrenias is a dancer and a poet. She splits her time between Athens, Greece and New York City. Before she became a professional dancer and writer, she studied Classical Greek at Columbia University where she obtained her Master's Degree. *Her Breath Built a World* is her debut poetry collection written in honor of the modern Priestess. She is currently in a sacred container on Amorgos the Dragon working on her second poetry collection and new choreographies.

Follow her @ioannamalandrenias

Made in the USA
Monee, IL
07 April 2023

31542284R00121